A BILLIONAIRE'S VOW

THE CALLOWAYS
BOOK ONE

LAURA RILEY

Copyright © 2022 Laura Williams
All rights reserved.

ISBN: 9798358806115

Cover Artist: Steamy Designs
Photographer: Wander Aguiar
Model: Lucas Loyola
Editor: RJ Locksley
Formatter: Champagne Book Design

Published by
Laura Williams
www.authorlaurariley.com
Sign up to my newsletter and never miss a release.

No part of this publication may be reproduced, stored in a retrieval system, copied, shared, or transmitted in any form or by any means without the prior written permission of the author. The only exception is brief quotations to be used in book reviews. Please don't steal e-books. This novel is entirely a work of fiction. All places and locations are used fictitiously. The characters are figments of the author's imagination, and any resemblance to real people is purely a coincidence.

This book is written by an English author, and all spellings are British English.

For Aoife Marie Proudfoot, for being an amazing friend, and being with me every step of the way through Lucian's story.

A BILLIONAIRE'S VOW

THE CALLOWAYS
BOOK ONE

PROLOGUE

Lucian
Two years ago

"You can't go in there!"

The frantic tone of my personal assistant causes me to look up from the contract I'm revising. The door to my office swings open and my brother charges in.

Malachi is Calloway royalty in my father's eyes, and it's for this reason I sit up in my chair. I'm half-expecting to see a full brass band, a red carpet or at the very least for him to have a courtier in tow, but instead he's accompanied solely by my PA, Christine. Platinum strands of hair whip across her face as she stumbles in her rush to get ahead. She clasps the wall-mounted bookshelf to steady herself.

"I'm so sorry, Mr Calloway," she pants. Her eyes—those tiny browns hidden behind ginormous red-framed glasses—are wide. "I had no idea that…"

I lift my hand, cutting her off mid-sentence. Christine knows better than to let anyone enter my home office unannounced, especially when I'm sifting through million-pound contracts. But it doesn't appear as though my brother gave her much say in the matter.

"As you were," I say simply, nodding my head in the direction of the door.

Regaining her composure, Christine smooths down her maroon pencil skirt. Her heels click against the polished wooden floorboards as she leaves.

I glance at Malachi, who at over six foot tall towers over me as I sit. Whatever the hour, my brother's beard is always neatly trimmed and his jet-black hair perfectly styled. His dark grey suit jacket hugs his lean frame, and I know he spares no expense when it comes to tailored suits.

"Good evening, brother. How's Scotland treating you nowadays?" I ask, noticing that he has traded his kilt and sporran in for a pair of black Armani trousers. As tempted as I am to make a snarky comment, I don't. I have a full night ahead of me with documents to read and contracts to sign. Still, I haven't seen my brother since our poker night almost a month ago. It would be rude if I didn't at least offer him a drink. I'm about to ask if he'll join me for a Scotch, but his glare tells me this isn't a social call.

This ought to be good.

The corner of my eye twitches in irritation, and with nothing but silence passing between us I contemplate a warmer greeting. I should at least try to look as though he isn't inconveniencing me. I place the paperwork I'm holding on the mahogany desk in front of me. Then, nonchalant as ever, I lean back in my chair. "Mal, to what do I owe the pleasure?"

"Save it," Malachi spits out. He retrieves a folded-up magazine from under his arm and slings it across my desk.

I open the pages and regard the bright pink cover with fading interest. "Thanks, but *Cornwall Gossip* is not on the top of my list of reading material." I place my index finger in the cleavage of the busty blonde cover model and slide the magazine in my brother's direction. I figure this is a joke, that is until Malachi slams his fist down on the magazine, stopping it in place.

"Page nine." His tone is sharp, though his tight expression gives nothing away.

I make a point of sighing heavily before pulling the magazine from his hold. As requested, I turn to page nine. The heading is bright and in a bold font.

Samantha Matthews tells all about her sordid affair with Cornwall's most eligible bachelor, Lucian Calloway.

My hand shakes and I fight the need to tear the page from the glossy spread. But instead of letting needless emotions get the better of me I keep my expression neutral. I glance up at my brother and shrug. "I wouldn't exactly say it was a sordid affair."

Malachi grunts, throwing his arms up in the air. "She was engaged!"

I yawn, using the back of my hand to cover my mouth. "Of which fact I was ignorant. Thank God for our cousin finding out when he did and bringing the matter to my attention. Upon finding out, I broke things off."

Malachi runs his fingers over his sleek black beard, not once but several times. It's a little trait he's grown up with, and something he often does when stressed. "Don't you think it's about time you ran background checks on future conquests?"

"None of the ladies I have dated have been 'conquests', and the very idea of running background checks is not only unethical, it's downright immoral."

Malachi's brows knit together. "Ethics and morals don't come into this. You're a Calloway, damn it. Start acting like one and stop wasting your time with penniless airheads."

Anger courses through me, but without an outlet I have no choice than to keep it bottled up. I allow my gaze to rove over the article; it's mostly gossip, though I home in on one paragraph, the one Malachi has conveniently highlighted yellow.

A close source has expressed concerns about Mr Calloway's blatant inability to juggle his personal life along with running Calloway Housebuilders.

Beneath the quote the writer concludes with several condescending questions. *Will Lucian fall at the first hurdle? Or will he put his love life on hold? With the spotlight shining on him and his reputation hanging by a thread, will he be forced to choose between love or money?*

I let the words float over my head, for anyone who truly knows me knows that I work my fingers to the bone for the property business. Money and work will always come first. Always.

The article was written by an old friend of mine, Darren Moore, a person I now intend to get reacquainted with in the near future. I bypass the text and my gaze lands on the photograph spread over the top of the page. It looks as though Samantha and I are deep in conversation as we walk hand in hand along the moonlit shoreline. I run my index finger over the image, and over Sam.

I'm snapped out of my reverie when Malachi snatches the magazine away. His knuckles turn white as he squeezes the pages tightly together. My attention shifts to the gold ring he wears. But it's not just any ring—it's a band with the Calloway crest that he and our brother, Gage, were each gifted from our parents on their eighteenth birthdays. A family heirloom I was not fortunate enough to receive when my time came.

There's a loud thud when Malachi drops the magazine into a wastepaper bin beside my desk. "This is the first and last time you bring publicity like this our way."

His comment fractures my last nerve. I stand abruptly, sending the chair I was sitting on hurtling back. "You have no right to stand there and lecture me. I will date who I want, when I want. I do not need your or anyone else's permission. And seeing as though the press are so interested in my private affairs, I will make sure to smile for the camera the next time they decide to run a story on me."

"Lucian—"

I shake my head. "I'm done with this conversation. You need to leave. Go back to Scotland."

"No can do, little brother. Father has requested that I stick around to keep an eye on you."

I clench my fists. "Malachi, I'm not asking."

Seeing my fists, Malachi stands tall. "Should I go grab my duelling pistol?"

"Funny," I say, rolling my shirt sleeves up. "We deal with this the old-fashioned way."

Malachi and I fought a lot as children. At five years my senior he would always win, but time has turned my body from a scrawny boy's to a man's, and at twenty-seven and thirty-two the size difference has diminished, making this fair game.

Malachi smiles triumphantly. "Always so angry." He tsks. "But I'm not here to fight. I'm here because you're my little brother, and I love you."

His words strike me harder than a blow ever could. Despite our differences, I love my brother fiercely. Defeated, I fall back into my chair. "Leave."

"Not until I've talked some sense into you."

I retrieve a fountain pen from the top drawer of my desk. "You've talked, I've listened, there's nothing else that needs to be said—"

A knock at the door silences our conversation. Christine lingers in the doorway.

"I'm sorry to interrupt," she says, pulling at the sleeve of her white blouse. "But a Miss Chelsea Janssen and a Miss Amber Janssen have arrived along with their significant others."

Chelsea Janssen is the only person of interest. She is the most exquisite creature to have graced this earth. "Excellent. I'll personally see her in."

Christine nods once before hurrying away. I round the desk when Malachi captures my wrist. "Who is Chelsea Janssen?"

"No one."

Malachi studies me for a beat. "From the look on your face I'd say she *is* someone."

"She's only here so I can purchase a photograph called 'Timeless Beauty.'"

Malachi's expression is unchanged.

"Didn't you hear Christine when she said Chelsea is spoken for?"

"Perhaps, but that didn't stop you when it came to Samantha."

"Get off me," I seethe, and yank my arm free from his grasp. "She's a friend of Cole's. Nothing more, nothing less."

With a wry smile, Malachi perches himself on the edge of my desk. "Cole, as in the contracts manager who works for our father?"

I fold my arms in front of my chest. "That's correct."

"Interesting." Malachi opens his jacket, pulls out his phone and scrolls through the list of contacts. He stops scrolling when he lands on Cole's name and hits the call button. Cole picks up on the fourth ring, and Malachi transfers the call to loudspeaker. My brother isn't one for greetings, and in true Malachi fashion jumps straight to the point. "It would seem Lucian and I are at odds with one another."

The line goes quiet before Cole speaks. "Hello to you too, and I'm fine, thanks for asking." Sarcasm drips from his words. "Now if you don't mind, I'm busy."

Malachi must sense Cole is on the verge of hanging up, and quickly adds, "It's in regard to your friend, Chelsea Janssen."

"Stay away from Chelsea," Cole warns.

Malachi smiles, and casually makes his way toward the window. He stands back and lifts the vertical blind just enough so that he can see out onto the driveway. "That may prove somewhat problematic, seeing as she and her party have pulled up outside my brother's home."

Cole's breath is loud as he blows out. "What do you want to know?"

"Just a little about Chelsea, is all."

"She has a boyfriend, if that's what you're asking."

Malachi looks at me and then back to the phone screen. "Go on."

"She and her sister Amber used to own a shop."

"Used to?"

"It was recently burnt down. I don't know why I'm telling you all of this though when Lucian can fill you in himself."

Malachi's brows rise. "Poor girl must be strapped for cash."

"You could say that. They're desperate to reopen."

Malachi's stare leaves the window and we lock gazes. "And I guess Chelsea would do anything to get her hands on the funds to make that happen."

"What are you insinuating?" I grit out.

"If this life has taught me anything about the fairer sex it is that girls without title or wealth are gold-diggers. I simply want to know if Chelsea is cut from the same cloth." Malachi taps his chin several times. "I'd be willing to bet she'd do just about anything for a life-changing sum of money."

I'm about to say how utterly absurd my brother's statement is when Cole speaks. "She'd do anything to get the salon back up and running."

Malachi smiles sardonically. "I rest my case. Thank you, Cole."

"The pleasure is all mine," Cole says before hanging up.

Malachi tucks his phone away in the breast pocket of his jacket. "There, my point proven. Why don't you allow me to take you out for the evening and introduce you to the sorts of women you *should* be spending your time with?"

"I appreciate you coming all this way to check up on me, but I'm afraid you've been labouring under a misapprehension. I don't need dating advice any more than I need a babysitter."

"That is not my intention. I simply want you to know in advance the kind of women you are getting involved with. What you do with that knowledge is entirely up to you, but I'd like to think you'll do the right thing."

Our gazes lock and I stand tall. Stubbornness is an inherent trait that runs through our veins. It's Malachi who breaks the stare. He runs his fingers over his beard and sighs heavily. "Prove me wrong. Offer her one million pounds to spend the night with you. Ask her and I'll leave."

Never have I paid for a woman's company. The very idea is not only vulgar, it's beneath me.

"When you go, remember that my door only swings one way," I say, gritting my teeth as I head out of the office. My steps are heavier than normal as I make my way down the long corridors. I'm far too busy with work to have Malachi breathing over my shoulder.

I'm rich enough to buy whatever I want. I want Chelsea, and I want my brother to leave, and I'm presented with a way to make both of those things happen.

As much as it pains me to admit, deep down I know my brother is right. Everyone has a catch and a hidden agenda. To hell with thinking that one day I could win Chelsea's heart. Love is a myth, everything in life is a transaction.

Tonight, I will make Chelsea an offer she simply cannot refuse.

I stroll along the corridor toward the front door. Out of all the properties I own, I must admit that my South Devonshire estate is one of my finest. The exterior of the opulent white building makes a statement, with its hand-carved spiralled pillars supporting a large overhanging balcony that offers an uninterrupted view of the ocean. Calacatta marble runs through the rooms of the ground floor, and an array of artwork I have collected over the years hangs from the walls. But as beautiful as the property is, this isn't a house I personally call home.

I open the front door and make my way out onto the driveway, which is lit up due to the ornate glass lanterns I had Christine light prior to Chelsea's visit. Attention to detail is everything when the most bewitching woman to have lived is dropping by.

I waste no time opening the door to the Bentley. My gaze bypasses everyone except for Chelsea. Her long blonde hair cascades over a figure-hugging black dress, which stops just above her knees. With our eyes locked, I capture her hand. "My timeless beauty, how are you?"

I don't miss the curiosity in her stare, nor do I miss the subtle way in which her hand trembles in mine. She takes in a deep gulp of air before breaking eye contact. Her gaze connects with her sister's before she seeks out reassurance from her boyfriend. This isn't going to work. Her little entourage serve merely as a distraction.

"McKenzie," I say to my driver. "See the others to the sitting room." As the last syllable leaves my lips I tug on Chelsea's hand and without question she steps from the car. I rest my palm on the small of her back and lead her into the house.

"The photograph," she says, reminding me as to the reason she is here. But why settle for a photo, an image captured within the tightly knit fabric of time, when I can have the real thing?

"We will get to that later," I say, and walk her through the corridor toward the grand staircase. I planned to speak to Chelsea in my home office, but with Malachi's untimely visit that is no longer an option. I lead her to the next best place.

The air is warm as we step out onto the balcony, and although the view of the sea is shrouded in darkness, we can still hear the crashing of the waves in the distance. Chelsea steps from my hold, and I unwillingly let her go. She doesn't speak and just stands at the stone handrail peering out into the dark nothingness.

Craving her touch, I stalk close behind. I stop walking when I am only inches away and stand perfectly still as the wind whips up long tendrils of her hair.

"Chelsea." I whisper her name and capture her shoulders in my hands.

"What are you doing?" She flinches, and immediately pulls away.

"One million pounds," I say simply.

Chelsea's eyes widen. "For my photo?"

"One million pounds for the photo, and—"

"And what?" Her words are filled with hope, hope that I will be able to give her the funds to reopen her shop.

I step forward and swallow away any remaining reservations. "One million pounds for 'Timeless Beauty', and a night with you."

She doesn't speak, and I wonder if it's because she is overwhelmed. I open the lapel of my jacket, about to pull out my chequebook when Chelsea takes in a sharp inhale. "No."

I quirk a brow. My brother put me up to this, but still, her one-word answer leaves me somewhat baffled. "No? Is that all the answer I am to expect?"

The wind blows more fiercely now, whipping up her hair from all different directions. In this moment she looks strong, empowered, and tantalisingly sexy. "I hate you, Lucian Calloway, and no amount of money would ever tempt me into your bed."

CHAPTER ONE

Chelsea
Present day

"I can't believe you're leaving me," I say, sinking down on the bed.

My roomie, Tyler, glances at the clock on the wall and waves exaggeratedly. "Yes, darlin', in exactly thirty-three hours I will be boarding my plane. I'll be back before you know it."

I capture his hand and pull him onto the mattress so he's sitting beside me. With our fingers interlinked, I look straight into his eyes. "Are you sure you're doing the right thing? Cleaning out your entire life savings to fly halfway across the world is crazy when you've only known Mason for six weeks. I mean, how can you really know a person in that time? How do you know he isn't some kind of crazed serial killer?"

Tyler shrugs. "I guess I don't. But what is life for if not for living? And you can't live life to the full without first taking a little risk."

A shiver skates the length of my spine, chilling me to the core. "You can take risk without being decapitated, cut into tiny pieces and thrown into the ocean."

Tyler's laugh is explosive, and it travels to the pit of his stomach, causing the mattress to bounce. His eyes crease at the corners as he makes a fist with his hand and gently nudges my cheek, turning my face to the side. "You watch way too many murder documentaries."

Tyler stands, and from this I gather he is done with the conversation. I, however, am not. I won't sleep at night knowing I haven't at least tried to talk some sense into him.

"Maybe I do watch too many murder documentaries. But can I remind you that they are factual?" I tell him, or rather his back as he turns away from me and begins emptying clothes out of the dresser. "Meaning they are based on true events," I add.

"So, write me a eulogy," Tyler says, waving me off. He pulls a polo shirt from the drawer and throws it for me to catch, my cue to fold it and place it in his suitcase. I fold it backwards, making sure to keep the defined neckline of the collar.

I'm about to speak but jump as heavy material lands on my head, sending me into a kaleidoscope of colour.

"Sorry, my bad," Tyler calls.

Yanking the item off, I notice it's his sequinned onesie. "You aren't seriously taking this?"

"Of course I am, darlin'. You made it for me, so I shall wear it with pride."

Pride is exactly the reason I made the multicoloured onesie for him in the first place.

"It's not the outfit, it's just… won't it be a little warm?" I ask, thinking how much hotter it is in the States than the U.K.

Tyler shakes his head. "I'm not planning on wearing much of anything," he says with an exaggerated wink.

I smile but know Tyler can see through my façade. "I'm going to miss you," I admit.

Pushing the suitcase aside, Tyler flops onto the bed and taps the empty space to his right. Straight-backed, I sit beside him and welcome the arm he wraps around my shoulder, pulling me into his chest. I relish the warmth and feeling of safety he packs into his hugs.

"Come with me," he says.

I gasp and look up. "What?"

"You heard. Come with me. Mason has a roomie. Patrick is hot and one hundred percent heterosexual."

I consider his words for a moment, but quickly shake my head. "Neither you nor I have that kind of spare cash just lying around."

It's not a lie. I'm broke and have been living on the little savings I have. But savings only stretch so far, and I can't afford to waste a single penny.

Tyler taps the end of his nose. "Let's just say I've stumbled upon a rather substantial windfall."

I laugh, though Tyler does not. "What windfall?"

"A little something from my parents." Tyler wags his brows, and I gather that is all I am going to get out of him for now. Our eye contact is unbroken, and he clears his throat. "So, what do you say?"

A trip across the pond would be amazing, and travelling is something I want to do in the future, but now is not the time to be swanning off when I have so much to sort in England. "I start my new job today; it wouldn't look good if I ask for time off already."

"I have no idea why you accepted a job milking cows—"

I narrow my eyes and fight the grin tugging at my lips. "I am not…"

"—when you have a perfectly good job here."

A job I don't get paid for.

Burt, Tyler's father, owns the building, and Tyler manages the clothing boutique downstairs. There are aisles for everything from vintage to glamorous. Like him, his taste in clothes is a little on the eccentric side.

Tyler offered me a part-time position when I moved in, and I was grateful for the hours and extra cash. That was until another clothing boutique opened across the street and Sparkle for

Men's profits took a nosedive. How quickly I went from getting a reduction in pay to working 'voluntarily'. Tyler would recompense me by covering the rent and bills. But it isn't the same as having money in my pocket when I need it, and I need money now more than ever.

"I'll still help out downstairs," I tell him, but he knows I can't help out forever. "Once the work on my salon is complete, I won't need to work at the farm. It's only a temporary summer job."

"Forget about the farm, come with. What an adventure we'll have. You can stay for a few weeks and be back with more than enough time for your best friend's wedding." Tyler nudges his elbow into my side. "What do you say?"

I smile, because although Tyler may have listened, he hasn't heard a single word I've said. "Look—"

Tyler places his finger over my lips. "Promise me you'll think about it."

I don't speak for a second, I just stare into his eyes. His blue irises are the colour of sapphires, framed by long sweeping lashes. His skin is bronzed, his lips full, he's so attractive it isn't fair. He's beautiful inside and out, and I know he'll make some guy very happy one day. Selfishly, I don't want that day to be anytime soon. I like what we have and I'm not ready to lose it yet. "Okay, I promise." I nod and try to sound genuine.

Tyler stands and continues packing his suitcase, occasionally trying on outfits to garner my approval. With a feathered boa draped around his shoulders, he prances around the room as though he's on the catwalk.

After showcasing the entire contents of his suitcase, Tyler strips down to his boxers and pulls out the tiniest pair of swim trunks I think I've ever seen. With his fingers gripping the waistband of his briefs he begins working them down, and that's my cue to leave.

I jump off the bed and hurry from the bedroom, grabbing

my denim jacket from the arm of the sofa as I pass through the open-plan lounge.

"Got to run," I call, stuffing my arm into my jacket sleeve.

"Already? A little keen, aren't we?"

I hear Tyler's words, and as I turn I notice him standing in the doorway of the bedroom, stark naked.

I lower my head as I slip my shoes on, letting my long blonde hair fall forward and act as a curtain. "I'm meeting my sister at Timms café for a coffee before I head to work."

"Can you drop by before you leave? My father has called for an urgent meeting."

I roll my eyes. No doubt he wants to raise the rent again. "When?"

"Over breakfast."

Breakfast, supposedly the most important meal of the day, and yet a meal I generally skip. I flash a glance at my wristwatch—it's still early. I guess I could pop back for a slice of toast before leaving for work. At which point Tyler should be more appropriately dressed.

I nod. "Sure, why not." I side-eye the bedroom door and get the perfect view of Tyler's toned ass as he disappears into the room.

"Love you, darlin'," he calls as I round the corner to the hallway.

"Right back at you." My fingers curl around the brass handle. I open the door, then push it shut behind me. I make my way down the narrow flight of stairs and out through a side door.

I look at the mannequins in the shop window in passing and stop walking when I notice Royston—Tyler's fifty-year-old assistant manager—manning the till. It's pretty hard not to notice Royston with his bottle-dyed electric-green hair and colourful motif T-shirts he wears to work each day. The bell above the door dings as I enter.

"You're in early," I comment, brushing my fingers along the clothes hanging on the racks.

Royston shrugs. "Boss wants to talk to me before the shop opens."

"You too?" Maybe Burt isn't raising the rent after all? I figure he wants to discuss the running of the business in Tyler's absence, but he really needn't involve me when he has Royston manning the fort.

It's now that reality starts gnawing at me. Tyler will be gone, and I will be here all alone. In all of my twenty-six years I've never been alone. I've either lived with my parents or had a roomie. It'll feel strange coming home every night to an empty flat. It'll feel strange not being woken by Tyler's terrible shower singing, and it'll feel strange not seeing his face every morning.

Exiting the shop, I head toward Timms café, which is across the street. I pass my beauty salon en route. My salon is two doors away from Tyler's clothing boutique. The 'closed' sign still hangs in my shop window thanks to the arson attack a few years back.

For the first time in what seems like forever it feels as though my life is right on track. I have an appointment at the bank tomorrow to discuss a business loan to get my salon back up and running. Granted, the insurance company paid out after the fire, but after all of the structural and external works were carried out, there simply wasn't enough to cover the costs of the interior. All that is soon to change.

Humming, I walk with a spring in my step. The café is quiet when I enter. My sister Amber is sitting at our usual table, and a steaming mug of coffee is waiting for me on a coaster. Her head is bowed as she glances down at the screen of her phone. Like me, my sister has long blonde hair and crystal-blue eyes. She's wearing a green summer dress, and her baby bump is hidden beneath the table.

I make my way over to her and pull out the chair opposite. "Hey."

"Hey, yourself," Amber says, resting her chin in her hands. "So, I hear you start a new job today. Tell me all about it."

It seems good news travels fast. "I'm going to be waitressing at a farm café. It's only temporary."

Amber nods once and lifts the menu from the centre of the table. "Breakfast? My treat?"

Amber knows I don't eat breakfast, but, forever the mother hen, she insists on feeding me.

"Sure. But I can't stay long; Tyler wants to see me before I leave for work. He's trying to talk me into going to America with him, how crazy is that?"

Amber spirals a strand of hair around her index finger. "I mean, it's not the worst idea. Have some adventure before the salon opens and you're committed to late nights and a ton of work."

I raise my brows, feeling somewhat outnumbered. "When did you speak to Tyler?"

Amber looks away, a smile tugging at her lips. "I don't know what you're talking about."

I toss a sachet of sugar her way, and, laughing, she glances back up at me. "He said there is a cute roomie with your name written all over him."

There it is right there. "If you're here to lecture me about my nonexistent love life, please save it. The only man I want to talk about is the one in there." I nod my head in the direction of her stomach.

Amber sits back, placing both hands over her baby bump. "I can't wait to meet him."

"Me too," I admit. Unbeknownst to my sister, I've been making outfits for the baby when he arrives. The clothes that Tyler doesn't sell he gives to me. Be they black suit jackets or colourful shirts, I cut them up and with my sewing machine make them into bespoke garments just for my nephew.

Amber leans forward in her chair. "Remember we have the dress fitting on Friday."

The dress fitting for Lizzie's wedding. Amber and I are to be bridesmaids. "I'm sure my dress will be fine, I haven't gained a pound since the last fitting." I narrow my eyes and glance at her baby bump. "Not sure about you though."

Amber laughs. "Ha-ha."

My sister is massive, considering she is only four months pregnant. She could easily pass for six, but what would I know? I've never been pregnant before and nor do I want to be. I'm comparing her baby bump to when she was carrying her daughter, Freja. With Freja on my mind, I ask, "So, how's my niece?"

"You know," Amber says with a knowing smile. "Giving Rick hell, braiding his hair and painting his nails."

I snort into my mug.

Amber orders our breakfasts. I sit quietly and listen to her talk about how amazing her fiancé Rick is, and how lucky she and Freja are to have him in their lives. Before I know it, an hour has passed. Our coffee mugs are empty and the plates bare, with only breadcrumbs and the remnants of tomato sauce left behind. I kiss my sister on the cheek and literally run from the café and head to the flat. So much for Tyler and I talking over toast. I've got to make this quick.

Rounding the corner, I stop dead at the sight unfolding before my eyes. What the hell is he doing here?

Lucian Calloway is standing outside Tyler's shop. A man in a navy suit stands hammering a sign to the wall. I can't see what the sign says because Lucian's big head is in the way. I take a few steps to the right, the large letters of the sign becoming apparent.

The word 'sold' hangs in bold red lettering.

My stomach twists in a way that is painful, and for a second, I'm sure the ground is moving beneath my feet. Sold. Seeing as Lucian is standing out front, it doesn't take long for me to put two and two together.

Burt has sold the shop to Lucian.

The Devil.

CHAPTER TWO

Lucian

I take a few steps back and shake my head. "No, it still isn't right. Try a few inches higher."

Josh glowers at me and wipes his sweaty brow with the back of his hand. "Remind me why I'm hanging this bloody sign?"

I clap my cousin on the shoulder. "You should know by now that everything I do has a purpose."

I open the lapel of my jacket and retrieve my grandfather's gold pocket watch. He was a stickler for punctuality and arriving at meetings ahead of time. It is for this reason the time has always been set ten minutes early, a tradition my grandfather started, and a tradition that to this day I continue.

"Lucian."

I smile because I recognise her voice immediately. I don't turn to face her, not yet. I offer her my profile whilst continuing to glance down at my pocket watch.

She's right on time.

"Lucian," she repeats. In my periphery I notice her standing with her hands placed firmly on her hips.

I close the lid on the watch and wait until the clasp clicks shut before placing it in my jacket pocket. I glance past Chelsea and briefly look at Josh. His mouth hangs open as he takes in the girl directly in front of him. *My damn girl.* Now that he has had a second to appreciate her beauty, it's time to remind him of the fact.

I lean in to him and nudge his chin. "Ogling is unattractive on you, and do I need to remind you that you are already spoken for?"

Snapping his mouth shut, Josh swallows loudly. "I was not ogling."

I dismiss his reply and, in a whisper, continue. "I believe the answer to your previous question is standing right in front of you. *She*, dear cousin, is the reason we are here."

I'm pulled from my conversation with Josh as Chelsea pulls on the sleeve of my suit jacket. It seems that she doesn't like to be kept waiting, a trait she and I share. I turn casually. Only now do I offer her my full attention.

I fight to keep my expression neutral, but it's clear to see why my cousin's jaw dropped. She is utterly captivating. She is wearing a brightly coloured floral summer dress. Her blonde hair hangs freely around her face and falls to the hem of a faded denim jacket. Her features are in perfect proportion, but what has my attention is her eyes. Utterly riveting, her eyes are as blue as the Mediterranean Sea, a sea I would willingly drown in.

I capture Chelsea's dainty fingers and guide her hand toward my lips. "To what do I owe the pleasure?"

Gazing into her eyes, I'm about to place a chaste kiss on her skin when she pulls away. Her expression hardens and her eyes, those beautiful blues, are as angry as a tempestuous sea.

"What are you doing here, Lucian?"

I look from Chelsea to the 'sold' sign. I believe the answer to be pretty obvious. Still, I like the game of cat-and-mouse and decide to humour her. "Is that a rhetorical question?"

"Don't tell me you've bought the shop."

Nonchalantly, I shrug. "As you wish. I won't tell you."

"This isn't a joke, Lucian," Chelsea scolds, rubbing her hands over her eyes exasperatedly. "People's livelihoods are on the line."

Relaxed, I lean against the wall. "No, I haven't bought the shop."

Chelsea draws in a long breath. At the same time colour seeps into her cheeks. "Thank God."

Her lips lift into a smile before they come crashing down. Her gaze is locked on the 'sold' sign as confusion washes over her face.

I don't doubt the girl's intelligence for a second, but it's taking her longer than I had anticipated to form the next question, so I'll make it easy for her. I push off the wall and close any remaining distance between us. She doesn't look at me, and I know why. Truth is a bitter pill, a bitter pill I will take great satisfaction watching her swallow. I capture her chin between my thumb and index finger and gently tilt her head. With nowhere else to look she is forced to meet my stare.

"Do you really think I'd set my sights so low? I have little interest in retail."

"Then what…" Her words are a hushed whisper.

"What I want is something money can't buy," I breathe into her ear. Or more specifically a million pounds can't buy, although I keep that thought tucked away for now.

For every problem there is a solution, and mine is simple. If I can't own the bird, then I will own her cage.

Chelsea trembles in my hold, be it fear or anticipation I'm not sure. I won't drag this out any longer than necessary. "I own the building."

She steps back, and I release her chin. I expect her to shove me, to get upset, to do anything but instead she does nothing. It's as though it is taking longer for realisation to hit her.

"You're bound to have a lot of questions," I say, and rock on my heels, awaiting her reply.

Silence.

"Chelsea?"

After a couple of long and slow exhales, she raises her right hand, whilst the left is cupped over her chest. "Just stop talking."

I'm well versed in emotionally erratic women; I've had to deal with them plenty of times in the past when ending relationships. But this, this complete lack of emotion is uncharted territory. She isn't yelling, isn't cursing, isn't doing anything. A foreign feeling overwhelms me, that being the unexpected need to comfort her. I advance toward her, but my path is blocked when Josh steps in my way.

"I see you've already met my cousin," Josh pipes up. Shouldering past me, he takes Chelsea's hand. "I'm Josh Ambrose. Pleased to make your acquaintance."

My jaw ticks at his untimely interruption, and I want nothing more than to yank him back by the collar of his shirt. I don't, of course. If being a Calloway has taught me anything it's never, under any circumstances, to make a scene publicly.

Chelsea doesn't pull her hand free. I wonder if Josh's words have even registered with her. Josh places a kiss on her hand (the bastard) whilst at the same time peering up into her eyes. Though her gaze does not meet his, and she just stares at me, or more specifically through me.

Josh clears his throat, and just like that she is snapped out of her trance. Chelsea eyes my cousin with scepticism, her expression giving nothing away in regard to whether she likes what she sees. Josh is three years my senior, tall, good-looking with thick black hair. Chelsea smiles politely before wiggling her hand free from his grip.

"Excuse me," are the words she leaves us with as she sweeps past and disappears into the shop, leaving me only with the aromatic scent of her lavender shampoo.

After several deep breaths I glower at my cousin.

Josh shrugs. "What?"

I loom closer and, placing my hand on his shoulder, I squeeze. I'm about to speak but instead we are forced apart when the shop door swings open and Tyler, the previous owner's son, storms out.

"Jesus, not him again," Josh spits out. He slaps his palm to his forehead and drags his fingers down his face.

Tyler discovered the building had been sold when we let ourselves in earlier and began measuring up. To say he hit the roof is the understatement of the century. He demanded we leave and when we didn't oblige he began charging around like a man possessed, yelling and tearing clothes from their hangers. Needless to say, he was causing quite the scene for passers-by, who gathered outside the shop peering in through the large front window. Having an audience is the last thing we want, and for that reason alone, Josh and I stepped outside. Tyler's little outburst worked to his advantage as he quickly locked the shop door behind us and has been on the phone ever since.

"What the fuck are you still doing here?" His voice is erratic, his cheeks beet-red. "No, Dad, I will not bloody calm down!" he yells into the phone before cutting the call.

Tyler begins barking profanities at us, by which point I have lost interest. Conflict doesn't interest me in the slightest, and squabbling in the street like old fishwives is beneath me. I dust down my suit jacket before turning my attention to my cousin. "I will leave young Tyler in your capable hands."

Josh's nostrils flare. "Where the hell are you going?"

"I have an urgent meeting with my father and brothers." I pull the pocket watch from my jacket and glance down at the domed face. "And would you look at the time."

Smiling to myself, I take my leave. I head to where McKenzie, my driver, is parked up in my Mercedes. I open the rear passenger side door and slide onto the rich leather upholstery.

"Where to, sir?"

"The Calloway Hotel in Truro."

I can't help wonder what my father deems so important that I had to cancel all of my morning appointments.

CHAPTER THREE

Lucian

The drive is pleasant, and with time to spare I ask McKenzie to take the slightly longer, more scenic route. I'm so used to the hustle and bustle of life, work meetings, and trying to be in a hundred places at once that when I do get the chance to have an uninterrupted drive, I savour every second.

The unspoilt terrain and lush greenery are soon replaced by red-brick buildings and cobblestone paths. Truro is renowned for its remarkable Georgian architecture, though the true show-stealer is the cathedral, which reaches high in the skyline.

The city is popular with locals and tourists alike, and for this reason was the perfect location for a Calloway hotel.

The car slows as we reach the hotel car park. I wave my hand in the air like royalty. "No, McKenzie, you know the drill. Drop me out front."

Flicking the indicator, he sighs. "Certainly, sir."

My driver has always been a man of few words. At seventy-five years of age, McKenzie Osborn is our longest-serving staff member. He drove me to boarding school as a boy, and from the back seat of the car I have watched his thick black hair thin and grey as time claimed his once-youthful appearance.

McKenzie's hazel eyes meet mine in the reflection of the

rear-view mirror. Perhaps he's hoping I've had a change of heart. I haven't. Without a word he parks up on the double yellow lines outside the hotel's entrance while I recline back in my seat.

It's the same old thing every time we meet in one of the hotels. We discuss profits and expansion, during which time Father tries—but fails—to talk Gage and me into manning one of the other Calloway businesses.

I casually slide my way along the back seat of the car. McKenzie is holding the door open, but I do not rush. The sound of horns and angry drivers is music to my ears. I do not do this for any other reason than to irritate my father. My father, who is keen for me to one day run the hotel chain. With millions, if not billions, of pounds on the line I feel the need to show him my utter disregard for this particular business endeavour. My intention is that he'll leave me alone to focus my attention on what I am good at, and that is the Calloway housebuilding empire.

I draw every second out, taking my phone from my trouser pocket and punching out a memo to Christine.

"Sir…" McKenzie prompts with his hand angled toward the building. I wait a few extra minutes before sliding out of the vehicle. McKenzie holds his hands up in apology to the building queue of traffic behind and hurries to get back in the car.

It is now that I notice my father standing in front of the hotel's revolving door. He's wearing his signature brown suit, matching tie, and off-white shirt with elasticated trouser braces. His thick grey hair is like a beacon as it reflects the morning sun. I smile and nod in acknowledgement, though he does not return my pleasantry. His body is rigid and his arms are crossed firmly in front of his chest.

Excellent.

Now that I have his attention I crouch down and lean my elbows on the front passenger side window. The window is partially rolled down, thus allowing me yet another opportunity to hold up traffic and prove to my father what a bad choice I would be for this company. "Before you go, be sure to pick me up in one hour. I have somewhere I need to be afterward."

Deep furrows form on McKenzie's brow. His gaze is fixed on the rear-view mirror and the building traffic. Just when I'm about to suggest we synchronise watches, a hand grips my arm from behind.

"That's quite enough, Lucian," my father snaps. He guides me toward the hotel, and, like McKenzie, holds his hand up in apology to the motorists.

He releases me and together we step through the large revolving doors. Cool air whips around my face from the overhead air-conditioning unit as we enter the grand marble foyer. In-house restaurants flash by as I hurry to keep up with my father's quickening steps. He's muttering under his breath again, something he always does when he can't say aloud what is really on his mind in fear of being overheard.

"Insubordinate little sh…"

I zone out because I gather his hushed rants are about me. Staff pass us by, cleaners and a few of the hotel porters. They smile warmly; however, I give them the same treatment as I gave to the drivers out front, which is to completely ignore their existence.

From the corner of my eye, I notice two young boys squabbling. They each pull the end of a stuffed toy, tug-of-war style. The taller of the two appears to have the advantage, that is until he unexpectedly releases the toy and sends it catapulting in the air. The toy falls to the floor and slides across the polished marble, coming to rest directly in front of my father, who, stepping over it, continues on his way.

"Here." Crouching down, I scoop up the stuffed cat and toss it to the younger child. His gap-toothed smile is short-lived as their game of tug-of-war starts over. I proceed to the conference room.

The doors are open, and my brothers, Gage and Malachi, are already inside sitting at the long table, along with Father's lawyer. What is Edgar doing here?

I meet my father's stare. "I take it that we're not here to discuss profits and marketing strategy?"

My father claps me on the back. "No, son, we are not."

We enter the room, and Father closes the door behind us.

Desperate to know what this is about, I make my way to the table where my brothers are sitting and pull up the chair beside Malachi.

Edgar Arnoult, Father's lawyer, is sitting opposite. A stack of papers lie in front of him. Edgar is balder than a newly hatched chick and the fluorescent lights above reflect off his polished scalp. But what he lacks on his head he makes up on his face with thick grey eyebrows and a long, neatly tended beard.

"Now you are all here, I will begin," my father says, his hands clasped behind his back. He narrows his eyes, his attention on me and my brothers. "There are several upcoming charity events I want you all to pencil into your diaries. Sponsors and shareholders will be in attendance, and as ever I want you all to make a good impression."

Malachi snorts, his stare burning into me. "Which doesn't mean turning up to each event with a different girl on your arm."

I laugh bitterly. "I'm hardly a womaniser."

"Not according to *Cornwall Gossip* magazine," Malachi drawls.

I clench my hands into fists. Two years on my brother still throws that damn article in my face.

"Behind every successful man is an equally strong woman. You'll do well to remember that," Father says, his brow furrowing. I know he is thinking of our mother, though he will never admit to the fact.

I clear my throat and pick up the conversation. "Is it really necessary that we all go to the charity events? Gage attended last year, and I the previous. I believe it is Malachi's turn to—"

"It isn't common knowledge yet. But I'm retiring," Father says simply. "So the answer to your question is yes. I require all three of you to attend."

Retiring?

My eyebrows shoot up. I can't have heard him correctly.

"Don't all look so shocked," Father says, with humour in his voice. "As much as I want to, I can't go on forever. It's been fun, but I don't want to be sat behind a desk my entire life."

I glance past Malachi to Gage, who in turn glances at me. I can't help noticing he's rotating his ring around his middle finger, a habit that serves as yet another reminder that I am the only Calloway brother who isn't in possession of the family crest.

At four years my senior, Gage is the most rebellious of us brothers. His mousy hair is a little unkempt, the top button of his shirt is undone. It's as though he takes pleasure in the subtle 'fuck yous' to conformity.

Publicly, Gage is the perfect gentleman, but there is so much carnage beneath waiting to be unleashed, I only hope my old man isn't around to see it when Gage finally snaps.

"I'm going to level with you, sons," Father says. "The Calloway empire needs some changes. I can't have all three of you working on Calloway Housebuilders. I've decided that going forward we are going to do things a little differently. I want to dissolve the company and split it into three. Seeing as there are three of you, it makes sense to each take ownership of one third, whether that's the property chain, Calloway Hotels, or Calloway Cruises."

"Fath—" Gage begins, to which Father cuts him off.

"Regrettably, I can't have all three of you running the housebuilding chain. My fear is that with no one at the helm of the other companies they'll lose profits and eventually cease to exist. And I will not sit by and watch businesses that I built up from nothing fall into bankruptcy."

"This is ridiculous," Gage snaps. He and Malachi begin to speak amongst themselves.

The housebuilding chain is everything. Gage, Malachi and I share a passion for the company and the three of us working together have seen profits skyrocket.

"No," I say, sitting back in the chair.

Father lets out a slight laugh. "No?"

"We've demonstrated that we are stronger working together. Splitting us up would be suicide for Calloway Housebuilders."

Father takes a few controlled steps closer. "I don't think you're hearing me, son. You have until the second Saturday in July to decide between yourselves who will run each company. If in that time you cannot decide then you will each come before me and

Edgar and present your case as to why you would be the best candidate for the business."

I pull my phone from my jacket pocket, click onto my calender app and count the weeks before tucking it back away. "You expect us to make such a big decision in a little over a month?"

Father nods. "As that is the official day of my retirement, then yes, I want all loose ends tied up before then."

I drum my fingers on the oak table. All those times Father suggested that I run the hotel chain and Gage the cruise liner business makes sense now. He was hoping that with a push in the right direction we would come to the decision ourselves.

"And if we don't?" Gage asks.

"Then I'm afraid you will all be disinherited, and the companies will be sold off, the money donated to charity."

A blanket of silence falls around us. Father smiles, because he knows that he has our full attention. Smirking to himself, he walks back and forth. "A while back I requested you all put in an offer for the land at Hazelwood Farm."

I sit tall, because it was my offer that was accepted by the farmer.

"Lucian has been fortunate enough to secure the option on the land. Now, what he does with that land I am curious to see."

"That's a fair point, Father," I say, my mind wandering back to the boys in the hallway. "We aren't children any more; we don't have to play tug-of-war with the company."

"What a beautiful analogy, Lucian," Gage mocks, his palm over his heart. "Did you come up with that all by yourself?"

I raise my hands, not wanting to start an argument. "All I'm saying is, why don't we leave it to fate and let the best man win?"

"Best man win!" Malachi taunts. "This is ridiculous. *I* am the best man. Not only am I the oldest son, but I'm the hardest-working. Therefore, the property chain should naturally fall on my shoulders."

Father shrugs. "You each have time to gather evidence and present your case."

"I can't believe you're even considering Lucian," Malachi

huffs. "The son who only a few days back bought a crummy shop for no other reason than the girl who rents the flat above."

I clench my fists under the table. I knew I shouldn't have confided in my brothers, but my tongue is loose when vast amounts of alcohol are consumed during our monthly poker nights.

Father's gaze lands on me. "What building? What girl? Lucian, why am I always the last to know?"

I force a smile at the same time my mind goes blank. Buying myself precious seconds to think, I cross one leg over the other and rock my foot back and forth. And just like that the answer presents itself. "Yes, I purchased a business premises in Heller St Claire. My intention is to convert the shop downstairs into an estate agency, where we can showcase all of the Calloway catalogue." A blatant lie, but a lie that nonetheless builds my case.

Father raises his chin. "Intuition, son, that's what I like and what makes you the shining candidate for the property company. Malachi and Gage, you would do well to take a leaf out of Lucian's book."

"Father!" Malachi's voice booms around the large room, but Father raises his hand.

"I have said everything that needs to be said. The rest is up to you. If you cannot come to an amicable decision amongst yourselves then the decision will be made for you. Edgar has brought with him three contracts. You are to read over the full terms and conditions before inking your signatures. I expect all documents signed and returned to me within the hour."

Edgar stands, separating the stack of papers in front of him into three neatly-laid-out piles. Without another word Father leaves the room with his lawyer running to keep up with him.

Malachi's eyes narrow. "You lying little shit. You only bought those premises because of Chelsea."

I clap him on the shoulder. "Perhaps. A girl who, thanks to you, I know doesn't just want me for my money."

Malachi leans in close. "Correction, little brother. A girl who doesn't want you. Period."

"We'll see about that."

Chelsea isn't just the shiny new toy I've been trying to get my hands on. No, she's more than that. So much more. Since the first day I laid eyes on her she's dominated my thoughts, and for that reason I have watched her from afar. I need to see her flaws up close and personal so I can finally stop obsessing over her.

I place my hand on my chest as my phone begins to vibrate. Perfect timing. I pull the device from my jacket pocket and briefly make eye contact with my brothers.

"I'm really sorry, but I'm going to have to take this." I hurry from the conference room and glance down at my phone. Josh is calling. I slide my finger across the screen.

"You better be dead or dying," I say because Josh knows he isn't to call me during a meeting unless it's urgent.

"Burt has returned, and all hell has broken loose. You need to get back here. Now!"

Not an emergency, but my interest is sparked. Having seen Tyler's temper first-hand, I can only imagine the fireworks going off inside that shop. But I don't care about the shop or its contents. There is only one thing in that building that is worth my consideration. "Where's Chelsea?"

"She's in the staff room with the staff, why?"

"Good. I have a few things that require my attention here, but it shouldn't take long. No one leaves until I get back."

The line goes quiet for a beat. "How am I meant to do that? Lock them in?"

I laugh and re-enter the conference room. "See how easily you answered your own question."

"Lucian!"

"No one leaves," I repeat, and cut the call.

CHAPTER FOUR

Chelsea

I jump at the slam of a door. The force causes the thin walls around us to vibrate. Raised voices from the shop filter in, and muffled words dance around us.

Time passes painfully slowly. But rather than watch the hands of the wall clock tick by, my attention is fixed on the fluorescent ceiling light, which flickers on and off.

"I don't know about you guys, but I can't just sit here twiddling my thumbs," Eve says. Getting to her feet, she makes her way to the small counter and flicks the kettle on. She peers over her shoulder, causing her thick ebony locks to rustle against the collar of her jacket. With a sombre smile she motions her hand toward the ceramic mugs hanging on the stand.

I shake my head. "No, thank you."

Royston stands and on tiptoes makes his way toward the door.

"You can't go out there," I whisper-shout.

"I'm not," Royston says, flapping his hand for me to be quiet.

I frown and lean forward in my chair. "What are you doing?"

"What's it look like?" Royston presses his ear to the door and closes his eyes.

Eve lets out a sigh. "Well, it was good while it lasted. I guess it's time to look for another job."

"We don't know anything yet," I remind her, trying my best to sound optimistic.

Eve rolls her eyes. "I think the 'sold' sign out front is clarification enough."

Forever the pessimist.

I open my mouth but have nothing to say in reply. Pursing my lips together, I sandwich my hands between my thighs. How can I stay upbeat and convince Eve and Royston everything will be fine when I have doubts myself? I slump back in my seat and look up at the ceiling light. The damn thing keeps flickering. Dust escapes from around the long fluorescent bulb as footfalls sound from above. I gather Tyler and his father are continuing their conversation in the flat.

"Hey, don't you start work on the farm today?" Royston asks, and I follow his gaze to the wall-mounted clock.

I nod, feeling guilty that I'm starting a new job just as Eve and Royston could be losing theirs. "I need to be here for Tyler."

"We're here," Royston says and opens his arms. "Please, go. We don't all need to be unemployed after today, do we?"

I smile awkwardly and glance at Eve, whose expression sours. "Girl, you better leave before I whoop your ass."

I let out a stifled laugh and get to my feet.

"Thatagirl," Royston says, and opens the door for me. My smile is replaced by a frown when I notice Lucian standing on the other side. He's dressed in a perfectly fitted grey suit and salmon tie. The guy hasn't so much as breathed a word and yet all eyes are on him. He stands with purpose and exudes confidence. Unlike any man I've ever met, Lucian possesses an aura that both bewitches and intrigues. His presence alone demands attention.

"Excellent timing, Royston," Lucian says, and enters the staff room. "We haven't all been formally introduced. My name is Lucian Calloway. I am a proud co-owner of Calloway Housebuilders."

Eve's and Royston's jaws drop. Everyone who's everyone has heard of the Calloways, but it's not every day that you meet one in the flesh. But neither his name nor wealth impress me, and I find my attention better spent checking my acrylic nails.

"Now that we are all here, I think it best I tell you where you stand going forward. Sparkle for Men will be converted into an estate agency. I hope that you will continue to work here, but be aware that I want reliable staff whom I can depend on to sell a vast range of properties."

"But—" Eve interrupts.

"Before you ask, I don't expect this to happen overnight. You will start at the bottom filing papers and work your way up. Full training will be provided. If successful, not only will your hourly rate be increased, but you will receive commission on every sale you make." Lucian motions with his hand. "The door is right there; I suggest you go if you want to find another job. But I encourage you to stay if you want the chance of a lucrative career."

I'm floored. As far as speeches go, Lucian sure can deliver. As much as it pains me to admit, he managed to drag my attention from my nails. Eve and Royston talk quietly amongst one another. As for Lucian, his gaze never deviates from me.

The clock ticks melodically in the background, reminding me that—despite what my brain is telling me—time has not stood still.

"Miss Janssen, about your tenancy—"

I raise my hand. "I'm sorry, but I'm going to have to take a raincheck. I start my new job today and I'm already running late."

I head for the door, but am stopped when Lucian lifts his arm, blocking the frame. Standing feet away, he leans in closer. "I don't recall a single spot of rain on my journey here."

Instinct tells me to back away, but I don't. My gaze travels down to the perfect Cupid's bow of his lips, lips that are inches from mine. I have no option other than to breathe him in. His breath holds a minty freshness, the essence of coffee lingering with each exhale. We lock eyes, and for a second, I imagine us to be the only people in the room.

How can someone so conceited and self-absorbed look so good? His features are strong, accompanied by a trim beard that frames his jaw and mouth. His skin doesn't appear to have been kissed by the sun but possesses a naturally bronzed hue, his hair a dark brown with flecks of gold running the length. But his eyes, his eyes are what have me hypnotised. Vibrant and intoxicating, they're the deepest shade of green I have ever seen. I stand, completely absorbed by the moment, completely absorbed by him.

"The rain is metaphorical," I stutter, trying to slow the erratic beating of my heart. "Much like the metaphorical storm I'll bring home with me if I lose my job."

"We wouldn't want that, would we?" Lucian says with an amused expression on his face.

"No," I answer quickly. My gaze is transfixed on his eyes and their many shades of green.

"So then, leave."

I blink and notice his arm is no longer blocking my way. I hurry from the staff room and wonder how long I stood lost in the moment, gazing into his stupid, hypnotic eyes.

"I'll be seeing you, Chelsea," are the words that follow me as I exit the shop.

I pull into the car park at Hazelwood Farm and park outside the café. It is a cute one-story building, the walls pink like candyfloss.

I turn off the engine and slide out of my car to be greeted by Wren Richardson, the farmer's daughter. I had the pleasure of meeting her a few days ago when I came for an interview. At first she seemed reluctant to give me the job, but my friend Cole managed to talk her around.

Her long auburn hair whips in the breeze as she extends her hand. When it comes to introductions I am usually more of a hugger, but from the rigid way Wren holds herself I know she is not.

I take her hand and shake enthusiastically. "Thank you so much for giving me the opportunity to work here. I promise I won't let you down."

Wren's eyes widen and she wriggles her hand from my vice grip. "Like I told you on Friday, the job isn't permanent, and the position will be on a rolling six-week contract."

I tuck a lock of hair behind my ear. "Honestly, that's perfect."

The corner of Wren's mouth quirks up, and she spins around. "Follow me. I have your uniform laid out ready and paperwork for you to fill in. I'll show you the ropes. I'll have to leave you to go check on one of the beehives, but I won't be long…"

Wren continues talking about her bees. She talks while I fill out the paperwork, all the way through the induction video and doesn't stop talking until—like her—I am clad in a green Hazelwood Farm T-shirt and shorts.

Before Wren leaves to check on her hives, she introduces me to her sister, Avery Connors, and her husband Joe, who work side by side in the kitchen. I will be waitressing along with their daughter, Brooke, whilst Maddie works the till. As well as my duties, there is a lot to remember. I don't have a chance to think as orders come in. Luckily, it doesn't take long for me to memorise table numbers and deliver food in a timely fashion.

Wren arrives just in time for the afternoon rush. Customers line up at the till. The queue is so long that it spills out of the door.

"The café never used to get this busy," the elderly lady I am serving complains. I'm unsure if she is speaking to me or the woman who is sitting opposite. I don't know what to say in response, so smile as I place their Caesar salads down in front of them.

I take a step back, and in doing so nearly crash into Wren. She flashes a glance at the elderly woman before turning her attention to me. She gestures for me to follow her, and I do. When we are out of earshot, she speaks. "Mrs Andrews is right. The café used to be quiet, that is before the construction workers began work here." Although her expression remains neutral, something about her tone tells me that she isn't happy about the fact.

"I'm friends with three of the construction workers," I tell her. "Rick is my sister's fiancé, and Seth is marrying my best friend Lizzie next month. Her big brother is the project manager…"

"Cole," Wren answers for me. I don't miss the way her cheeks flush red at the mention of his name. She doesn't wait around long enough for me to ask questions, and hurries to take her next order.

Humming to myself, I make my way around the café. I carry a plate containing a ham sandwich to table nine. At the same time, my gaze sweeps the room to see if any tables need cleaning in readiness for the next customer.

I stop dead, my heart slamming into my chest. Sitting alone at a window table is none other than Lucian Calloway. I've been so busy that I didn't see him come in. But he has seen me and makes a point of keeping his gaze trained on every move I make.

He followed me, there is no other explanation for why he is here. I'm about to head over to him and demand answers when Cole sits at the seat across from Lucian. They appear to be deep in conversation, though Lucian does not take his eyes off me. Blocking Lucian out of my mind, I continue to serve and am relieved to see Wren deliver a silver tray containing drinks to their table.

All I have to do is ignore him and pretend he isn't even here. *How hard can that be?*

I do just that, and after a while I flash a glance over my shoulder. To my delight, I see Cole sitting alone. I'm about to take my next order, but stop, feeling a presence looming behind. I don't need to turn; I know who it is.

Lucian takes a deep inhale before speaking. "Seeing as you will be working here, I have had my PA cancel all of my morning appointments for the foreseeable."

I turn around and our gazes meet. He's so close, too close, and yet I can't bring myself to step away.

"I will be seeing you, Chelsea Janssen," he says, before strolling out of the café.

Lucian Calloway is everywhere I turn. At home, at my work. Is there no escaping him?

After a disaster of a first day at work—thanks to Lucian Calloway—I'm happy to be home. I pull up in my usual parking bay at the rear of the building, but know something is wrong the second I step out of the car. The heavy bass of dance music fills the air, and if I'm not mistaken, it's coming from my flat.

My heels click against the cobblestone path as I hurry to see what is going on. The door leading upstairs is wide open, and I'm shoved out of the way by the conveyor belt of people making their way up and down the narrow flight. Faces pass in a flash, faces I have never seen before in my life, and I'm pretty sure Tyler hasn't either. The heady bass of the music intensifies, and I can feel its beat vibrate right down to my core as I hurry up the stairs.

I step into the hallway and glance around. The lights are off and all of the curtains have been drawn, cloaking the place in darkness. The open-plan lounge and kitchen are alive with strobe lighting that bounces off the walls. Bodies, there are so many bodies—people dancing, making out and gyrating in time to the music.

Instinct tells me to turn around and go back, but what am I thinking? I can't leave without first making sure Tyler is all right.

This is a break-in, it has to be because I know my roomie would never allow a party to take place here. This is Tyler, who bought a five-thousand-pound sofa and projector set for our movie nights. The kitchen cupboards are filled with his grandma's fine china, and he's still paying a monthly finance bill for our television. He wouldn't let this crowd of people pile in and ruin all of our stuff. I know he's going to America, but he's coming back.

Isn't he?

I try to push away the doubt clawing at my mind. I know Tyler, I know him. I tell myself that over and over as I push through the crowd in search of my roomie.

My eyes sting from the thick smoke cloud that hangs in the air. I look at people as I pass but the strobe lighting makes it hard to distinguish between faces.

"Tyler!" I yell. But I can't see him anywhere.

Once in the kitchen I twist the cord on the blinds and open the window. The light from outside filters in and gives me time to survey the damage. My eyes are wide when I see our week's worth of food either eaten or discarded on the floor. The fine china is smashed and lies in a mountain of pieces in the sink.

With bodies crashing into me from every angle, I walk around the room's perimeter to get to the lounge. I pull back the heavy curtains and light pours in. Grumbling dancers cover their eyes. The music is turned down and people begin to leave. I figure they've taken the hint.

"That's right, the door is over there!" I yell and watch in delight as the room begins to clear. Though my small victory is short-lived and the smug smile on my face falls when I see the puddles of beer staining our cream sofa and the tipped-up bottle of red wine bleeding into the Persian rug my sister bought me.

"Where are you all going? The party isn't over!" Tyler hollers. My jaw drops as he appears in front of me. This is a guy who usually lives on a strict alcohol- and gluten-free diet, but is now gorging on pizza and guzzling down beer.

"Tyler." My voice is drowned out by the music as it's once again turned up. The group of people who were making their way out pile back in and the room is soon filled to its full capacity again.

"Leave me, woman, I'm getting my funk on."

"Tyler, stop," I plead, running after him and tugging on the sleeve of his neon shirt. He turns to face me but can barely stand still. His eyes roll as he sways from side to side.

I yank on his arm. "Oh, my God, Tyler. Are you high?"

"I'm high on life, darlin'," is Tyler's reply. "To you, Daddy dear." He lifts the bottle he's holding into the air before chugging back the contents. Pulling his arm free, he moves in time to the music and disappears into the crowd.

I stand, completely floored. It would appear my roomie is throwing a 'fuck you' party, in honour of his father. But Tyler is not the only person who lives here, and if he won't put a stop to this madness, then I will. I pull my phone from my pocket and glance down at the screen. Of course the battery is dead.

That's fine, nothing ten minutes on charge can't fix. I fight my way to my bedroom, and once inside I flick on the light. I gasp, my phone falling to the floor as I take in everything around me. A young couple are making out on the bed. *My* bed. And if I'm not mistaken, the woman is wearing my favourite dress.

My body is shaking in anger and adrenaline. "Get out!" I holler and, crossing my arms, I wait while they stagger to their feet. It takes all of my self-control not to help them out of the room with a complimentary shove. I don't of course, and instead wait for them to leave and slam the door behind them.

With my arms wrapped around my waist, I pad around the room. My clothes and personal items have been discarded across the floor. Cigarette butts are everywhere. Most are out, others hold their amber glow as they slowly smoulder.

My heart hammers and my breath quakes as I make my way to my free-standing wardrobe. I pull open the door to find bare hangers lining the rail. My shoes that were neatly stacked in boxes are in a heaped mess, and our holiday jar is gone. Granted, it was mostly Tyler's money inside, but it was money we were saving for our dream trip to Paris.

I side-eye my dressing table and the place my jewellery box once sat. It's gone. I sink down and perch on the end of the bed. The state of our kitchen and lounge was bad enough, but it hurts me more to know strangers were in my room and going through my things. This is my personal space.

Panic courses through me, and I stumble over to the small ottoman beside my dresser. I prise open the lid, and my heart instantly breaks at what I see. The bag full to the brim of bespoke garments for my baby nephew has been torn open. The clothes that were folded neatly inside are screwed up into balls.

Through blurry vision I flick through the outfits one at a time. Apart from being creased, they appear to be okay—all but one, which incidentally is the outfit that took me the longest to make. The little outfit I had envisioned my nephew wearing on his first birthday. The navy suit jacket I made has been torn and the sewn-in shirt is without its buttons. I fist the material between my fingers.

How could someone do something so cruel?

I fight the tear threatening to fall. These weren't just clothes, no, they were outfits I spent hours hand-crafting, and they were made with love. If stealing from me wasn't enough, whoever did this took great pleasure in trampling all over my heart. I can't deal with this right now, so place the baby garments back into the ottoman and close the lid.

Tears fall from the corners of my eyes as I look around. Everything in this room will need bagging up and either throwing away or sterilising. I need a new bed, a new mattress, carpet, and as for my clothes, I will have to take them to the dry cleaner's in the morning. But I have the interview at the bank first thing. What the hell am I going to wear?

The walls begin to spin before very slowly closing in around me. My lungs are getting tighter by the second, and it's becoming harder and harder to breathe.

I should put my phone on charge. I should call the police, call Royston or Eve, I should call anyone. But all I do, all I'm able to do is scramble to my en suite to retrieve my cleaning products.

When life gets hard cleaning makes everything better and stops anything else bad from happening. The first thing I do is remove the bedsheets. I spray the mattress with antibacterial cleaner. I toss the old bed linen to the corner of the room—incidentally the place my bin is located. Then I bag up all of my personal belongings. Feeling like a small weight has been lifted, I drop to my knees and pick up and discard every cigarette butt. With the dustpan and brush I sweep up every remnant of ash. But my room isn't clean. It'll never be clean now.

I scrub my room from floor to ceiling. I scrub until my hands are sore and blood oozes from tiny cracks. I clean until I can clean no more, and with the bottle of antibacterial spray hugged tightly to my chest I cry myself to sleep.

CHAPTER FIVE

Chelsea

I wake up early the following morning and begin the arduous task of cleaning up, though time soon runs away from me and I'm hyper-aware that I have to get ready. With nothing to wear for my appointment at the bank, I drop in at my sister's and she kindly lends me one of her suits, a suit she hasn't worn in some time. I figuratively brush off the cobwebs and shake off the dust before slipping it on. I have just enough time to kiss my sleepy niece on the forehead as she's getting ready for school before I leave.

I make it to the bank right on time and a member of staff points me in the right direction. But she needn't have bothered, because I know where I'm going. My heels click on the wooden floor as I make my way to Bob's desk. I smile and wave when he comes into view behind the frosted glass partition. He nods in acknowledgment but doesn't smile back, which I try not to read too much into. If anyone is going to approve my business loan today, it'll be Bob Winters.

I've known Bob as far back as I can remember. He is the guy who dressed up as Santa and visited our school at Christmas. Like good old St Nick, Bob has long white hair and a white beard he grows in time for the festive season. Bob approved my parents' mortgage twenty-four years ago and approved my and Amber's joint business loan when we bought the shop. Bob is a yes-man and a real pillar of our community.

He stands when I near and offers me his hand, which, frowning, I accept. I don't remember him being this formal in the past. But things change all the time, and maybe it's protocol now.

"Miss Janssen," he says, and, when he releases my hand, we sit.

"Please, call me Chelsea." I flick the clasp on my handbag and reach in for my lucky pen. "So where do I sign?" I pull out the fountain pen and unscrew the lid. "If possible, can we hurry this along? I have so much I need to do today."

By 'so much to do', I mean I have so much cleaning I need to be getting on with before I have to leave for work. I'll pop in the corner shop on the way home and pick up more cleaning products. Then I have to…

"I'm sorry, Chelsea, I can't give you the loan today."

"What?" My voice trembles as I lower the pen onto the desk.

Bob shrugs. "If it was up to me, I'd give you the money in a heartbeat. But I've entered all your information onto the system, and unfortunately your application has been rejected. If I could do anything—"

"Do it," I say. My tone is verging on desperate, but Bob's sombre expression tells me that this is out of his hands.

"Thank you for your time." I close my handbag and get to my feet. I'm about to leave when he calls after me.

"Chelsea, your pen."

I don't turn. "Keep it. Seems it's all out of luck."

After a slow walk home, I have a hot shower. Once I am dressed in my work uniform, I make my way to Tyler's bedroom. I'm not in the least bit surprised that he is in the same position he was in when I left him, his legs wrapped around the quilt and his ass on display.

"I love you, Tyler, with all my heart. But I will never forgive you for what you did last night. Do you hear me? *Ever.*" Disappointment courses through me as I look at my severely hungover roomie whilst at the same time thinking back to the events that led up to this moment. His auburn hair partially covers his eyes, which I see are closed.

"Wake up!" I say, agitation clear in my voice. I'm not angry at Tyler, not any more. I'm just disappointed.

"Five more minutes," Tyler groans and, holding his pillow over his head, turns away from me. Beer cans litter the bedside table, and partially eaten pizza slices stain his white bedlinen.

"Time to wake up," I say, nudging his butt with the pointy toe of my shoe. "You have a plane to catch. And if I'm being honest, I can't bear to look at you right now."

Tyler slowly turns to face me. The pillow he was holding falls to the floor. "What time is it?" he asks, rubbing his eyes. Cans of beer topple over as he blindly searches the bedside table. More specifically, he's feeling for where his phone usually lies on charge. I wonder if that was stolen last night too, though I can't say I'd have any sympathy if it was.

I fold my arms in front of my chest. "It's eleven a.m."

"The bank appointment?"

I shrug and laugh at the same time. "Well, if my life wasn't falling apart enough…"

"You didn't get the loan?" Tyler's voice is filled with concern.

"No, I didn't get the stupid loan." I turn my back toward him, haul his duffle bag from the floor and sling it onto the bed. "As I said, you have a plane to catch, and I have to leave for work."

Tyler sits up, the strong scent of vomit wafting up from the sheets. "Shit, Chelsea, what happened last night?"

I laugh, this time louder. "I don't know, Tyler, where do I begin? You threw a party until five o'clock in the morning. We got robbed, our TV is smashed. They took our Paris fund, my jewellery…"

Tyler stands and attempts to wrap his arm around me.

"Don't," I say, holding up both hands, signalling that I need space. "As if I wasn't nervous enough this morning, with nothing to wear I had to rush to my sister's house just so I could borrow an outfit."

"I'll replace it, all of it."

I shake my head. "There are just some things money can't replace. Like my grandmother's gold brooch."

"I'm so sorry. I will make it up to you, I promise. Please don't hate me." Tyler juts his bottom lip out while at the same time holding his palms together as if praying.

"I could never hate you. You've been my rock. But right now, that rock is nowhere in sight and I'm drowning."

Tyler flashes a glance at my hands, hands that are red raw and throb with pain. "Tell me you haven't? We worked so hard with your therapist to cure you of your OCD."

I bite back a laugh, because he must know as well as I do that OCD cannot be cured. There isn't a magic switch that I can just flick on and off. The need to clean and keep cleaning is always there. I've just got better at hiding it from him. When my life falls apart, the mask I wear slides down and the OCD takes over. That's when Tyler gets a glimpse of the real me. It feels like a rope tightening around me, tighter and tighter till I can't breathe and the only way to loosen the ropes is to clean.

"It'll be okay," I say and nod my head. "It was just a blip. Now come on, you have a plane to catch."

I turn and leave the room.

"Love you, darlin'," Tyler calls after me.

I stop and wrap my arms around my chest. "I love you too. I just don't like you very much at the moment."

Floorboards creak, and I can sense him drawing near. "We're

okay though, aren't we?" His voice breaks with emotion, and I can hear the uncertainty in his tone. "Tell me we're okay?"

I blow out and give his question some thought. Part of me wants to say no and teach him a lesson. But then I remember that Tyler is catching a flight to America, and after the sale of the building I don't know if he'll come back. I'd never part ways on bad feeling, so for this reason alone I nod. I rest my chin on my shoulder, offering him my profile. "Of course we are okay. Now get showered."

My phone vibrates in my pocket. I pull it free and leave the room while trying to convince myself that the day can't possibly get any worse. Then the Devil's name flashes on the screen.

My shoulders slump as I answer. "Lucian—"

"Chelsea, hi. I'm just calling to check in with you."

"Check in with me?" I walk into the living room, picking up cans and bottles along the way, and toss them into a bin bag.

"I woke up to several messages complaining about the noise last night. I come here this morning to find the shop has two smashed windows."

My palms become clammier the longer I'm in the flat. There is just so much dirt, so much clutter. The phone shakes in my hand, and without thinking I cut the call. I glance around at all the mess. My OCD is demanding that I clean, but I know that once I start, I won't be able to stop. My fingers itch to grab the bleach, the hoover, anything.

Remembering the techniques my therapist taught me, I try to push the overwhelming urge to the back of my mind and prioritize what is important. I can't lose my job, I need it now more than ever seeing as the bank refused to lend me the money I need to open my salon.

The mess isn't going anywhere, it isn't going to get worse. Nothing bad is going to happen. I can clean when I get back, I say over and over in my mind. I take a slow and controlled breath in and head for the door. Exhaling slowly, I pull down the handle and come face to face with Lucian.

The intensity of his gaze leaves me speechless. A few seconds pass before I muster the confidence to speak. "I'm sorry about the window, but I can't talk now. I have to go to work."

Lucian smiles knowingly. "Then we'll continue our conversation there."

I fling my arms out in question. "Why are you stalking me?"

"Stalking is a little strong, don't you think?"

"Really?" I fold my arms indignantly. "First you buy the building where I live, then you follow me to my first day at work. I may not have as many letters after my name as you, but I know the definition of stalking."

It angers me that Lucian doesn't reply, and rather than looking at me, I get the feeling he is watching me. His gaze follows my hand as I tug on the ends of my hair, and he focuses on my lips when I talk. It's as though he is taking a mental snapshot of me, and all I want to do is erase the picture of me from his mind.

Lucian takes a step forward, and I immediately step back. "What are you doing?" I ask, my heartbeat accelerating in my chest.

Lucian wraps his index finger around a lock of my hair before tucking it behind my ear. His touch causes my traitorous body to react with an explosion of goosebumps on my skin.

"It was a pleasant surprise bumping into you yesterday," Lucian says. "I am in the process of acquiring the option on the land at Hazelwood Farm, and my being there was to check on my investment. Due to the nature of the business I have with the farmer, it's imperative that I visit regularly, and who's to tell me I can't enjoy a coffee whilst admiring the scenery when I am there?"

By scenery I know he isn't talking about the land. Him being there at the same time as me does seem coincidental, but I know one thing is not. I pin him with an accusing stare. "And buying this building had nothing to do with me?"

Lucian shrugs. "I saw a failing business, and with it an opportunity."

"An opportunity for what?"

"For—" Lucian begins, though our stare is broken when he looks past me and into the flat.

I want answers, so instinctively try to close the door behind me. Lucian steps forward and pushes the door open. His expression sours.

"What the…" His words trail off, and I'd say for once he is at a loss for what to say. He steps past me and walks into the open-plan lounge.

"I can explain," I say, and follow closely behind. There's urgency in my tone. I don't care about Lucian, but I do care that he'd think I'd treat my home with such disrespect.

He takes his time, stepping between empty beer bottles and half-eaten food that has been smeared into the cream carpet. After a full inspection of the lounge and kitchen he turns to face me. "May I remind you that I am now the owner of this establishment? And although I fully support maintaining an active social life, this utter disregard for my property is unacceptable."

My body begins to quake, and the coping techniques I have in place for my OCD falter. One by one my demons begin to appear. It's as though they've placed a magnifying lens over my eyes, and all I can see is dirt, mess, and clutter. My fingers itch to clean, itch to scrub, itch to polish.

Lucian continues to speak, though I do not hear a word. Instead, all I hear is the constant lull of his voice. I run my fingers through my hair and fist them at my scalp before finally exploding. "It was Tyler!"

Lucian's jaw slackens and he looks at me with wide eyes.

"I'm sorry, I just—" My words trail off, and I make a mental note of where the bin bags are positioned around the room. I started throwing stuff out first thing this morning. I began with anything that was broken, be it glass or the china set. I moved on to…

"This isn't your fault," Lucian says, pulling me from my thoughts.

My usual happy-go-lucky self is nowhere to be seen. I feel on edge, I feel like I'm going to self-destruct any second. I need to count to three, I need to focus on my breathing.

One. I inhale slowly.

Two. I exhale.

Thr…

It's no use, the walls are closing in. The rubbish scattered around is turning into mountains. Mountains of bottles and food that'll rain down around me and bury me alive. I'm trapped, I can't move, I can't breathe. Every feeling I fought so hard to suppress is jolted forward, and I press my internal self-destruct button. "No, this is your fault!" I yell, and pant heavily as my words detonate.

"My fault?" Lucian places his hand over his chest, clearly taken aback. But still he stands, as cool as a damn cucumber and completely unaffected by my growing agitation.

My breaths come sharp and heavy. *Leave, Lucian, leave before I say something I can't take back and you make me homeless.*

I purse my lips together, but it's no use. "Everything was fine until you bought this building behind Tyler's back. You've taken everything from him. I'm glad the flat has been trashed and the windows smashed. Do you want to know why? I'll tell you. Because people like you think you can buy anything you want, and everything comes with a price tag. Well, I have news for you, it doesn't!" My words echo around the room.

And there I go. Everything that was on my mind came tumbling out with zero filter. I should back down, apologise for my outburst, but I can't. I stand tall, my hands placed firmly on my hips.

Lucian studies me for a beat, like I am a piece of a jigsaw he can't quite place. He smiles devilishly. "Fascinating."

"What is?"

"I need you to move out."

"What?" My façade crumbles, and the confidence I exuded moments ago is gone. Lucian is kicking me out, and now I am officially homeless. Why did he have to come here today of all days, and why did he have to keep goading me?

"Only for a few days," Lucian adds, and taps his chin in thought. "I have a team of builders starting work on the shop. I will have them sort the mess out up here, after which I'll arrange for my interior design company to spruce the place up."

"You don't have to do that," I say, my words sheepish.

"Yes, I do. You have no idea what lengths I would go to to ensure your happiness." He speaks with earnestness, and for the first time it's as though I'm seeing a totally different side of Lucian.

He tugs at the lapels of his pristine black jacket before clearing his throat. "Have you got somewhere you could stay? If not, you're welcome to stay at one of the Calloway hotels."

I shake my head and swallow the hot lump building in my throat. "No, thank you. I'll crash at my sister's for a few days."

"Very well." Lucian motions his hand in the direction of the bedrooms. "I encourage you to spend the evening packing away your possessions."

My gaze lowers to the floor and I shrug. "There's nothing to pack. Anything of sentimental value was taken. The outfits I made for my baby nephew will need to be dry-cleaned and pressed. And as for my clothes, they are mostly ruined, and those that aren't need sterilising."

Warm fingers capture my chin, and Lucian lifts my head. "You are not going into work today, not after what has happened. You're not in the right mindset."

"I'm fine," I lie. Warm tears roll down my cheeks. I have no idea why I'm crying. I step back and lower my head so he can't see, but it's too late. "I can't miss time off work," I say, my voice cracking.

"Chelsea, I'm not asking."

CHAPTER SIX

Lucian

Never have I seen her look so vulnerable or so lost. All I want to do is scoop her up in my arms and carry her to my car. I'd take her away, far, far away where no one could hurt her, no one could touch her. I'm tempted to suggest it but fear it would concrete her earlier assumption of me being a stalker. I don't want to add 'kidnapper' to her list, although the idea itself is more than a little tempting.

Chelsea Janssen is mine, even if she doesn't know it. Every tantalising inch of her belongs to me. I have no way of articulating the depths of my feelings for her, I just know they're painfully real.

Chelsea turns her back on me. Her shoulders rise and fall jerkily, and I know she's crying. The floorboards creak as I advance toward her.

"Don't."

Her one word cements my feet to the floor. Chelsea spins around, her expression devoid of emotion. "I'm fine," she repeats with more certainty. Though try as she might, she can't hide the mottled pink patches on her cheeks or her bloodshot eyes.

"Very well," I say. If she doesn't want me to comfort her, I won't. But there is something I will do. I reach into my jacket pocket and retrieve my phone. I search for Kenneth Richardson's name and shoot over a quick text.

"Done," I say simply.

Chelsea's expression falters. "What's done?"

"I texted the farmer to let him know that you had a break-in yesterday, and subsequent to that you will not be at work today."

Chelsea's eyes narrow. She doesn't speak but I can see there is so much she wants to say. Awkward seconds pass, and she opens her mouth to say something when her ringtone sounds out. She pulls her phone from her pocket and taps on her screen.

I lean forward. "The farmer?"

"He's given me the day off," she says between gritted teeth.

"I will recompense what you have lost today."

"I don't want your money, Lucian. I didn't want it two years ago, and I don't now."

Finally, we're addressing the elephant in the room. I run my fingers through my hair. "About that—"

Chelsea shakes her head. "You asked me to your house that day so you could purchase my photograph, but instead offered me a million pounds to spend the night with you. Do you really think so little of me?"

I advance toward her, but she doesn't step back. She's facing me head-on, which I find more than a little intriguing. I capture her hands and hold them between mine. "I just wanted to prove a point to my brother. I promise you, my intentions were honourable. I would not have expected…"

Chelsea's expression is unreadable, and instead of pulling away she laces her fingers with mine. "Expected what?"

My breath hitches in my throat and my cock twitches in my trousers. "Don't play games with me," I bite out.

"If I'd been willing…" She steps closer.

I dip my head so my lips brush against the shell of her ear. "If you'd been willing…" I take a sharp inhale. "Then I would have fucked you all night long. In every position. In every room of my estate."

Electricity sparks around us. I want nothing more than to fist my fingers in her hair and claim her mouth. Her crystal-blue eyes meet my greens, and I can feel her retreat. I don't release her, not right away, and for a second I tighten my hold. I take in everything her body has to offer—her scent, her touch, her warmth—before finally releasing her.

I don't see anger in her stare, but something else. She looks at me in a way she never has before. "My point exactly, Lucian. If something is offered to you, you take it."

I shrug and try to fight back my desire. "I'm a red-blooded male, Chelsea, what do you expect?"

"Nothing, Lucian. You're the same as everyone else out there. The same as Thomas, the same as—"

I raise my hand. "Thomas, as in your ex-boyfriend who burnt down your salon? Tell me, how am I the same as him?"

"He wanted my shop, and you want my body. There is no sincerity behind your motives, everyone wants something from me."

I rub my hand over my beard. "Foolish girl. I don't just want your body. I want you, all of you."

The silence is louder than it has ever been. I'm waiting for her to say something, anything, but she stands with her lips pressed firmly together.

I don't know what to say to alleviate the tension between us. I ball my hands into fists and push them into my trouser pockets. I glance toward the hallway and back to Chelsea. "I think I'm going to—"

The bedroom door swings open and Tyler strides out. Steam rises from his bare chest. A pink fluffy towel is secured around his waist. He beams at Chelsea, but his expression sours when he looks at me. "What is *he* doing here?"

Chelsea motions to the door. "He was just leaving."

She doesn't stick around to hear my reply. She disappears

into one of the bedrooms and reappears with a tray full of cleaning products. She lays the bottles out on the kitchen worktop, along with a selection of rags for cleaning.

"Not this again." Tyler hurries over to Chelsea and puts the bottles back into the tray. "I said I'd clean up," he insists.

"You have a flight to catch. The taxi will be here any minute."

I take a step forward. "May I make a suggestion?"

"No!" Chelsea and Tyler holler in unison. They continue to argue about who is going to clean up, and, zoning out of their argument, I make my way to the window and peer out onto the street. From up here I have the perfect view.

Heller St Claire is a quaint yet busy town. People stop walking in the street to greet one another, shop owners help carry customers' bags to their cars and small crowds gather to gossip on street corners. From this small snippet of time I can feel a real sense of community. I know that in order to make the estate agency a success I will have to make a good impression with the locals. Which only reinforces that I made the right decision about Royston and Eve, the previous employees. Keeping them on and training them up in a lucrative career should work in my favour.

I home in on a black taxi, which parks up out front. "As much as I hate interrupting," I pipe up, "I believe your taxi has just arrived."

"Shit!" Tyler yells, and runs to his bedroom to get dressed. A smile creeps its way up my face from knowing that he is leaving and I will have Chelsea all to myself.

I don't move from the window and listen as Chelsea and Tyler say their goodbyes.

"Please call me the moment you've landed. I want Mason's home address. And if he gives you any serial killer vibes, I want you to get out, do you hear me?"

I watch them hug through the reflection in the windowpane. Tyler is gay and I know I have nothing to worry about, yet it bothers me seeing another man with his arms around her.

They break their hug and head downstairs. From the window I have the perfect view of their goodbye. They talk briefly before they hug again and Tyler slides into the taxi.

I step back and grab my phone from my pocket. I shoot an email to Cornwall's Merry Maids, a local cleaning service, and wait patiently for Chelsea to return.

I take a moment to look around the flat. The living area is small, a lot smaller than I'm used to. I ignore the mess and take in the actual room. I'm surprised that they don't have a breakfast bar or a dining table. Where the hell do they eat?

The open-plan living room and kitchen are decorated in a dull cream. Except for the kitchen, which has a cheap laminate floor, the same tired cream carpet appears to be fitted throughout. Everything looks so clinical, not like a home at all. I notice pictures hanging in a collage-style photo frame. I bypass photos of Tyler and focus on Chelsea. There are several of her and her sister, Amber, whom I am acquainted with. There are photos of Chelsea and a group of friends, all of whom I recognise, her niece, and finally two scraggy-looking black cats. Chelsea doesn't strike me as a cat person.

"Take a picture, it'll last longer," Chelsea says.

"If you insist." I lift my arm, my phone still in my hand.

"Lucian, don't."

Chelsea appears beside me and her fingers pull at the sleeve of my jacket. She's standing so close, so damn close. I push my phone into my pocket. Clearing my throat, I loosen my tie. "Get dressed. I'm taking you out for lunch."

Chelsea laughs and holds out her arms. "This is all I have."

Although the Hazelwood Farm T-shirt and skimpy shorts are somewhat appealing, they are not the right attire for the place I have in mind. "I'll take you shopping first."

"Thanks, Lucian, but no. I really have to tidy the flat."

I ignore her comment and instead think about where I could take her to get food. I'm sure she'd appreciate me taking her somewhere local. It's then I remember the little café on the street corner. I turn, about to suggest that, only to find Chelsea on her hands and knees gathering cleaning products. "That is unnecessary. I have arranged for a local cleaning company to come out and take care of the mess."

I fish out my pocket watch and look at the time. I was meant to be viewing a plot of land in Bristol this afternoon, but I will send Josh instead. "I have a few hours free," I lie. I make my way toward Chelsea and hold out my hand for her to take. "If you won't let me take you shopping, or out to a swanky restaurant, I guess I could lower my impeccably high standards and join you at Timms Café. What do you say?"

My comment was intended as a joke, but Chelsea doesn't laugh. I'm leaning forward with my hand poised in front of her as I wait for her to take me up on my offer. I clear my throat and Chelsea glances up. "You don't understand, Lucian. I *have* to clean."

My arm falls to my side. "I don't understand." My gaze follows her hand. Her skin is bright red and split in places. Her right hand appears redder, particularly in the place she's holding the rag. "Let the cleaning company do it."

"I can't!"

I take a few steps back and take in everything in front of me—the mountain of cleaning products, and the frantic way she scrubs at the carpet.

"Now you've seen crazy Chelsea doing what she does best, you can leave."

I side-eye the door, which is open. Without a word I head toward the door and push it shut. I pull my arms out of my jacket and hang it on the coat hooks in the small hallway.

Chelsea's eyebrows knit together. "What are you doing?"

I unfasten the buttons around my wrists and roll up my shirt sleeves so the fabric hugs my elbows. "What's it look like?" I advance toward the kitchen and grab a bottle from the worktop. "I'm helping you clean."

A smile tugs at Chelsea's lips, and she lets out a small chuckle.

"What's so funny? Not seen a posh boy clean up before?"

"It's not that."

"Then what?" I say, crouching down and joining her on the carpet.

She nods her head toward the bottle in my hand. "That's the de-icer for the car."

I laugh, and for once she laughs along with me. I get to my feet and sift through the cleaning products. I narrow my eyes to read the small print to work out exactly what each bottle is used for. Maybe I'd be more useful first throwing all the empty beer bottles away. I tear off a bin liner from the roll and open up the bag. With my back toward her I proceed in tossing the rubbish in.

"Lucian," she calls.

"Yes, Chelsea?"

Her eyes sparkle in a way I've never seen before. She nibbles on her lower lip for a beat before smiling. "Thank you."

CHAPTER SEVEN

Chelsea

Friday soon comes around, and after a long day at work I find myself in Starlight bridal shop.

"How do I look?" Amber asks. My sister is standing in front of three floor-to-ceiling mirrors. Pouting, she turns left and then right. Her focus is on her protruding stomach.

"Beautiful," I say, taking a seat on the plush leather sofa. Laid out neatly on the small glass table to my right is a selection of finger foods and canapés. A bottle of wine and a jug of non-alcoholic cocktail wait for us after the fitting.

My mouth waters and my stomach rumbles loudly. Lizzie, the bride to be, would kill me if I dropped so much as a crumb on my dress. But the thought of swiping one of the canapés is so tempting. To distract myself I lean forward and pull my phone from my bag. I'm surprised Tyler hasn't texted today, but remind myself he's six hours behind. With nothing else to do to pass the time I snap several photos, one of the platters of food and the other of my sister.

I smile down at the phone screen. Amber and I are so similar in appearance it's scary. From a distance we are identical, but up close is where our similarities begin to fizzle out. Amber's looks are more whimsical than my own and verging on pixie-like. Her features are smaller than mine, her nose is upturned, and her ears have a slight point.

"The dress doesn't make me look fat?" Amber pipes up.

"You're pregnant." I smile at how the peach bridesmaid dress hugs her baby bump.

"Don't tell me you took a picture?" Amber says, her hand on her hip. "Delete it. Now."

"Being pregnant is beautiful," I remind her. "It's a time in your life you want to look back on."

Amber's expression remains unchanged, and, sighing, I click on my camera roll and press 'delete' on the photo. I hold my phone in the air as if somehow she'll be able to see the screen from where she's standing. "There, happy?"

I'm about to place my phone in my bag when I notice a text message flash on the screen.

Lucian: The works are complete. You can return home tonight.

I breathe a sigh of relief. I've stayed at my sister's house for the past few days, and although she and her fiancé Rick have been most accommodating, in the back of my mind I know I'm a guest, and as a guest the last thing I want to do is overstay my welcome.

I type back a quick reply.

Me: Thanks.

I lean forward and clasp the champagne flute in my hand. The strawberry that floats on top bobs as I bring the glass to my lips. "Amber, I have some good news," I begin, meeting my sister's gaze in the mirror's reflection. I'm about to tell her that I'll be moving out when Tori, the shop manager, steps out from behind the changing room curtain.

"Are you ready?"

Lowering the champagne flute to the table, I get to my feet. Without hesitation she pulls the curtain back and Lizzie steps out.

I hold my hand over my mouth. "Oh, my God, you look stunning."

Lizzie's cheeks glow red and, looking to the floor, she smooths the front of her dress several times. "Do you really think so?"

"I do," I say with a smile so big it hurts. "Seth is one lucky man."

Tori crouches, and, with the dress' train in her hand, they walk over to where Amber is standing. Lizzie steps onto the raised platform in front of the mirrors. Everything is clear one moment and hazy the next. I have to wipe away the tears forming in my eyes so I can better appreciate my best friend. Lizzie is wearing a slim-fitting A-line gown, so simple in design yet perfectly elegant. She combs her fingers through her shoulder-length brown hair. Her movements are on the mechanical side because Lizzie has never liked being the centre of attention. But like it or not, on her wedding day all eyes will be on her.

"I can't believe I'm actually doing this. I'm getting married."

Tori lowers Lizzie's train and steps back. Amber stands to Lizzie's right, and, seeing my cue, I hurry over and stand to her left. Amber and I look like two bookends in our matching peach bridesmaid dresses. Smiling at our reflection, Lizzie takes our hands.

"I never thought I'd get here, you know." Trembling, she squeezes my fingers. "I have the perfect life, amazing children, the most wonderful husband-to-be, and the best friends anyone could ever ask for. I need someone to pinch me so I know this is real."

My lips quiver as I fight to keep them turned up. The smiles on Lizzie's and Amber's faces are genuine, because they both have their happily ever after. But what about me? I don't have anyone waiting for me at home. My roomie is thousands of miles away.

I've had my business loan rejected by three different banks, and I have used up nearly all of my savings. They say every cloud has a silver lining, but all my cloud seems to do is rain down on me.

I try to shake away my negativity, because my life is going to get better.

It just has to.

I return to my sister's house after the dress fitting. I pack the few belongings I have, after which I read my niece a bedtime story—*The Fairy and her Wings*, a book my sister wrote a long time ago. The story highlights the importance of not giving up, no matter how hopeless things seem. Freja is snoring before I say, "The end." I place a kiss on her forehead, tuck her in and, after thanking Amber and Rick for letting me stay with them, I leave.

Rain pelts against the windshield as I drive back. Back to the reality of an empty flat. Money is particularly tight until I get paid, and without Tyler I'm going to have to pay the bills myself. I can cover everything, just about, but I'm going to have to be careful.

I pull into the car park at the rear of the building. I don't rush to get out of the vehicle, instead look out through the window, which is hazy due to the heavy downpour. The hum of the engine is washed out by the pitter-patter of rain as it bounces off the car roof. The sky rumbles fiercely, and I jump. Looks like we're in for a storm.

I glance up toward the flat and am sure I see light filter out of my bedroom window. Leaving lights on isn't an option when I'm on an electricity meter. With that in mind, I hurry out of the car. The rain is unforgiving, and in the small distance between the car park and the entrance of my flat I'm drenched from head to toe.

Music fills my ears the second I enter the narrow hallway. Music that could only be coming from the flat. I hurry up the narrow flight of stairs. My nose is greeted by the strong scent of paint.

The front door to my flat is open, and bright light spills out onto the hallway. Music *and* lights? My stomach churns as I imagine how much electricity is being eaten up. I run inside and head straight to the meter to see how much, if any, credit I have remaining. Out of breath, I gasp when I notice the meter has had a fifty-pound top-up.

"What kind of a gentleman leaves a lady without electricity?"

I jump, turning suddenly on hearing Lucian's voice. How did I not see him when I came in?

Because I was in such a blind panic to check my meter, that's how.

My eyes go wide as I take him in. It is the first time I have seen Lucian clad in something other than a suit. Granted, he's wearing a shirt. The top buttons are undone, and the sleeves rolled up, but what has my attention is he's wearing a pair of jeans, actual jeans!

He places two glasses down on the kitchen island—an island that wasn't there before—and advances toward me.

"I thought we should celebrate. I have ordered food from my favourite French restaurant." He looks me up and down, pausing momentarily at my breasts. I follow his stare and am horrified to see the outline of my nipples protrude from my white T-shirt, a white T-shirt that—thanks to the rain—is completely see-through. Dithering, I hug my chest and turn my back toward him.

"It will arrive within the hour, so you have plenty of time to get ready," he continues.

Plenty of time to get ready? Get ready for what?

My head's in too much of a spin to process everything. So, taking a calming breath, I glance around the room. A candlelit table is positioned in the new dining area, the centrepiece being a small vase holding a single red rose.

I can't have dinner with him, it just isn't right. Even with all the effort he's put in, I just can't. "Lucian—"

He holds up his hand. "Hold that thought." He hurries to the new state-of-the-art American-style fridge and opens the door.

"Red or white?" he says, pulling out two bottles. "I know red is meant to be kept at room temperature, but I prefer it chilled."

I take in the fridge and all its contents. The colourful array of fruits and vegetables is the first thing I notice, then a selection of meats, cheeses and fish. The door is stocked with eggs, milk and a variety of juices.

I look around and am floored by what I see. The flat has been decorated like something out of a magazine, with grey walls, a brand-new sofa, TV and an electric fireplace. The old kitchen has been ripped out and replaced with new. The units are gloss-white with a stunning black granite worktop.

"This is too much," I say.

Lucian looks from me and to the fridge. "I couldn't very well have this beautiful kitchen fitted and not fully stocked for you."

Tears sting my eyes. I'm not happy, nor am I sad, I'm just overwhelmed. I hurry past Lucian and head straight for my bedroom, and am again blown away.

A gold-leaf bed sits in the centre with rich satin sheets. A beautiful red gown is laid out on the bedspread. A gown he obviously wants me to wear this evening.

Not going to happen.

The walls are painted in a deep blue, and thick gold curtains hang from the window. An integrated mirrored wardrobe hugs the back wall, and I instinctively hurry over and slide the door across. Everything that was once inside is gone and has been replaced new for old. Clothes for every occasion fill the rails. A selection of trainers and stilettos have been placed neatly on a shoe rack. Handbags—half a dozen, maybe more—line the top shelf.

This must have cost a fortune. Anger courses through me at the sheer presumption of the man. How could he think that I would want any of this stuff? I've never accepted charity, and I won't start now. But it's not just that that's bothering me. This place feels more like a show home than my home. Lucian said he was going to spruce the place up, not change everything. This isn't Barbie's dream house and I am not a doll he can dress up.

With my hands on my hips, I march to the door, but stop when I see my ottoman. Finally, one thing that he hasn't changed. The ottoman contained all the clothes I handmade for my nephew; no doubt Lucian has taken it upon himself to change them too. The walls may as well be painted red, because that is all I see right now as I march to the ottoman and pull off the lid.

Layer upon layer of blue tissue paper has been placed inside, which rustles as I flick through. After lifting the final sheet, I am able to see what lies beneath. My anger instantly dissolves at what I see. All the clothes I handmade have been folded and stacked neatly. The scent of fabric softener fills the air as I lift the small outfits one by one. I don't stop until I reach the navy suit that was damaged. Buttons that were torn off have been replaced, and the sewn-in shirt has been restitched. There isn't an imperfection in sight. My heart warms to see that the baby clothes haven't been replaced and instead have been washed and ironed.

As much as I want to hate Lucian, I don't in this moment. I feel something, something I've never felt for him before. I fold the little outfits and place them back in the ottoman, and then I do something I swore I'd never do. I swallow my pride.

I peel my T-shirt and trousers off en route to the shower. The sodden material slaps against the tiled floor as I discard each item of clothing. I slide the glass panel across and, reaching in, I turn the tap. I wait a beat for the water to heat up, and when steam begins to fog the bathroom mirror, I step under the shower head.

I glide the bar of soap over my body and then wash my hair. I dry off and slip into the towelling robe, which is hanging up on the back of the door. After towel-drying my hair, I pad into the bedroom. My gaze lingers on the wardrobe before finally landing on the red dress. I rock on my heels several times before advancing toward the bed.

This doesn't mean anything. Having dinner with Lucian just shows him that I am grateful for everything he has done, and I won't feel indebted to him.

I'm surprised how light the chiffon material feels as I lift it up. The fabric gently caresses my skin as I pull it over my head and down into place. The dress is on the conservative side, with a high neckline and a modest skirt that falls inches below my knee.

I look at myself in the wardrobe's mirrored doors and wonder who the person is looking back. The Chelsea I know wouldn't be joining Lucian for dinner, not now, not ever.

I swallow away any last-minute reservations, and with tentative steps I head toward my bedroom door. Counting to three, I take a deep calming breath, first in and then out. With my fingers clasped around the brass handle, I turn and push it open.

Lucian's back is toward me when I re-enter the lounge. The curtain's thick velvet material is clasped between his fingers as he stands and peers out onto the moonlit street.

With my hands held firmly behind my back I make my way across the room. The confidence that accompanied me moments ago dwindles with every passing second. Each step I take feels heavier than the last, and each breath harder to inhale.

I stand still for a beat and try to calm my nerves. Instead of advancing toward him, I'm walking back, back toward my bedroom and familiarity.

The floorboard creaks and Lucian turns to face me. Silently he watches me, and I can feel his gaze drinking me in. Though the admiration in his eyes is quickly replaced by disappointment and his brows slam together the second my fingers connect with the handle of my bedroom door.

"Chelsea, wait." His tone emits authority, the kind that has my feet rooted firmly to the spot.

I close my eyes to block out everything around me, and with my arms wrapped around my waist I shake my head. "I'm sorry. I thought I could do this, but it's too much."

I take a moment to bask in the silent emptiness that

surrounds me, but jump at the sensation of warm skin brushing against my face. My eyes snap open to find Lucian standing inches from me. He gently caresses my cheek with the back of his hand.

"Don't," I whisper. I tilt my head away, though his hand follows. For a split second I forget who I am, I forget who he is. I lean into him and it's as though I melt into his touch. The contact sends shards of electricity whizzing from my head right down to my toes. I've been touched before by a man, but never like this.

"I can't do this," I say, with more certainty.

CHAPTER EIGHT

Lucian

"You have made me wait two years for tonight. You're going to have dinner with me."

She swallows loudly before stepping back. "Fine. But when we are done, I want you to drop the magician act."

"Excuse me?"

"You know, magically popping up in my life."

I laugh and, brushing past, I capture her hand in mine. "No promises, because like it or not, I own the building where you live." And, taking the lead, I walk us toward the table. I pull out her chair and she sits.

"I'll find somewhere else to live. Then I'll be rid of you."

My smile doesn't falter as I sit in the chair opposite. "For a short while, perhaps."

Chelsea holds out her arms exasperatedly. "What are you going to do? Buy every building I rent?"

"If I have to."

Her jaw goes slack. "Tell me you're joking."

I smile devilishly. "Perhaps."

She gives me a lopsided grin before shaking her head. "I don't get you, Lucian."

"And that is how it will remain. Transparency in most cases is boring."

"Am I transparent?" Her question is so quiet I barely hear. It's as though curiosity got the better of her and the words tumbled out of their own accord. I could feign ignorance and pretend I didn't hear. But where would the fun be in that?

"Are you transparent?" I repeat her question and let the words rest on the tip of my tongue before answering. "As a pane of glass, although you are yet to bore me."

My reply has the desired effect as her cheeks turn a delicious shade of crimson. I break eye contact with Chelsea and glance down at my phone. I scroll through my contact list and stop on my butler Ronald's number. Without hesitation I open up a new message.

Me: My date has arrived. See to it that our food is brought up.

My finger hovers over the send button before I return my attention to Chelsea. "I wonder, is it presumptuous of me to refer to you as my date?"

"Does my opinion really matter? You're Lucian Calloway the Great." Chelsea makes a point of air-quoting 'the Great'. "You do and say as you please."

She has a point; I wouldn't have changed the word even if she objected. Chelsea leans forward and takes the glass of wine I courteously filled for her a little while back and drinks the entire contents.

I hit send on the text message and push the device into my pocket.

Chelsea grabs the wine bottle by the neck and pulls it from the ice bucket. I lean forward and place my hand over the rim of her glass before she has time to refill. "You may want to pace yourself."

Her eyes widen with indignation. "Move your hand."

I quirk my brow. "Or what? You don't strike me as a drink-from-the-bottle kind of girl."

"You have no idea what kind of girl I am."

"Of course I do, Chelsea."

Her expression falters, a ghost of a smile tugging at the corners of her lips.

Am I finally making headway with her?

I'm about to tell her how utterly breathtaking she looks when wine spills onto the back of my hand and seeps between my fingers. Instinctively I pull my hand away.

With a devious grin on her face, Chelsea continues to pour the wine into her glass. "Like I said"—she tips the glass back and finishes her drink in one—"you have no idea what kind of girl I am."

Her eyes twinkle with mischief, and the urge to pull her over my knee and spank her tight little arse has me shifting in my seat.

"Transparent enough for you? You didn't see that coming, did you?" Her tone is light-hearted, though I know I've hit a nerve. I could continue with the direction of our conversation and see just how far I can push her. But I don't want to ruffle her feathers just yet, there will be plenty of time after we've eaten.

"You beguile me," I say simply.

Chelsea's mouth forms a cute little O. "What the hell does that even mean?"

The sound of the front door opening causes us to break eye contact. Ronald and a team of caterers pile in with our food. Ronald is tall and gangly, and his long auburn hair is secured into a tidy man-bun. He is wearing a black suit with an off-white dicky bow secured to the collar of his shirt. He acknowledges me with a curt nod of the head and stands back whilst the catering team begin laying the food out on the kitchen island. Silver clangs together as domed plate covers are removed. The air is filled with the aromatic scent of a French restaurant.

Chelsea's eyes are wide as she looks over the sheer mass of food. "We're never going to eat all of that."

She is right, of course. I ordered two of everything on the menu. I can already feel the judgement in her stare. She thinks that because I am rich that I'm wasteful, but she couldn't be further from the truth. "All the leftovers will be hand-delivered to the nearest homeless shelter."

Chelsea's expression softens. She looks at me differently now and, tilting her head to the right, she lowers her glass onto the table. "How do you do it?"

"Do what?"

"Be a dick as well as a half-decent guy at the same time?"

I keep my expression neutral. "Skill."

An explosion of laughter erupts from Chelsea's lips. Her whole face comes to life when she laughs. What I'd give to be the man to put a smile on her face every day. Slowly her laughter dies down. She looks from me to the catering staff as they begin to pile out.

Her body hunches forward and her fingers begin to circle around a long lock of her hair, not once but over and over. It amazes me how quickly her body language shifts from jovial to uncomfortable. "So, what's on the menu?" she asks, and I suspect her question is a way of filling the silence.

I nod toward the kitchen island. "For starters we have escargots a la Bourguignonne, duck pâté en croûte, tartare de filet de boeuf…"

She raises her hand. "Please, speak English."

"Life would be very boring if we had all the answers. Don't you prefer a little mystery?"

Chelsea curves an eyebrow, her gaze homing in on the tray Ronald is carrying over. "Not when that mystery includes eating bugs."

I figure Chelsea is referring to the eight large snail shells that are heading our way. "Invertebrates," I say, matter-of-factly. "Snails are not bugs, nor are they insects. They are invertebrates, they have no backbone and—"

Chelsea raises her hand. "I don't need to know a snail's anatomy, Lucian. The fact is they're slimy and slither around in the mud. I am not putting that in my mouth."

I make eye contact with Ronald just as he is about to present us with the escargots. I give a discreet shake of the head, and within seconds the starter is back on the kitchen island and the domed plate cover is placed over the top.

I lean forward. "Tell me, Chelsea. What do you like to eat?"

She swivels and sits up in her chair to get a better look at the food. "I don't know, anything normal, I guess. Insects and snails are a no-no. I also don't eat any kind of unusual meat."

"Define unusual," I challenge.

Chelsea hitches a shoulder. "I don't know, Lucian."

"Am I right in my assumption that frogs' legs are off the table? Because it's true what they say, they taste just like chicken."

Chelsea slaps a hand to her mouth, the look of disgust written all over her face.

"You don't get out much, do you." Though my words hold a question, it is meant as a statement.

When Chelsea doesn't answer, I glance at Ronald. The ceiling light highlights the sweat gathering at his temples. He stands awkwardly and awaits instruction. "You heard the lady, bring the 'normal' food over. Nothing too audacious."

We eat our starters in silence. The only words spoken are from Chelsea when she asks for an English translation of the dish. No matter how beautifully presented the food, if there is a single ingredient she is unfamiliar with she turns the plate away.

There is a break between courses, and as the caterers swap the starters out for the mains, I see this as an opportunity to get better acquainted with the fair-haired vixen opposite. "Tell me a little about yourself."

Chelsea regards me sceptically before shaking her head. "No."

My chest quakes with a chuckle. "No?"

"You heard me. I'm transparent, remember, so I figure telling you about me would be a waste of my time. Why don't you tell me about you?"

"Okay." I shuffle in the seat, silently deciding which facet of my life to share with her. "I grew up in London. It was there where along with my brothers I attended Ravenhill boarding school. Naturally, I excelled at school and completed my studies at Eton. I have several degrees, one in—"

"One in finance, and another in business studies, I know. I don't want you to tell me what I can read in an article. Tell me something personal. Tell me something real. Tell me about you. Your childhood."

I rub my hand over my chin, the coarse stubble digging into my palm. "I imagine it comes as no shock to you that I had a privileged upbringing—"

"Understatement of the century," Chelsea teases.

"—but privilege comes with a price. I was brought up in a superficial world dictated by rules and structure. By eight I was sent to Ravenhill boarding school and those were the worst days of my life. The only time I can say I was genuinely happy as a child was the summers we spent in our family estate." I smile and remember back to the mischief my brothers and I would get up to. "Freesdon Hall is the only place I felt like I could let loose and just live. As boys we'd climb the gates that led out to a small park and play cricket with the local children. When I hit fourteen, we would go to the skate park and chat up girls."

I fail to mention that Gage was often getting high and doing a little more than just 'chatting' to the girls.

Chelsea waits for me to continue with my tales of Freesdon Hall, but the truth is our adventures ended abruptly the following year when Gage decided to steal a car. Things from then on went from bad to worse.

Chelsea places her elbows on the table and rests her chin in her hands. "Tell me about your parents."

"My mother." I take a deep breath and think of the best way of describing her. There isn't a word that can do her justice, so I settle on the first thing that pops into my head. "She was wonderful, she worked in fashion, and she was an amazing cook. Her signature dish was cottage pie. As for my father, he tried his best but being a parent just didn't come naturally to him and discipline always came before love."

I fail to mention that I would have received a sharp clip around my ear for daring to place my elbows on the table. I like the fact that Chelsea didn't grow up in my world and is ignorant of the many expectations we had thrust upon us at early ages.

"I guess privilege really does come with a price," Chelsea says, her gaze laced with pity. Pity, such a patronising emotion.

I shrug her comment off. "But we had everything that money can buy, and money is what life is all about."

Chelsea shakes her head. "No, Lucian, it isn't. Making special memories with the people we love is."

Her words stab me in the heart. I am so used to discovering other people's weaknesses that I'm not used to someone discovering mine. I'm entering unfamiliar territory and I don't like it. I clear my throat and shake my head. "Ronald will be serving our main courses shortly; you should remove your elbows from the table."

Chelsea does as I request. She lowers her arms to her sides and places her hands in her lap. Although my comment was abrupt, the upturn of her lips shows that she hasn't taken offence.

"What are you smiling at?"

Chelsea sucks her lips into her mouth before replying. "It's nice to see that you too are a mere mortal."

My jaw clenches for a second before I withdraw the tension.

It's not pity dancing in her gaze, but interest. I swallow hard, swallowing my pride in the process. I raise my glass of wine. "I'd like to make a toast."

Chelsea raises her glass immediately. "What are we toasting to?"

"To you, for agreeing to have dinner with me this evening."

Chelsea blushes and we ping our glasses together.

The mains go down a lot better than the starters. Although Chelsea still refuses to try anything that she refers to as 'odd'.

I hover my cutlery above the plate of coq au vin in front of me and stab my fork into a roasted cauliflower wedge. "You know, as children we would be made to eat every last crumb from our dinner plates before we were excused."

"Wow, it really sucked to be you."

I look up from my plate and notice how Chelsea's entire demeanour has changed. Although the cagy version of Chelsea is a hoot, I must admit that I like this side of her—the side of her that engages in idle conversation and doesn't see me as akin to something she's stepped in.

After she rejects three main courses, I'm surprised to see Chelsea say yes to one. It would seem we have found something that she likes: deep-fried chicken wrapped around cheese and ham. A dish so simple, yet utterly delicious. I point my fork toward her plate. "How's the chicken cordon bleu?"

She nods and uses her napkin to dab the corners of her mouth. "It's so good. Tyler would be proud of me. Before he left for America, he set me the challenge to try new things and live a little."

This girl doesn't know the definition of living, but I'm hoping to change that in the near future.

The wine flows easily, and one bottle quickly becomes two. I am not much of a wine drinker. After a few glasses I would normally move on to brandy. But tonight is different. I'm enjoying the wine as much as I am the company. Everything feels nice, feels natural.

Our conversation started off on matters such as business and her beauty salon, and quickly turns to series she likes to watch on Netflix. Her steady tone is swallowed up by laughter and intermittent hiccups.

"So, tell me why you bought the farmland?" Chelsea hiccups.

I shrug. Although I feel the alcohol loosening my tongue, it hasn't pushed me into the realms of being tipsy yet. "Long story short, I want the housing company."

Chelsea pops a profiterole into her mouth, her head swaying from side to side. "And owning the farmland will help?"

"No. Converting the farmland into high-spec Calloway houses may. But I don't think it's enough. I feel like Father wants more from me."

"Like what?" Chelsea says, her hand covering her mouth as she chews.

"I suspect that our father wants to see at least one of us brothers accomplished in every aspect of his life. Both in the business sense, and personally. It is he after all who keeps reminding us that behind every successful man is an equally strong woman."

Chelsea lets out a grunt and when she moves her hand from her face, I notice a small dollop of cream on her chin. "So, he wants you married with kids?"

I hold my cutlery out in an 'I don't know' gesture. "I think if I had a wife, or even a fiancée, that I would be taken more seriously."

"Good luck with that." Chelsea reaches for her glass of wine, but I remove it from the table.

"I think you've had enough."

She gives me a thumbs-down gesture. "Not cool."

I signal Ronald to bring over a jug of water and point not so subtly to Chelsea.

"It would seem we will only be happy when we have our working lives sorted," Chelsea continues.

As drunk as she is, her statement is true. Chelsea will only be truly happy when her beauty salon is open, and I when I'm flying the Calloway Housebuilders flag.

I place my elbows on the table and use the tip of my index finger to balance my chin.

Hiccupping, Chelsea cups her hand around her mouth. "You're not allowed to put your elbows on the table."

"I won't tell if you won't," I tease and lean in close. I reach out across the table and with my finger wipe the small dollop of cream from her chin and without hesitation I suck my finger into my mouth. "What if I told you there was a way we could solve both of our dilemmas?"

Chelsea mirrors my gesture and attempts to balance her chin on her index finger. "I'm listening."

"How do you feel about becoming the next Mrs Calloway?"

Chelsea snorts. "I'm nowhere near drunk enough to agree to marrying you."

I snap my fingers. "Ronald, another bottle of red."

Chelsea laughs. "Nice try."

"Nice try indeed. But I'm serious. Come to a few public outings with me and pose as my fiancée. Do that and in return I will give you the money you need to reopen your salon."

A faint line appears between her brows as she studies me. I think the realisation of what I've asked her has sunk in. "One hundred thousand pounds to attend a few events with you? Sure, why not? I've been blacklisted from every bank in Heller St Claire."

Ronald's timing couldn't be better. He appears to my right and refills my glass, which I lift. "I believe a toast is in order. After which we will discuss the full terms and conditions of my very generous offer."

CHAPTER NINE

Chelsea

Sunlight filters through the curtains, and I wake up with a start in a bed I don't know, in a room I don't recognise. Then, fuzzy-headed, I remember that Lucian has revamped my bedroom and I figure it's just going to take me a while to get used to.

I swivel around on the soft mattress. The digital clock on the bedside table tells me it's one o'clock.

In the afternoon! I never sleep in this late.

I'm about to start my morning cleaning routine when flashes of last night fill my mind. I remember the meal with Lucian and snippets of conversation. We talked and we drank, but my throbbing head tells me that we mostly drank. The taste of stale wine lingers in my mouth, causing nausea to creep its way up my throat. I hold my breath and try to swallow it down. The action causes not only my mouth to water profusely but nausea to creep its way back up with a vengeance.

Oh, God, I'm going to be sick.

I leap from the bed and stumble my way to my en suite. Except where the hell is the door?

I turn three hundred and sixty degrees and notice that my

en suite door is nowhere to be seen. I know I'm hungover, but not that far gone that a door would disappear, surely? With my hands cupped over my mouth, I glance around frantically for something, anything to throw up into. A bronze slimline bin beside a mahogany chest of drawers catches my attention. I hurry across the room in a last-minute ditch attempt not to spill my guts out on the carpet. The room spins, but I shut it off. When the bin is within reaching distance I fall to the floor, crawl on my hands and knees and hug it to my chest.

I don't throw up, but the feeling comes and goes in waves before my stomach settles.

I sit for five minutes, maybe a little longer, to ensure I'm not going to be sick. I place the bin back where I found it and slowly stand. I pad my way around the room and stop in front of an antique-looking freestanding mirror.

"You look terrible," I say to my reflection, and it isn't a lie. Hair that is usually vibrant and full of life lies flat and dull. My eyes are bloodshot and my skin a sickly white, with a subtle shade of green. My gaze lowers. I'm dressed in a large shirt; the buttons are only partially fastened. I don't remember putting this on. Hell, I don't remember taking my dress off. My heartbeat picks up and I pull the fabric out so I can see what lies beneath. I'm still wearing my bra, and releasing the shirt I feel for my underwear, which is still intact. It is irrelevant. Anything could have happened last night, and I'd never know.

Stupid, stupid Chelsea. How could I have been so careless as to put myself in this situation? The irony is that I drank to gain confidence and gain control, but by drinking far more than my limit I couldn't be more out of control.

Through the mirror my gaze meets the reflection of a dark wooden door. The doors at the flat are eggshell-white. I glance around and take a proper inventory of the room. The carpet under my feet is red, the walls that surround me are cream except for the wall directly behind the bed, which is covered with an intricate tapestry. The room is considerably larger than my bedroom at the flat, in fact my entire flat could probably fit inside these four walls and still have room to spare. *Where the hell am I?*

What if someone broke in whilst I was sleeping and kidnapped me? My gaze dances around the lavish room, and I quickly surmise how unlikely that scenario is. I've got to be at Lucian's place, it is the only feasible explanation. Was this his plan all along, to get me drunk and bring me here?

I've been kidnapped.

But then I vaguely recall Lucian telling me to slow down and stop drinking. Of course I wasn't going to listen, because he's Lucian Calloway.

With unanswered questions flooding my mind I hurry toward the bedroom door, fastening every button on the shirt along the way. I stop for a beat, because regardless of anything else, I can't leave this room dressed only in a shirt. I look around and notice a pink robe laid out on a small armchair. Without a thought as to who the robe belongs to, I quickly pull it on. If Lucian has kidnapped me, I want answers. Hell, I'm going to call the police and get rescued by a helicopter and…

I take a breath and try hard to let the rational Chelsea take charge, but rational Chelsea is seriously hungover. I march from the bedroom, walk down long corridors and pass door after door. I wonder how many rooms are in this house, this mansion. I begin counting and only stop when I happen upon a grand staircase. It is like something out of a fairytale, with a golden banister. I hold onto the handrail as I make my way down. The handrail finishes on the bottom stair, where it transforms into a life-sized carving of a lion. It's hauntingly beautiful and disturbingly lifelike. I stand still for long seconds, my gaze transfixed on the works of art that surround me. An array of artwork hangs from the walls in large gilt-edged frames, and Greek sculptures line the grand hallway on tall hand-crafted stands.

Everything looks so clean, so polished, and so expensive. It would be so easy to get lost in this place's charm, but no, I have to stay focused. I exit the grand hallway and once again find myself in a long corridor. I can hear the faint sound of voices echoing around me, which tells me I am heading in the right direction. Light filters in from every room. I pass a library, a study, a room that is home to a snooker table, and finally I reach the dining room.

A crystal chandelier hangs over a large rectangular table. I eye the long row of seats. All are empty and are pushed beneath the table, all except two.

Bingo.

Dressed in a pristine navy suit, Lucian is sitting at the table. A dark-haired man is reclined back in the seat opposite, his back toward me. They make idle conversation whilst sipping tea. I stand in the doorway and clear my throat, yet neither acknowledges me. Lucian's attention seems to be taken up with an article in the newspaper he's reading.

Anger pools in my stomach. "How dare you," I say, my words sharp.

Lucian glances up and is seemingly unaffected by my entrance. His face remains expressionless as he sips from his mug. "Ah, sweetheart, I wondered when you would finally grace us with your presence."

"Sweetheart?" My voice rises an octave.

The man at the table turns, and I recognise him immediately from the papers as Lucian's older brother, Malachi Calloway. His hair is as black as the night sky, and when touched by natural light, flecks of midnight blue appear throughout. He offers a tight-lipped smile, a neatly cut beard framing his angular jaw.

There is a harshness in his dark gaze that makes me feel uneasy. He possesses an aura and a coldness that demands respect. "Nice to finally meet you, Chelsea. I believe a celebratory drink is in order."

"A celebratory drink?" I'm waiting for the punchline.

Chair legs squeak against the wooden floorboards as Lucian gets to his feet and makes his way toward me. "Come." He grips my arm and I attempt to pull myself free, though his grip is firm. Without a word he walks me into the hallway and toward a nearby room. Once we're inside he closes the door behind us.

"Let me explain—" he begins, but I don't allow him to finish. I reel back and slap his cheek.

"Bastard. You kidnapped me!" I hiss.

A red handprint mars Lucian's perfect face. He does nothing to acknowledge the blow and instead folds his arms in front of his chest. "I did not kidnap you."

"Liar." I raise my hand again, about to slap him for a second time when Lucian catches my wrist in mid-flight.

"I will let you have the first one. But if you strike me again, so help me God, I will throw you over my knee and grace your milky white behind with a red handprint of my own. Do I make myself clear?"

His words are firm and authoritative. Though his eyes, his eyes are daring me to defy him. I sigh heavily. "Where am I?"

"In my Surrey estate."

My mouth dries instantly. "Surrey? As in Surrey near London?"

"That is correct."

"But that's…" I begin, but fall silent for a beat. "That's a four-hour drive from Heller St Claire."

"Four and a half hours, to be precise."

I can't help wondering what time we arrived. No wonder I slept in. Lucian walks around the room, which I see is a home office. He perches on a large desk and motions for me to sit in the swivel chair. I don't move, not so much as an inch. I place my hand on my hip and tap my foot against the floor. "Why are we here?"

"I'm here because I have a few prior engagements penciled in that require me to be in the City." Lucian looks me up and down before continuing. "You are here because you asked to come back with me, practically begged."

I laugh. "I would never…"

"Let me finish." His tone is sharp, and I immediately stop talking.

"You said you didn't want to be alone. I couldn't very well stay in your flat with you. It would have been highly inappropriate to share a bed given the state you were in, and I didn't fancy sleeping on the sofa. You coming home with me was the only logical thing to do. You had no objections and came of your own free will."

"I was drunk, you tool."

"Yes. Very much so. Another reason why you shouldn't have been left alone. I had my female staff members check on you on the hour. Just to make sure that you hadn't choked on your own vomit."

"How thoughtful of you," I deadpan.

Lucian nods. "Yes, I thought so too."

A wicked smile tugs at Lucian's lips. I lower my hand to my side, realising that I may have overreacted. "Thank you," I mumble.

Lucian holds his hand to his ear. "I'm sorry, I didn't quite catch that."

"I said thank you," I say, loud enough that he can hear.

"You're welcome."

I shift my weight from one foot to the other. The last thing I want to do is overstay my welcome. I nod my head toward the door, about to ask Lucian if he knows where my phone is when he clears his throat.

"You should get ready and shower. I can't have you wandering around the estate wearing a robe. I'll have my maid Bessie accompany you to your room and help you change into something a little more appropriate."

Appropriate? I feel the need to say something, but in this

instance Lucian is right. I've never been one to wear nightclothes during the day, and there is no way I am getting into a taxi dressed like this. But did I hear correctly? Lucian wants someone to help me get dressed?

"I'm very capable of dressing myself." Which reminds me. "Who dressed, or rather undressed me last night?"

"I carried you up to the guest bedroom and helped you out of your frock."

I gasp. "With your hands?"

"No, Chelsea, with my teeth," Lucian deadpans.

Pause. I don't blink, don't breathe. I was drunk last night, possibly passed out, and Lucian, he, he…

"Of course with my bloody hands. Don't worry, your modesty was kept intact, and Bessie was at hand. Together we removed the shoulder straps of your dress and guided your arms through the sleeves of the shirt. Only when you were covered up did I pull the dress down and remove it."

"How do I know you didn't touch me…?" My voice trails off.

Lucian's expression hardens. "Because I am a gentleman, and as a gentleman I wouldn't lay a finger on something that did not belong to me."

My shoulders fall, and for the first time in a long time I feel incredibly small. Lucian has shown me nothing but kindness. I don't have to like the guy, but I don't need to be rude.

"I'm sorry, that was cruel of me. I know you wouldn't have. I mean, what I'm trying to say is thanks." I nod once, and, turning my back on Lucian, I make my way to the door.

"Now, as per our agreement," Lucian calls after me.

My fingers are wrapped around the door handle. I could leave, I'm about to leave, but curiosity has me spinning around. "Agreement?"

Lucian is no longer leaning against his desk. He is making his way toward me with slow, confident steps. The air temperature rises the closer he gets, and I find myself taking a few steps back.

I stop when the cool brass handle digs into my back and I have nowhere else to go. I expect Lucian to stop, but he doesn't. He doesn't stop walking until he is standing directly in front of me.

I can't bring myself to look into his eyes and find it much easier to focus on the floor and our feet. My body jerks when he taps my forehead with his finger. "Tell me you remember."

My eyes snap up, and foolishly I meet his gaze. I don't like Lucian, not even a smidgen. But his stare causes something inside me to tingle and my stomach to clench. *Attraction?* I wonder. Hell no! It's the colour and intensity of his eyes, nothing more. Those emerald greens alone have the ability to melt the Arctic, of that I'm sure.

"Remember what?" Feeling flustered, I reach beneath the robe I'm wearing and pop open the first two buttons of my shirt.

Lucian captures my hand and brings it to his lips. "Our arrangement," he says, and kisses my knuckles. That is when I see it. The delicate gold band on my ring finger. An elegant diamond sparkles up at me, each tiny facet reflecting a different colour.

Dread, nausea, and fear cocoon me and I'm flooded by so many emotions all at once. "Oh, my God, Lucian, tell me we didn't get married? This isn't even legal, it will be annulled right away. I can't, we can't. This can't be happening."

My hands itch and my fingers shake with the need to regain an ounce of control. I didn't sign up for this, I didn't say those two little words 'I do', because I don't! "I don't!" I screech.

Lucian laughs and places his palm over my mouth. "My God, you are as subtle as a wailing banshee."

"Get off me," I demand, wriggling my head from side to side. Though my words come out muffled under Lucian's palm.

"No, Chelsea, we did not get married."

My racing heart begins to slow, and air comes a lot easier. Lucian lowers his hand and cages me in with both of his arms. "Last night I concocted a plan for how we could both get exactly what we want, you the beauty salon and me Calloway Housebuilders."

I swallow loudly. "Go on."

"I offered you the money you need for your salon in exchange for…"

"Exchange for what?"

"Your hand."

His words floor me. I feel trapped all of a sudden, like the walls around us are closing in. "That's ridiculous," I spit out.

"What's even more ridiculous is that you agreed." Lucian lowers his arms, giving me the space I desperately need.

I turn my back on him and grab the door handle. I have to get out of here.

"Aren't you the least bit curious to hear my full terms and conditions?"

I place my chin on my shoulder. "Give me one reason why I should entertain this craziness."

The corners of his eyes crinkle. "Why settle for just one when I can give you a billion reasons why?" Lucian's tone, although low and controlled, is daring. Perhaps daring me to hear him out and agree. Or daring me to defy him.

"I can't marry you." My words tumble out.

"And that's the beauty of it, you don't have to." His breath is warm against the side of my face, causing a shiver to skate the length of my spine.

I don't move, and when I say nothing, Lucian continues. "All I ask is that you live here with me for one month. You can live in a separate wing of the estate if you want. Think of it as a mini-holiday of sorts."

This is beyond ridiculous, but I will humour him. "Why a month?"

"That is how long my father has given me to prove I am the right person to run the housebuilding company. After the month is over, we separate and you can go back to your normal life. With only one difference—you'll finally be able to open your salon."

Lucian is offering me the funds I need to open my salon in exchange for a month of my life. It doesn't sound so bad.

I can't believe I'm even considering this. I shake my head, rational Chelsea returning.

I spin around and jab Lucian's chest with my finger. "Let me get this straight, you're going to pay me a hundred thousand pounds to be your fake fiancée?"

Lucian nods. "I guess that is the sum of it, yes. We will be expected to attend several charity functions together."

I let out a high-pitched laugh. "You expect me to leave my life and move in with you for an entire month? What about my job? What am I meant to tell my family, my friends and my sister?"

"You can tell them we've fallen madly in love and you've decided to move in with me."

That comment earns him an eye roll. "Amber wouldn't buy that for a second."

Lucian pauses for a beat, as if in thought. "Why don't you tell her that you've decided to join Tyler in America for a few weeks?"

I narrow my eyes. It is as though Lucian has this all planned out right down to the finest detail. "You're crazy. Insane. I'm sorry, I can't be around this madness." I clasp the door handle and push it down. "Have a nice life."

I inch the door open, and Lucian leans into me. His firm chest presses into my back and without hesitation he pushes the door closed. "This is a bit of a pickle we are in, because my family have received news of our engagement."

I narrow my eyes. "Oh, I bet you couldn't wait to tell them the good news."

Lucian shakes his head. "I haven't breathed a word to anyone. Someone close to me has big ears and an even bigger mouth. I can of course tell my family they have been misinformed."

"So do that," I quip.

"I could, but I'd like to think you'd at least consider my proposal. Or rather my *fake* proposal."

As much as I want to throw his offer back in his face, I don't. I stop for a moment to consider that this may be the only opportunity I have to re-open my salon. I draw my lower lip between my teeth before sighing heavily. "I need time to think."

"Time is not a luxury we have. You see, I'm expecting my sister any moment. and her sole purpose for visiting here today is to meet you."

I squeeze my eyes tightly together, shutting out this craziness I have woken up into. "You can't expect me to decide on a whim."

Lucian rubs his palm over the back of his neck. "I will stall her. You have one hour until I tell Farrah this is one big misunderstanding. Think about my offer, Chelsea. I mean really consider what that kind of money could do for you."

And just like that he releases the door and I seize my moment to escape. I yank the handle down and run as fast as I can through the long winding corridors, desperately trying to retrace my steps. I dart up the grand staircase and scamper into the safety of the bedroom. My heart hammers, and I do the only logical thing I can in this moment. I run and swan-dive onto the bed, pulling the thick duvet over my head and momentarily disappearing from the world.

One hour to give Lucian an answer.

One hour to decide if I sell my soul to the Devil.

One hour…

CHAPTER TEN

Lucian

The door slams, and just like that Chelsea is gone. This is what I get for drunkenly proposing to a woman who has no interest in being my fiancée, even if the proposal was a sham.

I curl my fingers around the door and squeeze the wood. I wait till my knuckles turn white before releasing.

Time to face the music.

I leave my home office and head down the corridor. I stop walking and retrieve my grandfather's pocket watch from my jacket pocket. I flick the clasp open to reveal the domed face and watch the hands silently tick away. I make a mental note of the time, because in one hour from now I will know Chelsea's decision.

I re-enter the dining room and can't miss the shocked expression on Malachi's face. "Blimey, she couldn't get away fast enough. She sped past the kitchen like a fox escaping a hound."

I should tell Malachi that this has been one big misunderstanding, to save myself the embarrassment. But I can't help but cling onto a tiny molecule of hope. I hitch a shoulder while making my way to my seat. "I informed Chelsea that Farrah is joining us for lunch. She went to freshen up."

"Oh, right. That would explain it." The cloud of doubt from moments ago seems to evaporate. "But you're going to have to explain it to me again. I just can't get my head around it. How one second she hates you, and the next you're engaged. Have you even bothered to run a background check on her? Is it financial or social gain she wants?"

"I've told you already. It was a whirlwind romance, now stop asking." Of all days my brother could have dropped by unannounced, he chooses today. Of course he just happened to overhear the maids gossiping about the woman in the guest bedroom and the fact she's wearing our grandmother's engagement ring.

"Why did you have to go and tell everybody that I'm engaged?" I blurt out. "It wasn't your news to share." But what I'm really saying is, *You've royally landed me in it*. With the exception of my father, who is away on a golfing weekend, my family are staying nearby in readiness for the charity gala this evening. They will no doubt expect me to turn up with my fiancée on my arm.

Malachi's brows draw in as he tries to look serious. "I didn't tell everybody, only Farrah."

By telling our kid sister Malachi may as well have broadcast it on every bloody television station from here to Timbuktu.

I sit down in the chair, pick up the newspaper and continue from where I left off. A full twenty minutes pass before the doorbell chimes.

I squeeze the page in my fist whilst forcing a smile. "Excellent, that will be Farrah."

Lucky for me, my sister likes to arrive fashionably late—a trait that I usually hate, though in this instance I'm grateful for every minute. Malachi and I leave the dining room and head to the hallway to greet her. I haven't seen my little sister in months. My hope is that it will be easy to fill the time with conversation before I address the subject of Chelsea.

Malachi's steps are sprightly, whereas mine are slow and controlled. I pull off arrogant and blasé daily, because those two emotions come so naturally to me, but not today. Today I'm on edge, my hands tremble of their own accord and a thin layer of sweat gathers at my temples because I have so much riding on what happens during the next four weeks. One wrong move could ruin my chance of securing the business I so desperately want, and that is simply not an option.

Malachi peers around several times and frowns. I suspect he wonders why I'm not at his side. This doesn't prompt me to walk faster, only to drag my heels. He rounds the corner to the hallway, and I stand still, gathering my thoughts.

"Malachi!" my sister squeaks, and the warm sound of her voice is all the incentive I need to join them. I pick up my pace and see Farrah in Malachi's arms. Her long black hair takes flight as he spins her around.

When her feet are back on the marble floor, she turns toward me. "Lucian!" Her squeals echo around the grand room as she runs toward me. I open my arms wide and envelop her in a hug. "I've missed you," she says.

"You too, sis." I make eye contact with Dante, my sister's leading bodyguard. He is a little taller than me, and a lot wider. His hair is cropped short and he's wearing a black suit and tie. "I'll take it from here." I'm surprised when he doesn't leave. "I said I'll take it from here," I repeat, unsure if Dante has momentarily lost his hearing or is being blatantly rude. My father is somewhat overprotective when it comes to my little sister, so much so that she has a bodyguard who accompanies her everywhere she goes. But Dante's services aren't required for the short amount of time she is here.

Dante folds his arms in front of his chest. "Your father informed me that I'm to stay. He said you have a spare bedroom in the servants' wing."

I quirk a brow. "Spare bedroom?"

I look down at my sister, who is looking up. Her ivory complexion is pink and blotchy. She snorts loudly. "I was so excited when Malachi said I am going to have a sister. So much so that he suggested I stay for a little while to get to know her. Isn't that exciting?"

In other words, Malachi has arranged for Farrah to be his little spy. I release Farrah, just as three of my maids, Flossy, Nancy and Claire, enter through the front door with Farrah's cases—all six of them.

"Exactly how long do you plan on staying?"

Farrah shrugs. "I don't know. A week, maybe two."

Alarm bells are ringing in my head. I told Chelsea she could stay in another wing of the estate. If she agrees to our little arrangement she will have to keep up the pretence whilst Farrah stays. This is turning into a nightmare. I need to call the whole charade off, and sooner rather than later. I need to speak to Chelsea immediately. I clear my throat whilst at the same time loosening the collar around my neck. "Please excuse me for a second. I will be back."

Without a backward glance I hurry to the staircase and place my hand on the banister. I stop and am physically frozen to the spot. Chelsea is standing on the top stair. She has undressed out of the robe and is wearing a yellow summer dress. The hem caresses her knees as she makes her way down.

She looks—my God, she looks magnificent. A painful reminder of the most beautiful thing in this world I want but can't have, and more specifically can't buy.

"This must be my sister-to-be!" Farrah squeaks, unable to contain her excitement.

I turn to my sister and Malachi. "About that..." I take a deep calming breath and think about the words that are to follow.

This is one big misunderstanding; Chelsea and I aren't engaged.

I open my mouth to speak when a hand snakes around my waist. I turn to see Chelsea standing at my side. She leans up on the tips of her toes and places a kiss on my cheek. "I'm sorry I took so long."

The scent of strawberry shampoo fills my nose, along with the subtle fragrance of coconut body wash. Her scent and warmth are all around me and cast a spell on my reasoning. I forget all the reasons why I should call this charade off, and focus on all the reasons why I should continue. I turn around, capture Chelsea in my arms and pull her close.

"It's okay, sweetheart, you're here now. That's all that matters."

Her body tenses and her eyes go wide as I lean in for a kiss. She could kill me with her stare alone, but at least I would die a happy man. My lips are inches from hers when she quickly turns her face away and I kiss her cheek.

She laughs theatrically and shimmies out of my hold. "Lucian, sweetheart," she says through gritted teeth. It amuses me that behind her annoyance she attempts to look lovingly at me, and bonus points as she even used my term of endearment. "You'll smudge my lipstick."

She laughs playfully and turns to our audience. She leans into me for a second, and to anyone watching it would appear she's whispering sweet nothings into my ear.

"Try that again and I will personally castrate you." She backs away with a smile so wide it would rival the Joker.

I laugh and flick the end of her nose. "You are so funny."

Her smile falters, and I know that was a step too far.

"Chelsea." I reach for her hand. Our fingers interlink for a second before the link is broken. She isn't used to me touching her, but that is something she will need to get over and soon.

"Relax," I say, though her painted-on expression and doe eyes are swallowed up by raven hair as my sister quite literally jumps on her.

"I'm so happy to meet you! I've always wanted a sister." Farrah bounces up and down in their embrace. Wide-eyed, Chelsea looks at me for help, and I of course step in.

"Sis," I say, peeling Farrah off Chelsea. "Carry on without us, we will be right behind you."

Farrah frowns and, crossing her arms, she pouts. This small gesture reminds me that my sister is only a teenager. At seventeen she is the baby of the family and is very much used to getting what she wants. "But I want to get to know Chelsea."

"And you will," I say, spinning her shoulders around and giving her a nudge toward our brother. "I just want a second in private to tell my fiancée how utterly ravishing she looks."

Farrah laughs and skips away, her bodyguard and Malachi on her heels. "Hurry up and make out so you can join us," are the words she leaves us with as she disappears around the corner.

I side-eye Chelsea, who side-eyes me.

"Please, let me apologise," I say, taking a step closer to her.

Chelsea holds up her hand, and as she does I get a strong waft of bleach. I'm about to ask whether she's been raiding the cleaner's cupboard when she speaks. "I don't want your apology. All I want is to reopen my salon. One month, Lucian, one month and I never see you again." She holds out her hand in a gentleman's handshake gesture. But it would be unfair to shake based on our previous discussion because things have changed, like the fact Farrah intends to stay with us. Like the fact Chelsea will have to play the doting fiancée twenty-four seven.

I run my fingers through my hair. "About our agreement. There are things we need to discuss before you commit."

Chelsea shakes her head. "I thought about your offer, and it didn't take me long to conclude that you are the only chance I have of opening my salon. I will put up with a month of hell if it means I get my life back. I will be your fake fiancée, I will hold your hand in public, laugh at your jokes, and kiss you on the cheek when the time calls for it. My terms are as follows. You do not kiss me on the lips without my consent, and I'm not having sex with you."

I lift my arm; our palms meet for a second and we shake,

sealing the deal. "To the temporary Mrs Calloway-to-be." With my free hand I make a sweeping motion around the grand hallway. "Mi casa es tu casa. My house is your house."

"Lucky me," Chelsea says, though I can't miss the air of sarcasm in her tone as she pulls her hand free.

Out of the few women I have brought to my Surrey estate, Chelsea is the first who doesn't look impressed, not even in the slightest. Her lack of admiration baffles me, because I have no idea how I'm to impress this girl. No idea what makes her tick, but I'm looking forward to spending this time together discovering all of her little idiosyncrasies.

"So what now?" she asks.

"We are going to have lunch with my sister and brother."

We make our way down the corridors to the dining room, and, as expected, the table is empty.

"Where are they?" Chelsea asks and holds out her arms exaggeratedly.

"I have no idea," I lie. Farrah is a sun-worshiper, and during the summer months spends her time outdoors. No doubt she is sitting on the rattan sofa outside drinking freshly squeezed orange juice whilst my maids wait on her hand and foot.

With Chelsea all to myself, I see now is as good a time as any to fill her in on our new arrangement. I tell her that Farrah intends to stay, and she will have to spend a great deal more time with me.

"I am not sharing a bed with you. You'll have to tell your sister that you are honouring my virtue and we're waiting until our wedding night."

I quirk a brow. That may have been believable in the nineteenth century, but not today. Women in their mid-twenties are not virgins. I could stand here and argue with Chelsea until I'm blue in the face, but frankly I do not have the time. Instead of getting into a discussion I decide it's best to keep my reply brief. "No."

Chelsea looks at me as though I've suddenly sprouted a second head. "What did you say?"

"You heard me, I said no. You will sleep in my bed."

Chelsea laughs, although there is no humour in her tone. She looks me up and down and places her hand on her hip. "And where will you sleep?"

"If you want to back out of our agreement, now is your chance. The front door is literally right there." I pause and jut my chin in the direction of the hallway. I give Chelsea a chance to speak, a chance to leave, but when she does neither, I continue. "As to our sleeping arrangements, that is a matter we will discuss this evening. But right now, my sister and brother are waiting for us to join them, and I do hate to keep our guests waiting."

I turn my back on her and make my way toward the door. I stop walking, hold my hand out and wait.

CHAPTER ELEVEN

Chelsea

I flash a glance at Lucian's palm, a palm that incidentally holds the solution to all of my problems. But what am I going to tell my family, my friends, Amber and finally my boss? As much as it pains me to admit, Lucian's idea of me telling them I've joined Tyler in America isn't terrible. Problem is Amber will see right through my lie. I will have no option other than to limit my contact with her, at least initially. But in any case, I will have to at least contact them to let them know I'm okay so they don't worry. But I can't contact them at all if I can't find my phone.

"I need my phone," I say finally.

"Isn't it in your room?"

If it were, I wouldn't be asking. "I couldn't find it."

"I will ask Bessie. She took your clothes last night after we helped you into bed."

"My best friend Lizzie's wedding," I blurt out.

"When are the nuptials taking place?"

"July tenth."

Lucian pauses for a second, and, taking his phone from his jacket pocket, scrolls to the calendar. "Perfect. That falls on the same day the meeting with my father and brothers takes place. I will go to Truro and sign the contracts and I will arrange transportation to take you to the church." Lucian pauses and studies me for a beat before continuing. "Unless by that time you have fallen madly in love with me and want me to attend as your plus-one."

I try not to laugh. "That's not going to happen."

"In that case we part ways amicably, and you can go on to reopen your salon."

Lucian really does have all the answers. It seems this crazy plan of his could actually work.

One month and I can reopen my salon.

One month and I'll have my life back.

One month…

I take a tentative step forward and slide my hand into his. I gaze into his eyes, wanting, or rather needing, reassurance. Lucian doesn't utter a single word. He doesn't so much as look at me. The subtle upturn of his lips is confirmation enough that he is pleased. He saunters forward and I follow his lead. We walk from the dining room to the kitchen, into the adjoining orangery, and from there step into the gardens.

It's a hot afternoon, but instead of glancing at the sky I keep my gaze trained on the ground. My ears are greeted with birdsong and the melodic sound of running water. Coarse stones crunch beneath my feet as we amble along a shingled path. The scent of pollen explodes into my senses as we pass a colourful array of flower beds.

"Do you like horses?" Lucian asks. He lifts my hand and points in the direction of a large courtyard, which I'm assuming is home to the stables.

"I guess." I don't tell him how I loved to ride as a girl. I figure the less he knows about me the better.

We walk in silence for a little while, reality hitting me with every step I take. I am in this situation for a month. I mean, how many times in my life am I going to be staying in a multimillion-pound estate? Maybe Lucian was right, maybe I should look at this as a holiday and a break from reality.

Finally, I allow my gaze to wander up and am floored by what I see. Grass like a thick carpet stretches as far as the eye can see. A mass of trees and hills shape the horizon. Without a house or car in sight it is as though nothing else exists.

"This way," Lucian says as he gently tugs my hand. We continue down another path, only this one is narrower. A long line of trees runs along each side. They are connected by their foliage, which gives the illusion that they are one. From the tree-lined path we pass an ornate fountain, its centrepiece a stone-carved gargoyle that spits water high into the air.

I imagine spending my days in the gardens, horseback riding or doing something as simple as picking flowers. I quickly surmise that staying here for a month won't be so bad.

"I used to ride as a girl," I admit, hoping Lucian will agree to show me the tack room where the riding equipment is kept. I can picture it now, horseback riding just as the sun begins to set. I almost feel the wind lapping against my face and imagine my hair as it is whipped back as we pick up speed.

"Excellent, we shall go horseback riding tomorrow."

My vision of riding into the sunset starts to distort because I didn't imagine there being two horses. I don't have time to reply as Farrah and her bodyguard come into view. Her bodyguard is standing beneath the shade of a nearby tree, seemingly giving her space, yet close enough should she need him. Farrah is lying on a cream sofa, her black hair fanned over her back as she snaps selfies of herself on her phone.

I tense with each step I take, and the need to run away has me dragging my heels. It's not that I don't like Lucian's sister, she seems pleasant, but what I don't like is lying to people. The problem with lies is that they blur the lines between what is real and what isn't. Lies are dangerous. The only way to not get found out is to tell more lies, thus creating a sticky web of deceit.

Lucian peers at me from over his shoulder, and I figure he can feel my uncertainty. He wraps his arms around me, and I stiffen as he pulls me into a hug. I rest my head against the soft fabric of his shirt and breathe him in. Damn, he smells good. The heady scent of his cologne, mixed with the subtle scent that is him, is all around me. His chest is firm and warm. I feel safe, safe in his arms and safe with him. He bows his head, and his lips find the shell of my ear. "Relax, I will do all the talking."

He pulls away, and from the heat in his gaze I'm sure he's about to kiss me. Maybe the thought flashes in his mind but, releasing me, he turns his attention to Farrah. "Where's Malachi?"

Farrah spins around on the sofa and faces us. She has a pretty face—full lips, high cheekbones and Lucian's green eyes. She is wearing a pair of jeans, fashionably ripped at the knee. The strap of her purple T-shirt slides down her arm as she shrugs. "I don't know. He said he'd catch up with us." With her gaze on me she taps the empty space to her right. I take a deep calming breath.

I'm Lucian Calloway's fiancée. I'm Lucian Calloway's fiancée, I tell myself over and over. Trying to exude confidence, I stand tall, flick my hair over my shoulder, and join her. I expect Lucian to be right behind me, but it doesn't appear as though he's moved a single inch.

He pushes his hands into the front pockets of his trousers and looks over his shoulder. I follow his gaze to the estate. It's the first time I've seen the building from the outside, and I don't know whether I'm looking at a house or a museum. The building is magnificent, three storeys high and made from traditional red bricks. The window frames are made from a dark wood, with far too many to count.

"Is he still inside?" Lucian finally asks. It's as though he waited a moment for Malachi to appear.

Farrah shrugs. "I guess so."

Lucian looks from me to the estate as though conflicted, but, sucking in a breath, he joins me on the sofa. This is it, the moment of truth. We will know after this conversation whether we can pull this charade off. Farrah is Lucian's sister after all. Surely she'll be able to see through his lies.

"Tell me everything, from the beginning," Farrah says, her attention on me.

"We met—" Lucian begins.

"I was asking Chelsea!" Farrah chastises.

"It's okay," I say to Lucian. But I'm not okay. My breaths are coming fast and sharp. I meet Farrah's gaze, and she looks about ready to burst. I hate lying, so I figure I'll stick as close to the truth as I can. I tug at the ends of my hair. "We met a little over two years ago at my sister's photo exhibition."

Farrah clings on to my every word. "Was it love at first sight?"

"Definitely." Lucian squeezes my fingers.

I force a smile. "Oh, your brother certainly made an impression."

"Go on…"

"I fell in love with Chelsea through a photograph of her, called 'Timeless Beauty'," Lucian says. "She was the most exquisite creature I had ever laid eyes on, and I knew from that moment I had to make her mine."

"It must have been one special photo. Can I see it sometime?" Farrah asks, her and Lucian's attention on me.

I shrug, feeling on the spot all of a sudden. "I mean, you could. But I donated it to the farm where I work. My boss is selling it at the next farmers' market."

"We'll see about that," Lucian says under his breath.

"So, what happened then?" Farrah prompts, eager to find out more. She sits forward and rests her chin in her hands.

Lucian's gaze smoulders into me, and he smiles. "I spent the weeks and months that followed trying to convince her to let me take her out for dinner. She of course played hard to get—"

I nod along as Lucian speaks, thinking back to all the times I turned him down.

"—until finally she said yes. We enjoyed a meal from my favourite French restaurant in the comfort of her home. Things from there happened incredibly fast, and I guess you could say the rest is history."

'Incredibly fast' is the understatement of the century. But I smile, grateful that Lucian hasn't deviated too far from the truth. He merely stretched it a little.

Farrah clasps her hand to her chest and sighs exaggeratedly. "That is so romantic."

"No, little sister," Lucian says, his eyes burning into me. "It is only the beginning; the romance is yet to come."

"How did you propose?"

I can feel my eyes widen, but Lucian's expression remains unchanged. He is taking all of this in stride.

His gaze shifts as he looks past me. I turn around to see one of his maids carrying a platter of sandwiches on a silver tray. A second maid walks closely behind, glasses in one hand and a glass jug filled to the brim in the other. Thinly sliced lemon pieces bob up and down as she lowers the jug onto the wicker table beside the platter of sandwiches.

The maids look identical as they stand side by side as though awaiting further instruction. They are wearing matching black tunics and trousers, and their hair has been pinned back into neat buns.

"Thank you, Flossy and Nancy. You may go. Please, if you see my idiot brother on your travels, tell him his company is required urgently in the gardens."

"Is there a problem?" Farrah leans forward and pours herself a drink.

"None, little sister. I just think it is incredibly rude of him not to have joined us. Especially seeing as you and Chelsea are here."

Zoning out of their conversation, I glance at the sandwiches. The crusts have been cut off and they have been cut into perfect triangles. They all have different fillings, from ham to chicken and salad. I hold my hand over my stomach as it rumbles, but it's not from hunger. Food is the very last thing on my mind. Still feeling queasy from my hangover, I don't think I could stomach anything.

"Here, allow me," Lucian says as he reaches for the tray.

"I'm not hungry, but thank you."

"You must eat. You will need your strength for the charity gala this evening," Farrah chimes in.

My head snaps around to Lucian. "What charity gala?"

Lucian wraps his arm lazily around my shoulder. "Only the one we've been talking about for the past week." His comment comes over as light-hearted, and Farrah laughs along with him.

I, however, do not laugh. "But I have nothing to wear."

"Chelsea has only recently moved in," Lucian explains, before Farrah has time to ask questions. "We were both so excited that I only managed to bring a small selection of clothes from her apartment." Lucian leans into me. "Don't worry about your dress. I will sort it." He takes out his phone from his trouser pocket and begins typing. I side-eye the screen, but the glass is distorted by the glare of the sun. When he has finished, he lifts up and tucks the device back into his pocket.

"Please, you must eat," Lucian insists.

I manage to eat half of a cucumber sandwich. It's not something I would usually choose but the scent of the cured ham and mature cheese turns my stomach.

The conversation flows well, and soon the awkwardness I'm feeling begins to evaporate. I tell Farrah about my beauty salon, my sister and my best friend. Farrah seems genuinely interested in everything I have to say.

The sun begins her journey in the sky. Time passes—how much I'm not entirely sure. Our conversation is interrupted when one of the maids comes to inform me that Marvin has arrived and is waiting for me in the master suite.

I frown, but think it wise I don't ask who Marvin is. "I guess that's my cue to leave," I say and get to my feet.

Lucian captures my hand, and I turn. "If you happen to see Malachi, ask him where he's been and what the bloody hell he's playing at."

"I will tell him to join you outside." My words trail behind me as I hurry to keep up with the young maid. I follow her into the house, up the stairs and toward the master suite.

"Here you are, Miss."

"Thank you"—my eyes lower to her name, which is embroidered onto her black tunic—"Flossy."

I wonder if Flossy is short for Florence. I'm about to ask her when the sound of a door opening catches my attention. Malachi steps out of the room, and, with his back toward us, flings his jacket over his shoulder. He strolls down the landing, humming to himself.

"Malachi," I call after him.

Malachi turns and raises his hand in acknowledgement.

Remembering Lucian's words, I ask, "Where were you?" I cup my palm over my mouth as the last syllable leaves my lips.

Malachi stops walking and offers me his full attention. "Excuse me?"

I suck in a breath. "What I meant to say is that Lucian wants you to join him and Farrah in the gardens."

Malachi nods once before tucking his phone into his trouser pocket. Although his smile is wide, there is something in the way he looks at me that makes me feel uneasy.

He glances at Flossy. "Please inform Lucian that I will join him and Farrah shortly."

I side-eye the maid, who passes us and makes her way across the landing. When she is out of earshot, he returns his attention to me.

"Forgive me, Chelsea, for I am going to be blunt." Malachi closes the distance between us. He doesn't stop until he is standing directly in front of me and I have to crane my neck to meet his gaze. He's tall, taller than Lucian. That, with the added weight of my lie, makes me feel incredibly small. "I do not approve of this union between you and Lucian. Surprisingly, it isn't due to your inferiority in rank or your lack of financial means. It's that I don't know what your agenda is with my brother. If your intentions are not genuine and it's money you seek, tell me the amount and I will write you out a cheque here and now so you can be on your way."

Malachi has called my bluff, and although outwardly I'm relaxed, inwardly I'm losing it. I have no idea what to say, so feign offence and say the first thing that pops into my head. "Do you really think so very little of me?"

"Based on the little time I have spent with you, I am yet to form an opinion. I'm just a man concerned for his younger brother; you must be able to understand that."

I nod, thinking of how protective Amber and my older brother, Phillip, are of me.

"It was my understanding that you despised Lucian. I'm just curious as to what caused the sudden change of heart. If it is money you seek, we can sort this out here and now."

My heartbeat accelerates in my chest. It would be so easy to take the money from Malachi and go about my normal way of life, the only difference being that I will be one hundred thousand pounds better off and able to reopen my salon without having to carry on with this sham of an engagement. I open my mouth, about to accept, but feel a strange kind of loyalty to Lucian. I hold my hand up. "Thanks for the offer, but—"

"Say no more." Malachi pulls his jacket from over his shoulder and searches the inside breast pocket. He pulls out a business card and presses it into my palm.

The card is cooler and harder than I anticipated, and without a word I curl my fingers around it. I'm expecting the corners to bend in my grasp and when they don't I glance down.

My eyes widen. "You have a gold business card?"

"Twenty-four-K gold-plated."

"What's wrong with good old-fashioned paper?"

Malachi doesn't answer and I run the pad of my index finger along the solid edges before tracing the outline of the calligraphy-style engraved lettering.

The card darkens, and I sense Malachi looming over me. "You're considering my offer, aren't you?"

"No." I keep my tone neutral. What I am doing in actual fact is deciding how best to dispose of this expensive piece of rubbish, seeing as I'm unable to tear the thin gold-plated card into tiny pieces or scrunch it into a ball before tossing it into the bin.

"I don't believe you." With his hands clasped firmly behind his back Malachi begins to pace back and forth. "I'm feeling in a generous mood today. Tell me your price, and I'll double it, triple it even. Have we got a deal?"

My gaze snaps up to meet his. I'm about to tell him what he can do with his money and his twenty-four-K gold business card when the door to the master suite bursts open. A man with shoulder-length blond hair and dressed in a flamboyant teal suit appears. "I thought I could hear talking."

"You must be Marvin," I say.

"Yes. And you must be the girl in urgent need of a dress. Come in. We haven't got all day. I have a range of gowns for you to try on."

I spin on my heel, about to enter the bedroom, when Malachi places his hand on my shoulder.

"We will continue this conversation another time."

CHAPTER TWELVE

Chelsea

Malachi's words play on my mind, but fade away the second I set foot into the room when Marvin attacks me with a measuring tape. His long blond hair flashes in front of my face as he gets to work.

A slender figure appears in the open doorway and a redhead with a notepad clasped to her chest hurries past and sits down on the window seat.

"Twenty-six-inch waist," Marvin calls to the woman. She nods once before retrieving a ballpoint pen from her messy bun and jotting my measurements down.

"How tall are you, flower?" Marvin asks, peering up at me as he circles the tape around my thighs.

"Five foot four," I say, glancing around the grand room. *Lucian's bedroom*. The walls are painted slate grey. Sepia photographs of landscapes hang in black frames. The room is ginormous, with a leather sofa and table one side and an opulent four-poster bed the other. Laid out on the duvet is a selection of gowns concealed by plastic covers.

"Can you walk in heels?" Marvin asks as he gets to his feet.

I nod. "Sure, what girl can't?"

My best friend Lizzie, that's who.

I smile as the memory of my best friend flashes in my mind. To watch Lizzie walk in heels is like watching a foal taking its first steps—unsure, unstable, and utterly adorable. I know it's only been one day, but I can't help wondering if Lizzie or my sister have tried to contact me. *I would know if I had my phone.*

"I know just the dress," the redhead says, pulling me from my thoughts. She makes one final entry in her notepad before snapping the pages together and pushing the pen into her messy bun. She stands from the window seat and makes her way over to the bed. Bending down, she flicks through the dresses as though she's flicking through pages of a book.

I can only imagine the thousands of pounds each garment must have cost. A girl like me doesn't wear gowns this extravagant. Now I know how Eliza Doolittle must have felt in *My Fair Lady*. I wouldn't say I'm the embodiment of rags to riches, but this doesn't feel right. I shift awkwardly from side to side because I'm in way over my head.

"I'm sorry, Marvin, and… I didn't quite catch your name."

"Valerie," the redhead says, looking up. "Valerie Cooper."

I rock on my heels several times before speaking. "Valerie, Marvin. I appreciate you coming to help me find a dress, but these are really too much. They must have cost a fortune."

Valerie and Marvin share a knowing glance before Marvin nods. "These gowns are priceless."

Plastic rattles as Valerie lifts a dress from the pile. She unzips the plastic cover to reveal the most beautiful white gown I have ever seen. "I'm sure Annabelle would be delighted to know you'll be wearing her dress."

"Annabelle?" The question rolls off my tongue.

"Annabelle Calloway. She designed all the dresses you see before you," Marvin says, making a sweeping gesture with his arm.

"Oh. Wow." My eyebrows shoot up. Annabelle must be Lucian's mother. I vaguely recall him saying she worked in fashion. *His mother is a dress designer?* I can't refuse to wear the dress now knowing that it is something she has put her heart and soul into making.

"I would be honoured," I say, fidgeting with the ends of my hair. "If you don't think Annabelle would mind?"

Marvin and Valerie exchange glances, and it's as though they are having a silent conversation.

"Annabelle Calloway, God rest her soul, passed away fifteen years ago." Marvin's expression is questioning as he meets my stare. Without a word he's asking how I don't know this already. After all, I am meant to be Lucian's fiancée.

"He has never mentioned his mother," I say, feeling the need to say something. To say anything.

Marvin raises his hands. "Please, don't feel the need to explain. Just focus on looking amazing in the dress. Here, allow me." Taking the gown from Valerie, he drapes the cool fabric over me.

I can't do this, I just can't.

"This is the last outfit Annabelle designed. She would be so happy knowing that Lucian's fiancée is going to be wearing it."

I couldn't feel any smaller than I do in this moment. My head that I held high moments ago lowers as guilt tightens its grip on me. If Lucian's mum was looking down right now, I'm sure she would be turning in her grave. I am not the woman who'll be marrying her son. I am nothing but an imposter.

"I couldn't. I mean, I can't wear this dress. Don't get me wrong, it's beautiful, it's just—" What the hell do I even say? *It's just I'm only pretending to be engaged to Lucian.* How can I possibly wear something that holds such sentimental value? "Is there another dress? We could go to the shopping centre and pick something new?" I clasp my palm over my mouth. I sound so ungrateful.

"You're nervous. I get it," Marvin says. He stands behind me and, taking the gown from the hanger, holds it in front of me. Without a word he walks us toward a full-length mirror.

Valerie's reflection joins ours, and she scoops my hair up and holds it in place. "So, what do you think?"

"It's beautiful," I choke out, and it truly is. The soft white satin is overlaid with a delicate lace. The gown has a sweetheart neckline and travels a few inches past my knees.

"And you will look beautiful wearing it." Valerie wastes no time securing my hair back with hair pins from a pocket in her tunic. "Lucian was most insistent that you wear one of the gowns from his mother's collection. Please, try it on, and I will make the required alterations. We will need to take a few inches from the bottom, take the sides in and—"

I lift my hand. "Wait. Once you make these alterations, the dress can't be changed back, can it?"

"That's right, flower," Marvin says, and spins me around to face him. Try as I might, I can't escape his gaze, and I figure that is the way he wants it. "Lucian wants the dress perfectly tailored to fit you, and only you."

Farrah insisted we get ready together in her bedroom, and we do. She is most insistent that I do her hair and makeup. This I don't mind, because it brings a bit of normality to this completely abnormal situation.

After I apply the final touches Farrah asks if she can do my makeup in return. This is something I like to do myself because I know which shade of foundation matches my complexion and which eyeshadow compliments my colouring.

I grip the makeup brushes in a chokehold, knowing she won't be able to prise them from between my fingers. I suck in my lips and try to think how I'm going to decline without hurting her feelings. That is until I see the excitement that is so evident in her stare. I grew up with a sister one year my senior, whereas Farrah grew up with three brothers much older than her. Doing one another's makeup was something Amber and I took for granted, but something Farrah never experienced.

One by one, my fingers loosen around the brushes. "Sure."

Farrah claps her hands together. "Fab!"

To my horror, Farrah spins the stool I'm sitting on around so I'm facing away from the mirror. Letting a seventeen-year-old do my makeup is one thing, but me basically being blind during the application spikes my anxiety. I smile and use the tips of my toes to spin the stool back around, but Farrah captures my shoulders and holds me in place. "Trust me. I know what I'm doing."

I shrug and laugh, though my laugh is devoid of any genuine humour. "Of course I trust you. A girl your age, I imagine you do your makeup all the time."

Farrah lets out a girlish chuckle. "I mean, no. That's what my stylist, Sandra, is for. But I watch her apply my makeup all the time."

Dear God. Any other day would be fine, but Lucian has told me repeatedly how important this evening is to him. I could end up looking like Bozo the Clown.

"Now hold still. I'd hate to make a mistake and have to start over."

I hadn't realised that while Farrah held me in place, my feet continued to move in a last-ditch attempt to spin the stool around. I would feel a little happier and a lot more in control if I could at least see what she was doing.

Farrah's expression transforms from excited to hurt, and I immediately hold my feet still. I take a deep breath in. Worst-case scenario I will take a pack of cleansing wipes in my clutch and redo my makeup in the restroom when I arrive.

"Okay, I'm ready," I say and watch as Farrah leans into me. Her eyes are narrowed and her tongue is poised on her top lip, the look of concentration evident on her face. I tilt my head back and close my eyes and sit in silence as Farrah gets to work.

"So, when did you fall in love with my brother?" she asks at the same time the foundation sponge glides across my cheeks.

Her question throws me, and I am grateful that I'm not looking at her. My eyes move rapidly from side to side under my lids. I hate lying to people but I can't say nothing. I think of the limited times I have been in Lucian's company, and the answer hits me.

I open my eyes. "It sounds hard to believe, but actually it was when Lucian helped me clean my flat."

Farrah laughs. "I don't believe you."

My stomach tightens and it feels as though I've been caught with my hand in the sweet jar. "I'm not lying."

Farrah lowers the foundation sponge and finds the powder brush. "I never said you were. It's just in all my life, I've never seen Lucian clean anything. You must have asked him very nicely."

"I didn't ask him," I answer honestly and smile at the memory. At how he used antibacterial spray to clean the windows. I didn't have the heart to tell him he was doing it wrong, and he didn't seem to notice the large smears across the glass. It didn't matter because he took time out of his busy day to help me, and that meant a lot. No, more than a lot, it meant everything.

"I can see it in your eyes." Farrah sighs and clasps the powder brush to her chest with a faraway look in her gaze.

"See what?" I wonder if she has managed to get makeup in my eyes without me knowing.

"The look of love," Farrah answers simply.

I laugh her comment off, but don't deny the fact. Not because I'm pretending to be in love with Lucian, but because, well, I don't know why. Despite our first meeting two years ago when we got off on the wrong foot, I'd be lying if I said that Lucian hasn't been the perfect gentleman since then. He had my flat decorated after Tyler's party and most important of all is that he had my baby nephew's clothes cleaned and placed back into the ottoman.

I close my eyes, contradictory thoughts of Lucian whizzing around in my mind. Time passes, and I'm not sure if I doze off at one point, but I'm awoken from my thoughts when Farrah shakes me.

"Finished," she announces. My eyes snap open and I jump as the stool beneath me jerks suddenly. I hold out my hands to try to steady myself as I'm spun anticlockwise to face the mirror.

The stool stops suddenly, and I come face to face with my reflection. Apart from being a little generous with the blusher, Farrah has done a really nice job. My eyeshadow is a mix of golds, not the colours I would have personally chosen, but it looks nice.

"What do you think?" she asks.

I glance up to meet her eyes in the mirror. "Looks fab," I say, and notice that she's even managed to glue the false eyelashes into place without sticking my eyes together.

Farrah squeaks in excitement. "I knew I was a wasted talent."

"Perhaps I'll employ you to work in my beauty salon as an apprentice makeup artist." I laugh, but Farrah does not. I of course was only joking, because an heiress working in a beauty salon is just unheard of. But Farrah's expression sobers, as does mine, and an awkwardness passes between us.

"I mean, you're welcome to work with me at the salon," I say, feeling the need to say something to fill the silence.

Farrah's gaze lowers and she runs her fingers through her long ebony locks. "Yeah. No. It's a terrible idea. Me working? My father would never allow it."

Her statement surprises me. Duncan Calloway is portrayed by the media as a hard-working man, and his sons follow in his footsteps. Yet here is his daughter, seventeen years old and not allowed to work? I'm unsure if her father is overprotective or chauvinistic.

Tears glisten in Farrah's eyes, and I know I've hit a nerve. I reach up and squeeze her fingers, which she has placed on my shoulder. "You're welcome to come to my salon any time, be it for treatments or training."

We hold one another's stare for long seconds, even when

Lucian knocks on the door to inform us that they are getting ready to leave.

"We aren't ready," Farrah calls and I follow her mirrored gaze to where our dresses hang.

"That's okay, we'll wait."

"Please, go ahead without us." Farrah quickly wipes at her eyes. "Chelsea and I want to arrive in style."

There's a beat of silence before Lucian speaks. "As you wish. The event starts promptly at seven. Don't be late."

"We'll be right behind you."

After changing into our dresses, we watch from the bedroom window as the Range Rover Lucian and Malachi are in leaves through the wrought-iron gates.

"I guess it's time to get the show on the road," Farrah says, checking her makeup one final time. Though she needn't bother, her makeup is flawless. Mine is too, now I've had a chance to blend the blusher when Farrah wasn't looking.

Farrah's bodyguard, Dante, escorts us from the bedroom and to the large driveway where the Mercedes is parked. The engine is purring like a regal cat when Farrah and I slide inside. With Dante sitting in the front passenger seat, we have the entire back of the car to ourselves.

I'm quiet during the journey, and Farrah is only too happy to fill the silence with reams of conversation. She talks about her studies and tells me about all the things she likes to do in her spare time, which ranges from singing to playing the piano and horse riding. I keep my gaze trained on my lap and focus on the intricately designed patterns made from the lace. I feel awful—no, more than awful, I feel like a fraud. Wearing this dress is dishonouring a dead woman's memory. I begged Valerie not to cut the material and pleaded with her not to shorten the length. She didn't listen.

"What do you think?" Farrah asks.

I look up and am met by her emerald gaze. She looks

stunning this evening, and a lot older than her seventeen years. She is wearing an off-the-shoulder maroon gown; the skirt falls all the way to the floor with a slight slit up her right calf. Her ebony locks fall in tight spirals and dance around her face as she talks.

"I'm sorry, what do I think about what?"

Farrah rolls her eyes and shakes her head. "About the handbags. Do I go straight in at ten thousand, or start lower?"

Ten thousand? For handbags? Is she insane? "Lower. Much lower."

"That's a good idea," Farrah says.

I notice Farrah meeting her bodyguard's gaze in the mirrored visor. She smiles at him. Dante's eyes don't crease at the corners, which tells me he isn't returning her smile, but he is looking at her. I wonder how old he is—my guess would be twenty-five. He isn't bad-looking, in a ripped gym-goer kind of way. His black dress shirt hugs his chest, showing the guy is in very good physical shape. His hair is dark, and his eyes…oh, my God, his eyes meet my gaze through the reflection, and I quickly look away.

Distraction over, I hold my head in my hands and say the words I've wanted to say all day. "I can't do this." I can't pretend any more.

"Stop the car," Farrah announces.

The driver adjusts the rear-view mirror. "I'm under strict instructions from Mr Calloway to get you there on time."

Farrah flashes me a smile before cupping her hand to her mouth. "If you insist, but just to warn you I get terrible travel sickness, and if you don't stop soon, then I'll…"

"Right away, miss." The driver indicates to turn off the main road and pulls into a layby. The driver and Dante jump out of the car and hurry to open our doors to let us out. That is, they would do, had Farrah not leaned into the driver's side seat and locked the doors from the inside.

"Finally, we're alone," Farrah says and sinks back into the leather upholstery.

The driver and Dante stand outside the car, the driver at Farrah's window and Dante at mine.

Dante taps the glass. "Open the door."

"Give us ten minutes," Farrah says, her smile wide as she does a shooing action with her hands.

Dante points to the face of his watch, making Farrah aware he is timing us, then he rounds the car and perches on the bonnet. As for the driver, he leans against a nearby bus stop and pulls out a pack of cigarettes.

"Now we're alone," Farrah says, shuffling closer, "tell me what's bothering you."

I let out a long breath whilst fidgeting with the lace on the dress. "Everything."

CHAPTER THIRTEEN

Lucian

"The event started at seven p.m., and it's now seven-thirty. Where are they?" I jab my index finger into the domed face of my pocket watch.

"Probably fifteen seconds closer than they were the last time you asked," Malachi says, whilst lazily rotating his golden dice cufflinks.

I pace up and down the hotel lobby, waiting for Farrah and my fiancée to join us. Cameras flash outside as the insanely rich and famous step onto the red carpet and enter through the large revolving door. Ballgowns in every colour imaginable whiz by as women, escorted by their dates, pass us and proceed to the function room. None of the women who pass are Chelsea. Damn my sister, who insists on turning up to every event 'fashionably late'. Farrah gave me her word that they'd be right behind us. She lied.

"There's my date," Malachi says, and he hurries to greet Lady Louise Whittington as she enters the lobby. Louise has a beautiful, bronzed skin tone and thick raven hair that is pinned back in a chunky braid. She is wearing a gold gown that hugs her voluptuous frame. She doesn't acknowledge me. Her attention is fixed on my brother as he takes her hand.

I take a few steps forward and peer into the function room. A string quartet plays quietly on stage as guests mingle. My father was right when he said there would be a ton of influential people in attendance this evening. From the media, to celebrities, to billionaires from all different walks of life, not to mention the mayor of Cornwall, they are all here to support the annual Pink Ribbon Breast Cancer Charity Gala.

Whilst skimming the sea of faces, I make eye contact with Austin Lake, an oil tycoon from across the pond. He nods in acknowledgement and, sighing heavily, I nod back. Obligation calls, and I know I can't stay in the lobby all evening. It's time to mingle.

The conversation with Austin is enough to condemn anyone to death via boredom. I talk when I need to and laugh at his humourless jokes. In the corner of my eye, I notice Darren Moore from *Cornwall Gossip* magazine. He sidles his way over to us. I have no interest in talking to him, so nod politely and make my way across the room to the beverage table. Empty glasses are stacked around a champagne fountain. I fill my fluted glass and lift it to my lips.

My gaze is trained on the lobby when striking blond hair and an offensive bright orange tan burn into my peripheral vision. I don't need to turn to know it's the same man.

"Darren," I utter.

Darren claps my back, causing me to jerk and the champagne to spill over the rim of the glass. The gold liquid mottles my pristine white shirt.

"Oh, how terribly clumsy of me." A ghost of a smile tugs at Darren's lips. "Maybe next time you won't be quite as generous when helping yourself to the complimentary champagne."

How very typical of Darren, forever the practical joker. But I am not laughing.

Darren's hazel eyes search mine. He waits for me to speak, and when I don't, he sighs heavily. "You've been avoiding me, friend."

"*Friend.*" I hold the last syllable for uncomfortable seconds before continuing. "Forgive me, but my definition of a 'friend' may differ slightly from yours. In my book a friend does not write a libellous article about you. No, Darren, you are an acquaintance at best."

"Don't be like that," Darren whines, squeezing my shoulder. "We have history."

It is true that once upon a time I considered this serpent of a man my friend. Darren's father, Bruce, was the groundskeeper at Freesdon Hall, our family estate in Knightsbridge. Bruce would often bring Darren along with him to work and as boys we would play together. Darren taught me how to play football, and in return I taught him how to ride and play croquet. But Darren tarnished any friendship we had by printing a story about me that he had no right to publish.

"My relationship with Samantha Matthews was no business of yours. You should never have pressured her into selling her story."

The day that story ran was the day I had dear Darren demoted from senior editor to a basic reporter. I threatened to sue the entire company for all they had, but I didn't under the strict understanding that they were never to run another story about the Calloways. Or, more specifically, me.

"I didn't pressure Samantha. It was she who came to me."

Lies. "You always had a talent for getting people to talk."

"Whilst we're on the subject of people talking, tell me, Lucian, how is the competition between you and your brothers going? The one where you're competing to win Calloway Housebuilders? I'm very curious to see how that'll pan out. It's a shame I can't write an article about it. I imagine we would have kept the piece running with daily statistics and polls as to who was the frontrunner."

How the hell does he know about that? Apart from Josh and Chelsea, I haven't told anyone. And it isn't like either one of my brothers to partake in idle gossip outside of our family. I neither confirm nor deny Darren's findings, and instead cover my mouth with the back of my hand and yawn. I'm bored of the conversation. I take a step forward, as does Darren.

I narrow my eyes, about to give him a snarky reply, when I see her. Chelsea is standing in the doorway of the function room. She looks... my God, she looks utterly breathtaking. She is wearing a figure-hugging white gown. Her blonde hair has been pinned back from her face, which accentuates her slender neck, making her appear as elegant as a swan. Heads turn from every angle, and guests talk amongst one another in hushed whispers.

I turn to Darren, whose mouth is agape. *Yes, he's seen her too.*

"It looks as though my fiancée has arrived. Take a picture, it'll last longer. Oh, that's right, I forgot, you're banned from running stories about us. What a pity, because this girl takes one hell of a photo, and I happen to be talking from experience."

The dark veins in Darren's neck are bulging and his pulse flickers rapidly. I imagine the story he would have written flashing by him, word by word, and there isn't a single thing he can do.

"Here, hold this," I say, and pass Darren my drink, or rather shove the stem of the glass into his unsuspecting hand. The liquid sloshes over the rim of the glass and soaks into the fabric of his shirt. "Oh, how terribly clumsy of me," I deadpan.

Without hesitation, I make my way across the room to my lady. A few people in the crowd try to catch my attention as I pass, but their efforts are futile. I'm surrounded by faces and yet hers is the only one I see.

Her gaze sweeps the room, stopping the moment our eyes meet. She doesn't smile, nor does she look away. The fire she ignites in the pit of my stomach is affirmation of how much I want this girl. She is really something—no, correction, she is everything. But my beautiful rose isn't without her thorns, ones I would gladly bleed for if it meant that I could one day have the flower.

I hold out my hand, which she takes. The sound of my

heartbeat hammers in my ears and for a second I'm stunned into silence.

"You look… my God, you look…" I choke out, unable to find a word that will do her justice. "Divine, and utterly breathtaking."

Chelsea's cheeks glow pink. She looks at the floor for a beat before meeting my gaze. "You don't scrub up so bad yourself."

I'm assuming she's referring to my Hampton navy three-piece suit. The suit was a gift from my grandfather and is one of the finer outfits I own. The jacket features luxury lapels, a subtly patterned matching jacket and trousers. Instead of completing the outfit with a tie, I have opted for a deep navy cravat.

I ignore Chelsea's earlier warning about kissing her and swoop down, claiming her lips. She doesn't pull away, she doesn't tense. To my complete surprise she parts her lips and kisses me back. I fight the desire to kiss deeper, harder, and the overwhelming need I have to own every single inch of her. Muffled voices and music from the string quartet play in my ears, and I remind myself that we are in public. I lean back, reluctantly breaking the kiss. It's not hatred swimming in her gaze, but something else.

"Change of heart?" I say, leaning in to her.

"No." Her one-word reply confuses me. What game is she playing? I would ask, but notice my brothers standing not too far away. Gage is with his date, Sophia Chase, and Malachi stands arm in arm with Louise. It's now I notice Josh with his long-term girlfriend, Natasha. There are too many ears around to continue with our conversation. So instead of pressing Chelsea for answers I take her hand.

"Where's my sister?" I ask, noticing Farrah is nowhere to be seen.

"She said something about getting first dibs on designer handbags in the auction room. She told me to carry on without her."

Farrah and her designer bag collection, God love her. I don't think she realises how a silent auction works but no doubt she has placed her bid and is doing her damnedest to discourage anyone from outbidding her. I know my sister is only seventeen, but I will not allow her to discourage people from bidding when the money raised is going to charity.

"What a coincidence she is in the auction room," I say, leading Chelsea toward a set of double doors. "Because that is exactly where we are heading."

"I've never been to a silent auction before."

And I smile, knowing Chelsea has lived a very sheltered life. I plan to be the person to introduce her to a lot of her firsts.

On entry we are handed a brochure that lists all the items being auctioned today, from artwork to jewellery, and a selection of gift cards ranging from weekends away to spa days.

"All the items here have been donated by guests and sponsors." I nod my head toward the long lines of tables that hug the room's perimeter. The tables contain a variety of hampers and gift cards, while a selection of artwork lines the walls. The expensive items such as million-pound necklaces and diamond-encrusted watches are displayed in tall glass cabinets, and armed guards keep watch.

"What have you donated?" Chelsea asks, her gaze fixed on an abstract painting of a child.

"Come, I'll show you." I saunter along the table. My gaze roves over the many items on display. I stop when we are standing directly in front of my donation.

"There." I point. My item is printed on a single sheet of paper and is displayed in a freestanding acrylic frame. Chelsea leans forward and peers at the writing.

"Plot eighty?" She looks at me briefly before her attention returns to the small print.

"That's correct. A plot of land at Hazelwood Farm. The highest bidder will have a choice of properties he or she wants."

"You're telling me you're giving away a house?"

I'm not sure if her question is rhetorical but I answer anyway. "It's for a good cause."

Chelsea shuffles from one foot to the other. "Breast cancer. Farrah told me all about your mother. Lucian, I'm so sorry."

There it is right there. The reason she reciprocated the kiss, and the look in her eyes I couldn't quite place. Pity. Pity is such a condescending emotion. To pity shows empathy, but to be pitied shows weakness. This is the second time I have been met by Chelsea's compassion, but there will not be a third.

"Love me, hate me or loathe me, but never pity me," I say as memories of my mother strike me deep, so deep that I can feel the cracks making their way to my heart.

"I'm sorry." Gazing up at me, Chelsea rubs her hand up and down the length of her arm. "I didn't mean to upset you."

"You didn't. I'm fine." I glance around the room, needing a momentary distraction, and that comes in the form of Angus Blackwell.

"Angus," I say, and with my hand placed on the small of Chelsea's back I walk a few steps forward and greet the old man.

Angus is quite the character, dressed in his signature pea-green suit and matching top hat. Angus lifts a monocle to his left eye and studies me for a beat. "Ah, young Calloway, how's life treating you?"

I flash a glance at Chelsea and smile. "Very well, as you can see."

"How's your old man doing?" Angus and my father go way back, though Angus's wealth is derived from pharmaceuticals. Growing bored of having all his eggs in one basket, Angus was more than happy to invest in Calloway Cruises. He is always dropping not-so-subtle hints that he wants to become a partner.

"You know my father. Busy working, and when he isn't in his office, he is occupying the golf course."

"Is he ever going to retire?" Angus presses, running his index finger up and down the length of his wiry moustache.

The news that my father is retiring isn't yet public knowledge, and that is how it will remain. "You know my father; he will take his laptop and phone to the grave. Tell me all about your new home in Swansea." I change the subject because as much as I like and respect Angus, the man's the world's worst gossip.

Chelsea stands in total silence as Angus and I talk. It isn't long before he invites me to join him at his private lake.

"Fishing? I would be delighted," I say.

"Will the young lady be joining you?"

I won't be able to join Angus in Swansea for a few months, by which time Chelsea's and my arrangement will be over. I fear that when our time is up I shall never want to let her go. My only hope is I can present her with enough of an incentive that she'll never want to leave.

Chelsea laughs. "Fishing isn't really—"

"She would be delighted," I answer for her.

When my conversation with Angus comes to an end, Chelsea and I take a quick turn around the room. I manage to locate my little sister, who is standing possessively in front of a trio of designer handbags.

I casually make my way over to where she is standing. "Sister dearest," I say only loud enough that she can hear. With an arm draped around Chelsea, I use my free hand to give Farrah a small nudge. "Why don't you step aside so that other people may admire the designer bags."

"Sure thing," she says with a smile so sharp it would slice through titanium. Though I give my sister credit for not reacting, because letting her mouth run away with her is a trait she has always been unable to control.

When Farrah's back is turned and she walks in the opposite direction I place a bid on the trio of bags. A bid I know won't be beaten. I request that my identity remain anonymous when the names of the highest bidders are announced at the end of the evening. I plan to surprise Farrah with the bags on her eighteenth birthday.

I fill out several additional ledgers, bidding on a wide range of items. From the auction I direct Chelsea through the double doors and back into the main room. From this moment on we are the perfect duo. Our relationship is so believable to the outside world that I almost believe it myself. Chelsea returns my glances, laughs at my jokes, and joins in on conversations with other guests. We mingle, drink champagne and snack on the hors d'oeuvres. With Chelsea on my arm, I glide around the room like a man who has everything, because in this moment I have.

I smile big as people pass me by but stop suddenly when I come face to face with a person, a woman I never thought I'd lay eyes on again.

"Lucian." Her voice fills my ears like liquid lava. She smiles at me, though glowers at Chelsea.

I swallow. "Samantha."

CHAPTER FOURTEEN

Chelsea

I smile and await a formal introduction, but my smile is met with a scowl.

"And who is this?" the woman says, her gaze sweeping over me as though I'm something she's stepped in.

I raise my brows indignantly. I may not be fluent in the ways of high society, but I know when someone is being blatantly rude.

But I can't think why for the life of me. What have I done? I stand purse-lipped and study our new acquaintance. She has long mousy brown hair, piercing blue eyes, and legs so long I have to crane my neck to meet her gaze. She's pretty, in a superficial, overly-made-up kind of way, and I bet her lips have had a ton of filler pumped into them. She breaks my stare, and that's when I see it. The way she looks at Lucian tells me everything I need to know.

Lucian clears his throat. "Forgive me. Chelsea, this is Samantha."

"Lucian's first and only love," Samantha adds, extending her arm.

Lucian's jaw clenches. "Samantha, this is Chelsea."

"Lucian's fiancée," I say and place my hand in hers. Her gaze travels down to my ring, and I smile. "It's a pleasure to meet you."

Samantha holds my hand and stares for a second before returning her attention to Lucian. It's as though she needs to hear the words from his lips as validation before she'll believe it.

"What are you doing here?" Lucian finally says.

"I was invited." Samantha looks down and runs her index finger along the scooped neckline of her long red ballgown. I figure her hope is that Lucian will look at her cleavage.

He doesn't, and instead narrows his eyes. "Who by? Wouldn't happen to be Darren Moore, would it?"

"Darren? No, why would he invite me here?" Samantha rocks on her heels before leaning forward and placing her hand on Lucian's arm. Anger courses through me at the sheer nerve of the woman. Didn't she hear me? I've literally just said that I am Lucian's fiancée.

"It's good to see you," she says, looking all doe-eyed at Lucian as if I'm not standing right here. "Could I speak to you, please? Alone?"

"I'm sorry, Samantha, but whatever you have to say to my fiancé, you can say in front of me." A possessiveness I have never felt before creeps its way into my gut. Lucian wrapping his arm around me couldn't come at a better time, and I wrap my arm around him in return.

"Have a good evening, Samantha. It was good catching up."

Or not, I think, but manage to hold my tongue as Lucian and I head in the opposite direction. I side-eye Lucian, who is wearing the most ridiculous smile I think I've ever seen.

"What?" I finally say and stop walking.

"Jealous, were we? Because, sweetheart, you were positively green."

I consider his words for a beat and then it hits me. Not once did the fake engagement cross my mind. It was like a red mist came down around me because in that moment I was Lucian's and he was mine.

Laughing theatrically, I wave his comment off. "Don't be stupid. I'm your fiancée, remember."

"How could I forget?"

I look up, and the second I do, he captures my chin between his thumb and forefinger. My heart hammers as he leans in for a kiss, but instead of turning my head to the side like I should do, like I need to do, I wet my lips in readiness. His gaze seeks approval, and I tilt my head in reply.

What the hell is wrong with me? Lucian has only been my fiancé, my *fake* fiancé for one day and already I'm getting lost somewhere between fact and fiction. This isn't real, Lucian isn't my fiancé. I need to—

My thoughts quickly melt away as Lucian's lips crash against mine. And fantasy or not, I kiss him back. His lips part, as do mine, and I grant his tongue entry. His hand spans across the small of my back as he pulls me into him. My head spins, my knees go weak, and I tremble in his embrace. The butterflies in my stomach that I thought were dormant fly around with gusto. He tastes of champagne and spearmint gum, sweet yet oddly refreshing. The kiss is firm and the coarse hairs on his face burn into my skin. He holds me with purpose and kisses me with everything that he is and, releasing all of my inhibitions, I kiss him back.

When the kiss risks being deemed socially unacceptable Lucian retreats. Our lips may be apart, but he holds my stare with an intensity that makes me feel connected to him.

"Tell me." He runs the pad of his thumb across my bottom lip. "Was that part of the act, or are you starting to feel something for me?"

I close my eyes and will my heart to stop beating so heavily and the butterflies in my stomach to stop flying around. This is ridiculous, getting jealous over a man who isn't mine to begin with and then kissing him.

"I'm acting, of course," I say in a whisper.

"Well, I give you top marks, Chelsea, because you had me fooled."

The music from the string quartet plays a little louder, and couples make their way to the dance floor. With our fingers interlinked we join them.

It's two a.m. by the time we say our goodbyes and head home. Malachi and Louise left the gala early and arranged with Lucian to take the Mercedes, leaving Lucian, myself, Farrah and her bodyguard no option than to share the Range Rover.

We leave the grand lobby through the revolving doors and wait to be picked up by Lucian's driver. We stand at the front of the hotel, but there isn't a Range Rover anywhere in sight.

"Perhaps he's just running late?" I say, looking left and then right.

"No. McKenzie is never late." Lucian whips out his phone and presses the screen to his ear. It rings for a while, and from the look on Lucian's face I imagine the call has been diverted to voicemail.

"McKenzie, we're outside the hotel. And guess what, you're not. I suggest that if you want to keep your position you get your backside here, and fast."

Lucian cuts the call, and I take his hand. "That really isn't necessary."

"He'll be parked in the car park," Dante chimes in. "It isn't too far, we can walk."

Lucian's jaw ticks as he glares at his sister. "In the state she's managed to get herself in? I thought you were hired to keep an eye on her," he scoffs, his nostrils flaring.

Dante shrugs. "She had a few glasses of champagne. It's no big deal."

"No big deal? She's seventeen." Lucian's voice rises, and I suspect this is as close as I'm going to get to hearing him shout.

Dante stands tall and straightens his shoulders. "Tell me, Lucian, did you wait till *you* were eighteen to enjoy your first alcoholic drink?"

Lucian doesn't answer.

"Your father pays me to keep your sister safe and out of harm's way. Not to be her moral compass."

I can feel the testosterone levels rising and quickly intervene before there's a fight. "She's fine. All she needs is some fresh air and a good night's sleep. Come on, Farrah."

The sky is tranquil and dark, lit up with sporadic twinkling stars. It's the perfect time to get fresh air. I walk ahead with Farrah, who may have had a glass of champagne too many. With her arm draped heavily around my shoulders, I attempt to steer her in a straight line. I don't think I'm doing too bad of a job, though my feet throb with each step I take and my calves burn. When Marvin asked if I could walk in heels I answered yes, but what I'm not used to is standing for hours on end whilst balancing precariously on two ridiculously thin six-inch points.

"Where's my handbag?" Farrah slurs.

"On your arm," I tell her and hoist her up.

"Did you catch the name of the thief who stole my designer bags?"

I laugh. "I think you mean bought. And no, I didn't catch their name."

"Pity." Farrah stumbles, and I struggle to support her weight.

"Here, allow me," a voice says from behind, and Dante appears at her side. He leans down and scoops her up effortlessly in his muscular arms. Her body goes limp and the second she is secure in his hold she allows her head to fall into the crook of his arm. I can't miss the subtle smile that tugs at her lips. I don't need to be a body language expert to know she is milking this moment for all it's worth. She may be obscenely rich and live a sheltered life, but Farrah Calloway is nobody's fool. Her long ebony locks hang over Dante's arm as he marches off in front.

I can see Lucian in my periphery as he quickens his pace. It isn't until we are walking side by side that he falls into a leisurely stroll. Without a word he snakes an arm around my back, his hand resting comfortably on my waist.

How easily the lines blur. Tonight, Lucian held my hand, and I held his. He wrapped his arm around me, and I let him. And then there was that kiss. I went to the gala tonight with a mask of pretence firmly in place, but as the gala drew to an end the mask had fallen and I was no longer pretending.

"I don't like how Dante is holding my sister," Lucian states, talking to me as if him having his arm around me is perfectly normal.

"He's helping her to the car," I remind him, very aware that we are alone and don't need to put on an act any more, but not doing anything to put space between us.

Lucian whistles, and Dante turns slightly. "That's enough, Romeo, put her down."

"No can do," Dante says, turning his back on us. "I work directly for your father. His orders are that I make sure Miss Calloway remains safe and out of danger. I don't want her tripping and breaking a bone, now do I?"

Lucian's arm tenses around me momentarily before he turns to face me. "Is something going on between Farrah and Dante I should know about?"

I love how protective Lucian is being over her, because it shows how deeply he cares. "No. I think it's just a case of a teenage crush."

"Good, because if I so much as get wind of…" Lucian stops talking, his gaze travelling down to our joined hands. *When did that even happen?* He leans into me. "You know that nobody is watching us now." I shrug, attempting to pull free, but his grip only tightens. "Whatever is happening between us, I would very much like it to continue."

"Nothing is happening," I say with humour, but by the expression on Lucian's face I can tell he doesn't believe me. *I* don't believe me. "We've both had a drink. Please don't read any more into this than me keeping up with my end of the agreement."

"Very well." Lucian releases my hands and slowly caresses the insides of my arms with the back of his fingers, the action so small, yet so incredibly sensual that it sends goosebumps rippling up my skin.

"Here." Lucian removes his suit jacket and drapes it over my shoulders. His scent is all around me as the warm material encompasses me in a hug.

"Thank you," I mumble.

Lucian nods once and we continue walking. He has been the perfect gentleman tonight, and on more than one occasion has made my heart go pitter-patter. But this is all an act, this isn't real. I can't allow my mind to get lost in the fairytale.

It isn't long before the Range Rover comes into view. The front driver's side is lit up by a flickering streetlight. It would seem Lucian's driver McKenzie is fast asleep with his head slumped forward over the steering wheel. I'm amazed he hasn't sounded the horn.

"I call shotgun!" Farrah calls, and I notice she no longer lies limp in Dante's arms but has her arms wrapped around his neck, much to Lucian's annoyance. He bypasses Dante—with a look that tells the bodyguard that they will be having words—and makes his way to the car window. Lucian balls his hand into a tight fist and knocks once, causing the old man to nearly jump out of his skin. The car door flings open and McKenzie stumbles out, apologising profusely.

"Don't mention it," Lucian says to his driver, yet his gaze is trained on me. "As it happens, we had a pleasant walk."

Dante helps Farrah into the front passenger's seat, and after fastening her in he joins me and Lucian in the back. It doesn't go unnoticed that the gap between Lucian and Dante is considerably wider than the gap between Lucian and me.

This is too much; *he* is too much. I feel as though I'm drowning, in a situation I have zero control over. I need to regain control and I need to put distance between us. Despite my best efforts to sit away from Lucian, I cannot get comfortable. Which is unsurprising when squashed awkwardly against the car door.

"Stop fighting it," Lucian whispers, and I do. I release my reservations and relax, finally allowing myself to sink back. On doing so my right shoulder fits snugly against Lucian's chest and my thigh overlaps his. Each time the car goes over a bump or hits a pothole we're jerked closer together. I relax my neck, and my head comes to rest directly below his chin. He places a kiss on my crown. "We'll be home in no time."

Home, what does that even mean? With Farrah staying with us Lucian has already made it clear that we are to share a room. There is no way in hell I am going to share a bed with this man. It's not because I don't trust him—the person I don't trust is me.

CHAPTER FIFTEEN

Chelsea

Cool air blows against the side of my face and causes my eyes to snap open. I immediately sit up. I'm in bed, Lucian's bed. The last thing I remember is Lucian escorting me to his bedroom. While he had a shower, I changed into a silk nightie and quickly slipped beneath the covers. With the duvet cocooned around me I lay awake and waited for Lucian to join me. My heart raced in anticipation because I knew that any second, he would be lying next to me.

I must have fallen asleep. Now I look around but can't see a thing, as everything is shrouded in darkness. As my eyes become accustomed to my surroundings, the darkened silhouettes around me slowly take shape. I'm in a large bed with a heavy duvet over me. There is a nightstand to my right and a tall glass positioned in the centre. A sliver of silvery light seeps in from between a crack in the curtains, curtains that move like the ebb and flow of the sea, the result of an open window or balcony door beyond.

I yawn and use the back of my hand to cover my mouth. I'm about to lie back when something takes shape behind the curtain and a figure of a man steps into the room. But not just any man, it's Lucian.

The curtain has been pushed all the way across, causing light from outside to pour in and highlight his bare chest. Dark shadows wrap around his pecs and the top of his arms. It takes a few seconds to realise they aren't shadows at all but Celtic tattoos. The positioning of his tats is hot as hell and could be easily concealed by a long- or short-sleeved shirt. My eyes widen, and the coldness I felt moments ago is replaced by a wave of heat. I squeeze the duvet in my hands and lean forward to get a better look. His body is lean and muscular and looks as though it has been carved to perfection. His stomach is a mass of rippling muscles leading down to a waist that tapers in. The trousers he wore earlier hug his waist.

I knew Lucian was attractive, and he sure does look good in a suit, but I've never seen him like this before. My gaze travels up and comes to a sudden stop.

My God, he's looking straight at me.

It feels as though my heart crashes into my chest as we lock gazes. He doesn't speak, neither do I. He just stands like a shadow in the darkness, silently watching me, as I watch him. After a few seconds have passed, he reaches into his pocket and pulls out a packet of cigarettes. He places one between his lips and heads toward the curtains. Inch by inch he begins to disappear behind the thick fabric.

"Wait," I blurt out. Lucian stops walking and turns to face me. What the hell do I say now? I sit purse-lipped and watch the slow rise and fall of his shoulders.

"Do you want something?"

I don't know are the words on the tip of my tongue, but I don't let them take shape. I pull the duvet up over my chest. I side-eye the pillow and bolsters beside me and notice they're plumped up and the duvet is untouched. I try to swallow down the question burning on my tongue, but it's too late, the words begin to take shape and I give them volume. "Where are you going to sleep?"

Lucian turns slightly and extends his arm to the sofa behind him. A sofa I sat on earlier during my dress fitting, and incidentally where Malachi's gold-plated business card resides, pushed somewhere between the lumpy cushions. I remember how the springs dug into my ass. To say it was uncomfortable is the understatement of the century.

"You can't sleep on that thing." My words tumble out. "The sofa is horrible."

Lucian takes the cigarette from between his lips and places it back into the packet, which he then tucks into his trouser pocket. "The sofa belonged to my late grandmother. It was once situated in her music room and was where I would sit and watch her play the piano. Call me a sucker for sentiment, but I happen to be quite fond of it."

I sink into the bed, wishing the mattress had the power to swallow me up. *Of course* the sofa belonged to his dead grandmother. "I'm so sorry, Lucian. It's not horrible, I didn't mean that. What I meant is that it's uncomfortable."

Lucian shrugs. "I've slept on worse."

Now that comment has me laughing. "I'm sure. A rich boy like you must have had it tough."

Lucian closes the balcony door and steps closer. "Chelsea Janssen. Are you mocking me?"

"No." I let out a snort-laugh and quickly place my palm over my mouth to cover that godawful sound. But I can't for the life of me stop laughing.

"I'm sure I could tell you a lot of stories about my past that would shock you." Lucian continues toward me with the stealth of a cheetah about to strike.

My laughter subsides when he stops at the foot of the bed. Without a word I lean across and lift the covers beside me, a silent invitation.

"You want me to sleep with you?" Lucian questions, almost in shock.

"This is your bed. It isn't right you're sleeping on the sofa."

"Yes. After all, you've already demonstrated your utter disdain for the piece of furniture that I hold so dear to me." His words slice through me because I feel awful for saying what I did about his grandmother's sofa. But if I'm not mistaken, I could swear he's laughing from the way his body jerks up and down.

"Not funny," I say, and, grabbing a pillow from behind my head, I launch it at him.

He reaches up and catches it mid-flight before approaching the side of the bed. The mattress dips as he sits down, and, with his back toward me, he takes a slow inhale of breath. "I am going to find it incredibly hard sleeping beside you and keeping my hands to myself."

"That can be easily fixed." I grab one of the large bolsters and place it in the middle of the mattress as a dividing line. "There. You will sleep on your half, and I will sleep on mine."

He turns his head to face me. "That kiss tonight, do you regret it?"

I consider his words for a moment, and in all honesty, I don't know how to answer. It's only been a day and yet everything is happening so fast, too fast. The fake engagement, being introduced to his friends, his family, and then attending a charity gala filled with the rich and famous—it's enough to make a girl giddy.

"I don't know," I answer honestly.

Lucian nods. "Thank you."

"For what?"

Lucian pivots around and places his legs on the mattress. "For giving me hope. I want to use our time together wisely and get to know you."

"As a friend?"

"No, Chelsea, I'm afraid I will never and can never be your friend." Cool air fans around me as Lucian pulls the covers over him. He lies on his back and stares up at the ceiling. "You have my word that I won't try to have my wicked way with you in the night. If you can promise me the same."

I stifle a laugh. I'd have elbowed him if the bolster wasn't in the way. Like Lucian, I lie on my back and stare up at the high domed ceiling. "I'm a virgin," I say, matter-of-factly.

"And I'm the king of England," Lucian says in a light-hearted tone. But when I remain silent, he turns his head and looks at me. "Are you serious? How is a twenty-something-year-old as beautiful as you still a virgin?"

With my gaze trained on the ceiling I let out a slow exhale. "I'm not going to lie, I've come close, many times, but something always prevented me."

Lucian doesn't speak, and his silence goads me to continue.

I blow out my cheeks. "Because I've never wanted to hand another person that kind of control before."

"Why are you telling me this? Are you worried I will try something in the middle of the night? Because you have my word that I won't."

"I want you to be my first," I blurt out, and pull the quilt over my face in fear my cheeks are glowing red like a beacon. To my surprise, Lucian doesn't pull the quilt from my head, giving me the time and space I need. Slowly, I lower the quilt and attempt to swallow away my embarrassment. "When the time is right, I want you to be my first."

"Why me?"

Lucian's question confuses me as much as my statement has undoubtedly confused him. I could answer with just about anything—that he is here, and he is now—but that would be a lie. The truth is that at twenty-six years old I feel ready to let someone in, I want to feel that closeness with someone. But not just someone. I want it with him. Lucian is the first man to have pulled me out of my comfort zone and taken away my control. To my surprise, I don't feel as though I am drowning. I feel as though I'm afloat, and he is my lifeboat.

It meant something that Lucian helped me clean up my flat, it meant something when he had my nephew's clothes dry-cleaned.

Against my better judgement, and despite everything inside me screaming at me to see sense, I have to admit that Lucian means something. I know our engagement is fake, and when I wake up in a month from now I will be alone in my own bed, but that doesn't matter. I don't want to wake up in a month as the same play-it-safe person I am now.

Lucian drums his fingers against the mattress, and I figure he is waiting for my answer. So I say the words that are burning on the tip of my tongue. "Because I trust you."

"Even after I propositioned you two years ago for sex?"

The pillow rustles as I nod. "Yes. Because I don't know who that Lucian was back then, but what I do know is that he isn't the same Lucian lying beside me now."

"I will be honoured to be your first, Chelsea, and every time after."

The quilt rises as Lucian reaches his hand across to my side. I freeze, about to chastise him because I didn't say I wanted to have sex with him *now*. But Lucian surprises me by linking his fingers with mine. Such a tiny move on his part, yet it sends shock waves coursing through me.

"Good night, Chelsea."

I smile and close my eyes. "Good night, Lucian."

Light filters in through the curtains and I crack open my eyes. Everything is fuzzy to begin with, and it takes several seconds of wiping sleep from my lashes to focus.

I glance around and realise that I'm lying on Lucian's chest. I try to sit up but am held in place by the weight of his arm that is wrapped around me.

"Lucian," I say while at the same time nudging him, but he doesn't answer. His eyes are closed and his breaths are heavy. I hold my breath and carefully remove his arm. Free from his hold,

I lie on my side of the bed, or at least I would if Lucian wasn't sleeping diagonally across the mattress. The bolster is nowhere to be seen, and I can't help wondering if it got tossed onto the floor when we were asleep or if Lucian secretly discarded it.

I may as well get up—there is no point trying to go back to sleep, at least not now. The conversation Lucian and I had last night replays in my mind. In the cool light of day, and with the evening's alcohol out of my system, I can finally reflect. It surprises me that I don't feel the smallest ounce of regret. Embarrassment, yes, but regret, no.

I slide out of bed, take the glass from the nightstand and have a sip of water. The drink catches in the back of my throat as I take a sharp inhale.

My phone.

The device is on charge and lying face down. I replace the glass on the nightstand, grab my phone and pad across the room to the en suite. The en suite is stunning, a long and rectangular room with spotlights running its length. The lights reflect from the white marble tiles, giving the illusion of tiny gemstones sparkling all around me. How easy it would be to get lost in the wonder of this place.

I lock the door behind me to make sure I won't be disturbed. I press the power button and glance around as my phone loads. There is a large walk-in shower with a waterfall-style showerhead. Not far from the shower is a jacuzzi bath, and a TV hanging above in a wall alcove. Everything is so clean, so white, and so big.

A few seconds pass before my screensaver appears. It's a photo of me, Lizzie and my sister during a night out. Amber is sticking out her tongue, I am doing a Marilyn Monroe pose, and Lizzie, God love her, is attempting to cover her face—she never has cared for having her photo taken. My screensaver image is there for only a second before my phone is hijacked by message after message filling the screen.

Amber, Amber, Lizzie, Amber, Amber, Tyler… Names flash

in individual text boxes for a split second before the box moves down and is replaced by another. I don't wait to be bombarded by any more texts, so open the message app. In total I have five voicemails and eighty-three texts.

Panic radiates through me. I've missed countless messages from my sister. She must be worried sick about me, and she's pregnant. I'll never forgive myself if I've caused her unnecessary stress. With shaky hands I open her messages and scroll all the way to the top.

Amber: Hey, sis, you'll never guess what? Rick surprised me and Freja with a weekend away in his motor home. I will send you photos.

My hands feel less shaky as I scroll down and see image after image of Amber and her family at the seaside, at the fair, and finally swimming.

The last message I received from her was at ten p.m. last night, and it reads:

Amber: Hey, sis, I've tried calling but your phone is off, is everything okay?

I waste no time in clicking on her name. The call rings out and she answers on the eighth ring.

"Chelsea?" Her voice sounds muffled, like she's still in bed, which is where I would be had Lucian the space invader not taken up the entire mattress.

"Hey, sis," I say, my voice unusually chirpy.

Amber yawns down the receiver. "I've been trying to call you, are you okay? Lizzie said she dropped by the flat to see you, but you weren't in."

My heartbeat begins picking up in my chest, because I can't lie to my sister. But what good will telling her the truth do? Amber thinks I hate Lucian, and I do—I did. Amber would never believe our lie, that I agreed to marry him. The truth that me being here is all an act would only hurt her, cause her to worry, which isn't good for my baby nephew, and that I will not allow.

I look long and hard at my reflection before turning my back on myself. "I've actually decided to join Tyler in America." The lie falls from my lips with ease.

"Oh, my God, seriously?" Amber says, her voice high-pitched.

"Yes, seriously. I'm just about to board the plane. I won't be able to message much when I'm in the States, but I will send you updates."

"You will be back in time for Lizzie's wedding, won't you?"

"I wouldn't miss it for the world. Right, sis, I've got to go, enjoy your weekend away and give my favourite niece a big hug from me," I say, and cut the call.

I message my friends, family, and finally my boss informing them all the same thing, that I have decided to go to America. There is only one thing left to do. I click on Tyler's name.

Me: I need to ask a big favour. If anyone asks, tell them I am in America with you.

By trying to protect my nearest and dearest, I've lied to them. My shoulders fall, and I slowly spin around and face the mirror. I take a long, hard look at my reflection, hating the Chelsea who stares back, because this Chelsea is a liar. Lies feel dirty, the kind of deeply ingrained dirt one can never get clean from. I make my way to the shower and turn the tap, causing the water to cascade down. I wait a couple of seconds for the temperature to heat up.

I'm about to place my phone on the vanity when it vibrates in my hand. Tyler's name flashes on the screen from an incoming text.

Tyler: If I am going to lie for you, I want to know exactly what you have gotten yourself into.

Two seconds later my phone rings, and I answer. "Tyler…" After a long and drawn-out conversation with Tyler, plus a lot of begging, he finally agrees. I'm under strict instructions to message him every day to let him know I am okay. I of course agree and cut the call. I have a shower and get changed into a blue summer dress—that has been laid out for me in readiness—and head downstairs to the kitchen for a glass of freshly squeezed orange juice. After which I'll grab the cleaning products and help the maids scrub the kitchen. I can't say they were overly keen on me cleaning one of the en suites yesterday, but when I wouldn't take no for an answer they let me do my thing

I'm halfway down the stairs when I hear a man clear his throat. I turn and see Lucian's cousin, Josh, standing on the top step.

"And how are you this morning?" He closes the distance between us and stands on the stair above. Josh is tall and heavily tanned with a good physique. Unlike Lucian, his face is angular, with a five o'clock shadow covering his jaw. He has the most alluring dark brown eyes I think I have ever seen.

"I'm fine," I say.

I'm about to continue on my way when he speaks again. "What made you agree?"

I turn and force a smile. I figure he's asking why I agreed to be Lucian's wife. I can do this, I just have to repeat what we told Farrah. Consistency is key.

I swallow, and swallow away my nerves. "I don't know really." My voice is higher-pitched than usual, but I can work with it. "It all happened so fast. I guess you could call it a whirlwind romance."

"Cut the pretence. I know."

My throat feels dry all of a sudden. "Lucian told you?"

"Of course. My cousin and I have no secrets. He seems to think you being engaged will help him secure Calloway Housebuilders, and if that's the case I'm all for this. Don't worry, I will not tell a soul."

"Is that Chelsea?" A sweet and chirpy voice ping-pongs off

the walls. Josh spins around as his girlfriend approaches. Her blonde hair bounces off her shoulders as she hurries down the stairs to join us. She is wearing the cutest pink summer dress and a smile so warm it would melt snow.

"Natasha, darling," Josh says and wraps an arm around her waist.

Natasha's blue eyes sparkle with excitement as she reaches for my hand. "Would you join us for breakfast?"

I tug on my earlobe, thinking of an excuse. "I, er, I don't really eat breakfast, and I really must—"

"Of course she will," Josh interjects.

"Excellent," Natasha says, not giving me a second to get away. Her eyes glimmer as she quickly links her arm through mine. "It's right this way."

I glance at Josh, who in turn glances at me, a knowing look in his eyes.

How am I going to get through breakfast?

CHAPTER SIXTEEN

Lucian

Two hours earlier

The conversation with Chelsea keeps me awake long into the early hours. I can't sleep, so instead watch her toss and turn. She fights with the quilt to get comfortable and often pushes it all the way down as if she is too warm, only to pull it back up to her neck seconds later and wrap it around her like a cocoon. It's in the briefest moments I notice how her nightgown hugs the swell of her breasts and can't help wondering what lies beneath.

I shift awkwardly, my hand covering the bulge in my boxers. Slowly I rub my shaft up and down, needing some kind of relief, if only for a moment.

"What time is it?" Chelsea mumbles. I remove my hand from my erection and notice her reaching for something on the nightstand. I know what that something is right away. Her phone.

I side-eye the digital clock. "It's six a.m."

Chelsea nods before sinking her head into the duck feather pillow and drifting back off to sleep. I have no such luck in the getting-back-to-sleep department. I'm highly aroused and wound so tightly I feel I'm about to explode. I slide out of bed. Already dressed in my trousers I wore last night, I pull on a T-shirt and make my way down to the servants' quarters.

The servants start their duties at five-thirty, and already this part of the house is a hive of energy. The cooks are in the kitchen preparing the day's breakfasts and luncheons. The maids set about the house with dusters and polish and from the large windows I notice the gardeners are busy tending to the lawns. Everything in my house works like a well-oiled machine, and I love it.

After checking each room, I stumble upon Bessie and Nancy doing the laundry.

"Sir," Nancy says.

"Mr Calloway." Bessie nods once before continuing to load the dirty clothes into the machine.

"Bessie, you were with me the evening I brought Miss Janssen home."

"Correct," she says, wiping her hands down the front of her tunic.

"You took her clothes with you to be washed. Amongst her things you may have come across—"

Bessie lifts her finger and reaches into the pocket of her trousers. "Yes, the lady's phone. It was seconds from going in with the washing. Luckily it started to buzz, and I slipped it into my pocket for safekeeping. Here," she says, retrieving the device and handing it to me. "I was meaning to give it to you sooner, but I've just been very busy with my work."

"Thank you, Bessie," I say and peer down at the screen.

"The battery is dead, sir. I'm sure one of the staff has a charger you could use." Bessie motions her hand toward the door. "If you like, I can ask around."

"That would be wonderful, thank you."

I join my cook Mrs Collins in the kitchen and have a cup of Earl Grey tea while I wait.

"Just to let you know, your fiancée insisted on cleaning one of the bathrooms yesterday," she says, her gaze locked on mine.

I expect she's waiting for me to chastise her, but I don't. I'd much rather Chelsea wasn't on her hands and knees scrubbing toilets, but I don't know much about OCD other than it's not something she can turn on and off. "If she wants to clean, let her clean," I say, though my hope is that I can find other activities for her to fill her days.

Bessie is true to her word and returns some ten minutes later with a phone charger in hand and I make my way up to my bedroom.

I place Chelsea's phone on the nightstand beside her and smile, knowing she will have her phone fully charged by the time she wakes up. The second I slide into bed, I notice the bolster is no longer on the mattress between us—she must have knocked it off in her sleep. I'm about to reach down to retrieve it when Chelsea turns over and places her head on my chest.

"Hey, Chelsea," I say, and gently begin to lift her.

"I'm comfy," she grumbles.

Well, if the lady is comfortable, I wouldn't want to move her. I wrap my arm around my Sleeping Beauty and place a kiss on her head before closing my eyes.

The first thing I do when I wake up is reach out my hand. The space beside me is cold and empty. Her side of the bed has been made and the duvet tucked neatly under the mattress.

I can't help the pang of disappointment that ripples through me, but what was I expecting?

After a shower and change of clothes I head downstairs in search of my fiancée. Laughter and conversations echo throughout the corridors, and I follow the voices to the orangery. I'm surprised to find Natasha and Josh are sitting on my wicker sofa and indulging in a continental breakfast laid out buffet-style on a chunky wooden table.

"Lucian, my man." Josh smiles before lowering his head to butter a croissant. The morning sun reflects in from the glass-paned roof, making red tones shine in his black hair.

"What are you doing here?" I ask.

"There was a leak at my place," Josh says. "I've had to get plumbers to fix the pipe, and a new carpet is being laid as we speak." By the way Josh's eye twitches, I know he's telling a blatant lie. Josh and Natasha have a long-distance relationship, and whenever she visits he always finds a reason to stay over at one of my estates. I can't say I mind seeing as I own numerous properties up and down the country. I suspect the only reason our paths have crossed is because this is the closest estate to where last night's charity gala was held.

"Won't you join us for breakfast?" Josh asks, a droplet of sweat working its way down his brow. He's nervous, but he needn't be.

"It's fine, stay as long as you like. I, however, will not be joining you for breakfast. I'm looking for my fiancée."

"Oh, Chelsea is so lovely," Natasha purrs. "You've chosen well because she's a keeper."

I nod in acknowledgement. How I wish that could be true because I want nothing more than to have Chelsea as a permanent fixture in my life.

I study Natasha for a beat. She is naturally pretty in a girl-next-door kind of way. She's a genuinely nice person, and loyal to a fault, which is hard to find in today's world. I can honestly say my cousin is lucky to have her.

Josh leans forward in the seat, inserting himself into the conversation. "Chelsea joined us for breakfast a little while ago, followed shortly by your sister. They started talking about horse riding, and that's when Farrah offered to show her the stables."

"Excellent," I say and reach down, stealing the newly buttered croissant from Josh's hand.

"Hey, that's mine," Josh complains.

The warm pastry crumbles as I take a bite and head out of the door. The sun is out and the sky is clear. It's the perfect day for riding.

I take a slow and leisurely stroll to the stables and notice two of the stable doors are open. It would seem the girls have taken Gypsy and Rebel for a ride. I catch sight of Tim, my stable boy, although I use the word 'boy' very loosely seeing as Tim is in fact in his twenties. He is tall and gangly, with a mop of curly red hair. He is clad in a checked cloth shirt and a tatty pair of jeans. Whistling to himself, he alternates between stables with the mucking-out shovel clasped in his hands.

"Tim." I click my fingers.

He meets my gaze and then, leaning the shovel against the wall, he hurries to meet me. "Yes, sir."

"Why aren't the horses in the paddock?"

"I was just about to let them out when Farrah insisted I show her and Chelsea around and introduce them to the horses. Chelsea was very interested in the animals."

"Tell me, Tim, how long ago did they leave and in which direction?"

Tim nods to his right. I use my hand as a visor and peer out as far as I can see. Two black specks move in the distance, and I know them to be my horses.

"Fetch my helmet and riding gear. I will be taking Whiskey."

Whiskey is my twenty-two-year-old stallion, dapple-grey in colour. He is the most muscular and has the deepest torso build of all of our animals. This, however, is not the reason I have selected Whiskey to ride. He was the first horse my mother bought me.

When Whiskey is tacked up for riding, I slide my foot in the stirrup and pull myself up.

"The horses will be in their paddocks and fully cleaned out by the end of the day."

I nod. "I don't doubt your work ethic for a single second."

Tim's face is bright red and shines as he smiles. This is a

common problem with my grounds workers. They think that because they work outdoors every day they are impervious to the sun's rays, but they are very wrong. I lost Dennis, my most experienced gardener, to skin cancer last year and since then have been most insistent that my grounds workers take regular breaks to top up on their sun cream.

"Take twenty," I tell him. "Go rehydrate, and while you're at it, apply some sun lotion."

Tim salutes me. "Yes, boss."

With the reins secured in my hand I squeeze both legs together and Whiskey begins to walk. From the slow walking pace I build Whiskey up to a trot and finally a canter as I make my way over to where the girls ride.

The fields around me pass by in a green flash as I close the distance between us. I tug the reins and Whiskey slows to a trot, and I gradually direct him to walk alongside Rebel and Gypsy, my black beauties. But what has my attention is not Gypsy but the beauty riding her.

"Are you enjoying the ride?" I ask. Whiskey and Gypsy are now trotting at the same pace.

"Very much so," Chelsea says, her face glowing, and I'm sure she would hide behind her hair if her helmet didn't prevent her from doing so. Riding horseback is the most alive I have seen her, and she certainly looks the part. She is clad in a pair of tight-fitting tweed breeches, a matching hunt coat, white dressage gloves and even the stock tie with its signature pin around her neck.

"I'm going to leave you two lovebirds to it," Farrah announces.

I can't miss the disappointment on Chelsea's face.

"Please, don't go on my behalf," I say with zero enthusiasm.

"No, really, I have somewhere I need to be."

"Excellent." I quickly cough. "I mean what a pity."

I meet my sister's gaze. She seems overly made up given the hour. And by overly made up I mean bright red lipstick and enough foundation on she may have used a trowel.

"Farrah?" I question, but Farrah turns Rebel around and he canters in the opposite direction.

I look at Chelsea, who grins and looks away.

"So where is my sister off to in such a hurry, and may I ask what happened to her face?"

Chelsea sits tall, and I watch how her body moves with Gypsy. The action is very sexual if one were to ask me, and I find my attention drifting to her arse. "She has decided that she wants to become a makeup artist."

A makeup artist. My initial reaction is to laugh. "If that is how she plans to apply makeup she may be better looking for a job at a circus."

Chelsea doesn't laugh and it would seem that my joke has not been well received. "We all have to practise somewhere."

"Forgive me, I am not criticising your line of work. And if Farrah wants to practise makeup on her own face, then who am I to judge? It's just my father would never allow it. He won't allow Farrah to do any form of work." And as awful as my comment is, it is true. My sister was put on this earth to look good, carry the Calloway name and further the bloodline.

"That's so sad," Chelsea says.

"It is," I agree. "My father's heart is in the right place, and in his eyes, he is protecting her."

"Protecting her from what?"

I consider Chelsea's words as I direct Whiskey to slow down to a trot. "There is a small stream ahead. Why don't we let the horses rest and have a drink, and we can find somewhere to sit? We can talk and get to know each other a little better."

What I'm actually asking is to find somewhere to sit so I may get better acquainted with her curves, those luscious lips, and may I dare to imagine that one thing may lead to another?

Chelsea squints in the distance, probably looking for the stream. "Okay, sure, why not."

I smile to myself. *Excellent.*

CHAPTER SEVENTEEN

Lucian

We dismount when the stream is within walking distance and remove our riding helmets. With the reins clasped in our hands we walk the horses along the water's edge. After the animals have had a drink I secure their reins to a nearby tree, and Chelsea and I sit beneath another.

This is my moment to lean in to her and go in for the kill.

"So, about last night," I say. I side-eye Chelsea, but she isn't looking at me. She is picking tiny daisies from the grass. She fidgets with the flowers for a while before I notice her feeding one stem through another.

I shift awkwardly because my cock envisioned a slightly different scenario, but instead I'm given the cold shoulder. A little presumptuous of me to assume we would jump right back into that kiss. I surmise that Chelsea may need a little time to warm up to the idea. With nothing but awkward silence passing between us, I decide to ask the question that's been on the tip of my tongue. "Tell me, is my estate not clean enough for you?"

Chelsea sucks in a breath. "I'm sorry, what?"

"Keep cleaning as you are and I'll have to start paying you a wage."

My words are meant in jest, though Chelsea's expression is one of shame. "You can't stop me from cleaning, Lucian. I can't stop me." She stops making her daisy chain momentarily.

I smile. "Nor would I try to. If you'd like to speak to someone…"

"Not another therapist." Chelsea's words are sharp.

"As you wish. If it's something you need to do, I will not get in your way. I'm here if you want company, though you know as well as I do that my cleaning skills leave a lot to be desired."

With her head bowed she lets out a small laugh.

"When did your OCD start?" I ask, genuinely interested.

Chelsea shrugs. "I guess I've had it from an early age. For years I was able to hide behind the title 'clean freak'—that was, until the fire. As well as cleaning, I became fixated on turning off electrics. That was something I was able to get in control of with the help of my therapist, but not the cleaning. I think that's just a part of who I am."

I lean in a little closer. "Are you a germaphobe? Or is it the need to control that has you cleaning the way you do?"

"Maybe a bit of both," she admits. I nod, wanting to know more, needing to know more, when Chelsea speaks. "What is your father protecting Farrah from?"

My father has never given a direct answer to this, so I can only answer her based on my assumption. "Life, reality, getting hurt."

"But if he protects her from life, she is never going to live. Well, not really."

I shuffle closer to Chelsea and push a lock of hair behind her ear. "Try telling my father that. He is as stubborn as a mule, and once he has made up his mind there is no changing it."

Her body deflates a little. "It's a shame someone can't talk to him."

"Maybe you'll have the opportunity to voice your opinion on Wednesday when he comes for dinner."

Chelsea's eyebrows shoot up. "I was referring to you or one of your brothers. I can't, I mean I won't say anything, it's none of my business."

I lean in for a second time, sweeping her hair away from her face. Her gaze leaves the daisies momentarily and she frowns. "What are you doing?"

"You always let your hair hang loose around your face. Your hair is beautiful, but you should wear it back more often."

"Oh, yeah?" She shakes her head in defiance, causing her hair to fall messily in front of her eyes.

I capture her chin and turn her face. "I see you, Chelsea. See the way you use your hair to hide behind. But you should never hide because you truly are exquisite."

Chelsea sucks in her lips, but I can see she's attempting to stop herself from smiling. She shakes her head again, snapping us out of the moment. "Tell me, Lucian, what's the deal with Josh?"

I raise a brow. "The deal with him?"

"Yes. He did all the talking over breakfast and was telling his girlfriend all about me, like we were old friends who go way back."

I cringe inwardly. I may have been a little too open when sharing information about Chelsea with my cousin over the years.

"That doesn't bother me," she continues. "But you want me to play the part of your fake fiancée, but failed to mention that you told Josh the truth. Can you even trust him?"

"I can trust Josh," I say with one hundred percent certainty.

"Really? Well, either way I'd like to know more about your cousin, seeing as he knows everything there is to know about me."

I consider her words and don't know what she wants me to say. "There really isn't much to tell."

Chelsea folds her arms, and I suspect she isn't going to let this go. I let out a sigh. "My uncle married Josh's mother when Josh was two. My aunt and uncle went on to have three boys of their own."

Facts about my family are on a need-to-know basis, and the

fact is that there are things that Chelsea doesn't need to know. Like that at the age of three Josh's surname was changed to Calloway, or that Josh changed it back to his mother's maiden name at eighteen when his stepfather died and excluded him from his will. Josh has had to start from the bottom and work his way up, though thanks to me he has never gone without. Things will vastly improve for him when I acquire Calloway Housebuilders.

"Is he close to his brothers?"

I consider Chelsea's question before answering. "I wouldn't say they aren't close, just that they're at different stages of their lives at the moment."

As in, his brothers are living the high life, while Josh works a low-paid office job and relies heavily on handouts from me. I let him stay in my estates whenever he pleases.

"I guess that is enough information for now." Chelsea is silent for a beat as she continues to pick daisies. "So, what's the story with Jupiter?"

"The planet or the horse?" I ask, knowing I'm being obtuse but buying myself time to think.

Chelsea rolls her eyes. "The horse."

"What about her?" Jupiter belonged to my mother. She is unbroken, unruly and unridable. The less Chelsea knows about her the better, because knowledge brings with it curiosity, and if I'm not mistaken, it was curiosity that killed the cat.

"Tim said I wasn't allowed to ride her. When I asked why he said I should ask you, so I am."

I sit tall, brushing strands of grass from my brown breeches. "You can't ride her because she's dangerous."

Chelsea lets out a laugh, and I get the feeling she thinks she can prove me wrong. "I don't believe that for one second. Any horse can be broken in, they just need time and perseverance."

"And with any other animal I would agree with you. But not Jupiter."

Her expression remains unchanged, like my words have

floated over her head. "My mother was a professional jockey," Chelsea begins, "and as a child I would ride all the time. Mum taught me everything there is to know about horses, from grooming to breaking them in, and I know that if…"

I raise my hand. "No." And by 'no' I consider the subject closed.

"No? Just no? That's all I'm going to get?"

"I'm afraid so."

Chelsea stands, a small chain of daisies dangling from between her fingers. "Giving up on people or animals is the easy option. You surprise me, Lucian. I thought you had more about you."

She has a look of determination and defiance in her eyes that terrifies me, because it's a look I know too well. Chelsea turns her back on me and heads toward Gypsy. I jump up to my feet, capture her hand and spin her around to face me.

"Three days," I grit out. I'm angry because I'm terrified, terrified that she will do something stupid like attempt to ride that damn horse.

Chelsea's eyes are as wide as saucers as she takes me in. "Three days?" she repeats.

"I was in a coma for three days after the injuries I sustained from riding Jupiter. My head injuries were so bad that the doctors told my father to prepare for the worst. But the stubborn sod I was, I refused to die and against the odds I survived."

Chelsea laces her fingers with mine. I lift our joined fingers to my mouth and kiss the back of her hand.

"But it's not like I woke up and jumped straight back into my old life. I had to learn how to do everything again—walk, talk and even feed myself. And do you know who was there with me every step of the way?"

Chelsea shakes her head.

"Josh. He sat by my bedside day and night until I woke up from my coma. I know he is a bit of a pillock, and at times he drives me insane. We aren't related by blood, but I consider him more of a brother than Malachi and Gage. So, coming back to your previous question about whether I trust Josh or not, the answer is yes. With my life."

Chelsea stills and finally I think I'm getting through to her. "Don't give up on Jupiter," she says softly, a sentiment I know my mother would share. I should have agreed to let my father euthanise Jupiter after the accident, but something, something always told me she was worth saving and worth fighting for. Maybe it's this moment.

"Six months," I say under duress.

Chelsea's lip quivers. "What?"

"Jupiter is a wild horse, Chelsea. If you're serious about breaking her in, then my terms are that you spend every day with her over the next six months. Six months of handling her, six months of getting her used to having a bridle on her face, a bit in her mouth and a saddle on her back. But no one is to ride her until she is ready and the six-month time period has elapsed. And the person who will be sitting in the saddle will be me. Together we will teach her to obey simple commands."

I must be a glutton for punishment but the saying 'get right back up on the horse' springs to mind.

"Six months is a little excessive just to saddle-break her, don't you think?" A frown washes over Chelsea's face as realisation hits her. "Six months? I won't be here then."

I shrug. "Then I guess Jupiter will remain as she is."

"You'll have to do better than that if you're trying to coax me into staying."

"Oh, I'm sure I can—" I stop talking when Chelsea leans forward and places the daisy chain she made on my head. Such an innocent gesture.

I laugh and raise my hand to remove it. "Thanks, but this isn't a good look for me."

She captures my hand in hers. "No, leave it." My focus shifts from the ridiculous flowers that dangle over my brow to Chelsea.

Her face is alight with a smile as she looks at my daisy crown. "It looks good."

We lean in to each other like the attracting ends of two magnets. Our gazes are fixed, her breaths silent, though her lips are puckered. I place my hand around the small of her back and pull her into me. Her chest is pinned to mine, our breaths gliding into one another's.

"I'm going to kiss you now," I say, closing any remaining distance between us, but instead of a kiss what I get is whipped in the face by long strands of her hair that are picked up by the breeze.

"This is one of the reasons you should tie your hair up." I laugh and take a step back. I release the small of her back, and just like that the moment is gone. I take the daisy chain from my head, and for some bizarre reason I stuff it into my pocket.

Chelsea doesn't move from the spot, and, taking a hair tie she has around her wrist, she reaches up and secures her long tresses into a high ponytail. "Better?" she asks and, looking down, shifts awkwardly from foot to foot.

"Much better," I say, and place my hand around the back of her head. Her ponytail fits snugly between my fingers as I pull her into me. Our lips crash together. I'm walking forward, causing her to walk back until her back collides with a nearby tree trunk. My erection presses into her, leaving her in no doubt how much she is affecting me.

Her eyes are hooded and her lips red and swollen.

"You want me." My words are not a question, but a statement.

CHAPTER EIGHTEEN

Chelsea

I gaze into Lucian's piercing green eyes. The way he looks at me takes my breath away.

I swallow the lump in my throat. I'm afraid he's going to try to fix me. Put together all my broken pieces. The problem is he's placed me on a pedestal and that means I have a long way to fall. As cowardly as it sounds, I don't want to fall and break all over again.

I reach for Lucian's hand, but I have no idea what exactly I want other than more of him and more of this. It's been months—no, years since I've been this close to a man and felt a man's desire. Everything inside me is charged and every nerve ending heightened.

"You're mine." He is standing so close to me that his words escape into my mouth, and it's as though I absorb every syllable.

The leaves above rustle and sway in the soft breeze, causing shards of light to shine down around us like tiny laser beams. Pretty pink petals from the tree's blossoms float down around us. Everything is perfect. Everything.

"You were mine from the moment I first laid eyes on you," he says and, fisting my ponytail between his fingers, pulls me into him for a kiss. In my mind I'm telling him I don't belong to anyone. But in reality, I say nothing. I leave all of my inhibitions behind and kiss him back with matching synchronicity.

Our bodies are so close, and it's as though on instinct that he grinds against me. I meet his pressure with my own unspoken desire and push my hips forward, chasing his touch.

"You're playing with fire," he scolds.

"I'm not afraid of getting burnt." My words are a lie. I'm terrified, and yet I can't help but goad him.

This thing I have with Lucian isn't real, I repeat in my mind. But then why is my heart hammering in my chest? Why are butterflies racing around in my stomach? Why do I feel this way if Lucian means nothing? But who am I trying to convince? Lucian does mean something, he means a lot, and giving someone that much power, that much control scares the hell out of me.

Lucian's kisses linger on my lips as I wake up the following morning. I've been kissed in the past, but never like that. Never has a man held me with such want, such desire and such need. It felt as though sparks of electricity travelled the length of my body from my head and all the way to my toes. My core awoke and tingled in a way I never thought was possible.

Unfortunately, I haven't spent any more time with Lucian since yesterday afternoon. Upon returning to the house, he was called away on an urgent business matter. I didn't see him again until late last night when I was going to sleep. He informed me that he would be up early because he and Farrah have a family matter to take care of. He didn't tell me what time he would be back, and I didn't ask. Instead, he lay behind me and wrapped me up in his arms.

Now, half asleep, I roll over, remove the flattened-down

bolster from the middle of the mattress and reach over to Lucian's side of the bed. The space is empty, and the sheets are cold.

I can't help the pang of disappointment that courses through me. Yawning, I slide out of bed and pad across the carpet to the en suite. I brush my teeth and jump in the shower. Dressed in a towelling robe, I re-enter the bedroom.

I step into the walk-in wardrobe. My eyes widen as I glance over all the clothes Lucian has hanging up for me. On first inspection I would think these are average shop-bought dresses. They don't scream expense, and certainly don't look as though they each cost a small fortune. Though upon flicking the labels, I can see they all come with names—Louis Vuitton, Gucci and an Italian name I can't begin to pronounce.

My gaze travels to the opposite side of the wardrobe where Lucian's clothes are stored. I look up and down the long lines of shirts, trousers, cupboards, and drawers of varying sizes. I know I shouldn't touch, but I can't help but take a look. Ties of all colours are folded neatly in long thin drawers. Gold and diamond-encrusted cufflinks are displayed in a flat glass cabinet with a lift-up lid. All the drawers are open, with the exception of one that is locked. I trace my index finger around the keyhole. Curiosity has me tugging on the small brass handle one final time before giving up.

My gaze skims his suit jackets and I walk slowly along the rail, running my fingers over the rough fabric. One of the jackets falls from the hanger and slithers to the floor, where it lies partially held up between clothes either side. I crouch down and lift the garment by the shoulder cap. I'm about to place it back on the hanger, but instead lift the cool fabric up to my nose. I close my eyes and take a long and deep inhale. With my eyes closed I wrap the thick sleeves around my waist and hold it close to me as though I were holding Lucian.

Lucian, the man I once called the Devil. Lucian, the man I think I'm slowly starting to like, and possibly more than like.

I release the jacket, the arms falling back into place as I place it on the hanger and back on the rail. I slip on a pair of navy jeans and grey T-shirt and leave the bedroom. With Lucian and Farrah out all day I can't help but wonder what I'm going to do with myself in this huge house.

After cleaning the kitchen for an hour, the need to keep cleaning is replaced by something else, or rather someone else. I spend the morning with Jupiter in the paddock. Jupiter is a beautiful horse, and the most unusual orangey-yellow colour I have ever seen. But as beautiful as she is, Jupiter is wild. She bolts whenever I get close, and so instead of overwhelming her I spend much of the morning walking around her enclosure. My hope is that she'll begin to feel more at ease in my presence.

It's a beautiful day, the sky is blue, and the sun is shining. I look back to the house, and that's when I notice Josh making his way toward the paddock and Jupiter's enclosure. Smiling, I lean against the fence post and with my arms behind me I weave them between the slats.

"Morning," Josh calls with a wave of his hand.

I nod as he leans against the fence directly behind me.

"Looks like you've tasked yourself with the impossible job of training Jupiter. But may I say, you aren't well equipped for riding." Josh's gaze travels over the thin material of my T-shirt and then my jeans. I'm not embarrassed to admit they are on the tighter side, which would make riding somewhat uncomfortable.

I remove my arms from the fence and dust my jeans down. "Lucian said I'm not allowed to ride her. He wants me to saddle-break her first."

"Ah, I see. Though I would advise you to quit whilst you are ahead. Jupiter is unridable."

"Lucian told me all about the accident and the three days he spent in a coma."

Josh grimaces and closes his eyes, as though looking at the

horse is bringing the painful memory back. "Those were the worst three days of my life."

I feel as though I should do something, like place a reassuring hand on his shoulder, or offer words of comfort. Yet there is an invisible shield preventing me from displaying any genuine emotion. After all, how can I act genuine while wearing Lucian's *fake* ring?

Josh opens his eyes, a pained expression on his face. He clears his throat before reaching into his jacket pocket. "Here." He retrieves a small box wrapped in blue paper. "Would you be able to give this to Lucian for me? I'm taking Natasha home, and then I have to travel to Cornwall to oversee the progress being made on the estate agency. Therefore I won't be able to wish him happy returns in person."

Josh holds out the box, and I take it from him. "Today is Lucian's birthday?" I'm not sure if I'm asking or stating the fact. Either way, I had no idea.

"Not just any birthday. Today Lucian is thirty." Josh emphasises the word 'thirty'. "Don't worry, Chelsea, I didn't think you'd be privy to the fact. It's not like you're really engaged. You're only with my cousin because he's paying you."

Josh's words hurt, but he isn't being cruel, no, he's being honest. I feel the need to tell him that things between me and Lucian have changed.

"It isn't like that, not any more." I scuff the toe of my trainer into the dirt. "The thing is," I begin, but stop when Josh raises his hand.

"Please don't feel as though you need to explain. All you need to know is that today is hard for Lucian. Please be there for him."

I have no idea what to say, so keep my gaze trained on Jupiter, who is standing at the other side of the enclosure.

Why is today hard for Lucian? And why didn't he tell me it was his birthday?

After dinner, and a glass of wine, I head into the lounge and wait for Lucian to return. I hold a bottle of rosé by the neck and it swings to and fro as I pad across the room. I sink down into a plush leather sofa, grab the remote for the TV and turn on a murder documentary to watch while I am waiting.

One episode turns into two and two into four. I sporadically refill my glass and watch as one by one daylight shadows are taken captive by night. It becomes harder to stay awake and, leaning my head back, I close my eyes and welcome sleep's silent embrace.

I jump on hearing a loud bang. I'm lying down with my head on the arm rest of the sofa. It takes me several seconds to get my bearings before I shuffle to an upright sitting position. The television screen is black and is on standby. The crystal clock on the hearth tells me It's two a.m.

I get to my feet and head into the hallway to check out where the noise came from. On my way I catch sight of Lucian as he makes his way up the stairs.

"Lucian," I call. He must not have heard me as he continues to scale the stairs.

"Lucian," I call again, and this time he turns. His face is pale, so pale that I wonder if he's ill. His hair falls unkempt around his face and his eyes are bloodshot. "My God, Lucian, are you okay?"

I reach for his arm, but he retreats. "I'm fine, Chelsea. I just need a good night's sleep."

I can't miss the subtle scent of alcohol and tobacco that clings to him. "You're drunk."

"No," is Lucian's one-word reply.

"It wasn't a question." I really look at him. His movements aren't unsteady, nor is he drunkenly swaying. He isn't drunk, he's upset. But it's more than that, he's hurting. Lucian is too proud to admit something is wrong, so I don't probe. "Come on, I'll help you into bed."

Lucian drapes an arm around my shoulder, and I can't help noticing how much heavier the weight of his arm becomes with each step we take. It's like each step brings with it more hurt, more pain, and it's killing me inside because I don't know how to make his pain go away.

He releases me upon reaching our room, and without a word makes his way toward the bed. He yanks at his tie, causing it to hang loosely around his neck, before he falls back onto the mattress.

I rock on my heels, once, twice before turning on a bedside lamp and joining him. I open the nightstand drawer and retrieve the gift Josh gave me earlier and hand it to Lucian.

"From Josh," I mutter, and watch as Lucian rotates the small palm-sized box around several times, not once attempting to tear open the paper.

I turn on my side and am met by Lucian's profile in the darkened room. "Why didn't you tell me it was your birthday?"

No answer. With the gift clasped between his fingers, Lucian reaches across and places it on the nightstand.

"Where were you today?" I ask, my voice as low as the ticking clock.

Lucian turns so he too is lying on his side and is facing me. "What caused you to have OCD?"

I open my mouth, but where do I start? Because it isn't as simple as a cleaning addiction. No, it's entirely about regaining control. I purse my lips together but they begin to part. If I want Lucian to confide in me, then I will have to first confide in him.

I take a deep breath and prepare to do something I have never done before, and that is to open up.

"My parents," I begin and pause to clear my throat. "My parents always argued. I believe it stemmed from my mum wanting to come to England to pursue her horse-riding career, whereas my father didn't want to leave Holland, but he came to England because it was what my mum wanted, and he resented her for it."

The memory hits me hard, and I can feel my breaths quicken. I remember as a child how my parents would argue. While my siblings slept, I would sit at the top of the stairs and listen. The spiral curve of the banister spokes spring to mind, how vividly their outline imprinted on my palms due to how tightly I gripped them. With my face wedged between the narrow gaps I'd sit amongst the shadows and listen. I recall the salty taste of tears as they rolled one by one down my cheeks. Some would seep into my mouth, whilst others would roll past my chin and rain down into the empty hallway. The hallway was always dark, with only faint light like a silhouette surrounding the lounge door. It didn't matter that the door was closed, or that their arguments began as hushed whispers, because the volume always got cranked up and I could hear every word they were saying.

"My father would get drunk, my parents would argue and he would pack his things and leave. He would be gone for a few days, a week, sometimes longer. My mother would tell us he was away for work, but I knew the truth. As a child it was so unsettling not knowing if or when my father would be coming home. He often said he was stressed, so I always did what I could to make his life less stressful, by eating all of my vegetables, doing all of my homework and behaving. I was the perfect little girl, but it made no difference."

One argument in particular springs to my mind. "I overheard my father say he was leaving because the house, like his life, was a complete mess. That was it, the solution to all of our problems. If I could keep the house clean my father would stay. I spent hours polishing, hours cleaning, hours making sure the house was spotless." I smile poignantly because it very quickly became less about cleaning and more about regaining control of the situation. A situation that I would never get control of.

"And did that work?" Lucian asks.

"Hm?" I say, lost in my thoughts.

"You cleaning the house, did it work?" He sounds almost hopeful, but I suspect he already knows the answer.

I shrug. "No. Each time my father left I blamed myself for not doing a good enough job and not giving him reason enough to stay. And the sad part is that each time he walked out of that door he took a small part of me with him. A part I can never get back."

It never fails to amaze me that my parents have stayed together. They still argue, Dad still leaves and eventually returns with his tail between his legs. The only difference is that the landing and banister lie empty, and I'm no longer the little girl sat at the top of the stairs.

"I want better for myself," I admit. "I think it's one of the reasons I've been scared to commit to another person."

Lucian watches me. "If you let me in, Chelsea, I promise that I will never hurt you."

"Don't make promises you have no way of knowing you'll be able to keep."

"At least let me try."

Let him in? The concept is foreign to me. Foreign, terrifying, and would mean me giving up any last semblance of control. "You don't know what you're asking of me."

"Perhaps I do, perhaps I don't. I would very much like the opportunity to show you what love could look like. If you will let me."

CHAPTER NINETEEN

Chelsea

Somewhere deep down I want to believe Lucian and I could be more. But how can a relationship, an engagement built on a foundation of lies develop into something real?

Lucian's breath warms the side of my face as he leans in for a kiss. But I place my palm against his chest. "Why didn't you tell me today is your birthday?"

"It's two o'clock in the morning. My birthday was yesterday if you want to be pedantic."

I pin him with a pointed stare. "Not funny."

Lucian shrugs. "I'm not laughing." When I say nothing, Lucian continues. "I'm just not big on celebrations."

Ignoring my palm, which is still flat against his chest, he leans in for a second time. His lips press against mine, and he waits patiently. When I don't pucker my lips in response he opens his eyes and our gazes meet.

Waves of pain travel the length of my body as I stare deep into his emerald greens. But those emerald greens are gone in a flash as he looks away, seemingly unable to hold eye contact. I know what it's like to shut people out, because I've done it for most of my life. Like the tip of an iceberg, there is only so much the outside world can see, but there is so much more hidden beneath the surface. I want him to allow me to get close enough that I can dunk my head underwater and see what no one else can. But the tide between us has turned and, as opposed to him letting me get closer, I can feel him pushing me away.

Apart from my therapist, Lucian is the only person I've opened up to about my past. That means something, and it hurts deep inside that he doesn't feel able to confide in me. "What aren't you telling me?"

"Nothing." His response is immediate.

"That's precisely my point, you're telling me nothing," I fire back.

Lucian sighs and his expression changes. The mattress dips as he shuffles away and sits on the edge of the bed.

"I just want to know—" I begin but stop talking when Lucian flings out his arms.

"Want to know what?" Lucian's voice rises an octave, and I can hear the annoyance in his tone. "That my mother had cancer, and that she died on my fifteenth birthday? Is that what you want to know?"

Oh, my God. What the hell do I say? Why did I keep pushing him? Birthdays are inherently days filled with celebration, but instead for Lucian they are filled with sorrow. I scrape my fingers through my hair. Each word he said replays over in my mind, like tiny blades digging deeper and deeper into my subconscious.

"I'm so sorry," I choke out, my throat burning.

Lucian shakes his head. "I don't want you to be sorry. I don't need your pity."

He may not want my pity, but he needs me in this moment, more than he realises. I shuffle forward and reach out to comfort him when he jerks away. "Please, don't touch me."

His rejection hurts, it hurts like a sucker punch to the stomach. In this moment his pain becomes my pain. A solitary tear spills from the corner of my eye and makes its slow journey down my cheek.

Lucian doesn't so much as look my way. His chin is resting on his hands, which he has clenched into tight fists. His body is so rigid. His jaw is tense, causing the muscle to tick. He looks so tightly wound that one wrong move would cause him to snap.

Physically Lucian and I are so close, yet mentally we couldn't be further apart. Emotions like bullets shoot at me from every direction, and I can't bear the pain of the onslaught.

"Lucian," I whisper. "I know what it's like to keep all your feelings bottled up. I know what it's like to shut people out. It's a lonely place to be. But you don't need to do that any more. I'm here and you can—"

"I can what?" Lucian laughs, but it isn't with humour. "Share with you my innermost thoughts, and we deal with everything I've bottled up together?"

I suck in my lips. He has taken the words out of my mouth, but they don't have the same sentiment coming from him.

Lucian shakes his head. "You won't force emotion from me. I'm a Calloway, it simply is not and was not allowed."

Allowed?

"From Mother's prognosis we were given strict instructions from our father that she was not to see us cry. Not a single tear."

"Oh, Lucian." I lower my arm onto the mattress, inches from him. I don't make any further attempts to touch him. He knows where I am, where my hand is if he wants comfort. If he wants me, I am here.

Silence.

Nothing but the sound of a whistling breeze forcing its way through a partially open window. Lucian remains perched on the edge of the bed. He stares at the walls, perhaps replaying childhood memories in his mind, or perhaps thinking of nothing at all.

The lamplight flickers sporadically, and it seems to snap Lucian out of his trance. Slowly, he turns his attention to me.

"So now you know everything there is to know about me, am I right in saying there is nothing else that needs to be said?"

There is so much more that needs saying, but instead of giving my thoughts volume I simply shake my head.

"Good." Lucian leans toward the nightstand and switches the lamp off. Now that we're shrouded in darkness, my eyes become tired. My outstretched arm is feeling numb and heavy. A pins-and-needles sensation prickles at my fingers. I reclaim my arm and hug it into my chest because, for the first time since I've known Lucian, he doesn't want me. He wants—no, he *needs* space, and if it's space he needs, it's space I will give him.

It's too painful to look at him any longer, so I plump my pillow and turn in the opposite direction. I close my eyes, squeezing my lids tightly together in the hopes of drying up my stupid tears. But they're relentless and fall like miniature streams down my cheeks. Silently I'm breaking, and there isn't a single thing I can do to make the hurt or the pain go away.

Seconds pass, minutes, maybe an hour, I have no idea. I think I'm all cried out, and there isn't a single tear or emotion left inside me. I feel so empty and so numb. I want sleep to take me away, to somewhere happy and less complicated.

More time passes, and I can feel myself slowly starting to drift off when an arm wraps around my waist.

Finally, he needs me. Being lost in your own grief is a lonely place to be. You can only stay in the darkness for so long until you search for light. I wonder if I am the light Lucian came in search of, the light he needs to slowly heal, because I am convinced that Lucian hasn't dealt with the death of his mother. But I will be here for him, I will help him heal.

"Lucian," I whisper.

His touch, I need his touch, and I need the closeness with him. I can't feel his body, so shuffle back. My back meets his warm chest, and the backs of my legs brush against his bare thighs. Lucian is undressed and is quite possibly naked. Instead of feeling nervous, and instead of pulling away, I lean my ass back. Sure enough, he is wearing boxers. The hard bulge digging into me leaves me in no doubt as to his intentions.

"I'm sorry," he whispers, and tightens his hold on me.

"You've got nothing to be sorry for," I say, and, linking my fingers with his, I lower our joined hands between us, down past my bellybutton, and stop directly over my sex.

His lips find my earlobe, and I melt into him as he kisses me, long and sensually.

"Lucian,"

Releasing me, he pushes his fingers beneath the armhole of my dress. Without a word he takes my left breast in his hand. His hips roll forward as he fondles me. Feeling a tingly sensation below, I begin to roll my ass back and grind into him.

Lucian's hand leaves my breast and is inching below the hem of my dress. "Tell me to stop, and I'll stop," he whispers.

"Don't stop," I groan, and part my thighs.

But Lucian's touch is gone. I'm about to glance over my shoulder when he flips me over onto my back.

Heart racing, I watch as his head disappears beneath the bedding.

"What are you doing?" I ask, lifting the quilt up to see. His head travels down the length of my body and stops directly between my legs. Without a word he prises my thighs apart.

His fingers move my panties to the side, and I let him. I arch my back when his finger rubs over my clit, and I cry out when his tongue takes over.

"Oh, my God." My body jerks as his tongue circles my clit. My legs stiffen and I immediately tense. I've never been kissed down there before, so intimately, so… so… God, this feels good, better than good. As much as I can feel my cheeks heat with embarrassment, they heat with something else. Desire, lust, and pure need. I relax my head back into the pillow and buck my hips. I weave my fingers through his hair and can't help but pull his face closer.

"Lucian," I say and squirm as the pressure he applies intensifies. The strokes of his tongue are unrelenting. He fucks me with his finger and pleasures me with his tongue. I'm hit by an intoxicating cocktail of pleasure that I cannot get enough of.

My stomach clenches, my legs tremble. Lucian doesn't stop when I reach my climax, and instead he increases his pace and exerts more pressure. Together we ride my waves of pleasure. I feel hot and tingly all over. But Lucian continues to work my clit. God, this is too much. I squirm and, fisting his hair between my fingers, I give it a gentle tug.

His tongue laps my clit one final time before he peers up. "Do you want this?"

I know what he's asking, and my answer is a no-brainer. "Yes."

Lucian kisses his way up my body. He bunches the skirt of my dress between his fingers and pulls it up with him. He kisses his way up my stomach and up the valley of my breasts. Of course he stops at each nipple and sucks it into his mouth before finally his lips are on mine and he kisses me hard. He kisses me like this is our first kiss, he kisses me like this is our last. We kiss one another with everything we are.

"We don't have to do this," he says. "If you're not ready we can just—"

The pillow rustles beneath me as I shake my head. "I. Want. This," I say, slow and controlled.

Lucian's lips meet mine, and he smiles into the kiss. "You don't know how long I've waited for this."

He slides off me and off the bed. I lean back on my elbows and watch as he takes a condom from the nightstand drawer. He removes his boxers and sheathes his cock. I'm met by a rush of excitement and a rush of nerves as he braces himself over me. With his knee between my legs, he prises my thighs open one final time before lowering himself down.

"It will hurt at first," he says, positioning the head of his cock over my entrance. "But it will start to feel good, I promise." Slowly, he begins to slide into me. My thighs tense at the burning sensation. Each inch deeper feels like fire.

I turn my head to the side, close my eyes and fist the bedsheets between my fingers. I want this, I want him, I just have to get through this burning sensation before I can enjoy this.

He's going slow, so slow that it's making the pain last forever. Without thinking, I loop my leg around his ass and pull him into me. My body jerks and the burn is immediate as I take every inch of him.

"Are you okay?" Lucian asks, his body still.

I nod, realising that I am no longer a virgin. "Yes."

Lucian kisses me on the forehead before lifting up. He thrusts in and out of me. Having him inside me is excruciating, but very soon the sensation morphs into pleasure and it feels good.

I remove my fingers from the vice grip I had on the bedsheet and wrap my arms around Lucian's back. I hold him as he makes love to me. Our lips connect, our gazes burn into each other, and we are as close as two people can be. Emotionally and physically, we are one.

In and out he thrusts. Deeper and faster. His kisses turn from sensual to demanding. Each thrust brings him closer to the edge, until finally he climaxes and he stills. Inside me, he rolls us over so I am lying on top of him. He wraps me up in his arms, and as crazy as it sounds, I feel safe in his embrace.

"I love you, Chelsea," he says, and kisses me on the head.

"I, I…" My words trail off. *I love you, Lucian* is what I want to say. The syllables are literally on the tip of my tongue, but try as I might, I can't gather the courage to join them together to give those three little words volume.

Lucian takes a deep breath. "I hope that one day you can love me, and one day you can wear my grandmother's engagement ring for real."

"Your grandmother's ring?" I question, having had no idea.

"That's right, she was a very special woman, and I'd only give her ring to someone I'm serious about. Our engagement may have started off as fake but be under no illusion, I have no intention of it remaining that way. I'm done with pretending. Chelsea Janssen, I want you to be my wife."

CHAPTER TWENTY

Lucian

I wake up at six a.m. with Chelsea wrapped up in my arms. As much as I want to stay, there is somewhere I need to be, and that somewhere is the Calloway London offices for an important annual meeting.

It doesn't matter that I'm the first to arrive at the offices because arriving early is a Calloway brother tradition. A tradition I plan to keep, if only for one final time.

I spend the best part of an hour on the building's rooftop lounging on an al fresco-style bench. I remember all the times my brothers and I would come up here before and after a long day's work in the office. We were kings of our castle, masters of our empire and the streets of London our playground. But everything changed when Malachi announced he was moving to Scotland. Malachi was our foundation and without him the cracks in our relationship began to appear. Our bond crumbled and the three of us drifted apart. To this day Gage sporadically works in the offices, Malachi commutes a couple of times a month and, as for me, my time is much better utilised in my home office.

By eight a.m. the city comes alive with the sound of

pedestrians, honking horns and engine noise. The door to my right opens. Malachi steps out onto the rooftop to join me.

I nod my head in acknowledgement and gesture toward the table where I have laid three unlit cigars. Malachi leans down, takes a cigar and sits beside me.

He really looks the part today. His black hair is sleeked back with not so much as a single strand out of place. He is wearing a grey Armani suit with a matching silk tie. His outfit is completed with golden ribbon cufflinks. Why would he look anything less than perfect? Today is the day all the company executives get together and discuss the previous year's profits and forecasts for the following year. It's a morning of number-crunching, followed by an afternoon spent with our marketing team.

I should be excited to see the figures, but I'm not. Talking to Chelsea about my mother struck a chord with me, because after she passed we weren't allowed to talk about her. My father told us we needed to rally together and keep our business heads on. Scheduling our companies' annual financial meeting the day after she passed away was my father's way of achieving just that. Contrary to popular belief, Duncan Calloway isn't cold, nor is he uncaring, he's just a man buried deep in his own grief and denial.

Lost in our thoughts, Malachi and I sit and wait. With nothing else to do other than twiddle my thumbs, I retrieve my grandfather's golden pocket watch and watch the minutes silently tick away.

"Do you still have it set ten minutes early?" my brother wonders aloud.

I nod. "Of course. It's tradition."

Malachi smiles and claps me on the back. "Grandfather would have been proud of the man you have become."

"Thanks, Mal." Malachi and I have our differences more often than not, but he is a good guy.

The door swings open for a second time, and we're joined by Gage. His hair is dishevelled, his suit is creased, and there is a suspicious stain on the collar of his shirt. As blasé as my brother is, he is never this brazen. But here he is, walking around in public in what looks to be yesterday's suit with a lipstick stain smudged on his collar.

"Rough night?" Malachi asks.

"Not at all," Gage replies, making his way toward us.

"Jesus, Gage, you look awful," I say, noticing how flushed his cheeks are and how wide his pupils appear. "Have you been doing drugs?"

It's a good job that no one from the press has dared write a story about us since my little altercation with Darren Moore and *Cornwall Gossip* magazine. But it's only a matter of time before someone from the press is feeling brave and one of us appears on the front spread of a newspaper. I just hope the story they print isn't too damaging to our name.

"It is not a crime to indulge in a little debauchery," Gage protests.

I meet Malachi's stare. "He cannot go into the meeting in this state."

"It doesn't matter," Gage interrupts. "Because I'm not going to be joining you."

Frowning, I lean forward. "What do you mean, you're not going to be joining us?"

Gage sits between us and takes the cigar. "Call it what you will, a change of heart or a conflict of interests. Either way, I no longer have any desire to pursue Calloway Housebuilders. Yesterday evening I had a lengthy conversation with our father where I withdrew my stake in the company." Gage claps Malachi and I on the back. "It's a two-horse race. I wish you both the best of luck."

Malachi and I say nothing. We're both waiting for the punchline, because this has to be a joke. Gage has wanted nothing more than to work for Calloway Housebuilders since he left university. Why would he just give up without a fight?

"Gage?"

Gage shakes his head. "It isn't up for discussion. I just want to smoke this damn cigar for old times' sake, and when I'm done, I'm going home to get shitfaced."

I shrug at Malachi, who in turn nods. I reach in my pocket for my nineteen-twenties vintage lighter and light all three cigars. We inhale at the same time and blow out rings of smoke into the morning air. The rings link together, and I can't help likening them to the Calloway crested gold bands my brothers wear, a band I myself should have and be wearing. The smoke circles unite and are as one for the briefest of seconds, before the link is broken and the smoke fades into nothing. I hope that isn't a representation of things to come, that by going our own separate ways in business that our brotherly bond doesn't begin to disappear.

Today is the last day all three of us will sit together on the rooftop. The next time this meeting takes place only one of us will be sitting on this bench and there will be only one cigar. Call me sentimental, but today marks the ending of an era.

"Welcome to team thirty," Gage says, and side-eyes me.

I nod once, but don't acknowledge the fact.

"Yes, about that." Malachi reaches into the inside breast pocket of his jacket and retrieves a crisp white envelope. "Seeing as you will not accept gifts, Gage and I have booked a skiing weekend away to Switzerland."

Smoke catches in the back of my throat and I cough. "As in for the three of us?"

"No, as in you and the bloody Tooth Fairy. Of course the three of us."

I could swear by the way his eyes crease at the corners that Malachi is smiling, but I can't see his mouth due to the position of his hand, which is strategically placed.

Skiing in Switzerland with my brothers just like old times. It has been years since we have been away as a trio. "When is this trip taking place?"

"We leave on Saturday after the contracts have been signed and we know which one of us will be running Calloway Housebuilders. Whatever happens with the business, we are still brothers."

That weekend just so happens to be when my fake engagement with Chelsea will come to an end, and the weekend of her best friend's wedding. Is it presumptuous of me to hope to be her plus one? I rub my hands over my beard. "I think Chelsea and I have plans."

What I should say is that I *hope* we have plans. My hope is that we are still together. I made it abundantly clear that I'm sick of pretending. I want her to be mine. I'm not sure if I've intrigued her or scared her off because after my proposal, she did not say a word. But silence is better than a flat-out no. She knows my intentions; she just needs time to decide what she wants to do with them.

"Nonsense," Malachi says, waving me off. "We're going. She is welcome to join us."

Chelsea on the slopes, now that's something I want to see. I laugh, picturing Chelsea as more of a sun-worshipper. "I'll make sure to mention it to her."

"Yes, make sure that you do." Malachi stubs his cigar out on the side of the bench and stands. "Right, Lucian, it's time. Come, Gage, I will see you out."

Malachi heads toward the door to re-enter the building with Gage close on his heels.

"Go ahead," I call to my brothers and, when the door closes behind them, I pull out my phone. I flick through my list of contacts and stop on Farrah's name.

Me: I want you to take Chelsea out today. Go shopping, to the spa, anywhere. But don't bring her home until after seven p.m. Please inform the staff that they are all

relieved of their duties from five p.m. I do not want a soul setting foot in the main house.

I hit send and, getting to my feet, I head toward the door. The sooner we get this meeting out of the way, the better.

The meeting runs over and we leave the presentation room at five-thirty. Malachi and I shake each executive's hand on their way out of the door.

"Why do you keep looking at the time?" Malachi asks.

"I'm not," I say, discreetly pushing my pocket watch back into my pocket.

Malachi frowns, shakes Roger's hand, and returns his attention to me. "If you have somewhere you need to be…"

"I don't," I say to Malachi, and when Roger stands in front of me, I take his hand. Although he's frail, his grip is firm as we shake. "On behalf of Calloway Housebuilders, I cannot thank you enough for your hard work."

Roger Silverstone is our marketing team leader. He has been with our company for over thirty years. Thanks to his diligence and dedication we have seen profits soar. It's unfortunate that Roger is retiring in a few short weeks. There is so much more I feel I need to say to the old boy, but words are simply not enough. My brothers and I have however arranged a retirement party for him, which is our way of showing our appreciation.

Roger leaves through the door, and with Malachi's attention on another member of staff, I seize the moment to sneak a peek at the time.

Five thirty-five, damn it.

When I look up, Malachi's dark gaze is already on me. "Will you just leave? I can wrap things up here."

I want to say no, because I really should stay. Work and money have always been the centre of my universe, everything and everyone else naturally slotted into second place. But not Chelsea.

"If you're sure?" I ask, not waiting for an answer because my feet are already starting toward the door.

"If you look at that watch one more time, I'm going to shove it—"

I don't stick around long enough to hear Malachi's words. I'm out of the building in no time and hurry to where McKenzie is parked up in the Mercedes.

"Where to, sir?" he asks as I slide into the back seat.

"Surrey estate," I say, and, pulling my phone from my trouser pocket, I search for Mrs Collins, my head cook, and dial her number. She picks up on the tenth ring.

"Hello, Mr Calloway," she says, her voice always so chirpy. It's a trait I know my mother adored in her.

"I know I said you could finish early," I begin.

"Oh, yes. I was just about to enjoy a soak in the bath and read my novel."

I can hear water running in the background. I squeeze my phone in my grip, hating that I'm about to ruin her evening. "I don't suppose you could postpone your bath and novel to tomorrow? I will give you the day off, with full pay."

The sound of the water running quietens before eventually stopping. "Certainly, what do you need me to do?"

I flash a glance at the small clock on the dash. I told my sister to return with Chelsea at seven. There just isn't enough time to do what I had originally planned to do myself. "I planned to cook a three-course meal for Chelsea, but time appears to be slipping away from me. Therefore I would greatly appreciate your assistance."

"No problem, what's on the menu for this evening?"

I switch the call to loudspeaker as I search through my cloud file. I hurriedly swipe through album after album until I find the file I am looking for.

"Cottage pie." I click on the file. "My mother's famous recipe. I'll send you the list of ingredients," I say, whilst at the same time taking several screenshots.

"That sounds wonderful." Mrs Collins knows what that dish means to me, to my family. It hasn't been cooked since my mother was alive. "Any preference for the other dishes?" she asks.

I recline back in the seat. "I had envisioned a soup to start, and something sweet to finish."

Mrs Collins is silent for a beat. "How about I make a start on those, and put the ingredients on the side ready for you to cook the main?"

It is like the woman has read my mind. "Perfect," I say, and cut the call.

Never in my life have I cooked for a woman. I've never cooked, period. But something about making Chelsea dinner this evening feels right.

How hard could it be?

"Oh, my God, Lucian, this is amazing." Chelsea stands with her hand cupped over her mouth as I guide her into the dining room. The table has been laid with a selection of candles and a beautiful orchid centrepiece. "You did this all yourself?" she asks as I pull out a chair for her.

"With a little help from Mrs Collins," I say, and after she sits, I push her chair under the table. "We have homemade tomato and basil soup for starters, followed by my mother's famous cottage pie and a chocolate soufflé for dessert."

Chelsea lays her hand over mine. She doesn't need to say a single word because she knows what a big deal it was for me to cook something so personal to my mother. It's my way of including her and keeping her memory alive.

"I can't wait to taste it," Chelsea says, and rubs her palms together.

"I can't wait to taste *you* later." I lean in close and kiss her neck. She lets out a long breath and closes her eyes. I slowly work my way around to her lips whilst at the same time lowering my hand into her lap. She is wearing a pink polka-dot dress, which when she sits rucks up. It isn't hard for me to slide my hand under the hem and work my fingers up her thigh.

Higher and higher. Chelsea doesn't stop me. Her body is relaxed, and slowly she opens her legs wider for me, granting me perfect access. The pad of my index finger brushes against the material of her panties.

"Oh, my God, Lucian, stop. What if someone walks in?"

"You have nothing to worry about. I have given all the staff the evening off. All except Mrs Collins, who I have informed not to disturb us until I tell her we are ready." I press my lips to hers. I'm about to slide my finger inside her panties when there is a knock at the door.

I break the kiss. "Go away!"

Silence. It would seem whoever it was has gotten the message. Returning my attention to Chelsea, I slide my finger into her underwear just as the door swings open.

"Go away? That is no way to address me."

Jumping away from the chair, I stand bolt upright. "Father!"

CHAPTER TWENTY-ONE

Chelsea

F*ather?* Did I hear right?

Oh, God, oh, God. Did Lucian's father see where his son's hand was? Where it was about to go?

Needing something to do, I pull at the hem of my dress and work the cotton material down my thighs. What I'm wearing isn't overly revealing, but I'd have worn something a little more conservative if I'd known Lucian's father was visiting.

I'm too embarrassed to meet his father's eyes, so I keep my gaze trained on Lucian. He brushes his hands down his grey suit jacket. I figure it's his way of regaining his composure. "What are you doing here?"

Footfalls echo, and when I glance up Lucian's father is pulling out the chair opposite to where I'm sitting. The place that has been set for Lucian. "You invited me for dinner."

"On Wednesday, Father. Today is Tuesday."

His father waves him off, picks up a napkin folded into the shape of a rose, squeezes the rolled-up stem between his thumb and forefinger and shakes it vigorously in the air. The linen petals lose their shape, and when the napkin is just a napkin, he places it in his lap. "What's for dinner?"

Lucian meets my gaze, and I smile. We can't be rude and kick his father out. I'm sure there is enough food to be split three ways. I take a short inhale before answering. "We have tomato and basil soup for starters, followed by—"

"Say no more," Lucian's father interrupts, and, sitting back in his chair, rests his hand over his stomach, which rumbles loudly as if on cue. "I'm famished."

Sighing, Lucian pinches the bridge of his nose. "I will ask Mrs Collins to set another place."

Lucian turns to walk out of the room but spins around just as suddenly. "I'm sorry, where are my manners? Chelsea, this is my father, Duncan Calloway. Father, my beautiful fiancée, Chelsea Janssen. I will leave you to get better acquainted."

I don't miss how loudly Lucian's shoes tap against the wooden floorboards on his way out of the dining room. Nor do I miss the heavy way the door closes in its frame, not quite a slam, but I know he isn't happy. Tonight was meant to be for us, and I'd be lying if I said I didn't feel a pang of disappointment.

My gaze connects with Duncan's blue-green eyes, trained on me. The shock of thick grey hair is the first thing I really notice about him. He's older than I had imagined, possibly late seventies. He's dressed in a maroon suit, with a white shirt and trouser braces peeking out from beneath his jacket. "So, Clarissa, tell me about yourself."

"It's Chelsea," I say. My voice cracks and I clear my throat and continue. "I own a beauty salon—"

"A businesswoman, that's what I like to hear. Tell me the name of your chain and how many establishments you run."

How many establishments? I gulp, and at the same time sink in my chair. "Just the one, sir. One salon in Cornwall. It's currently being refurbished." I don't tell him I can't afford to reopen, that's information he doesn't need to know. "But I plan to branch out in aesthetics and offer courses to train upcoming therapists."

"Oh." Duncan's brows furrow, and he doesn't utter another word. I try desperately to think of something to fill the silence but can't think of a single thing.

Our eye contact is broken when the dining room door swings open and Lucian re-enters. Mrs Collins follows closely behind. She's an elderly lady dressed in a black uniform with a white apron secured around her waist. She is carrying napkins, several pieces of cutlery, and a soup bowl. She's quiet as she sets Lucian's place beside his father. I feel somewhat intimidated sitting alone and facing two such powerful men.

"Clarissa was just telling me that she owns a salon."

"Her name is Chelsea," Lucian corrects and takes his seat. "And yes, she owns a soon-to-be-very-prestigious beauty salon in Cornwall."

"Soon-to-be?" Duncan questions.

Lucian looks to me and then back to his father. "It's a work in progress."

"I will go fetch your starters," Mrs Collins says, and leaves the room.

Both men are openly staring at me. I didn't realise how hot the room temperature was until right now.

"Tell me about your upbringing. Did you attend private school?" Duncan asks.

I can't even begin to imagine how much private school in England costs. My parents didn't have two pennies to rub together. "Mainstream."

"And what of your education?"

What does that even mean? Is he asking how I did at school? I shrug. "Average, sir. I passed all my exams—well, the important ones anyway." I fail to mention the two F's I received.

"Where are you from? Do you have siblings?"

Laughter erupts from Lucian, and he places a hand on his father's shoulder. "Next you'll be asking her her blood type and religious beliefs."

"I had planned to, yes," Duncan answers, and I can't tell if he's being serious.

"Don't overwhelm the poor girl."

I lift my hand. "It's okay," I say, and I mean it. I'm an open book, and have nothing to hide. It's nice that he wants to know more about me. "I'm originally from the Netherlands. My parents moved to England when I was a baby. I'm AB positive, and I grew up in a Christian household. I have two siblings, Amber and Phillip."

Lucian places his elbows on the table and leans in close. "I didn't know you had a brother."

I let out a small laugh. "There is a lot about each other we don't know. But I look forward to learning everything about you."

Lucian smiles, and it's a genuine smile. He looks at me with pride, and it makes me feel all fuzzy inside. I could stare into his eyes all night, but I tear myself away from their hypnotic pull, reminding myself that we have company.

"Tell me about yourself," I say to Duncan, deciding to flip the conversation around.

Duncan's eyes gleam. "Certainly, young lady. What is it you want to know?"'

I'm sitting in front of one of the richest men in the country. A million and one questions flood my mind. But where do I even begin? At the beginning is as good a place as any. "Tell me about you, your childhood. What made you the man you are today."

Duncan's eyes roll back, as though he's trying to recall a past memory. "I have fond memories of my childhood. I had the best education money could buy. All of us Calloways attended Ravenhill boarding school in Kent. It's where your children will one day go."

My body stiffens. "Children? I don't know if I want children," I answer honestly, and am met by silence. It surprises me that Lucian says nothing. What is he expecting? I entered into this agreement just days ago, and he's already asked me to marry him for real. And now children? Everything is moving way too fast.

While I'm lost in my own internal turmoil, Duncan turns to his son. "Did I tell you that I play golf with Simon Matthews?"

"I was not aware," Lucian answers. He picks up a glass of wine and swirls the liquid around. "Matthews, where do I know that name?"

The dining room door opens and Mrs Collins re-enters carrying a crock bowl. She places the bowl between us and, pulling a ladle from her apron pocket, begins dishing out our starters. My stomach instantly rumbles at the scent drifting up to my nose.

I glance down, about to pick up my spoon, except there are three. Three knives and forks also. Wide-eyed, I look at Lucian for help, and he subtly gestures toward the first spoon to my right.

"As I was saying," Duncan pipes up, buttering a bread roll. "Simon Matthews is an IT giant, and Samantha's estranged uncle. The family are back on talking terms, and since he has no children of his own, Samantha has become a big part of his life."

I recognise that name immediately. Samantha Matthews, Lucian's ex-girlfriend from the charity gala.

"That's great," Lucian says, though his words and tone are contradictory. If anything, he sounds bored.

I make a point of keeping my elbows off the table as I take my first taste of soup. The tomato and basil flavour explodes onto my tastebuds. Looking heavenward, I sink into the chair. "Oh, my God, this is seriously good."

The corners of Lucian's mouth quirk up, and he nods in agreement. My cheeks heat, only this time for the right reason, and that being that I love the man sitting across from me.

I don't know when it happened, or how, I just know that I can't picture my life without him in it.

"As I was saying, Samantha will be at the next charity gala. Simon said she talks about you all the time."

I choke on the soup and end up spilling it on my dress.

Glasses rock back and forth as Lucian hurriedly grabs a napkin. "Here, allow me."

But it's too late, I have pushed the chair back and am already on my feet. "It's okay," I say, and, grabbing a rose-shaped napkin, begin to dab my mouth. I gaze down to be met with mottled red patches. My dress is ruined.

"I'm going to go change." I don't look at Lucian's father, I'm too embarrassed. The pink polka-dot dress I am wearing falls a few inches above my knee with a slit up the right side. The dress is sweet and playful, but not something I'd have worn in Duncan Calloway's presence.

"Would you like me to join you?" Lucian offers.

"No, no," I say, tripping as I hurry toward the door. "I'm fine." I grab the handle and let myself out, not once turning back.

I hurry down the long corridors, power-walk up the stairs and run to my room. Once inside I dart to the walk-in wardrobe and yank open the door.

Hangers clink together as I flick through the long line of gowns. My hands still as I lay my eyes on the most beautiful purple number. The neckline drops to a subtle V. I take the hanger from the rail and hold the dress against my body. The long chiffon skirt falls easily to the floor.

Perfect.

When I have changed, I flash one final glance in the mirror and smile at my reflection. I can't run, not in this dress, but, walking quickly, I make my way out of the room, down the stairs, and toward the dining room.

I feel like a million pounds in this dress. The right amount of sexy with a hint of sophistication. I plant a big smile on my lips just as my fingers wrap around the cool brass handle.

"What is your problem?"

I freeze on hearing Lucian's terse words.

"My problem, son, is that I came here tonight expecting to be introduced to a lady, but instead you introduce me to a commoner who dresses like a floozy."

A floozy? A commoner? I'm not one for eavesdropping, because these are words I am not meant to hear. But as much as I know I should walk away, I can't prompt my legs to move, not so much as an inch. I lean in closer and press my ear to the door.

"How dare you. There was absolutely nothing wrong with the way she was dressed, and correct me if I'm wrong, but our mother wasn't born from money."

"No, but your mother had a business head on her shoulders. We were the perfect team."

"Were you not listening when I told you Chelsea owns her own business?"

Duncan laughs, but it isn't with humour. "A rundown backstreet salon is not a business. That I may have been willing to overlook, but she doesn't want children. No, son, this simply won't do."

I can't listen for a moment longer. I release the door handle and step back, away from the dining room. I spin around, about to go anywhere that isn't here when I come face to face with Mrs Collins.

Her face appears drawn and her cheeks flushed red. But still she paints on a smile. "I'm sorry, Chelsea, I was just about to see if everyone was finished with their starters."

I sniff loudly, trying to sniff away all my emotion, but it's no use. My bottom lip trembles and my eyes become cloudy with unshed tears.

"I'm feeling tired all of a sudden." I feign a yawn. "I think I'm going to have an early night." I wipe the tears from my eyes.

"An early night?" Mrs Collins' voice is high-pitched as she takes my arm. "You'll do no such thing. Lucian has gone out of his way to make this evening special for you. Now I will not have you disappoint Lucian"

She begins to tug me in the direction of the door, but I pull back. Lucian and his father can't know that I've been crying. I need time to pull myself back together.

"The dress," I blurt out. "It's too tight."

Mrs Collins smiles warmly. "Come with me. I'll have you changed and sat back at that table in no time."

CHAPTER TWENTY-TWO

Lucian

My father remains seated beside me and eats his starter as though we are discussing something as trivial as the weather. I want to get up and walk to the other side of the room to put distance between us. But running away is not how we Calloways deal with our problems. We face them head-on, like men.

Father passes me a sideward glance. "End your engagement with Chelsea and marry Samantha. Marry Samantha and Calloway Housebuilders is yours. Not only will your union see the merger of two affluent local families, but Samantha herself informed me that she wants children one day, thus continuing the Calloway name."

My eyebrows shoot up. It would seem my father and Simon are very well acquainted, and I have been the hot topic of conversation. "My, my. My ears are positively burning. Has it slipped your mind that the last time Samantha and I were together we hit the tabloids due to her philandering ways?"

Father waves me off. "That's all water under the bridge," he says and proceeds to dip what is left of his bread roll into his soup.

"Samantha was under the same impression when our paths crossed on Saturday." I pause and something occurs to me. "It was you. You invited Samantha to the Pink Ribbon Breast Cancer Charity Gala."

Father dabs the corners of his mouth with his napkin before addressing me. "I will not deny my involvement. I thought that perhaps if you were to see her again that—"

"That what? I'd fall madly in love with her? That I'd forget all about Chelsea, and Samantha and I would just pick up from where we left off? I'm engaged, Father. Now I know that didn't deter Samantha, but I'm in love with Chelsea and our engagement means something." I speak with such earnestness that I almost believe my own lie. The engagement may be fake, but my feelings for her are not.

"You weren't engaged when I approached Samantha." He spends long seconds working his spoon around the inside of his bowl, collecting the dregs of soup.

"Perhaps, but still you deemed it your place to interfere in my love life." With a shaky hand, I grab my wine glass and gulp the rosé down in one. I reach across the table to where the ice bucket and bottle of red is stored.

Father takes hold of my wrist. "Slow down, son."

I glower at my old man. "I respect you, Father, and your wishes. But I am more than capable of choosing my bride."

I break eye contact and finish my soup in silence. I place my spoon in the empty bowl when it dawns on me that Chelsea is yet to return. I glance across the table and notice her starter, which lies virtually untouched. I push back the chair, about to excuse myself, when the door to the dining room opens and Chelsea walks in.

She is wearing a teal gown; the skirt falls to the floor. If I'm not mistaken, this is a gown from my mother's collection, and it fills me with pride seeing something she designed on the woman I love.

"What took you so long?" I ask, hurrying around the table to pull out her chair.

Chelsea shrugs. "I couldn't find the right outfit to wear."

"You chose well," I say, and when I retake my seat notice Mrs Collins lingering in the doorway.

"Are you ready for the main course?" Mrs Collins asks.

"Chelsea's soup will need reheating."

"It's fine." Chelsea pushes her bowl forward. "I'm ready for my main." She sits quietly and fidgets with the tablecloth. She looks so awkward and so on edge.

"Please, reset my place beside Chelsea," I say, and get up from my seat and walk around the table. I sit in the chair to her right as Mrs Collins switches my place over and clears away our starters. She returns moments later with our main course, my mother's famous cottage pie. Mrs Collins has presented the dish in the same way Mother used to. The cottage pie has been cut into small rectangular helpings with a sprig of rosemary placed diagonally over the top.

I stiffen as she lays a plate down in front of my father. I'm unsure if he'll be angry or hurt that I have resurrected Mum's signature dish. I await his reaction, but he doesn't utter a single word.

Chelsea clears her throat. "I remember reading that the Calloway legacy started many generations ago."

My father nods. "That is correct. My grandfather fancied himself as a bit of a chancer. It started when he bought his first property. He sold it at the right time and made a significant profit. My grandfather made it his life's work buying and selling houses. One day he stopped investing in property and started buying land. Over the years he gained several partners and investors. Bored of working in just the property market, he decided to branch out and invest in hotels, and, well, you could say the rest is history."

"That's amazing. Your legacy began with the sale of one house," Chelsea purrs. "It gives me hope that my business will grow over time. Who knows? One salon today, a chain of shops tomorrow." She smiles sweetly. "Once I am settled in business, maybe one day I'll be settled enough to want children."

I can't help wondering if her words are genuine, or if she's saying the words she thinks my father wants to hear. My father smiles, but it doesn't crease the corners of his eyes, because it isn't sincere. Duncan Calloway is a first impressions kind of guy. Whatever Chelsea does and whatever she says from here on out is irrelevant. He has made up his mind, and it will remain unchanged.

His gaze lands on me. "Samantha and her uncle plan to attend the Hope for Children Charity Gala. It would be nice if the two of you could catch up."

I stop listening as Father drones on. He talks about Samantha as though Chelsea wasn't sitting right beside me. I side-eye her and notice she isn't eating. Her body is rigid, and her hands remain tightly sandwiched between her thighs. I lower my fork and place my palm over her hands. She flinches immediately and pulls away and angles her thighs so they're facing in the other direction.

This is the first time in my life that I find myself standing at a crossroads. I'm standing between a woman I'm pretending to be engaged to and a company I've committed my life's work to. My knife and fork clink against my plate as I cut into the cottage pie.

If I break up with Chelsea, then Father will hand me the company. If I break up with Chelsea, I get everything I have ever wanted. Everything except the girl. How easy it would be to fall back into my old way of life without Chelsea in it. The problem is that I'm more like my old man than I care to admit. I'm greedy and stubborn to a fault. I want the company *and* the girl. I just need to figure out a way I can have both.

I look up and meet my father's stare. "Certainly, Father. I will speak with Samantha at the charity gala." I fail to mention that it will be to tell her once and for all that there is no hope of a future for us.

Chelsea hasn't touched her main and it hasn't escaped my attention that she hasn't had more than a bite to eat all evening. When Mrs Collins comes to take our plates, Chelsea complains of a headache and excuses herself. I hate that my father is here, and I can't accompany her to our bedroom.

Lucky for me, we only have one course remaining. My only hope is that Father doesn't suggest retiring to the study with a bottle of Scotch and concluding the evening with a game of chess. A game of chess with my father can last hours, and hours is something I simply don't have when there is a beautiful woman lying in my bed.

"So, what are your plans for the rest of the week?" I ask, trying to keep a light conversation flowing.

Father relaxes back in his chair and regards me for a second before answering. "Now that we are alone and won't be disturbed, I have to tell you, son, that I have decided to part with Freesdon Hall. I plan to sell the property via a private auction house."

Pain ricochets around me, and I have to squeeze my hands into tight fists to prevent them from shaking. Freesdon Hall is the place I grew up, the place where all my childhood memories with my mother are stored.

A war is raging in my mind, and it takes all my self-control not to strike my fist on the table. Trying my hardest to keep my composure, I take a deep and calming breath. "Not only would it be wrong, but it would be immoral to sell our home."

Father sighs. "I'm a little long in the tooth to live my life based on sentiment. The house, like your mother, is dead. It's a beautiful property, and it's about time it had a new lease of life with a new family. It's time to move on and close that chapter in our lives."

"Father, you can't."

He shakes his head. "It's already done."

The soufflés arrive and we eat in silence, or rather Father eats as I wait patiently for him to leave. I don't meet his stare and instead watch the hands of the old grandfather clock tick away.

"I'm tired. It's time I head home," Father says and gets to his feet.

Finally.

"I'll see you out." I stand and follow Father into the hall. The sensor lights come on the second we step out onto the driveway.

Albert jumps out of the Mercedes and helps my father. Once he is inside the car, I turn my back to leave when he calls after me.

"I hand the keys over next week. I'm planning to visit the house on Friday if you want to join me. Feel free to look around and take anything sentimental."

The whole damn house is sentimental, I want to say in reply. But I don't. I keep my lips sealed. It is a coward who is unable to face his problems head-on, but in this instance I'm unable to turn to meet my father's stare.

I take a slow and controlled inhale. "No, thank you. I will not be setting foot back inside that house." I can't, knowing it'll be the last time.

"That's a pity, because Farrah, Gage and Malachi will be joining me in the afternoon for a family get-together in the gardens. I would really like it if all my children were in attendance. I have arranged a small buffet-style spread and some drinks. I would like us to raise our glasses for a toast in memory of your mother before I lock the doors one final time."

How wonderful. An intimate family get-together while Father rips out my fucking heart and soul. I bite down hard and grind my teeth.

I'm a Calloway, I remind myself, *and Calloways face their problems head-on.*

"I will see you Friday," I grit out. I don't wait until the car is off the property to re-enter the house. I hurry back inside, slamming the door behind me. I pass Mrs Collins on my way to the stairs.

"What do you want me to do with Chelsea's food?"

"Keep it covered," I practically growl. I hurry up the stairs and make my way across the landing to the bedroom.

I push open the door and step inside. The main light is off, and the room is lit solely by a six-foot lamp in the corner. The room appears to be empty. I check the en suite and walk-in wardrobe. They too are empty.

Where is she?

I've got to keep it together. I'm a Calloway, and I cannot let emotion get the better of me.

I take a few long and calming breaths, regaining my composure. The only person I can think of now is Chelsea. I need her arms, I need her kisses. Damn it, I need her. I'm about to head back downstairs to ask Mrs Collins if she's seen her when I notice slight movement from the curtain leading out onto the balcony.

I push back the curtain, and sure enough she's here. She has her elbows on the stone railing and is staring out at the night sky, a sky that is lit up with neon lights in the faraway distance from a travelling fair.

"Chelsea?" I say and, making my way toward her, rest my palm on her shoulder. She doesn't pull away, but she doesn't acknowledge me either. I take another step toward her, take both shoulders in my hands and breathe in the scent of her hair. Finally, I have found my calm. I'm about to wrap her up in my arms when she speaks.

"I can't do this any more, Lucian."

"Do what?"

Chelsea spins around. "Fit into your world. I don't belong here. What was the point of this fake engagement when your father wants you to marry Samantha?" She squeezes her eyes shut before continuing. "Eventually you're going to patch things up with her, and where does that leave us? There's no point dragging this out. I've called a taxi, and it'll arrive within the hour."

She is not doing this to me now. I want to grab her and physically shake some sense into her. Can't she see how much she damn well means to me?

I've got to alleviate the growing tension between us before I snap. "Cancel the taxi," I breathe into her ear.

"You're not listening." Her eyes snap open. "I can't do this any more."

"What can't you do?" My voice trembles as I fight to keep calm.

She tilts her head. "Pretend. I can't pretend to be your fiancée,

I can't pretend that one day I'll want children and I can't pretend to love you."

"So then don't pretend." My voice rises an octave. "Tell me you'll marry me. Tell me you'll think about children in the future. But above all, tell me you love me."

Laughing, she shoulders past and hurries into the bedroom. I hurry after her and grab her wrist. I try to spin her around, but she pulls the opposite way and does everything in her power not to face me.

"Take your hand off me." Her voice is strained.

"No, I will not. Not until you talk to me." Anger fills my voice. My body shakes with adrenaline. Not only is my father selling my childhood home, but the only woman I have ever loved is slipping away.

My blood is boiling, and I'm close to goddamn madness, and to my surprise my cock is hard. So damn hard. I need a release before I self-combust.

I take hold of her shoulders and spin her around so she has no choice other than to face me. She trips and falls into my chest. I lasso my arms around her and hold her close.

"Let go!" she demands.

"Never."

I capture her fists as she pummels them against my chest. I hold her tighter as she wriggles and squirms to get out of my embrace. When she stops striking me, I hold her at arm's length. Her cheeks are flushed, her eyes bloodshot. Try as I might to get her to look at me, she won't.

"What the hell has gotten into you?" I bite out.

CHAPTER TWENTY-THREE

Chelsea

His breaths are hot, rapid, and beat against my cheek.

I fight in his hold, twist and pull to break free, but it's no use. There is no escape from this or from him. With emotions so strong and no way out of this situation, I do the only thing I can. And that is to explode.

"Everything is wrong!" I yell. My hands are shaking and my body hums with adrenaline.

I'm spiralling out of control, and there is no way to steady myself. Finally, I glance up and meet Lucian's stare. His gaze has my insides twisting and my heart hammering in my chest.

"Talk to me, Chelsea," he says, but I can't. I'm too mad, though not at him. I'm mad at myself for agreeing to be Lucian's fake fiancée, because deep down I don't want this to end. But our arrangement isn't permanent, nor can it be. We're classes and worlds apart and there is no way our two worlds can magically blend into one.

"This isn't working," I choke out. His father wants him to marry Samantha, and why wouldn't he? She and Lucian are cut from the same cloth and walk in the same social circles. I'm a commoner, an imposter, and I don't belong here.

"Then we'll make it work." Lucian's expression is pained.

I've got to end this now, before one of us gets hurt. The words 'Lucian, this is over' are on the tip of my tongue. I take a deep breath in, and mentally psych myself up.

He raises his brows expectantly, but I can't do it. I can't say the words. Instead, I throw my arms around his neck and pull him into me for a kiss. With his arms wrapped around me he charges forward and gives me no option other than to stumble back. Fingers that seconds ago were clasped around me are now unfastening my dress.

We stagger toward the bed and drop items of clothing on our way. My dress, his suit jacket, my bra, my panties…

The back of my legs collide with the mattress and it's here we stop walking and start exploring one another. There is no softness to his touch, nor is there softness to mine. My nails dig deep into his back, indenting, clawing and scratching. His beard burns my face as he kisses me deeper and harder than he has ever kissed me before.

My arm shakes as I tentatively reach between us and take his cock in my hand. I grip him firmly and start to work his velvety shaft up and down. Without warning, he slides a finger between my folds and begins circling my clit. Waves of pleasure course through me as he hits the spot.

"I want to see you come," he growls into my ear. Warm breaths lap against my cheek as he works his free hand up my back, my spine and my neck. I gasp as he fists my hair. My eyes snap open as he holds my head back and gives me no choice but to look straight into his eyes.

He offers me a smile that ignites a molten fire in my stomach and leans in close. Instinctively I pucker my lips and try to meet him halfway, but he doesn't plan to make it that easy for me. My lips are inches from his, and I figure this is how he wants it to remain. I try again to close the distance between us, but his grip on my hair tightens, preventing me from getting closer.

Embarrassment very quickly tightens its hold on me, because I literally have nowhere to hide. I suck my lower lip in and close my eyes.

"Look at me," Lucian demands, and I do. Piece by piece I fall apart, until my legs tremble beneath me and my breathing becomes heavy.

Finally, his lips crash onto mine. He kisses me long and hard, sucking my bottom lip into his mouth. This isn't a kiss, no, this is something entirely different. He's drinking in my orgasm.

"I've got to be inside you." He gives me a nudge. My gravity shifts as I fall onto the bed. I prop myself up on my elbows and watch as Lucian takes a condom packet from the nightstand drawer. With a savage look in his eyes he tears the packet open with his teeth and slowly works the latex down his length. When every inch of him is sheathed, he grabs my thighs and drags me toward him. I squeal as he lifts my legs, places them on his shoulders and eases his cock inside me.

"Lucian," I cry out. He isn't gentle, nor is he slow. His thrusts are hard, savage, deep and demanding. Pain and pleasure become one and, lowering my leg, I hook my calf around his ass and demand more. With his free hand he grabs my hip and moves me in time to his quickening pace. Faster and harder, he's merciless in the way he takes me. I feel his release, and he holds me in his arms for long seconds after.

"I love you, Chelsea," he says, before slowly pulling out. He leans down and kisses me, slow and sensual, which is a complete contradiction to how he has just taken me.

His teeth graze my lips in a soft bite, and he breaks the kiss. "I should go clean up."

"Maybe I should help you."

Lucian quirks a brow. "You should definitely help me. Right after you cancel the taxi."

I smile and do just that. I call the taxi firm to cancel my booking and, with our fingers laced together, I follow him to the shower. The warm water cascades over our bodies and he grabs the bar of soap, lathers it up and glides it over me. Over my back, my chest, and in slow sensual circles over my stomach. He places the soap back in the chrome dish and reaches for the bottle of shampoo.

"Turn around," he whispers, and I do. With my body flush against his, he lathers my hair up. I bite back a smile at his erection that is pressing into my back.

He gives my arm a gentle squeeze, and together we step under the shower head. The water washes over my hair and over my body, transforming the products into a white foam that puddles around our feet before disappearing into the plug hole.

I take the soap from the dish. "Your turn."

Once dry we lie in bed, wrapped up in one another's arms. With my head against his chest, my ear is met with the melodic beat of his heart. I like being this close to Lucian and having him this close to me.

"Tell me," I say, and at the same time run my hand over his broad chest. "Out of all the buildings in Cornwall you could have bought, why mine?"

Lucian raises a brow. "I thought the answer was obvious."

I smile and am filled with a rush of heat. Though the heat is soon replaced by guilt that bubbles in the pit of my stomach. "That shop was Tyler's livelihood."

Lucian frowns. "I'm sorry, I never meant to hurt anyone. I only wanted the building. It was never my intention to transform the shop into an estate agency."

"So why did you?"

"Because I thought it would give me the upper hand in acquiring Calloway Housebuilders."

"And did it?"

Lucian shrugs. "Honestly, I have no idea. But I would like to think so. I've put my blood, sweat and tears into that company. Calloway Housebuilders is who I am, and without it…"

"What?" I prompt.

"I'll lose my identity."

I take in a sharp inhale. It saddens me to think that Lucian feels this way. "There is more to life than work and money."

Lucian brings my hand to his mouth and kisses my knuckles. "I'm beginning to realise that."

"But this… me…" I pause. "What I guess I'm asking is, am I enough?"

"You are everything," he says with his lips still brushing against my skin. We lie in silence for a while before Lucian releases my hand and turns his back on me. It isn't like Lucian to turn away from me unless something is on his mind. So I shuffle closer and drape an arm around him.

"Is everything all right?"

Lucian sighs. "No, and the sad thing is it never will be."

"Lucian," I whisper.

"My father is selling Freesdon Hall."

I don't press him to talk about his feelings, because that didn't go well last time. Instead, I decide on a different approach. "Tell me about it."

Lucian stills for a beat. "What, my home?"

I nod. "Yes. Tell me about the place you grew up."

"Freesdon Hall is beautiful and I have a lifetime of memories packed between those walls, be it horseback riding with my mother, piano lessons with our grandmother or sneaking out when the opportunity presented itself."

I smile, thinking back to the memories Lucian shared with me of the cricket matches he and his brothers would have with the local children and their time at the skate park. "And your father? Where did he fit in?"

Lucian pauses for a beat, as if thinking back. "Occasionally he'd call upon one of us to join him in his orangery for a late-night game of chess."

"That sounds fun." I meant my comment to come over as

sincere but instead it comes across sarcastic. I'm thinking of what to say next when Lucian clears his throat.

"As bizarre as it sounds, I really enjoyed our games. It was the only one-on-one time I had with my father. How I wished he'd join us in the gardens for a kickabout with a football or fishing in the stream, but Father couldn't tear himself away from work. We missed out on so much quality father-and-son time. We missed out on many things I promised myself that my children never will. I want to be that father who high-fives his son when he scores a goal. I want to be the father who sits in the front row of my daughter's ballet show. I want to be the father my father never allowed himself to be, and I want my children, *our* children to have the childhood I missed out on."

I suck in a breath at his words. In front of me lies the man of my dreams. He's painting a picture of a perfect future, one he envisions me being a part of. Indirectly he is expecting too much of me. I need to tell him I meant what I said earlier and I don't know if I want children. Frankly the idea scares the life out of me. I only said I may in the future to appease his father.

I place my palm on his back. "I—"

Lucian turns around and the palm I placed on his back now rests on his chest directly over his heart. "I had visions of taking my children to Freesdon Hall one day. To show them where I grew up, and tell them all about their grandmother. That dream is no longer possible."

"Why don't you buy it?"

"I couldn't. While I am all for adding properties to my growing portfolio, Freesdon Hall is different. The property has been derelict for long enough. It deserves a new lease of life, it deserves a family to move in and create special memories of their own."

He sounds conflicted as he speaks, and, taking my hand in his, he squeezes. "We have the opportunity to visit the house one final time before Father hands the keys over. Would you come with me?"

"Yes. Of course."

We lie staring at one another in the dimly lit room. Lucian is the first to close his eyes and it isn't long before he's asleep. I spend this small window of time looking at him, really looking. Naturally his Celtic tattoos are the first thing that steal my attention. My gaze travels up past his pecs to his high cheekbones and his strong jawline. My gaze hovers over his full lips and, lifting my hand, I trace my index finger over his defined Cupid's bow. With him asleep I have the courage to say the words that I will never say aloud when he is awake.

"I love you, Lucian," I whisper.

I love him because he makes me feel in control even when I'm spiralling. I love the kind person he is, beneath all that arrogance and self-importance. Damn it, I love Lucian Calloway, but I don't want to. I don't want to fall so hard that it'll destroy me when he leaves. And he will. I refuse to settle down, start a family and bring a child into the world who will watch from between the spokes of the banister as her father walks out of the front door and out of our lives.

The tears I fought so hard to fight spill down my cheeks. My tiny pearl-drop tears soak into the pillowcase, taking their unspoken secrets with them.

I bring my index finger to my lips, grace its pad with a solitary kiss and press my finger to his lips. Our arrangement is temporary, I remind myself, and temporary is how it must remain.

"Good night, Lucian," I say, and turn my back toward him. I reach across to the bedside lamp and flick off the light.

CHAPTER TWENTY-FOUR

Lucian

F riday soon comes around, and I find myself spending longer than is necessary in my walk-in wardrobe selecting a suitable tie and cufflinks.

"Are you nearly ready?" Chelsea calls from the bedroom.

"Hurrying, sweetheart," I call back, but hurrying is the antithesis of what I'm doing. The glass case that contains my cufflinks is open and they are scattered everywhere.

"Lucian." This time it's Farrah who calls, and I can feel my nerves fracturing.

"I'm coming!" It wasn't my intention to shout, but I can't bring myself to apologise, nor can I step away from this confounded mirror.

With shaky hands I wrap the crimson silk material around my neck and begin making the loop.

"Lucian?"

I look up, and in the mirror's reflection I see Farrah standing behind me. This is the first time I've looked at my kid sister and seen a woman staring back. She is wearing a slim-fitting turquoise dress, a matching cashmere shawl, and her ebony locks have been pinned back. She looks beautiful and in this moment is the image of our mother.

I blink and try to clear my mind. My gaze bypasses Farrah and I attempt to get a better view into the bedroom. "Where's Chelsea?" I ask, noticing the bed where she sat moments ago is empty.

Farrah takes a few steps toward me. "She's gone downstairs to tell Albert we're almost ready."

Albert is Father's driver, who Father sent to pick Chelsea and me up this morning, whilst McKenzie escorts Farrah and her bodyguard to Freesdon Hall.

My sister points to her wristwatch and taps the domed face. "It's eleven-thirty, so we're already late."

"So then go." I wave her off.

I can't help but wonder what her hurry is, for it's not like my sister to care about punctuality.

"Not without you." She steps forward and continues to fasten my tie.

I stand quietly whilst she loops one end around the other and slides the knot up to rest at my collar. When she has finished, she reaches into the glass case and picks out two cufflinks.

"There, done." She drops small gold dice in my palm and turns to leave.

I stare down while moving the cufflinks around. "You have no idea how hard today is for me."

"It's hard for all of us."

I stuff my hands into my trouser pockets and shake my head. "It's different for me."

I regret the words as soon as they leave my lips, but I've said them and it's too late to take them back.

"Just because I was a toddler when she died does not mean I love her any less. I was robbed, Lucian. Robbed of precious memories—the sound of her voice, the feel of her hugs. Just because I don't remember doesn't mean my pain is any less than yours."

I hurry to catch up with my sister and place my hand on her shoulder. "I'm sorry."

Farrah doesn't turn to face me. She doesn't have to. I know from the tremble of her body that I have upset her. "I'm sorry too, Lucian. But don't make today about you. We are all hurting, just in different ways."

Without a backward glance, she leaves. She leaves me alone, surrounded by a dozen ties and suit jackets strewn on the floor, alone with my thoughts. I spend a few more minutes staring into the mirror's reflection, straightening my tie and adjusting my collar, but most of all, I'm stalling.

"Lucian!" Chelsea calls for what seems like the hundredth time, and instead of putting on a different tie and fastening and unfastening a different set of cufflinks, I step out of my walk-in wardrobe and stroll along the landing and on down the stairs.

With each step I force myself to stand taller, and with each step I force a smile on my face.

I only have to get through a few hours, I remind myself as I set foot in the hallway.

Chelsea's hovering in the doorway leading out to the front of the estate. A long blue dress hugs her body, and her hair has been curled and falls to her waist. She hasn't seen me yet; her attention appears to be taken up with what's happening outside. Chelsea waves, and it's only when I step forward that I notice my Mercedes pulling off the driveway. My sister and Dante are seated inside.

"Lucian!" Chelsea calls again, her voice so loud it feels as though it goes right through me.

I take a few steps forward and place my hand on the small of her back. "I'm right here."

She spins to face me and at the same time clasps her hand to her chest. "Jesus, you gave me a heart attack."

"What?" I say, and, tilting my head toward her, cup my hand around my ear, feigning deafness.

Chelsea elbows me playfully. "I did not shout that loud."

I lower my arms and loop them around her back, pulling her in close. "Shout? No, wail would be more apt. I believe you'd give a banshee a run for her money."

Chelsea smiles, but like mine it's forced. I know she is nervous about today, though her reasons differ from mine. I've been so wrapped up in myself that I've completely overlooked how she's feeling.

"We will stay for an hour, show our faces and make our excuses."

Chelsea nods. "It's fine. I'll be by your side as long as you need."

It's over an hour's drive from Surrey to Knightsbridge. I'm taken down memory lane as Albert passes the old terraced housing estate and the park we would pass as boys on the journey to and from boarding school. With Albert driving it's like being thrown back in time. The park hasn't changed—the ice cream van is in the same place, and a tyre swing still hangs from the old oak tree.

We pass the park and the set of traffic lights, and I know we're getting closer. I squeeze Chelsea's hand in mine as the estate begins taking shape.

She squeezes my hand in return. "Are you okay?"

No.

I nod and attempt to smile. "I'm fine."

"When was the last time you came here?" Chelsea asks.

I don't have to think about my answer. "The last time I visited Freesdon Hall was on my birthday. It's tradition that my siblings and I come here on the anniversary of her death. We lay flowers under the tree she planted with us as boys, and we spend much of the day sharing childhood memories."

"Oh, Lucian." Chelsea shuffles closer toward me and places her arm around my shoulder.

Damn it, I love this girl. I capture her hand in my hand and kiss the backs of her fingers. My lips happen upon the engagement ring and her stare meets mine. She may be guarded as to what she says, and she may keep her feelings under lock and key, but there are so many emotions filling her crystal blues that I know there is more to us than a fake engagement.

Our stare is broken when the wrought-iron gates to the estate open and our car pulls in. There are two cars I don't recognise and a catering van parked out front. It would seem my father was true to his word when he said he was arranging a buffet-style spread. He can't do anything without alcohol and canapés. But food and drink only suggest one thing, and that is that we will be here for the duration of the day.

I look to the Georgian mansion and at the beautiful architectural design of the building. The front doors are open, and catering staff dressed in black are stepping inside.

The car stops, and the sound of the driver clearing his throat pulls me from my thoughts. The car door opens, and Chelsea slides out. A few seconds pass before Albert has made his way around the vehicle and opened the back passenger side door for me.

I don't remember getting out, and I don't remember walking up the asphalt driveway. It's like I'm on autopilot as I enter the grand hall.

Room to room I walk, and I take the time to really look. I glance around. Everything is the same, yet different. All of Mother's photographs and portraits have been taken down. The corner of the living room that was home to her grand piano lies empty. The only evidence of it ever being there is the flattened-down tread of the carpet. Colourful tapestries that once hung from the walls are gone. Ceilings with intricately designed patterns have been painted over. Furniture has been replaced and entire rooms changed around. It looks as though Father has already begun emptying the place, and that's exactly how it feels. Empty.

"Excuse me, sir." A red-haired woman carrying a silver tray approaches us. "Can I interest either of you in a chorizo, ham and cheese canapé?"

Chelsea smiles politely and reaches for a bite-sized treat.

"I need air," I say, and take Chelsea's hand before she has chance to take the canapé from the tray. Without a word I walk us toward the door.

"Lucian."

I sigh. So much for having a few minutes to myself. I turn and catch sight of Gage making his way toward us. His arms are outstretched as though something has perplexed him. "What time do you call this? I have a Scotch in the gardens with your name on it."

"Is it a double?" I muse, to which Chelsea elbows me.

"Triple if you like," Gage says, his eyes alive with mischief.

Chelsea glowers at my brother, who holds his hands up in surrender. "Don't worry, Chelsea. You have my word I won't let him get shitfaced and spew up over Mother's prized begonias."

I pat my brother on the shoulder. "No, Gage, I believe that is a party trick unique to you."

Chelsea looks between us. The scent of alcohol lingers heavily on Gage's breath as he stifles a laugh. "Guilty, but it was only once."

"After you set the trellises on fire and decided it was too hot to wear a stitch of clothing." I close my eyes, trying to block out the godawful image of my brother's bare arse.

"Wow," Chelsea all but chokes out, and I can't say I blame her. Whereas Malachi and I have etiquette, Gage does not. I'm sure his manners, like his tongue, reside somewhere in the gutter. "You're really something," Chelsea says.

Gage flashes a wolfish grin. "Thanks, I get told that all the time."

I'm sure Chelsea has him pegged as a class-A arsehole, and she wouldn't be wrong.

"In my defence," Gage continues, "I was only eighteen. And anyway, it would be counterproductive to get Lucian drunk today when I need him bright-eyed and bushy-tailed for our poker night."

"Poker night?" Chelsea repeats, and her gaze lands on me.

I run my hand along my jaw. *My God, how could I have forgotten?*

I hosted our boys' night in my Devonshire estate last month, and Gage in his Pembrokeshire mansion the month prior. Which only means one thing. I grab my pocket watch and make a point of looking at the time.

"Obviously it'll be too far to travel to Scotland by car," Gage says, picking up on my not-so-subtle gesture. "So Malachi has arranged for us to go to Dunmorrow Castle via helicopter."

I curse inwardly and shake my head. I can already feel the excuse on my tongue.

"It sounds like fun. You should go," Chelsea interrupts.

"I like her," Gage says, and, leaning into Chelsea's personal space, ruffles her hair. I'm seconds away from punching my brother in the face when Chelsea steps back. Long curls fall in front of her face before she pushes them behind her ear.

"I'm going to go ahead," she says, and, finger-combing her hair, hurries toward the door that leads to the gardens.

I watch Gage as he watches Chelsea, though more specifically homes in on her arse.

"Are you trying to get a black eye?" I enquire, my tone neutral.

Ignoring my question, Gage nods in approval. "Am I right in my assumption that Chelsea has a sister?"

I shove my brother. "Didn't you learn anything at Eton?"

Gage taps his chin a few times, as if considering my words. "If getting high and getting laid count, then yes. Women would naturally flock to us on our boys' nights out, and I can't say I blame them."

I shake my head and let out a laugh. "You're a real inkstain on the Calloway name."

"I know," Gage drawls. "But perfection is so drab and highly overrated."

The sun is blinding as we make our way outside. I shield my eyes as I look around for Chelsea.

One thing I always loved about Freesdon Hall is the immaculately tended gardens and beautifully designed landscape. When Mother became ill, she would spend hours confined to her bedroom. She would sit on the small balcony looking out onto the many acres of land. It was for this reason that Father paid a small fortune to have the most experienced gardeners work here. Every flower has a purpose, every stone and pebble have a place. The garden is like one intricately crafted mosaic, which when you stand back to look makes the most magnificent picture.

"I'll go grab your drink," Gage says and walks on ahead to where my family and the catering staff gather in a white marquee. Silk tablecloths have been laid out on long rectangular tables, and the food has been beautifully presented on an array of platters.

It would appear as though Gage has forgotten my drink. Without a backward glance he joins Malachi and Father, who are helping themselves to sandwiches. Farrah and Chelsea stand chatting with small plates of food in hands. I'm about to join them but instead stand, frozen to the spot, an observer, a bystander to everything and everyone I hold dear to me. I watch how easily Chelsea fits in with my sister, and despite Gage's less than tactful introduction, it would seem he was happy to welcome her to the family. I just need to work on my father. I need him to see what I see, and that is how wonderful Chelsea is.

I casually make my way toward Chelsea and my sister. Father turns and meets my gaze, and without hesitation calls everyone to gather around for a toast.

The staff grab the champagne flutes and hurriedly begin to

fill them. We are each handed a glass and stand in a semi-circle inside the marquee.

Father raises his glass. "I would like to raise a toast to family, old and new." He pauses and, frowning, looks over our faces one at a time. I can't help but wonder if his reference to 'new' had anything to do with Chelsea. One can only hope.

"To the future, and the past," he continues. "To Annabelle Calloway, may we never forget the amazing woman she was."

"To Mum," Gage says, lifting his glass.

"To Mum," Malachi, Farrah and I say in unison.

An arm snakes around my waist, and I glance down at the top of Chelsea's head. Everything about this moment is perfect. Mum isn't here physically but being here makes me feel as though she is here in spirit.

Glasses chink together as the others toast. Everyone's attention lands on me, and it's now I realise I haven't lifted my glass, not so much as an inch. I shake out of my reverie, about to complete the toast, when a blonde-haired woman in a teal maxi dress hurries to my father's side.

My jaw clenches at her untimely interruption. I'm about to tell her this is a private family get-together when Father turns his attention to the woman, his face transforming into a frown.

She leans into my father and presses a kiss to his lips. "I'm so sorry I'm late. My meeting ran longer than I expected." She wipes a red lipstick mark from his chin.

My mouth hangs open as I look from Gage to Malachi. They wear the same look of confusion I imagine to be displayed on my face.

My body tenses, my jaw sets so tightly I feel my teeth crunch. "Father? Who the hell is she?"

CHAPTER TWENTY-FIVE

Chelsea

Silence.

Nothing but silence fills the air. It is like someone reached for the volume control remote and turned the sound all the way down. The birds no longer grace us with their beautiful melody, the wind no longer whooshes and rattles the fabric of the marquee, and no one speaks, not so much as a single word.

Duncan looks around the sea of faces, and I figure he is waiting for someone to say something. Long uncomfortable seconds roll into long uncomfortable minutes, and finally there is sound, in the form of Duncan clearing his throat.

"This is Julie Ross." Duncan wraps his arm around the blonde's slim waist and pulls her close. "Julie is my—"

"I need air," Lucian announces before his father can finish. He hands his drink to Gage and leaves the small semi-circle. I turn and watch as he passes a large vegetable patch and disappears through an opening in a long line of bushes. I'm about to follow when fingers wrap around my wrist. I look up and am surprised to see Malachi standing at my side. He doesn't speak, just shakes his head, silently telling me not to go after Lucian.

My attention returns to Duncan, who, looking in the direction his son left, sighs heavily. "That is a disappointing start."

Malachi is still holding my wrist when Gage materialises to my right. In a split second he polishes off his own drink, along with Lucian's, and places them down on the table behind. Without much effort, he plucks the champagne flute from my hand and swallows it down in one. When the three empty glasses are lined up side by side on the table he nods his head in the direction Lucian left.

"I'll go after him," Gage announces, and walks in a not-so-straight line in pursuit of his brother.

"I think I better—" Farrah chimes in until her father pins her with a pointed stare.

"Stay," he commands, and she does. She stands perfectly still, her feet rooted to the ground. I look past Farrah to where dark green shrubs have been clipped into the shape of geisha girls. As still as Farrah is standing, I surmise she would only need a fan and an umbrella and she would easily blend in with the topiaries that stand behind her.

The pressure around my wrist is gone, and Malachi takes a step forward. "It is nice to meet you," he says, and, capturing Julie's petite fingers, he presses a kiss on the back of her hand. He releases Julie and passes Farrah a glance. Farrah stumbles forward and pulls Julie into the most awkward embrace I think I've ever seen.

Duncan smiles, seemingly happy with Malachi's and Farrah's reaction. He looks at them with an approving glint in his eyes, and it's now I realise that he hasn't once looked at me. Come to think about it, he didn't so much as acknowledge me when I arrived here today. It's as though he expects his children to make an effort and accept Julie, but he will not give his son the same courtesy and accept me. Somewhat hypocritical, but who am I to pass judgement?

I meet Julie's stare, and she smiles warmly. "And who is this beauty?"

Duncan scoffs.

A hand rests on the small of my back, a hand I know isn't Lucian's.

"This is Chelsea, our soon-to-be sister-in-law," Malachi says, and gives me a soft nudge forward. I feel hot all of a sudden. I feel as though I've been thrown to the wolves as all eyes land on me. I ignore the bile creeping its way into my throat and I ignore Duncan's glacial stare. My gaze locks with Julie's, and I hold out my trembling hand.

"Pleased to make your acquaintance," I say, trying to sound a little more upper class and a little more confident.

"The pleasure is mine." Julie takes my hand and shakes softly before releasing me. Julie is beautiful, and at first glance is difficult to put an age on. She has a mature vibe about her, though her skin is flawless and free of any visible wrinkles or imperfection.

I narrow my eyes and scan her features. "I know you. I mean, I've seen you somewhere before."

Her hair brushes against her shoulders as she leans her head toward me. Her eyes, which are the colour of light caramel, narrow as she takes me in. "I can't say I recognise you."

"Yes, dear," Duncan agrees. "I know exactly what you mean. Young Charlotte didn't leave a lasting impression on me either."

It's Chelsea, I want to blurt out, but keep my lips pressed tightly together.

"Father," Malachi scolds under his breath, but his father's expression remains unchanged. This is the second time I've had the misfortune of being in Duncan's company, and to say his personality leaves a lot to be desired is the understatement of the century.

"Where are you from?" Julie asks, as if trying to piece together where our paths may have crossed.

I straighten my back and force myself to stand tall. "The

Netherlands originally, but my family moved to Heller St Claire in Cornwall when I was a baby."

"Go on," she prompts.

I'm not sure what she wants me to say, so decide to tell her a little about me. "My sister and I used to own a photography shop in the town. We specialised in photography packages. She would take the photos and I would do the hair and makeup. There was a small room at the back of the shop where I would carry out a range of beauty treatments."

Julie taps her finger on her chin thoughtfully, and it's now that I notice the back of her hand. Dark veins protrude, and her skin is sunken and clings to the frail bones beneath. Her face suggests she is in her late forties, though her hands indicate she is much older. "I'm the owner and founder of the skincare company Lotus Flower. I wonder if you are familiar with our products. My face is on all the advertisements."

My mouth forms an O. Lotus Flower is one of the biggest skincare products on the UK market. If Julie is who she says she is, then she is a millionaire in her own right. "Yes, I used your products all the time, and I would always order an extra cleanser for myself."

Her eyes shine with pride. "Which is your favourite?"

"That's easy, the Monarda range. I love the uniqueness of the mint and oregano scent." The sick feeling from moments ago has completely dissolved as Julie places her hand on my shoulder.

"Tell me the name of your salon. I will come down for a treatment," she says, her smile wide, exposing a perfect set of pearly white teeth.

My stomach clenches. "Our shop was called Perfect Prints. We were forced to close after an arson attack a few years ago. The insurance didn't cover all of the damages, but I've been working hard to secure the funds I need to get back up and running."

The thought of reopening my salon suddenly feels less appealing because it'll be with Lucian's money. Money I will be given when our arrangement is over and I'm no longer bound to him. My heart tightens painfully at the thought.

"Oh, Duncan dear, this simply will not do," Julie announces. "I will give you the money you need to reopen your salon."

I smile, but quickly shake my head. "That is lovely, thank you so much, but no. I could not accept."

I flash a glance around the small crowd. At Farrah, whom in only a few short days I have grown to love. At Malachi, who no longer looks at me with indifference—his look is now one of interest. I go so far as flashing a glance at Lucian's father, a man whom I don't imagine I will ever grow to like, but a man whom I respect. I wonder what it would be like to be part of this family, and to be Lucian's fiancée for real. Even with Gage, as brash as he is, I can't say the idea of having these people in my life on a more permanent basis is the worst thing to imagine. In fact, it is quite the opposite.

With Lucian in mind, I take a few steps back. "Please, excuse me. I'm going to see where my fiancé has got to."

"Can you keep an eye out for Rocky, please?" Julie asks. "He ran into the gardens the second we arrived."

"Sure thing," I say and turn my back on them in pursuit of Lucian and I'm guessing a dog of some description.

The conversation between Julie and Duncan ebbs as I hurriedly make my way past the vegetable patch, toward the arched opening in the bushes and beyond. The land is vast, and I'm met with a rich explosion of colour from the shrubs and many different types of flowers. No matter which way I turn, my gaze is met only by unspoilt land. There is no sign of Lucian, Gage, or a dog.

Lucian isn't the kind of person to go walking in circles. I know Lucian, he's practical. He'd walk in one direction and keep going until he didn't want to walk any more. Or at least I hope that is what he would do, as I continue on in a straight line.

I pass bushes and trees, walk along a narrow, pebbled walkway and continue until finally something other than plant life comes into view. That something is a large tennis court.

"Fifteen-love!" Gage calls from one side of the net and does what I can only describe as a victory dance.

"You're cheating," comes the disgruntled sound of a child. A fair-haired boy whom I'd guess to be around eight or nine runs over to Gage. The boy is dressed in a royal blue T-shirt and matching shorts with a tennis racket wedged under his arm.

Gage crouches down so he is eye level with the boy. "No, lad, you just chose the wrong team to play on." sGage lifts his head and his attention shifts. "A hundred-pound wager, was it? Now pay up."

I stop walking and lean against the trunk of a large tree. I'm shaded from the hot summer sun and hidden from sight.

I watch as Lucian jogs over to where Gage and the boy are standing. His hair appears damp, and a thin line of sweat shines on his forehead. His pristine white shirt hugs his chest and, like his hair, appears damp, which causes it to mould to the rippling muscles beneath. Lucian reaches into the pocket of his trousers and pulls out his wallet. I can't see how much he takes, but he places an ample wad of cash onto his brother's awaiting palm. "Why does everything have to be a wager with you?"

Gage's tongue hovers over his lip as he flicks through the notes. Smiling, he counts the money. "Games are more fun when there's a little risk involved, don't you agree?"

Lucian rolls his eyes. "Come on, Rocky, let's show Gage how it feels to lose."

So Rocky isn't a dog.

Hidden from sight, I watch as they play tennis. I love seeing how competitive Lucian is. He and his brother have fire in their eyes as they backhand the ball over the net. I'm surprised to see how well Lucian can play. His movements are fluid, and he has excellent control of his racket. Lucian is a much more skilled player than his brother. The problem arises when Gage hits the ball to the boy in what I like to call a cheap shot. Rocky misses the ball by inches and it careens off the court.

"Thirty-love," Gage calls, shaking his hips from side to side and punching his racket high into the air. I hate cheaters, and although Gage isn't cheating, per se, he isn't giving the kid a fighting chance.

I step out from the confines of the tree just as Lucian pulls out his wallet. "Boo!" I call and give a thumbs-down, at which Gage, Lucian and Rocky turn to face me. "Foul ball," I continue.

Lucian's face transforms into a big smile. "We're playing tennis, not football."

I feign ignorance. "You can't play two against one with a weaker player. That isn't fair."

The truth is, I am very familiar with the rules and lingo of tennis. I played a lot of sport growing up—tennis, football, and even cricket. My mother called it my tomboy phase, but it was a way for me to spend some one-on-one time with my big brother when my father wasn't around. I was so desperate to have a positive male role model in my life.

Lucian raises a brow. "What do you suggest?"

I narrow my eyes. "What I suggest is that we play against Rocky and Gage."

Gage lets out a laugh. "You're hardly going to play tennis in that fine dress and those shoes."

I slip off my high heels and stand directly in front of Gage. "I mean, if you think you'll lose, then…"

Gage eyes me speculatively. "I'm not scared of losing. You're on, blondie." He grabs Rocky by the collar of his T-shirt. "Kid, you're with me."

We leave the tennis courts after two games. Technically Lucian and I won, but we may have let Rocky think he beat us. Either way, it was a good game, and Gage returned Lucian's money to him.

Gage and Rocky walk ahead while Lucian and I fall steps behind. Lucian's hand finds mine, and we walk like this is perfectly normal. As if he belongs to me, and I to him. How the lines have blurred in the small amount of time we have been together, but despite everything, I'm happy living in this blurred version of reality.

"She's okay," I say, and wait for Lucian to reply. When he doesn't, I continue. "Julie. You should give her a chance."

I look to Lucian and keep my gaze trained on his profile as we walk. Strands of wayward hair fall over his brow, and he pushes them back into place. "And I will, just not today. I don't know what it is, but being inside Freesdon Hall knowing it will be sold hurts more than I thought possible. Like Father, I thought maybe selling the house would finally offer some closure, but contrary to that, it feels like I'm losing my mother all over again."

His pain becomes my pain, and slices through me like the sharp edge of a blade.

"I admit that today isn't the best timing, but it isn't Julie's fault. You owe it to your father to at least try."

Lucian stops walking and faces me. "How do you do it?"

I rub my hand over my arm. "Do what?"

"See the good in people. Even if those people don't deserve your kindness. Tyler, my father, and even me, and yet you believe we are worthy of your time, worthy of redemption."

I shrug. "I guess I just like to believe there is good in everyone."

Lucian leans in close and strokes my cheek with the back of his hand. "If only I could see the world through your eyes. If only for a day."

If that were possible, he would know how truly magnificent he is to me. He would know how deeply I have grown to care. He would know my innermost thoughts and my weakness, and that is something I will never allow.

"Okay," Lucian says, and opens his arms. "I will speak to Julie. I will take the time to get to know her, but not for my father. I will do it for you."

Slowly we retrace our steps, through the opening in the long row of bushes and past the vegetable garden.

"Grandma," Rocky calls, and makes a beeline for Julie, who stands in the marquee chatting with Farrah and Malachi.

I look around for Duncan, but don't have to look far as he and two other men emerge from the house. One of the men I recognise as Josh, the other a tall elderly man with a walking stick I haven't seen before. Lucian's father and the old man stop walking, whereas Josh waves in acknowledgement and heads our way.

"What the hell is *he* doing here?" Lucian spits out.

"He's joining us to play poker," Gage chimes in.

"I wasn't talking about Josh," Lucian says. "Wait here, Chelsea, I'll be right back."

Lucian releases my hand and walks toward Josh, passes him and continues to his father and the elderly gentleman.

"Who's the old guy?" I ask as Josh joins us.

Gage shrugs. "I don't know, but I'm going to get a drink and introduce myself to Julie."

Gage heads toward the marquee, leaving me and Josh smiling awkwardly at one another. Part of me wishes Lucian hadn't confided in Josh about our arrangement, because when I am alone with him, I feel naked.

"That's Simon Matthews," Josh says.

So that is Samantha's uncle. I draw my brows together. "What's he doing here?"

Josh shrugs. "They were here when I arrived."

"They?"

Josh nods. "Yes, Samantha is inside looking around. Simon said he was in the area and was interested in purchasing the property for his niece. Duncan said something about Lucian giving her a private tour."

My gaze shoots to Lucian, who smiles at Simon and his father, but it's forced. Without a backward glance he heads into the house. The door opens and I get a flash of Samantha standing inside. Her mousy hair has been pinned back, a small strand coming loose when she straightens the skirt of her floral dress. Her gaze connects with mine and she smiles sweetly. Instinctively I step forward. If she's inside with Lucian, I want to be there.

Josh stands in front of me and blocks my way. "Please, don't get lost in fiction. What you and Lucian have, it isn't real."

Yes, it is! I want to yell in his face.

"You didn't see how happy Lucian was when he and Samantha were together. He was a different person when he was with her. Now, please, come with me, we'll mingle." Josh shoots a glance toward the house. "I would hate for us to step in the way of fate."

CHAPTER TWENTY-SIX

Lucian

Chelsea insisted I join my brothers in Scotland for our monthly boys' night. I'm not sure if she truly wanted me to go, or if she was just growing tired of Gage's constant begging. Either way, I am here, and plan on returning to my Surrey estate first thing in the morning.

My brothers, along with Josh, arrived at Dunmorrow Castle a little after five p.m. and were shown straight to the games room. The games room is an oxymoron if ever I've seen one, rustic yet contemporary, dark yet light. Antique carved wood panelling lines three of the four walls, and a full-sized domed aquarium has been built into the fourth. The ocean-blue light that is emitted reflects onto the wood panelling. That along with the movement in the tank gives the illusion of being submerged underwater.

Malachi, being Malachi, has the mammoth tank filled with only the rarest fish, from the pink and blue striped candy basslet to the masked angelfish and Neptune grouper. Amongst his prized beauties are less attractive yet still rare fish that swim in a synchronised shoal.

"Bloody hell, this is embarrassing," Gage complains, pulling my attention from the aquarium and back to the poker table. "Not only is Malachi winning, but he's wiping the floor with my arse." Gage's eyes widen as he takes in Malachi's hand.

A royal flush.

Malachi claims his winnings. "Good game," he says, clapping Gage on the shoulder.

Rather than watch my brother stack his chips, I turn my attention to Kevin, Malachi's very tall, very greying butler. He busies himself filling drinks and handing out cigars. He's doing a fine job seeing as no one's glass is empty and there isn't a single person in the room who isn't puffing on one of Malachi's imported Gurkha Black Dragons.

"Take the shot already. I have money to win back," Josh says, pulling my attention to the table.

Gage raises his hands in mock surrender before taking the shot of whiskey positioned in front of him. With unsteady hands he knocks it back. No sooner has the glass been placed down on the green felt than it is taken away and refilled.

The stakes are high, and as well as the many thousands of pounds we gamble away, at the end of each game the losers take a shot. We play into the early hours, only forfeiting when we're out of chips or we're too inebriated to form a coherent sentence.

"Bets in, ladies," Malachi says, referring to the blinds that two of the players make before any cards have been dealt. On cue, Gage and I push a handful of multicoloured chips into the centre of the table.

Straight-faced and the most sober of the group, Malachi begins to shuffle. He sighs heavily, as though he is somehow inconvenienced, before dealing two cards face down to each of us.

"How's the estate agency going?" Gage asks, lifting his cards to peer at what lies beneath.

"It's going great," Josh answers for me, his attention, like Gage's, trained on his cards. From his stoic expression it is impossible to tell what he is thinking. My cousin has one hell of a poker face, and without so much as a word he pushes his cards into the middle of the table. "Fold," he says, and takes another shot.

Leaning forward, I lift the corners of my cards. Two of clubs, seven of hearts. The hearts begin to float around on their pristine white background and it's now that I decide to call it a night. I have an early morning and I can't afford to spend it nursing a hangover. It's time to gracefully bow out. I grab my shot and knock it back. "Fold."

With Malachi and Gage's focus on the game I decide now is as good a time as any to answer my brother's previous question. "Everything at the estate agency is going swimmingly. It may just be the advantage I need to secure the housebuilding company."

Although I speak to Gage, my snarky comment is aimed at Malachi. My hope is that it'll annoy him just enough to throw him off his game and put an end to his winning streak. Malachi's brows draw together, and there is a flash of anger in his gaze. Our eye contact lasts seconds before he cracks his neck and returns his attention to the game.

Conversations continue, and Malachi wins yet another hand. I sit quietly and drum my fingers on the table.

"Another game?" Malachi asks, back to shuffling the deck.

I flash a glance at the time and notice it's after one. "Not for me, I'm afraid, old boy," I say and nod curtly at Kevin, silently requesting a Scotch. Requesting a Scotch is code for forfeiting any subsequent games.

Josh's eyes are drawn to his chips, or lack of. "Make it two," he calls.

I glance at Malachi. Glowering at me, he flips a red chip around in his left hand. "Hurry up and leave the table so that the men can play."

"Men?" I place my hand over my brow and, making a visor, glance around the room. "Let me know when you see any."

I dodge to the left as a flash of blue comes hurtling my way.

I'm not sure who threw the chip, but notice Josh is quick to reach down and claim the five-thousand-pound chip as his own.

"That's mine," Gage scoffs.

"Finders, keepers."

Kevin places my glass of Scotch in front of me. I take it and leave the room. Josh and Gage's heated words ricochet off the walls as I make my way through the corridors.

I pass the kitchen, the lounge, and stop briefly when I reach the ballroom. Why anyone would want a ballroom in this day and age is beyond me. Malachi, the indulgent ass, surrounds himself with the very best—countesses, earls, and viscounts. I see my big brother one day marrying a princess of some description, a duchess, a marchioness, or an heiress. A bunch of stuck-up socialites in my opinion.

I pass the ballroom and head for the study. On entering, I take up my usual position beside the marble fireplace. Handcrafted, the fireplace holds engraved images of scripts and angels' faces. It's a little peculiar if one were to ask me, but seeing as though nobody has, I keep my thoughts to myself.

Gertrude, Malachi's larger-than-life bulldog, is splayed out on a black leather sofa, her mouth partially open. I admit that I'm a fan of our four-legged friends, but Gertrude, God love her, is a ghastly, ill-tempered creature, with teeth that are far too big for her mouth and a rather peculiar lopsided face. But despite her disagreeable personality and hideous appearance, Malachi adores her. I make my way over to the dog, patting her head once before sitting in the empty space at her side. Opening her left eye, she peers up at me and lets out a guttural growl.

"Love you too, old girl," I say. Standing, I retake my place beside the fireplace. It isn't long before Josh enters the room.

"Blast, there goes another ten thousand big ones down the toilet," he scoffs, sidling up to me.

I shrug. "You shouldn't gamble with what you can't afford."

Or, more specifically, he shouldn't spend money he's 'borrowed' from me.

Josh loops his thumbs in his trouser braces, tugging at the elastic. "I just need to win a big hand, and then I can pay you back everything I've borrowed."

Gambling is the Devil's pleasure. And once you've been taken captive in its hold it's hard to break free. Josh has a major gambling addiction, and instead of letting him go to a bookie's or casino, we allow him to join us for our poker nights. I sub him ten thousand, which unbeknown to Josh is returned to me from the winnings at the end of the evening. I wouldn't call what my brothers and I do encouraging Josh to gamble—we're merely managing it within a controlled environment.

"So," Josh pipes up, a little too eagerly. "How are the chances looking of us acquiring Calloway Housebuilders?"

"Us?" I let the single syllable roll off my tongue. "The word 'us' suggests it will be evenly shared. I have offered you fifty percent of the profits made from the estate agency, but Calloway Housebuilders is mine."

Disappointment shines brightly in his eyes, and I want so much to hand him half of the company. But sharing is just not in my nature, especially something that has been passed down in the family from my grandfather. No, the housebuilding company has always been and will always remain in the Calloway name.

"Yes, I know that." Josh runs his fingers shakily through his hair. "But if you don't get the housebuilding company, then what use is Calloway Estate Agency? I can't run fifty percent of a business that doesn't exist."

A smile tugs at my lips, but I keep it at bay. "You're right, cousin. If I fail to acquire the housebuilding company, then I will rebrand the estate agency into a confectionery shop. We will sell everything from toffees to sticks of rock. The list is endless."

Josh's face sours. "That isn't funny. Natasha will never take me seriously if I'm running a bloody sweet shop."

I clap Josh on the shoulder. "Whatever business I acquire, I will theme the shop accordingly. The cruise ship business, for example—the shop would be a travel agency that will feature the Calloway Cruises. I will do the same with Calloway Hotels—the shop would feature our UK-based hotels for staycations."

"You have it all figured out," Josh muses.

I nod curtly. "Of course I do. I'm a Calloway, and no matter what, I always have a backup plan."

Josh nods, seemingly happy with my answer. "And I'll get fifty percent of the shop's profits?"

The desperation is deep-rooted in his voice, which has me turning my full attention to him. It hasn't gone unnoticed how drawn my cousin looks, the dark circles that encompass his eyes. Nor has it gone unnoticed that Josh has worn the exact same suit at least half a dozen times over the past few weeks. Just because he has chosen to accessorise with trouser braces does not hide the faded blue material of his jacket or the badly re-stitched buttons. I want to ask him how things are financially, but financial hardship has always been a frowned-upon subject.

"I've had a change of heart," I drawl, my words filled with boredom.

"Why?" Josh asks.

"I no longer have any interest in the shop or the building in Cornwall. Frankly it is a waste of my valuable time."

Josh pales and, squeezing his hands into fists, he shoves them into his pockets. "So just like that you're selling up? What about my share? Lucian, you can't do this."

"I can, and I am. The shop and the building." I pause, relishing in the look of sheer panic on my cousin's face. But I won't keep him agonising for long, and, clearing my throat, I continue. "They're yours."

Josh's mouth goes wide. "Lucian—"

I raise my hand. "Under the proviso that Chelsea and her

roomie Tyler are still able to rent the apartment upstairs and that the shop is to remain in keeping with the business I acquire."

My hope is that Chelsea will not return, but I can't rule it out. If life has taught me anything it is to always be prepared for any eventuality.

Josh nods, tears filling his eyes. "I accept, I accept."

If I'm not mistaken, I'd say my cousin is close to hugging me. Though my actions aren't entirely selfless. I simply do not have the time to take on any more business endeavours. As long as the shop remains in keeping with the Calloway brand, I am giving my cousin a full-time income. If he plays his cards right, he will be set up for life, and everybody wins.

"Is that everything?" he asks.

I rotate the glass in my hand and swirl the liquid lazily around before speaking. "If Chelsea's roomie returns from overseas I want you to offer him the job of shop manager."

"Done." Josh practically charges me and grabs me into a bear hug.

My body instantly goes tense and I wriggle to get out of his hold. "Honestly, it's nothing. I told you from day one that I wasn't interested in retail, or the building for that matter. I have what I want." I slowly begin to relax as my mind takes me to the blonde-haired vixen who will undoubtedly be lying in my bed this very second.

"Lucian—" Josh looks fit to burst.

"You're welcome." I keep my tone blasé.

"Are we interrupting you, ladies?"

I look up as Malachi and Gage enter the room. Josh releases me and, wiping his nose with the back of his hand, sniffs. "Lucian, my favourite cousin, has just given me the shop in Cornwall."

"Favourite cousin?" Gage says, placing his hand over his heart. "That hurt."

As much as I enjoy the back-and-forth between my cousin and brother, I have something, or rather someone, more pressing on my mind. My hope is I can catch her before she goes to sleep and spend a bit of time exchanging some flirty text messages. I plan to tell her in the most ungentlemanly fashion all the ways I want to fuck her. I may even go as far as throwing in some colloquialisms and light cursing. The girls seem to like it when I talk dirty, and who am I to disappoint?

"I really do have an early morning." Tipping my head, I finish my Scotch in one swig and place the empty glass on the fireplace. "Gentlemen," I say out of politeness.

I'm about to walk through the door when Malachi stands directly in front of me, blocking my way. "I spoke to Father earlier today. He told me he offered to sign Calloway Housebuilders over to you on Tuesday evening, but you refused. And now you're giving Josh the property and shop in Cornwall. This would have nothing to do with you surrendering your stake?"

"What does he mean?" Josh asks, clearly eavesdropping. I don't answer my cousin and instead keep my gaze trained on Malachi.

"No, brother, I am not forfeiting my claim on Calloway Housebuilders. I have just refused to marry Samantha."

Malachi studies me for a beat. "Even if marrying her earns you the company? I don't understand you, Lucian. You've had your sights set on that company since you were a boy. Why the sudden change of mind?"

"More a change of heart. You see, I've found something, or rather someone, whom I want with equal measure, and I am determined to get both." I lean in close. "You should know by now that I don't give up without a fight."

Malachi's face twitches, and I make a point of squinting. "Heaven forbid, don't tell me that's a trace of a smile I see? Anyone would think you have an actual beating heart beneath that stone chest and icy façade."

I shoulder past my brother and exit the study. I'm halfway up the stairs when my brother calls after me. "Lucian."

I turn around. "Malachi."

He takes a step forward and stops inches before the foot of the stairs. "I know you think you have some kind of penance to pay with Josh. But this has got to stop. By constantly helping him you're becoming a crutch."

"Some kind of penance? He was at my bedside while I was in the coma, and he was there with me through every step of my recovery. Where were you?"

Malachi rubs his hand over his beard. "I was at work, running the family business, where I needed to be."

"My point exactly." I'm about to turn my back on him when he clears his throat.

"By day I was working, and by night I was sat at your bedside while Josh went home to get some rest. I lived on coffee and stayed awake for the three days solid while you were in the coma, only grabbing the odd nap between meetings."

A lump forms in my throat, because I know how hard Malachi worked in the offices. He would be the first to arrive and the last to leave, often taking paperwork home with him that he would be sifting through well into the evening.

"I admit I wasn't there during your recovery, but that was only because Father sent me to Inverness to view a potential plot of land."

My being in a coma would have been an inconvenience to my father, who has always been a stiff-upper-lip and business-as-usual type of man. But despite his lack of emotion, he didn't send Malachi to Inverness until I had woken from the coma. I would like to think that this was no mere coincidence because as uncaring as Father portrays himself to be, I know he cares in his own way.

My father's true motives will remain a mystery, but that doesn't matter right now. What matters is that Malachi was there for me, he was sitting at my bedside when I needed him. I walk down a few steps and attempt to close the distance between us, at which my brother steps back. That's right, we're Calloways, we don't express emotion. I stop walking and keep my feet firmly rooted to the spot.

"Why didn't you tell me? Why did you let Josh take all the glory?"

Malachi shrugs. "Because glory was what Josh was seeking. Whereas I? I never wanted a thank you or any credit. I just wanted my little brother to wake up from his coma. That was all that mattered to me."

My eyes burn with emotion. I want nothing more than to charge toward my brother and pull him into a bear hug the way Josh did previously. The problem is years of expectation and conformity have cast an invisible forcefield around us and all I'm able to do in this moment is to meet his gaze. My eyes are saying all the words that I will never say aloud.

"Malachi," I say, and rub my hand over the sleeve of my suit jacket. "I—"

"I know," is his curt reply, and by that the subject matter is closed. Although we will never speak of this again, I shall certainly never forget.

"Is that all?" I ask, knowing the conversation is over, but feeling like there is more my brother wants to say.

"I was wrong." He grits out the words. I'm about to ask him to repeat his admission when he carries on. "Wrong about Chelsea. I watched you both today, the way you looked at each other. I see now that you do have something special. And, despite my initial reservations, you have my approval."

Although his approval is unneeded, it feels good to have it. "Thanks, Mal."

He rocks on his heels several times before jerking his head back in the direction from which he came. "I better go. I can't very well expect Josh and Gage to remain in the study without the host."

I smile at Malachi, and nearly fall down the stairs when he

smiles back—a big, open-mouthed smile. Just like that his smile dissolves into nothing. He takes his leave, and I take mine.

I take the stairs two at a time, pull my phone from my pocket and write Chelsea a text that would have any girl blushing. I re-read the text one final time, then finish the message with a promise. A promise that at the end of our month together, she will be mine.

CHAPTER TWENTY-SEVEN

Chelsea

My head is throbbing when I wake up the next morning. I partly have Farrah to blame for taking me to the fair last night. It was last night I discovered I get terrible vertigo from spinning. It was a pity I didn't discover this fact about myself *before* Farrah dragged me onto the waltzers. Needless to say, the ground was still moving long after the ride had stopped, and Dante had to carry me to the car.

I woke up around three a.m. to a ream of naughty texts from Lucian. By that time I was wide awake and began texting him back. We sent texts back and forth well into the early hours and I didn't get back to sleep until after six a.m.

Stretching, I let out an exaggerated yawn. I side-eye the digital clock on the nightstand. Ten-thirty flashes in bold red. I sit up with a start and jump out of bed. Not because I have anything I need to do, but I asked Tim to have Jupiter in the paddock ready for an early start. My hope is that we can get her saddle on today—it's a little ambitious, I know. If we don't get the saddle on, we can at least get her used to seeing me wearing the riding gear and the riding equipment lying around.

After a shower, I get changed into a pair of navy breeches,

matching hunt coat, and tall black boots. I sure look the part of a confident rider. Now I just have to convince Jupiter and gain her trust. After looking myself over in the mirror, I make my way downstairs.

The smell of freshly baked bread fills my senses as I walk down the corridor, and I will myself to continue toward the orangery to the gardens. It would seem my legs have other ideas and take me straight to the kitchen. My stomach rumbles loudly as I enter. Mrs Collins is standing behind a large oak table. She smiles in acknowledgement as she kneads dough.

"Go sit down. I'll bring you something to eat shortly," she says, rolling the dough into a ball.

I still can't get used to having people wait on me hand and foot. "It's okay, I can make myself a sandwich." I head toward the pantry. The doors are open, displaying the many shelves of preserves, spices, pasta and vegetables.

Heavy footfalls follow me, and fingers covered in flour wrap around my wrist. "You will do no such thing. Lucian will have my guts for garters."

I smile at Mrs Collins, who has a kind grandmother vibe about her. She is a small, well-built lady with bright rosy cheeks. Her grey hair is secured in a hair net, though a few strands are loose and fall around her face in tight spirals.

"Honestly, I don't mind," I say, but she refuses to listen and insists on making me something to eat. I take this moment to fish out the cleaning products from the cupboard directly below the sink. While I get to work cleaning the worktops, Mrs Collins butters two thick slices of granary bread. I listen intently as she tells me about her dear grandchildren: Molly, who's eight, and Paisley, who's nine. Although I smile, I can't help the sadness that runs through me thinking about my niece, Freja, and Lizzie's young children. I'm only here for a month, but I'll be missing out on so much during that time.

"There you go, sweetheart," Mrs Collins says, sliding a plate my way.

"Wrap it up, June."

I jump on hearing a gruff male voice from behind and turn to see Josh standing in the open doorway.

"Chelsea will be joining me in the gardens."

"Is everything okay?" I ask, peering around him to see where Lucian is. I'm sure he said that he and his cousin would be returning together.

"I'm afraid not. That is what I want to discuss with you."

While I replace the cleaning products back in the cupboard, Mrs Collins wraps a thin layer of foil around the sandwich and passes it to me. I thank her and push the sandwich into my jacket pocket.

I follow quickly behind Josh, who heads straight to the orangery and to the door leading out of the house. The strong scent of pollen attacks my senses as we pass the flower beds. I follow Josh through the tree-lined walkway, past the rattan chair set I sat on with Farrah the day of her arrival, and on. It isn't until I look back that I realise how far we have come. I stop walking and look around.

"Josh," I call, to which he stops. He turns to face me. His usually pristine hair falls unkempt around his face, his suit is creased and his shirt appears to be missing a few buttons. Heat blossoms at my brow, and my heartbeat begins to pick up pace. "Is Lucian okay?" I ask, though this time panic fills my voice. All I can think of is why isn't he here with Josh?

"Lucian is fine," Josh says. "When I woke up early this morning, he was still asleep."

I smile to myself, knowing I may have had something to do with that.

"Instead of waking him I decided to go ahead. The helicopter is on the way back to Scotland to pick him up when he's ready."

I let out a deep and calming breath. I allow my heartbeat to slow. "My God, Josh, you had me worried something was wrong."

I let out a laugh, but Josh's stoic expression remains unchanged.

"This isn't a laughing matter, Chelsea. Something is wrong, and that something is you."

My brows shoot up and, frowning, I wrap my arms around my waist. "Me?"

Josh takes a step forward, to which I step back. He reaches out and places his open palm on my shoulder. "Samantha was most upset yesterday given that Lucian wouldn't engage in conversation with her during her tour of Freesdon Hall."

"That's a pity." I try to sound sincere but fail.

"I know my cousin is smitten with you, Chelsea, but it's time to drop the act. Duncan will not give Lucian Calloway Housebuilders while he stays in this fake relationship with you. You've had your fun, lived in a billionaire's mansion and enjoyed the lifestyle. But now it's time to stop with the act and go back to reality because it's over."

None of this is pretend, I want to shout in his face, but instead keep my emotions tucked away in their vault. My emotions are all I have. By letting them go I'm giving up my control, and that is something I refuse to do.

"Lucian and I have already had this conversation. We both agree there is more to life than money." I stand taller. "So it would seem as though you've had a wasted journey. Aside from that, Lucian has asked me to be his fiancée for real."

Josh takes a step away and studies me. "Did he now?"

"He did, and not that it's any of your business, but I am considering saying yes."

Josh's jaw tightens, but he doesn't speak. I consider the conversation to be over, so I spin on my heel and head in the opposite direction toward the paddock when he calls after me. "I'll go to the press."

My body comes to an immediate halt, and I turn. Josh is continuing toward me. "I'm really sorry. I didn't want to have to do this," he continues whilst looking a million shades of smug. "I'm a close friend of Darren Moore. I'm sure the readers of *Cornwall Gossip* would love to hear all about Lucian paying you to be his fake fiancée. He will be made a laughing stock and you a whore. That isn't the kind of publicity a beauty salon owner wants, and as for Lucian, it will not just damage his career and credibility, but destroy it."

His words hit me like a thousand missiles. "You're bluffing."

"I never bluff. I have had several conversations with Darren in the past and may have played a part in the Samantha Matthews publication."

My eyes go wide. I remember that article well—it was a patronising and derogatory piece that portrayed Lucian as a womaniser who is incompetent at his job. "How could you?"

"She was a distraction. He needed to move on and get over her. The article was the only way for him to get his head out of the clouds and back to the family business. Though I must admit that article was a bad move, as I didn't know Samantha's estranged uncle was a gazillionaire."

I swallow the lump building in my throat. "Lucian's your cousin."

"Yes, I'm merely looking out for his best interests, and my own."

"I love him," I choke out.

"Then you'll let him go." Josh takes a deep breath. "You will tell Lucian you don't love him and you want to put an end to this ridiculous fake relationship. Do you understand?"

I don't answer, I just stand staring, waiting for Josh to laugh, to tell me this is all one big joke.

"I will have Bessie help you pack so you can return to Cornwall before Lucian gets home. As of today, I am your new landlord, but please don't worry about this month's rent. I expect you will need some time to readjust to your normal way of life."

His words strike me deep in my chest, so deep that they feel as though they've pierced through my heart and I'm bleeding out right in front of him.

"I release you from this contract," he says, with a wry smile. A smile that is telling me that I'm free from the shackles of this fake engagement.

A smile that is telling me to have a good life, though a life without Lucian doesn't seem bearable.

"You will receive the money for your services in due time."

My services. I sniff and fight harder to hold back my tears. "I don't want the money, not a single penny."

"Very well," Josh says, and leads the way to the house. My head and body feel disconnected as I follow him toward the building. With his back toward me, it's now I allow the tears to fall. One by one they roll silently down my cheeks. Each step I take toward the house marks a step away from Lucian. The man I love. I love him, and that is the reason I need to leave.

I straighten my hunched shoulders and wipe away my tears. *I am doing this for Lucian,* I tell myself. My foot lands on the step leading into the orangery, and I stop walking. I turn my head and from the corner of my eye make out the paddock. I can't see Jupiter from here, but know she's there.

"Chelsea?" Josh asks, and holds out his hand for me to take. I glower at his hand. He wants me out of the house and far enough away when Lucian returns, giving himself time to convince Lucian that my leaving is the right thing, the only thing to do in this situation.

I take a step back. "Go ahead. There is someone I need to say goodbye to."

"Breathe a word of this to Farrah, and you will see my wrath. Push me, Chelsea, and I will be cruel. The rent on your flat will be doubled and Eve, Royston and Tyler will lose their jobs."

My eyes narrow into thin slits. "Farrah isn't here, you jerk."

"Perfect. I will tell her the news of you leaving when she returns. Now, don't dally."

I nod my head in the direction of the paddock. "I want to say goodbye to Jupiter."

Josh pulls his phone from his trouser pocket and gazes down at the time on the screen. "Okay, but make it quick. I have arranged for McKenzie to take you back."

I raise my hand. "I've had enough of you telling me what to do. I'll pack my own bags, and I'll leave when I'm ready to go. Now, if you don't mind, I'm going to say goodbye to a horse I'm very fond of."

My hair whips behind me as I turn, and without a backward glance I head toward the paddock.

Birdsong follows me as I hurry along the well-trodden path. I look around me and take everything in. Everything is so beautiful, so green, and so big. I will miss this place, the grounds, Farrah, the staff, and above all, I will miss Lucian. Miss the time we spent together, miss the feel of his arms around me.

"Chelsea!" Tim calls, and hurries toward me.

I nod. "Tim."

I continue walking when Tim has caught up with me, and he walks backwards, matching my quickening steps forward. "You'll never guess what," he says, his eyes bright and alive with excitement.

"What?" I didn't realise how quickly I'm walking, nor how tightly I'm squeezing my hands into fists.

"Don't ask me how, but I managed to get the saddle on Jupiter."

I stop walking instantly. "You can't drop a bombshell like that and expect me not to ask questions."

Tim tugs at a strand of his hair. "I can't help it if Jupiter likes me better."

I slug his arm harder than I had intended.

"Ow!" Tim rubs his arm.

I slap my hand over my mouth. "I'm sorry, I didn't mean to—"

"It's fine," Tim cuts me off. "It's the carrots. Jupiter loves them. It seemed to distract her long enough that I was able to slip the saddle right on. The problem is that I ran out, and I was making my way to the house to get some more."

My throat burns with emotion. This is huge. After all these years, Jupiter is finally wearing a saddle.

"Carry on back to the house," I tell Tim. "I'll wait for you in the paddock."

Tim nods. "Now don't get any crazy ideas like riding her. She isn't ready for that just yet."

I laugh, but when Tim hurries past me I consider his words. Everything around me is spiralling out of control—my life, my future and my emotions. As a girl whenever I overheard my parents arguing, the next day I would beg my mother to let me ride. Riding was a way of finding my calm, of regaining some control.

I walk with quickening steps toward the paddock. My sight is set on Jupiter, who stands grazing on the vibrant green grass, and as Tim had promised, she has the saddle secured on her back. A saddle that has my name written all over it.

I enter the enclosure and keep a confident gait as I approach. Her head is down as she grazes on the carpet of grass below, but her eyes are focused on me. Our eye contact is unbroken as I close the distance between us. She doesn't bolt, doesn't back away, and an air of calm settles around us as she stands watching me.

"Thatagirl," I say, and when she raises her head, I place my palm on the bridge of her nose. I stand in silence for a beat to gauge her response. I haven't been this close to her before, and I know if she's going to bolt, it'll be now. To my surprise, she remains calm as her copper mane is whisked up in the gentle breeze.

From the bridge of her nose, I work my palm slowly across her jaw, down her neck, and onto her shoulder.

Jupiter isn't wild, and I don't think she's dangerous. Maybe it's reckless of me to try to mount her, but right now I just need this escape.

I drop the stirrup so it is easier to reach. I grab her mane with one hand and grip the saddle with the other. With my foot placed in the stirrup, I pull myself up.

I sit tall for a few seconds and take everything in. I am sitting on a horse who is deemed out of control, who hasn't had anyone astride her for over a decade. Today is monumental and I would hate to push her too far.

"Good girl," I whisper. I'm about to slide down when Josh catches my attention. He is running toward the paddock waving his arms frantically in the air.

"Chelsea, are you bloody insane? Get down this instant!" His voice is high-pitched and verges on erratic as he nears.

The air of calm that surrounded us moments ago is starting to evaporate. Jupiter's relaxed stance goes rigid, and the rate of her breathing intensifies.

"Josh, stop," I call, but it's too late. He continues to bark at me to dismount, waving his arms wildly as he runs toward us.

Jupiter neighs loudly. Seeing as she isn't wearing a bridle, I have no reins to hold onto and instead grab for her mane, but the coarse hairs slip right through my fingers as she bucks beneath me. I'm jolted forward and then back before I'm thrown to the ground.

Colours bleed into each other as the world around me spins. Josh's face comes into view for a split second before everything goes black.

CHAPTER TWENTY-EIGHT

Chelsea

I wake up to the high-pitched sound of beeping. I open my eyes only for my vision to be flooded with bright light, so bright that I have to hold my hand over my eyes to give myself time to adjust.

"Thank God." I hear a male voice to my right, a male voice that sounds remarkably like Lucian's. I lift my head, about to crack open my fingers to peer between them when my hand is pulled from my face. I squint as the bright light once again fills my vision and it takes a few seconds for my eyes to adjust. Slowly everything around me begins to take shape.

I'm lying in bed in a white room. Machines beep all around me, and an IV has been taped to the back of my hand with a needle going directly into a vein.

I have so many questions, but all I can focus on is the needle. I'm about to yank it out when Lucian takes both of my hands in his. "Leave it, the doctor said you need fluids."

I pull one of my hands free and rub my head, which is aching. I flinch immediately when my finger makes contact with some kind of dressing. "Where am I?" I ask.

"In hospital." Lucian takes a control and presses a button that lifts the top part of the bed into a sitting position. When my back is vertical, he plumps the pillow behind my head.

"I know that," I say, and make a sweeping motion with my arm. "Where?"

"In a private wing at St Anthony's."

I flash a glance around the room for a second time and take in the sheer size.

Lucian releases my hand and from the inside pocket of his jacket pulls out a small container. "Don't tell the nurses, but I snuck you in Mrs Collins' freshly made turkey salad." He stands and pulls out a tray that he positions directly over my lap.

"Why am I here?" I ask, trying to think back, but everything is fuzzy.

Lucian lifts the lid of the container and goes on to pour me a drink of orange juice. "I was hoping that was something you could tell me." This time when his gaze meets mine, I see a flash of anger on his face.

I rub my head for a second time and wince again when my fingers connect with the dressing. "I don't remember…"

"Please allow me to refresh your memory," Lucian says, and retakes his seat. "I told you Jupiter was dangerous, and I told you not to ride her without saddle-breaking her first for six months. I said then and only then she could be ridden by me and only me. You could have been killed today. What the hell were you thinking?"

"I, er…" I rub my head again and wince for a third time. I think back and remember waking up this morning and joining Mrs Collins in the kitchen. After that it's a little fuzzy.

"If Josh hadn't found you when he did, who knows what would have happened."

Josh.

Now I remember everything.

I remember the conversation I had with Josh in the estate gardens. I remember heading to the paddock and how easily I was able to climb onto Jupiter's back. It was as though she didn't even feel me as I got comfortable in the saddle. I remember leaning forward and telling her she was a good girl, all whilst running my fingers through her coarse mane. The next thing I remember is Josh running toward me, yelling for me to get down. And that was it. Josh spooked Jupiter and she bucked beneath me. My gravity shifted, and I fell.

"What were you thinking?" Lucian asks for a second time. "You didn't even have a helmet on."

"I, I…" My words hitch in my throat as the door leading into my room opens and two doctors walk in.

Lucian stands immediately and nods. "Gentlemen."

They exchange pleasantries before the two men approach the bed. "Hello, Miss Janssen. I'm Dr. Connors, and this is my assistant, Dr. Davis. You'll be pleased to know that after the preliminary checks we carried out everything looks as it should. We're going to keep you overnight for observation, and all being well you'll be discharged in the morning."

Home.

I zone out of the conversation and consider what that word really means to me. Home is the place I feel happy, the place I belong. For the first time since I was a child, I don't feel as though I belong anywhere, to anything or anyone.

"Thank you, Doctors." Lucian shakes both men's hands, and they leave the room. He retakes the seat beside me and stares down at his phone screen.

I lean forward to see what he is looking at when he angles the phone away from me. "What are you doing?" I ask.

Lucian lets out a sigh and lowers his hand, and with it his phone. "I am emailing a plastic surgeon whom my father plays golf with. Now I don't want you to be alarmed, but it is a nasty cut you have to your head. I just want to see what availability he has, should you decide to—"

I shake my head vehemently. "I am not having plastic surgery."

Our gazes connect, and it's now I look at him, really look at him. His face is drawn and his eyes are bloodshot, but as red as his eyes are, his gaze still holds a warmth I feel right down to my core. I love this man, I love him so much that I can't sit back and watch him lose everything he has worked so hard for.

I open my mouth, the words on the tip of my tongue, when Lucian jumps up from his seat and covers my lips with his. The kiss feels so good, soft yet demanding, passionate yet angry. His whole body trembles, and he snakes his hand around my head and pulls me closer.

"I'm sorry I yelled at you," he breathes into the kiss. "I thought... Jesus, I thought I lost you."

My eyes snap open, and I don't see Lucian as a cocky billionaire with the world at his feet. I see him as a man, a man who was close to losing all he holds dear, and that scares the hell out of him and that scares the hell out of me.

This is every little girl's fairytale ending, the part where they live happily ever after. But I am not a Disney princess, and this is not my story. Sure, I am a brief chapter in Lucian's life, but a chapter that needs to come to an end. I pull back. His lips fight to hold their claim on mine before he releases me.

"Lucian," I whisper, his face only inches from mine. His eyes snap open, and I'm lost in a vision of emerald green. I want to tell him everything that happened today and what a snake his cousin is. But if I do, Josh will ruin him.

What choice do I have?

"Yes, Chelsea?"

Lucian leans forward and waits for my reply, but I'm completely lost for words.

"You're exhausted." Lucian pulls the tray to the side so it is no longer over my lap and grabs the bedside remote. "Please don't let me stop you from going to sleep." He leans back in his seat, and I gather he is trying to get comfortable. "I have some emails that require my attention, not forgetting that I need to catch up with Christine, my PA, but I'll be quiet. Most importantly, I'll be here when you wake up."

No, you won't, and you never will again.

I force a smile as the top part of the bed is lowered and I am once again lying down. I force a smile though my heart is breaking in my chest, and I force a smile knowing what it is I have to do.

I open my mouth, about to speak, when Lucian's phone starts to vibrate.

He swipes his finger across the screen and holds it up to his ear. "Josh, your ears must have been burning. We were just talking about you."

I shut my eyes, and fist the sheet. Of all people to call, of course it would be Josh. No doubt he was hoping I was seriously injured or worse.

"Thanks to you, she's doing well. I cannot thank you enough—"

"Cut the call," I croak out. Lucian seemingly hasn't heard me as he continues chatting to Josh.

"I'm sure she'd be happy to speak to you, but make it quick. She's about to get some rest."

I crack open an eye, and sure enough, Lucian is holding the phone for me to take. All I can see is Josh looming closer, and all I can hear are the threats he made. My body begins to tremble as I recoil and push Lucian's hand away. "Didn't you hear me? I said cut the damn call."

My heart hurts knowing Lucian will remember the final moments we spent together were of me snapping at him.

Without question, Lucian cuts the call. "Forgive me, I wasn't thinking. You need rest."

He pushes his phone into his trouser pocket and then crouches down to place a kiss on my lips, though before his lips make contact with mine I turn my head to the side. As his lips linger on my cheek my stomach knots and a pain like no other courses through my body. I'm trembling—no, shaking in his hold because my whole world is shattering and there isn't a single thing I can do to stop it.

His lips leave my cheek, and I can feel him leaning over me. His breaths glide over my face in warm waves. I know he's close, and it's for that reason I can't bring myself to meet his gaze.

"Is everything okay?" he asks.

No, and it never will be again.

"It's over," I whisper as I force myself to make eye contact with him.

Lucian frowns and leans a little closer. "I'm sorry, I didn't catch that."

"It's over," I say with more certainty. My eyes burn from the tears I am keeping back. Whatever happens, I won't allow him to see me cry.

"This? Us? We are not over because, my dear, we haven't even begun."

I sit up on my elbows, trying to exude a little confidence. "But it's going to end eventually. What about our arrangement?"

"Fuck the arrangement." Lucian's voice cracks. "You are mine and you are going nowhere. Do you hear me, Chelsea Janssen? You are mine." He stands tall and dusts his jacket down. "You've had a nasty fall; you aren't thinking clearly—"

He may have heard, but he hasn't listened to a single thing I have said. I could try telling him again, but what good would that do?

"Why don't you get some rest while I pop back to my Surrey estate to pick up some of your things?"

"Okay, Lucian."

Lucian leaving isn't the worst idea. But I can't watch him walk out of the door, and out of my life, so I turn my head and look in the opposite direction.

All I hear is the soft tap of his footfalls and the click of the door as it shuts behind him. I sink back in the bed and allow myself this small window of time to grieve.

"Goodbye, Lucian."

CHAPTER TWENTY-NINE

Lucian

I'm in our bedroom packing a small overnight bag. Our conversation in the hospital room plays over and over in my mind. I have to remind myself Chelsea received a nasty blow to the head and wasn't in the right frame of mind, and it's for this reason that I deemed it best to give her space. But try as I might, I can't shift this feeling of unease I have growing in the pit of my stomach. I start off by folding each item of clothing neatly, but it isn't long until I'm throwing them into the bag

When her bag is packed, I make my way out of the house to where the Mercedes is parked. I slide onto the back seat. McKenzie's gaze meets mine in the rear-view mirror.

"Back to the hospital, Mr Calloway?"

"Please, but can you hurry?"

The closer we get to St Anthony's the more uneasy I feel. I may be to blame for two speed cameras that flash and the red light McKenzie drives through. I will feel a lot more at ease when I am sitting back at her side.

I jump out of the car before McKenzie has parked, and once inside the hospital I hurriedly make my way to Chelsea's room.

The bed is empty, and a nurse is changing the sheets in readiness for the next patient.

I count to ten, trying to remind myself I'm a Calloway, and as a Calloway I should never make a scene, but it's no use. I lose my temper and make a loud and very public scene when I call the staff incompetent for allowing Chelsea to discharge herself. From the hospital there is only one place she could be. Despite being given wealth and riches and the keys to my goddamn castle it's no good, for my little bird has returned to her cage.

A cage I own!

With McKenzie driving, we arrive in Heller St Claire a little after six. I jump out of the car and pass Calloway Estate Agency just as Eve is locking up. She meets my gaze and, much like a soldier, stands to attention.

"Mr Calloway. I cannot thank you enough for this job and opportunity," she begins.

"You're welcome," I say and hurry past her to the side door leading up to the flat.

"If you're looking for Chelsea, you won't find her," Eve calls after me. "She's in America with Tyler."

I turn and offer Eve a curt nod. "I am just checking on the flat," I lie, and, opening the door, make my way up the narrow flight of stairs. I stand outside Chelsea's front door and push my key into the lock. The key won't turn.

I bang on the door. "Open up, I know you're inside."

Silence.

"For God's sake, Chelsea, my key isn't turning which means one of two things. Either your key is in the barrel, or you've had the locks changed. Seeing as Eve is unaware of your return, it would suggest the latter. Now open up."

I've gone from knocking on the door to hammering on it. "If you don't talk to me then I'll be forced to break the bloody door down."

Silence.

I know the girl doesn't like confrontation, but this is ridiculous. "Very well, you've given me no choice." I pull my jacket off, unfasten the shirt buttons at my wrist and roll up my sleeves. I take a few steps back and prepare to charge. Breaking down doors is not the way I would usually conduct myself, but I would tear through bloody mountains just to get to her.

"Please, leave."

I drop my arms to my sides and walk toward the door. I press my palm against the cool wood. "Talk to me. Tell me why you're doing this."

Shadows take shape in the small gap at the bottom of the door and I can hear movement from the other side. I'd like to imagine that she too has her hand pressed against the wood, that despite it acting as a barrier we are connected somehow.

"I'm doing it for you." Her words come out as a sob, and all I want to do is tear the door from its goddamn hinges and pull her into my arms.

"Chelsea—" I press my forehead against the door and watch as something is pushed through the small gap. I bend down and pick up my grandmother's engagement ring. The gold band is still warm, telling me she hasn't long taken it off. I close my fingers around it and bring my fist to my heart.

"Tell me what I did wrong. Tell me how I fix this," I say, wanting, or rather *needing* answers.

"It isn't you."

I roll my eyes at the 'it isn't you, it's me' spiel. "Sorry, Chelsea, but you're going to have to do better than that if you don't want me tearing the door off its hinges or camping out here until you let me in."

"I don't love you, Lucian, and I never will," she calls, and her words stop me dead. "I'm done with pretending. Our arrangement is over."

My shoulders fall, and my mind takes me back to the break-up with Samantha. Samantha broke my heart, but the pain

I felt then doesn't come close to the pain I feel now. My heart hurts, so much so I bring my hand to my chest. I can't breathe, nor can I deal with this much pain.

"I hope you have a good life," I grit out, and stumble down the stairs. I trip as I make my way onto the street. I run across the road and to where the Mercedes is parked. I look to the shop and to the window of the flat above where Chelsea is standing.

She's there for a second before she disappears back into the darkness. I swallow the burning lump in my throat, open the door to the Mercedes and slide in.

McKenzie doesn't start the engine. He looks to the flat and back to me. "Where's Chelsea?"

"It's over," I say and slide my grandmother's engagement ring into the pocket of my trousers. Without another word McKenzie switches on the engine and we head back to my Surrey estate.

My phone vibrates in my pocket, and I feel a glimmer of hope, though the glimmer of hope is slashed when I see Samantha's name displayed on the screen. Damn my father for giving her my contact details, seeing as I had to deal with the inconvenience of changing my number two years ago when we broke up.

I slide my finger across the screen. "Now isn't a good time," I say and hang up.

The drive seems to take longer than usual. It's as though everyone is purposely driving slower so I have more time to wallow in my misery. The white clouds that hang in the sky gradually turn to grey, and large droplets of rain splash down on the windshield.

When the car pulls up outside my Surrey estate, the sky is black and angry with the promise of an impending storm. Rain pelts around me as I make my way to the front door. My white shirt is wet through and clings to me when I step into the hallway. I look around the vast space and realise how empty it is.

I take a deep breath in and get the subtle whiff of her. No matter which room I go in, her scent is all around me. So much so that I have Bessie make up one of the spare rooms for me to sleep in tonight because I can't bear the thought of sleeping in a bed that smells like her.

I had it all—the promise of owning a successful business, the girl, and billions in the bank. But it's irrelevant now. My business is there to make me more money, but money has no value if I don't have someone to enjoy it with.

I make my way to my office, and it's here I find Josh sitting at my desk.

"What are you doing in here?" I ask.

"Waiting for you to return, of course."

I suck in my bottom lip. "It's over, Josh. Chelsea and me, we're over."

I expect Josh to make a comment about our relationship not being real in the first place. But to my surprise, he says nothing and instead pulls out my secret bottle of Scotch I have stashed in the bottom drawer.

"Where would I be without you, cousin?" I ask as Josh fills two glasses.

Josh hands me a glass and raises his to his lips. "I dread to think. I've got your back, Lucian, and I will get you through this the same way I got you through the breakup with Samantha."

We talk and drink for hours. We drink until the bottle is dry and I have to get another from the wine cellar. Josh is asleep face down on my desk when I return. Instead of waking him and escorting him to one of the guest bedrooms, I leave him. I walk from room to room drinking vodka from the bottle.

I take this time to drunkenly ponder my life and wonder where it all went so wrong. Everything was fine until Chelsea decided to ride Jupiter. I squeeze my fingers around the neck of the bottle.

Jupiter.

Without a moment of hesitation, I head out into the gardens. I don't stop walking as the wind howls and rain pelts against my face. I don't stop as lightning lights up the night sky and thunder booms in the distance. I don't stop until I am standing directly in front of Jupiter's stable.

I can make out the horse's silhouette as she makes her way toward me. "You let me down, old girl," I say. Jupiter neighs as thunder booms. "What am I going to do with you? You can't be fixed, can't be saddlebroken. You don't want to be ridden. You don't want me to love you, protect you, or make you happy." I shake my head. "What the hell do you want?"

Jupiter rears back. Flashes of lightning illuminate the stables, and it's now I see the deep-rooted fear in her eyes. It's a look I've seen many times but until now failed to recognise. They say that animals, like humans, grieve. Perhaps she has not yet got over the death of my mother and is scared of getting attached to another rider. Maybe fear is the reason she is the way she is.

I've been so blind.

"Jupiter, I'm sorry," I say and, opening the stable door, make my way inside. She backs off as I approach. I keep walking until I have her cornered and I place my palm on the bridge of her nose. It surprises me how calm she is, though the calmness dissolves when lightning strikes again. I back off, giving her the space she needs.

"You were always terrified of storms," I say, sitting on a large bale of hay. "I remember how Mother would join you in the stables and sing to you for hours. Now I don't have much of a singing voice, but I have a classical playlist saved on my phone you might appreciate."

I pull the device from my trouser pocket. My body shakes from the cold and rainwater drips from my hair onto the screen as I flick through trying to locate the playlist. With shaky hands I click on the first song.

An incoming call flashes on my screen, and Samantha's name appears. I swipe my finger across. "Now isn't a good time," I say, about to cut the call.

"Don't hang up."

I flash a glance at Jupiter and back to my phone. "You have two seconds. Make them count."

"Josh told me you and Chelsea split up."

"It would seem good news travels fast," I muse.

"My thoughts exactly. Now, as to the reason I called. I have great news, Lucian." She pauses, and when I say nothing, she continues. "Okay, I'll come right out and say it. I am the proud owner of Freesdon Hall."

"Great," I say, my tone dripping with boredom.

"I'd really like it if you would help me move in…" Samantha carries on talking, though I no longer listen. They say things happen in threes. So far I've lost my childhood home, I've lost my girl, what next?

"Lucian." She pauses. "There is something important I need to tell you, something that will change everything."

I drum my fingers on my thigh. "I'm waiting,"

"This is something I need to tell you in person. Alone."

"You had plenty of time to talk to me yesterday when I was showing you around Freesdon Hall."

"I tried, but you kept talking over me and walking at a pace I had to run to keep up with."

I can't deal with this, not tonight. "Good night, Samantha." I cut the call and, switching on my playlist, close my eyes.

I wake the following morning when Tim opens the stable door to let Jupiter out into the paddock.

"Rough night?" Tim asks and holds out his hand to help me up.

I take his hand. Once standing, I dust myself down. "Something like that." I make my way out of the stables and en route pull wayward strands of hay from my hair.

"Your phone," Tim calls after me, to which I turn and he passes me the device. It's cold as it rests in the palm of my hand. The screen is blank, indicating my battery has died.

"Thanks, Tim." I push the phone into my trouser pocket and head outside. It's a dull day, and thick dark clouds hang in the sky. My shoes slip on the grass—still damp from last night's storm—as I make my way to the house. Although I've not long woken up, I feel in need of a proper sleep. My head throbs, my eyes are heavy, but more specifically I'm hungover.

I make my way through a side door, passing staff members as I enter the hallway. With my head hanging, I make my way to my bedroom and once inside I stand and look at the bed. A bed in which hours ago lay the woman I love. A woman who doesn't love me. I won't sleep in this room again until the bed and the mattress have been replaced.

I make my way to the walk-in wardrobe for a change of clothes. My eyes are hit with rail after rail of the dresses I bought for Chelsea. I pace forward and back, the hangers creaking against the rail as I run my fingers along the garments. Her scent explodes in the small space around me, causing anger to pool in the pit of my stomach.

Stupid, stupid Lucian, thinking I could buy my way into her affection. Stupid me for thinking that my love for her could be enough. My fingers fist a Dolce and Gabbana dress and I yank the soft material. Hangers and gowns fall to the floor as I pull each one from the railing and make a not-so-neat pile in my wake. I don't stop until the rails are free of every dress, every dress except for one. The white gown my mother designed, the same gown Chelsea wore to the Pink Ribbon Breast Cancer Charity Gala.

My mind takes an unexpected turn, and I wonder what my mother would think if she were here now. I look to the drawer that I always keep locked, because what's inside is too painful. And yet, in the face of true anguish and sorrow, I find myself growing closer. I locate the key hidden in the drawer below, push it into the small brass lock and turn.

The drawer is full of unopened cards and presents I received over the years on my birthday. My brothers stopped giving me gifts when I turned twenty-one, though Josh, the stubborn sod he is, refused to give up. The gift he bought me for my thirtieth lies amongst the pile.

I scan the many different shades of blue wrapping paper, some matt, others gloss, some with ribbons and some without. But the gift I am looking for is very specific.

I make a small pile to one side of the drawer as I move gifts aside until I find what I am looking for.

The gift wrapped in gold.

The last gift from my mother that she planned to give me on my fifteenth birthday. I lift the small box, so light in my hand, and yet it weighs heavily on my heart.

This gift represents years of keeping memories of my mother tucked away, years of me trying to forget because the pain of losing her was too hard to deal with. The box represents a grief I never faced head-on. Finally after fifteen years I feel ready, after fifteen years I need closure. For me to face the future, I need to first face the past. I have no idea what is inside and never wanted to know, until now. I take a long breath and slowly lift the corner flap.

CHAPTER THIRTY

Chelsea
Yesterday evening

I stand peering out of the lounge window and watch Lucian walk away from me and out of my life. My heart hammers loudly in my chest with each step he takes toward the car. He could look back at any second. I should move away from the window, but I can't. Part of me wants to run after him and take it all back, but I can't. I'm doing this for him, so that Josh doesn't destroy his reputation. Not only that, but Lucian wants children, and that is something I am unsure if I'll ever be able to give him. But instead of picturing a little girl sitting at the top of the stairs whilst her father leaves, I see something else. I see a girl with striking blonde hair watch as her mother kisses her father as he leaves for work. I see a boy with emerald-green eyes running down the stairs as his father returns home from a long day in the office.

What if he leaves, the question that has forever plagued my mind, is replaced by *What if he stays?*

Image after image plays in a loop in my mind, a motion picture of the life and children we could have had. Tears wash away my imaginings and pull me back to reality because a dream is all it can be, all it'll ever be.

My legs shake and my body trembles with emotion that I can't quash. When I think I couldn't feel any worse than I do, Lucian turns around and looks straight at me and it feels as though my whole world implodes in on itself.

This is too much. I can't end things like this. I hurry away from the window and head for the front door. I turn the key in the lock and run barefoot down the narrow flight of stairs. My feet are met with the icy chill from puddles and water splashes up my calves as I run out onto the street. Fat raindrops fall down around me and become one with my sorrow. Through a haze of tears burning in my eyes I watch as the Mercedes drives away, taking Lucian with it.

With shaky hands I pull my phone from my pocket and frantically search for his number. I'm seconds from calling him when the sound of someone clapping has me spinning around.

The door to the estate agency swings closed and Josh approaches. He looks so put-together this evening. He has a large umbrella sandwiched under his arm, keeping the rain from his suit, which appears new. His hair has been sleeked back and an aura of smugness surrounds him. "Bravo, Chelsea. You succeeded in hurting him so much that he'll never give you the time of day again."

"Bite me," I spit out, and hurry toward the door leading to my flat. My feet pitter-patter as they hit the cold metal beading on the stairs. But it isn't only my feet I hear. Heavy footfalls echo around me as someone follows closely behind.

My pace quickens as I reach my flat. I grab the door, about to slam it shut, when Josh steps up behind me. I freeze on feeling his warm breath against my cheek and, for the first time in a long time, I feel scared.

"Touch me, and I'll scream," I croak.

Fingers brush through my wet hair, and I squeeze my eyes shut as Josh takes a deep inhale. "I won't deny that I have always wanted what my cousin has. His wealth, his heritage, his business. Though not women." He releases my hair. "I won't deny that you are somewhat pleasing to the eye, but I'm in love with Natasha."

I relax a little at his words. "What do you want, Josh?"

He doesn't speak for a beat, and it's as though he's deciding on just the right words. "I wanted to thank you for doing the right thing."

I scoff. "Gee, thanks."

"And to show my appreciation I am giving you a year's free pass on one of the Calloway cruise liners. Courtesy of Duncan Calloway, of course."

Of course.

"I'll pass," I say, and try to dislodge his arm from the door. But he doesn't budge, not so much as an inch.

"I'm sorry, I think you misunderstood. Let me try that again. You have until the end of the month to pack up your shit and move out."

My mouth falls open. "You can't do that."

"I can, and I am. Lucian will be busy running Calloway Housebuilders, the biggest and most profitable Calloway chain. He doesn't need any distractions. I need you to move out so Natasha and I can move in. I will be running the business downstairs; it makes sense that I live close. As payment, I am giving you a year-long cruise. I've even thrown in an extra ticket if you want to take a friend."

I stand tall and raise my head. "I'll tell Lucian. I'll tell him everything."

"I would strongly advise against that. I have been kind until now, but don't be fooled because I can be cruel."

I spin around, my eyes narrow. "Are you threatening me?"

"You personally? No. I can hurt you and those you hold dear without lifting a finger. Your sister's photography business will be sued for fraud, her fiancé's construction business shut down due to health and safety. As for your beauty salon, you may want to consider relocating. It is far too close to my estate agency. I can't have my Natasha coming in to have her nails done and you gossiping about me behind my back."

Josh's arm is gone and without another word he casually makes his way down the narrow flight of stairs.

"Enjoy your cruise," are the words he leaves me with.

I stand in the darkened kitchen, which is sporadically lit up by a flash of lightning. I could swear the building shakes with the loud rumble of thunder. Tears stream down my face, and I wipe them away with my aching hands.

I have been cleaning the kitchen for the past five hours. I have been emptying out stale food from the fridge and cleaning the worktops. The lights have remained off whilst I clean because I don't want anyone to know I am back. Amber cannot see me like this. She will only worry, which isn't good for her, nor is it good for the baby. Tonight, I have used up every cleaning product I own, but it isn't enough. If I clean then everything will be okay and nothing else bad can happen.

My skin burns as I apply more pressure to the cleaning rag. Harder and harder I scrub the worktop, trying desperately to clean a surface that'll never be good enough.

I will never be good enough.

Shadows dance along the tiled wall as night turns to day, and then again when day dissolves back into night. One by one, days pass by. Days turn into weeks. I stay confined to my flat and completely shut off from the outside world. My phone remains switched off and I spend my time watching murder documentaries and cleaning. My OCD has consumed me and I don't know who I am any more.

The weeks pass in a flash. I thought the hole in my heart would begin to repair, but that has most definitely not been the case. I refuse to let myself dwell, or lose control of the situation, so instead do what I do best when my world's falling apart.

I wake up at six a.m., slide out of bed and head for the kitchen, where I begin my daily cleaning routine. After breakfast, I have a shower and spend an hour scrubbing the white ceramic base. Once it's clean I'm able to leave the room and return to the lounge, where I will watch an hour of Netflix. Dressed in my pyjamas and a towel wrapped around my head, I make my way into the lounge but stop suddenly when I see a dark figure looming in the hallway.

Someone has broken in, or is it Josh come to kick me out? I lower my head and slowly walk back; I keep going until my hand reaches the brass handle of my bedroom door. Without making a sound I let myself in and push it to behind me.

My heart thumps in my chest as realisation kicks in. I'm alone in my flat. Nobody knows I am here. With shaky hands I grab my phone, which is face down on the nightstand, and switch it on. It takes longer than usual to load. The second my screen photo is displayed it is bombarded with update notifications and text message after text message.

Texts from my parents, my friends, Amber, Tyler and Lucian. My hand shakes as my phone pings continually. I switch it to silent when my bedroom door swings open, and I scream, letting out every emotion inside me.

"Jesus Christ, Chelsea, it's me!" Warm arms surround me, but they do nothing to stop the emotion pouring out. "Chelsea, it's me."

I recognise the voice to be Tyler's, recognise his touch, his scent and his warmth. My scream is soon replaced by sobs, and for the first time in a long time, I release all my broken pieces. I allow myself to be seen for the broken mess I have become. For years I have bottled up the damage my parents caused, bottled up the damage my ex-boyfriend caused when he burnt down my shop, and bottled up every negative that life has thrown at me. I've bottled so much up that to the outside world I look like a fully functioning adult, but on the inside, I've been barely keeping it together. Since losing Lucian it has all become too much and I can't bottle it up any more.

Tyler doesn't say a word, and it's better that way. He holds me and lets me release all the pain I'm feeling.

I'm not sure how much time passes, but slowly, I pull out of Tyler's embrace. He looks like the same old Tyler, except with a slightly fuller face and a natural tan.

"I take it it didn't work with Mason?" My throat is so sore that my words come out in short gasps.

Tyler shrugs. "It happens. I guess it didn't work out with Lucian?"

My lower lip trembles, and sinking down on the bed, I tell him everything from start to finish.

Tyler jumps up. "Josh, that scheming bastard. I'll kill him," he declares, heading toward the door.

I stumble to my feet and run after him. I pull on the sleeve of his jacket and yank him back. "Getting into a fight with Josh won't solve anything."

Tyler pulls his arm free and flicks his hair back. "Perhaps, but it would make me feel a damn sight better." Tyler rolls his eyes when my expression remains unchanged. "Come on, darlin', I'll buy us breakfast." He links his arm with mine and pulls me toward the door. The room spins faster the closer we get to the hallway. Suddenly the idea of leaving the flat feels too daunting.

"Tyler, get off me," I say, and pull back.

"I know you don't eat breakfast, but I can get you an extra-strong coffee."

"Tyler, get off me," I repeat. My heartbeat is erratic when he opens the door.

"We need to tell Amber you're back. She's been calling me non-stop since—"

"Get off me!" I yell, and, snatching my arm free, I run into the kitchen and grab the bottle of antibacterial spray. With eczema-covered hands, I spray and scrub the worktop. "I can't leave, I have to clean, have to clean."

Tyler enters the kitchen and, folding his arms, stands watching me. "Lizzie is getting married tomorrow."

I shake my head vehemently. "I can't leave the flat, I can't leave."

We break eye contact when the ringtone sounds from an incoming call. Tyler pulls his phone from his pocket and looks at the screen. "It's your sister."

"Don't answer," I say, scrubbing harder now.

Tyler accepts the call and holds the phone to his ear. "Amber, darlin'. Yes, I am back in the UK." Tyler turns his attention to me. "She isn't back yet. Don't worry, I will let you know the moment she is home." He cuts the call, and his attention remains on his phone.

"What are you doing?" I ask.

Tyler taps the glass screen and holds the device to his ear. "I'm calling your therapist. I'm going to request an urgent home visit."

I laugh. "I don't need to see my therapist. I'm fine."

Tyler shakes his head. "No, Chelsea, you are anything but fine."

CHAPTER THIRTY-ONE

Lucian

"To us." Josh clinks his glass against mine.

"To us," I repeat, and swallow back my drink. Drinking brandy in my home office on a Saturday morning? Life doesn't get much better than this, or at least that is what I'm telling myself.

Since Chelsea left, I have thrown myself into work. Every day I called her and left numerous messages, but she is completely unreachable. She may only have been in my life for just over a week, but in those few short days, I was truly happy. She filled a void in my world I didn't know existed, and now she's gone the void has only gotten bigger.

"May our efforts be rewarded in the meeting this afternoon," Josh says. He swaggers around the large office space, plucks random non-fiction books from the built-in bookshelf and flicks through the pages, calling out arbitrary facts. It's becoming slightly tedious, but from the way he's struggling to stand still I know he's nervous. His nerves are making me feel jittery, so I suggested a brandy to help take the edge off. But if anything, the alcohol has only added to his restlessness.

"Will you take a seat already? I'm starting to get motion sickness," I say, my gaze following his every move.

"I'm so sorry," Josh says and walks toward the desk at a pace that would best fit a sloth. I laugh. Despite his irksome ways, I can't stay mad at my cousin for long. Josh has really stepped up. As well as running the estate agency, he has helped me secure some big building contracts. I didn't know he had so many contacts in high-up places. He never fails to amaze me.

"I was thinking about what you said when we were in Scotland," I say, and hold my glass out for a refill.

"And what would that be?" Josh asks.

"About giving you a small percentage of the company."

Josh's face lights up and he hurriedly fills my glass. "Lucian, I cannot thank you enough. We need to make it official and celebrate."

I pick up my glass and swirl the liquid around. "Yes. I will arrange for my father's lawyer to draft up a contract that will officially make you the proud owner of Calloway Estate Agency in Heller St Claire, and a five-percent shareholder of Calloway Housebuilders."

I haven't officially been handed the company, but I am confident that I am the front runner.

"Five percent?" Josh repeats, and I can't help miss the tinge of disappointment in his tone.

I know it doesn't sound like a great amount, but what I'm offering my cousin will set him up for life. "Josh, it is a multi-billion-pound company. Five percent for someone like you is huge."

Josh's jovial expression falters. "Someone like me?"

"Yes." I tip the shot back. "Someone with a humble upbringing."

Josh smiles, but it doesn't reach his eyes. "Very well, cousin. You have been so good to me over the years. And I you when you had that awful horse-riding accident. Remember, it was I who sat by your bedside day and night while you lay in a coma."

I narrow my eyes, remembering that Malachi told me he sat with me when Josh went home to sleep. "About that…"

A knock at the door pulls my attention away from my cousin. Christine, my PA, is standing in the doorway tugging at the sleeve of her blouse. "I'm sorry to disturb you, but the car is here."

Father sent Bentleys to pick me and my brothers up for today's meeting. But it isn't just any meeting, today is the day it is decided who will own Calloway Housebuilders and we officially sign on the dotted line. I stand up from my desk and check the time on my grandfather's pocket watch. I should get there with ten minutes to spare.

Truro is over a four-hour drive from my Windsor estate. I moved out of my Surrey home a few days after Chelsea left. The plan was to move back into my Cornwall manor, but with Chelsea residing in Heller St Claire I couldn't bear to have her on my doorstep. Josh was right, a clean break is exactly what I need to get over her. I'm not there yet, and I dare say I never will be.

"Knock them dead," Josh says, and claps his hand on my shoulder.

I leave Josh drinking in my office and follow Christine out of the estate and to the Bentley. She stands proud with her hands clasped behind her back.

I take the handle of the car door, about to let myself in, but stop. "Today was to mark the end of my and Chelsea's agreement."

Christine nods, but she has no idea what I am talking about.

"There is a photograph called 'Timeless Beauty' being sold at a farmers' market today. I want you to go and buy it. I will forward you all the details shortly." I open the lapels of my jacket and pull out my wallet. "There is a cheque already written out for a Miss Chelsea Janssen for the sum of one hundred thousand pounds."

Christine's eyes widen. "That's quite some money."

She's quite some girl, I want to say, but instead open the car door and am surprised to see Samantha sitting in the back seat.

Her hair has been curled seductively and her usual pale

complexion has been enhanced with a generous amount of makeup. A red halter neck hugs her voluptuous chest, so much so it causes her cleavage to spill out.

I look at Christine and back to Samantha. "What game is this?" I demand.

"No game, cousin." I turn as Josh approaches. "I asked Samantha if she would join you for the car journey. Now Chelsea is gone, I thought it was about time you jumped right back on the horse, so to speak."

I close the car door and square up to Josh. "She's my ex," I seethe.

"Exactly," Josh says, his voice high-pitched. "You have history. Not only that, if you get back with Samantha, then you will be guaranteed to secure the company."

"That was what years of hard work was for."

Josh winks. "I mean, you don't have to really get back with her. You can pretend. You've done it before."

My and Chelsea's fake engagement had nothing to do with business and everything to do with pleasure. I wanted her and saw an opportunity to make that happen. "I will not secure the company through lies and deceit." I open the car door and hold out my hand. "It was nice seeing you again, Samantha, now out. Josh will make sure you get home safely."

Samantha leans forward and looks from me to my cousin. "No. I will sit in the front if you don't want me in the back with you."

I look past the car and at my PA, who taps her wrist, telling me I need to make headway or I'll be late.

"I will sit in the front." I slam the car door shut and make my way around the vehicle with Josh fast on my heels.

"Remember your father wants you to marry Samantha. She is the only niece of Simon Matthews. Marry her and put her up in one of your estates. You can focus on work, and visit her during the quiet periods…"

I stop walking, causing Josh to crash into my back. I capture his shirt by the collar and I pull him close so our faces are but inches apart. "If you presume to go behind my back and interfere with my love life again the deal is off. I cannot go into business with someone I cannot trust. Do I make myself clear?"

Josh swallows. "Crystal."

I release his shirt and slide into the car. McKenzie indicates and heads down the large driveway.

"It's nice to see you," Samantha says from the back seat.

I nod and turn my attention to my phone. I scroll through the pictures I have of Chelsea, pictures I've been meaning to delete, but can't muster the courage to get rid of. Deleting the photos is closure, closure I am not yet ready for.

We drive in silence for an hour, so long that I almost forget Samantha is sitting in the back seat.

"Do you want to come by Freesdon Hall sometime?" she asks. "I know how special the house is to you, and because of that I haven't changed a single thing."

I angle the mirror in front of me so I can see Samantha. Maybe after all these years I will get the answer to the question that's been playing on my mind. "Why did you do it? Why did you go to the press and have an article written about me, about us?"

Tears glimmer in her eyes. "You wouldn't see me, and you changed your number. I knew if I had an article written you'd read it. I did it to get you back."

"Ha!" I can't help the sarcasm in my tone.

"I mean it." Samantha leans forward in her seat and wraps her arms around me. "What I said to Darren Moore isn't what was published. He twisted everything I said to make you sound bad."

I take her arms from me and sit forward. "Doesn't matter, you were engaged to someone else the whole time we were together."

I angle the mirror so she can't escape my stare. Her lower lip trembles, but she holds her composure. She looks down into her lap and fidgets with her charm bracelet. "That's just it," she says and looks up. "I wasn't. There was never anyone else, only you."

Now she's sparked my interest. "There wasn't another man?"

Samantha sinks back into the seat, her lips pursed tightly together.

My temper frays because more than anything I hate liars. "I suggest you start speaking before I stop this car and hurl your ass out onto the road."

"I had no choice."

I jump. Her words come out louder than I had anticipated.

"He threatened to ruin my family if I stayed in a relationship with you. He said he would have my father fired from his job and us living on the streets. That is the only reason I got back in contact with my uncle. I thought that if I wasn't just some poor nobody we could be together. I wanted to have the article retracted, but my uncle made it abundantly clear that he didn't want our name dragged through the papers for a second time."

I hold up my hand. "Samantha, you're going too quick. Who threatened you? Who was going to make you homeless?"

"Josh."

I pivot around in my seat and give her no other choice than to meet my gaze.

"I don't believe you." She has to be lying. Josh is my cousin, but more than that, he is like a brother. "I know Josh."

"Not as well as you think you do…" Her words trail off, but not once does she break eye contact. Samantha could never look at me when she was lying, whereas Josh on the other hand has always had the perfect poker face.

"Why don't we stop the car and go somewhere where we can talk?" she suggests.

I spin around in the seat and catch sight of a small country pub to our left. "McKenzie, stop the car."

CHAPTER THIRTY-TWO

Lucian

"Chelsea, open the door," I call, my fist pummelling the hard wood. She doesn't answer, and instead of waiting like a normal person, I push my key into the lock and let myself in.

I almost trip over the suitcases that are stacked in front of the door. I push them aside and make my way into the open-plan lounge. I know someone is here from the scent of toast lingering in the air. The TV plays but has been muted, and all I can hear is the sound of running water coming from Chelsea's bedroom. I make my way to the door, about to take the handle, when fingers wrap around my shoulders and pull me back.

"What the hell are you doing here?"

I turn and come face to face with Chelsea's roomie, Tyler.

"I need to see her," I say, and, rolling my shoulder free from his hold, I attempt to enter the bedroom.

"If you set one foot inside that room, I will kill you."

I turn and laugh at Tyler's threat. "I would love to see you try." I fish out my wallet and pass him a crisp fifty-pound note. "I would appreciate it if you could give us some privacy. Why don't you go somewhere and buy yourself something nice?"

The note falls from between his fingers and floats down to the floor. Tyler shoves me away from the door and my back crashes against the wall. I clench my fist, about to react, when Tyler continues. "She was meant to be at her best friend's wedding today, but is unable to go. Lucian, she's had a breakdown."

I unclench my fist. "What do you mean?"

"What I mean is your cousin has done a real number on her. So much so, he has not only sparked her OCD, but she has been unable to leave the flat this entire time in fear of bumping into him."

Anger courses the length of my body because I know that when everything is said and done, Josh will regret ever crossing me.

"I had no idea. Josh's lies and deceit have recently been brought to my attention. Please, I just want to speak to her. I just want to make this right."

Tyler shakes his head. "You can't, she isn't in the right headspace at the moment. With the help of her therapist, we have convinced Chelsea she needs to get away. She needs a change of scenery before it's too late."

I gaze at the suitcases stacked by the door. "Where are you going?"

"Not that it's any of your business, but I'm taking her to Paris for the week. I've been a shitty friend, and because of me the money we saved for our trip was stolen. Chelsea is in a real dark place, and she needs me now more than ever."

"I will drop everything and come with you," I say, not giving a damn about the meeting or the company.

Tyler shakes his head. "I'm sorry, Lucian, but you are the last thing she needs right now."

How I want to shove Tyler aside and tear down the door and take Chelsea away, far away. But in doing so, will I cause more hurt and more damage? If it's time away she needs, it's time away she will get. "Please, allow me to help." I open my wallet.

Tyler places his hand over mine. "I have all we need."

I nod, and Tyler backs away. "Tell her I will be back when you return. Just let me know where and when."

He lets out a long breath. "The Grovers Hotel, in two weeks."

I glance at the bedroom door one final time. The sound of running water still filters through the small opening. "Great. I'll see you there."

I clap Tyler on the shoulder and make my way to the hall to leave when Chelsea calls after me. "For our leaving party."

I still at the sound of her voice and at her words. "Your leaving party?"

"Yes. Your cousin is kicking us out," Tyler explains.

"He can't do that." I turn my attention to Chelsea. She looks so small swallowed up in a huge blue robe. Her hair has been secured in a towel, and that's when I notice the pale purple scar on her forehead from her falling off Jupiter. I want nothing more than to run my finger over the slight imperfection.

"Chelsea," I whisper.

She has a faraway look in her eyes, as though she's looking at me, but isn't seeing me. I take a step forward, only for her to step back.

"Josh has been good enough to let us stay here for an extra few weeks whilst we get our affairs in order." Sarcasm drips from every syllable. "After Paris, we are going on a year-long cruise, courtesy of your father."

"You can't." I can see everything crumbling down around me, and I'm powerless to stop it.

"That's just it, we can," Tyler interjects. "Chelsea has always wanted to travel, and seeing as though I have no business keeping me in England, well, there is nothing stopping me from joining her." He meets Chelsea's gaze, and she nods once as if silently telling him she's okay. Of course she's bloody okay, I'm here.

Bile creeps its way into my throat as I can feel Chelsea slipping away.

"Come back to me," I say, and it's killing me being this close to her, yet feeling so far away.

Chelsea looks to the floor and scuffs her slipper-clad foot into the carpet. "Lucian, I have been alive for twenty-six years, but I haven't lived. I've never travelled, never seen the world. I haven't done anything."

"If it's the world you want to see, I will show you. We can travel anywhere you want to go, just say the word."

Chelsea makes her way into the lounge and sits down on the sofa. I see my cue to follow and sit in the space beside her. Our knees touch as we sit side by side. The connection I feel is so strong, surely she can feel it too?

"I have feelings for you, Lucian, but in the long run we aren't going to make each other happy. Your business is here, and for the first time in a long time, I have nothing to keep me."

I grab her hand in mine and place her palm against my chest. "You have me. Your family. Your life."

The light that once shone so brightly in her eyes is gone, and there is nothing but coldness and ash in its wake. "It's not enough. Not any more. You and I have no future. As for my sister and family, they have their own lives."

"What about your salon? That shop means everything to you. It was the reason you agreed to get engaged to me in the first place."

"Pretend to get engaged to you," she corrects with a wry smile.

"I will make the calls now and have your salon up and running by Monday. What do you say?" I'm still clasping her hand, desperately willing her to say the words I want to hear. "Tell me to go on a year-long cruise with you. Tell me you'll stay. I don't care which. As long as I have you, nothing else matters."

Her hand slips out of mine, and the place in my heart that is reserved only for her is once again empty.

"When you love someone, you love them enough to say

goodbye." She stands, the towel falling from her hair, revealing a much shorter style. It's as if by cutting her hair she has cut away all her ties to her past, me included.

Without a backward glance she heads toward her bedroom, and I jump up to follow. "Chelsea," I call after her. The door slams shut in my face.

Tyler reappears as if by goddamn magic. "Now, if there isn't anything else, I would like you to leave. I have a long drive ahead and I want to spend some time meditating."

I pull out a business card from my wallet and press it into Tyler's palm. "I want you to contact me the second you set foot in Paris."

Tyler quirks a brow. "Now why would I want to do that?"

"Trust me when I say that you will be very interested in what it is I have to say."

"I seriously doubt that."

I leave the flat completely lost for words. How have I been so blind that I couldn't see what was happening right under my nose? I have given Josh so much over the years, and the whole time he's been silently destroying my life, and for what? Though the answer to that is simple. Greed. Greed drives people to do almost anything. But I trusted Josh, or at least I thought I could.

I exit the building and stand in the street for long seconds, looking up at her bedroom window in hopes she will peer out, but she doesn't.

I flash a glance at my grandfather's pocket watch. Two hours. I am two hours late for what was to be the most important meeting of my life. No doubt the meeting has gone ahead without me and Malachi is now the proud owner of Calloway Housebuilders.

I slide into the back seat of the Bentley and Samantha places a hand on my shoulder. We had a long conversation earlier, and despite her tears, she has accepted we are over for good. She said she wants to remain friends, but being friends with an ex is not a good idea. At best I have agreed to be amicable.

"Lucian, I'm so sorry." She is speaking as though I have already lost Chelsea, and perhaps I have. When Samantha lassos her arms around my neck, I don't pull away, but wrap my arms around her and pull her close, needing comfort in this moment, because in this moment I truly have lost everything.

Father, his lawyer Edgar Arnoult, and my brothers are sitting around a circular table when I stagger into the meeting room. In all honesty I'm surprised they're still here.

Father is dressed in his best Alexander Amosu tweed suit, with gold canary cufflinks and burgundy tie. His eyes narrow the second I step into the room. "What time do you call this?"

Ignoring his snarky comment, I make my way toward the table and pull out the seat beside Malachi. "Why didn't you start without me?" I whisper.

Malachi's cologne fills my nose as he straightens in his chair. "Father wanted to. He was so angry at your tardiness that he was going to hand the company over to me."

"So why didn't he?"

Malachi pulls out a pen from the breast pocket of his jacket. "Because I believe it is the best man who should win, and perhaps the best man wasn't here."

My brother's words strike me deep. Despite him wanting the company above anything, he waited, he waited for me to return so I would have a fair chance. For years I thought Malachi and I had a conflict of interests, but the truth is, conflicting or not, we have always been on the same team.

"I do apologise. Finish your conversation first. I've only been waiting three and a half hours, what's another five minutes?" Father says, and turns his attention to me.

"Sorry," Malachi and I say in unison.

Father takes his position at the head of the room and clears his throat. "It is with great pleasure that I announce Lucian to be the proud owner of Calloway Housebuilders. Congratulations, son."

Chair legs screech against the floor as Edgar gets to his feet and walks across the room with a large stack of papers in hand. He separates the papers into four neatly stacked piles in front of me.

Malachi claps me on the back and hands me the pen. "Well done, brother."

"I need your signatures on all of the dotted lines," Edgar says, and points to where yellow Post-it note arrows have been stuck down. "You will also find contracts drawn up for your agreement with Mr Ambrose. He called ahead this morning and informed me of your decision to give him ten percent of the company."

Ten percent?

Did Josh think I would be so wrapped up in securing the business that I wouldn't read over the fine print?

Father stands proud. "It is a very noble thing you're doing, son; on what I have seen so far, I believe you and Josh will make a fantastic team."

Anger pools in me as I scan over the first of the four contracts. A contract that meant everything, that promised to deliver everything I ever wanted, whereas now all I see is expectation. The expectation to marry a woman my father deems worthy and whom I do not love, the expectation to send my children to private school, and the expectation to become the carbon copy of my father.

"As soon as Lucian has signed the contracts, we shall discuss the hotel chain and the cruise liner company," Father continues.

"The cruise liner company. The irony of running something that is meant to stay afloat but is sinking," Gage scoffs.

"Well, I am certainly not running a sinking ship," Malachi argues.

"You may not have a choice," Gage fires back.

It would appear the most favourable company after Calloway

Housebuilders is the hotel chain, and why wouldn't it be? It is highly successful, and profits have almost tripled over the last ten years.

"Come on, son, we haven't got all day," Father prompts when I've made no attempt to put pen to paper.

Malachi places his hand over mine and brings the pen to the dotted line. "Hurry up, Lucian. We have a plane to catch for our skiing weekend."

Malachi freezes, and glances at my hand, or more specifically my finger. "I see you finally opened your present from our mother."

I scrutinize Malachi's blasé expression. "All this time, you knew?"

"Of course, I am the eldest after all, it is my duty to know everything," he says, and my gaze alternates between our matching heirlooms.

"Why didn't you tell me?"

"I couldn't. It was something you had to do when the time was right."

Like Malachi and Gage, I am the proud owner of the Calloway ring. The crest is subtly depicted within a chunky black gemstone. Rings signify the never-ending, like the bond between brothers.

Three rings, one eternal bond.

Malachi leans in close. "I just have one question,"

"And what might that be?"

"The engraved message from Mother inside your ring. What does it say?"

Father clears his throat, telling us it is time to resume business.

"Perhaps a conversation for another day," Malachi says, and for a second time guides my hand toward the dotted line.

The pen makes contact and the ink bleeds onto the paper as I make my decision.

CHAPTER THIRTY-THREE

Chelsea

Monday morning soon comes around. With a full day's itinerary ahead of us we wake up at the crack of dawn. Tyler and I hurry from our Airbnb and catch the Métro, better known as the subway, and hit the streets of Paris.

The tarmac walkways are alive with locals and tourists alike. The streets are lined with shops and restaurants. Colourful awnings stand proud, and business names are depicted in fancy bold lettering.

"Come on," Tyler prompts for what seems like the hundredth time. Whereas he hurries ahead, I amble behind and take everything in around me. He waits for me to catch up and, taking my wrist in his hand, gives me a not-so-soft tug.

"I have no idea why you've insisted on dragging me here. I don't even eat breakfast," I say, and follow Tyler into Café Blanche, a quaint French café located on the corner of Boulevard de Lefort. Green and white awnings hug the building's exterior, and chunky wooden chairs and tables are positioned out front for al fresco dining.

"Because, darlin', Jean-Paul just happens to make the best breakfast in Paris."

I quirk a brow and see the not-so-subtle glances passed between Tyler and the man inside who is standing behind the till. A man with sandy blond hair and dark brown eyes. I recognise him from last night when we hit the nightclubs. I didn't catch his name, but that was probably because Tyler's tongue was in his mouth.

"He's the chef, and occasionally works front of house," Tyler informs me.

"Nice," I say, and wave at Jean-Paul.

"Wait here. I'll see which table we have been allocated."

I take a step forward. "I'll come with you."

Tyler places his hand on my shoulder. "I've got this, and no offence, but you do this weird thing with your face whenever I'm talking to a guy."

I fold my arms in front of my chest. "What thing?"

Jean-Paul approaches and, leaning into Tyler, whispers something in his ear before making his way back to the till. When Tyler's gaze meets mine he gestures with his hand. "You're doing it right now."

I'm about to playfully punch the top of Tyler's arm when I catch sight of myself in the reflection of the café window. I place my hands on my hip. "I'm smiling."

"Yes, darlin', but in so doing, you look like the Joker."

I laugh and brush off his comment while at the same time relaxing my cheeks, which ache. "Okay, maybe I'm smiling a little too big, but it's because I'm happy for you."

Tyler claps me on the shoulder. "I'd rather you be happy for me from a distance, because it's distracting." Tyler waggles his brows and makes his way into the café. I don't need telling twice and wait behind as requested.

Romantic music from a street performer fills my ears, and, turning my attention from Tyler and Jean-Paul, I make my way toward the violinist. He plays a Spanish melody, and a ballet dancer dances to his right. The performance is beautiful and intoxicating, so much so that they have a decent-sized crowd gathering around them.

I join the crowd and am so enthralled with the performance that I can't stop the tear that trickles its way down my cheek. I feel a presence from behind and, without turning, step aside to allow whoever it is to pass.

"To watch a dance filled with emotion is like watching the soul as it bleeds."

My mouth falls open, and I spin around. "Lucian?"

Sure enough, it is none other than Lucian Calloway, clad in a black and white striped T-shirt and navy jeans.

"What are you doing here?" I choke out.

Lucian takes a step forward so he is standing by my side. "I thought the answer to that was obvious."

I sidestep away and cross my arms in front of my chest. "I've been in France for five minutes and poof, there you are."

"France is nothing. Believe me when I say that I would travel to the end of the earth for you."

His comment leaves me feeling warm and tingling all over. I want nothing more than to fall back into us and the way we were, but it just isn't that simple. "How did you even know where I was?"

Lucian looks toward Café Blanche. He and Tyler share a glance, and Tyler offers a two-finger salute before continuing his conversation with Jean-Paul.

"Great, so now you're in cahoots with my roomie? How much did you pay him?"

"Not a single penny." Lucian drapes an arm around my shoulder. "I asked Tyler to call me when you arrived in Paris. After which we had a nice little conversation regarding Calloway Estate Agency in Heller St Claire."

I guess that explains where Tyler disappeared off to when I was unpacking on our arrival. "What about the estate agency?" I ask, pulling out of Lucian's hold.

A round of applause breaks out around us as the performance finishes, and the violinist bows before flicking through the pages of his music book.

Lucian takes my hand in his. I'm about to pull away when he guides it to his lips. "Come back to me."

His words float on the soft breeze, while his eyes, those hypnotic greens have me hypnotised. How easy it would be to fall and let Lucian catch me. How easy it would be to wear his ring for real. The problem is my whole life I've been living in a cage of my own creation. It doesn't matter how nice the bars. It isn't enough anymore, I want out. I want to spread my wings, feel the breeze beating against my feathers as I soar.

I pull my hand from his. "Lucian, I can't."

Lucians' eyes glimmer, and for a split second I swear I see a tear. He blinks and nods his head in a kind of acceptance. "Will you at least have breakfast with me? I've come all this way and—"

"Of course I will," I say, and we make our way to Café Blanche.

My phone vibrates. I pull it from my pocket and see Cole's name flash on the screen. "I have to take this," I say and accept the call. "Hello, Cole?"

Lucian's eyes widen and he leans a little closer, as though trying to listen in. I smile and subtly turn my phone volume down.

"Chelsea. Hello! How the fuck are you, or better yet, where the fuck are you?" Cole asks.

With my palm over my eyes I shake my head. Cole is Lizzie's older brother. I can't tell him I missed his sister's big day in order to come to Paris. He wouldn't understand—none of my friends will. I'll tell them, I'll tell them everything, but not today and not over the phone. "I'm fine, Cole. I've called Amber and Lizzie to let them know I'm safe. I just need some time, you know?"

Lucian and I join the small queue of people being directed into the café. A waiter dressed in black shows people to their tables.

"You need to let us know you're okay from time to time," Cole says.

'I have,' I'm about to say, but I can't help the laugh that escapes between my lips. If I had a pound for every time Cole disappeared without so much as a courtesy call, then I would be a very rich lady. "Yeah, like you do when you go MIA?"

My attention is waylaid, and I continue the conversation, though feel a million miles away. I stand and look at Lucian, really look at him. How the breeze picks up loose strands of his hair, and how it annoys him and he is quick to push it back. My gaze lowers to his hand, one I could quite easily slip my hand into. Physically we are so close, and yet emotionally I am putting more and more distance between us. Just because Lucian and I aren't together anymore doesn't mean we can't be friends.

"When are you coming home?" Cole asks.

"Soon," I say, snapped from my thoughts.

The music from the violinist picks up, and I turn to see the ballet dancer start her next dance. Lucian was right when he said that dancing done right is like the soul bleeding in front of your very eyes. It's painfully beautiful.

"Votre table, madame," a waiter says. I look around to see where Tyler is—surely he will be joining us?—but he stands eating a pastry whilst deep in conversation with Jean-Paul.

"Sorry, Cole. I have to go; our table is ready."

"Is Lucian with you?" Cole asks right before I cut the call.

We follow the waiter to the table, and when Lucian pulls a chair out for me, I take a seat.

Lucian sits opposite. "Is everything okay?"

"Cole just asked me if I was with you. How would he even know?"

The waiter clasps his hands behind his back. "My name is Andre; I will be your waiter today. Would you like a French menu, or an English menu?"

"English," I say.

"French," Lucian replies, his gaze never leaving me. "You really should try ordering from the French menu. Languages can be fun."

I laugh. "Kijk nooit met je ogen dicht."

Lucian frowns. "That isn't French."

I place my elbows on the table and lean forward. "No, it's Dutch. It translates as 'never look with your eyes closed'. Which is basically what I'll be doing if I try to order from a French menu."

"Point taken." Lucian finally breaks eye contact and turns his attention to Andre. "Deux jus d'orange, s'il vous plaît."

I have no idea what he said, and nor do I ask. Andre bows his head, passes us our menus and leaves. We spend several minutes deciding what to have before Lucian clears his throat. "Do you want to hear something funny?"

"Sure."

"Since Saturday evening I've had Cole calling me non-stop accusing me of kidnapping you."

My mouth falls open. I'm too shocked to speak.

Andre returns with two glasses of orange juice and places them in front of us. "Are you ready to order?"

I'm not, but take this time to let what Lucian has told me sink in. I lower my menu card. "I'll have a croissant."

Lucian's expression remains unchanged, and I know he was inwardly hoping I would try something new. He points to his menu. "Pain au chocolat."

Andre jots our choices down on a small notepad and leaves.

Now I've had some time, I pick up where Lucian left off. "Cole thinks I've been kidnapped?"

"Mr Crowley seems to be under the impression that I am keeping you against your will. For the time being I've asked Christine to inform anyone who calls that I am away on business. As for Cole, I will deal with him when I get home."

I sink back into my chair. "This is all my fault."

Lucian takes a sip of his orange juice. "The next time you

speak to Cole, I would appreciate it if you could let him know I haven't taken you against your will."

"I will," I promise. "I'll speak to my friends tonight."

Lucian and I enjoy breakfast, and in the corner of my eye I notice Tyler helping out behind the till. He laughs and jokes with the customers as they pay, which baffles me seeing as Tyler doesn't know a single phrase in French, but he seems to get by with his quirky and endearing personality.

"Are you staying in Paris?" I ask.

Lucian dabs the corners of his mouth with a napkin. "I'm afraid not. I am actually on my way back from Switzerland. My brothers and I had a fantastic time on the slopes. I was hoping you would return to England with me." Lucian reaches across the table and places his hand over mine. "I am going to spend a few days in Swansea with Angus Blackwell. If my memory serves me correctly, he invited you to join us."

I pull my hand out of his grip and swallow deeply. "I can't."

"You don't have to join us at his lake, I know fishing is something you either love or hate." Hope shines in his eyes, but he must know my reason for declining has nothing to do with fishing.

"I can't," I repeat.

Lucian lifts up in the chair and pulls out a golden pocket watch. "In which case, I will have to leave soon."

Lucian and I leave Café Blanche. The violinist still plays in the background and the ballerina continues to dance. The crowd around them is starting to spill out onto the road.

"I hear you bought my photograph at the farmers' market," I say loud enough to be heard over the music.

"My PA Christine made the purchase, but yes, I am the proud owner of 'Timeless Beauty'. Your photograph will hang in my bedroom. Wherever I sleep, you will always be with me. Always."

There is an invisible pull between us. I can feel it, and I'm sure Lucian can too. But he doesn't attempt to step closer. It's like finally I've spoken and he's not only listened, he's heard me loud and clear.

Lucian clears his throat. "I trust you have sufficient funds to open your salon? If you need more you only need to—"

I raise my hand. "No, I have everything I need. So I guess this is goodbye?" I keep my gaze trained on the ground.

"For now," Lucian says, and when I look back up, he is gone.

CHAPTER THIRTY-FOUR

Chelsea

"Grovers Hotel is down there. You're going the wrong way," I tell Tyler as he continues down the motorway.

"Trust me, darlin', I know where I'm going."

I don't say anything else, because Tyler is going to look very silly when he pulls up outside a random hotel in the middle of nowhere.

I look out of the window and watch long stretches of field pass by. The last two weeks have gone by in a flash. One week in Paris to forget, accompanied by a week at home to remember. A week of daily appointments with my therapist, a week to explain to everyone why I've been MIA, and why I've been so vague on the phone, and, more importantly, why I missed my best friend's wedding.

I feel like a hypocrite having a leaving party and expecting people to turn up when I missed Lizzie's big day. But Tyler, being Tyler, was most insistent we leave in style, and a leaving party would give us the opportunity to say goodbye to everyone in one evening before we leave for Southampton to board our cruise ship in the morning.

My gaze connects with a brown road sign, and I point. "You can still make it in time if you take the next exit."

"Shush." Tyler waves his hand in the air. I can't help but laugh at the beret on his head. Although we're back in England, it feels as though we brought Paris back with us.

Since returning, Tyler has been pining over Jean-Paul, though the two have been in touch daily, and the French chef is keen to come to England to be with Tyler when we are back from our cruise. A year is a long time to wait for someone you've only spent seven days with, but if it's meant to be, it'll be.

My shoulders slump as my mind takes me back to the last conversation I had with Lucian. I was so sure I was doing the right thing for him, for both of us, but regret has never been far away.

Paris was amazing, though Lucian was always in my thoughts. He messaged me every day and left voicemail updates. The last message he left was to tell me he was still in Swansea. I'm not sure if he'll be back in time for my leaving party, but I can't help thinking that him not being in attendance may be for the best.

I sit in silence and watch as signpost after signpost pass by. "Wake me up when you realise we're lost," I say, and close my eyes for the remainder of the journey.

"Darlin', we are here."

I'm shaken awake. I sit bolt upright in my seat and peer out of the window. I frown because the car park is bigger than I remember, a lot bigger. My gaze shifts up to the large four-story white building and I read the words that sit proudly on top. Calloway Hotel.

My body tenses. "Tyler, why are we here?"

"Trust me, it'll all make sense." Tyler unfastens his seat belt and walks around the car to let me out.

He leans forward, holds one hand behind his back, and the

other he holds out for me. I shuffle awkwardly in the seat because this is the last place I want to be.

I shake my head. "Tyler, I can't."

The smile on his face dissolves, and he lowers his hand to his side. "Okay. You wait here while I go inside and tell everybody who turned up today that the guests of honour are leaving before their leaving party has even begun."

The irony of his statement is not lost on me. Tyler turns his back on me and heads toward the hotel.

"Wait," I call after him.

Tyler stops walking and I gather up the ruches of my gown and slide out of the car. Side by side we enter through the revolving door, and I lower my head as we approach the main reception area.

"Make it quick," I say to Tyler, who places his elbows on the polished marble counter. I know it's highly unlikely that I'll bump into Duncan or one of Lucian's brothers, but the thought of them randomly appearing has me on high alert.

"The alabaster gold suite," Tyler says, and the receptionist directs us.

My hair bounces off my shoulders as I hurry to keep up with Tyler, whose pace seems to quicken with each step he takes.

"What's the rush?" I call after him as he enters the suite. The heels of my stilettos slip on the floor as I reach the large doorway.

I take a deep inhale and paint a smile on my face. With my fingers wrapped around the brass handle, I let myself in. Cool air hits my face as I step inside. The room is massive, with high domed ceilings and beautiful crystal chandeliers. I'm so busy looking around myself that I hadn't considered our guests. I'm surprised that no one has come over to greet me. I glance around and notice people sitting down on chairs with a slim narrow walkway down the centre.

I stop walking. *Something is wrong.*

I hurriedly scan the backs of people's heads and faces, faces of people I don't recognise. We must be in the wrong room because this isn't a leaving party. If I didn't know better, I'd say this was a—

"Come on." Tyler appears out of nowhere and grabs my arm. "You need to change your outfit before the ceremony."

"Ceremony?" My mouth instantly goes dry as Tyler pulls me toward a door leading into a side room.

"Tyler." I yank my arm free as we enter what looks to be a storage room that has been transformed into a changing area. An oval mirror is secured to the wall and garments covered in black clothes bags hang on a portable rail. In my periphery I see Amber securing Freja's hair into a neat up-style. They are both wearing matching peach dresses. I walk deeper into the room. "What the hell is going on!"

All eyes are on me as I stand, hands on hips, glowering at my roomie.

"Perhaps I should explain."

I spin around and see Lucian making his way toward me. He is wearing a beige suit with a red silk cravat secured around his neck.

My eyes shoot daggers at Tyler. "You tricked me."

"Just hear him out, will you?" Tyler says, and he, my sister and niece leave the room, leaving Lucian and me alone.

I scoop up the ruche skirt of my dress and pace back and forth. "This is underhanded deceit. You can't arrange a wedding when the bride hasn't even said yes."

Lucian steps to the right and blocks my path. "Oh, but she has."

I look at Lucian from under my lashes. God, he looks and smells so good. Being this close to him, it's hard not to fall headfirst back into the fantasy. But a fantasy is all it was, and all it can ever be. I shake my head. "I said yes to being your fake fiancée. I never agreed to an actual wedding."

Laughter erupts from his throat and he erases any distance between us. "This isn't our wedding,"

Relief and disappointment course through me. "I'm confused. If not ours, whose?"

Lucian takes my hand and walks me a little way toward the door leading out into the large suite. I narrow my eyes and scan the sea of faces. "I don't recognise anyone."

Lucian lifts his arm and points toward the aisle. I squint and finally see a familiar face. "Is that Seth?"

"It sure is."

Seth is Lizzie's husband. "What is he doing here?"

Lucian sucks in a breath before speaking. "I can't help feeling responsible for you missing Lizzie and Seth's big day. So much, in fact, that I decided to bring their wedding here to you. Or rather the premature renewal of their vows."

I spin to face Lucian, my mouth hanging open. "You did all of this for me?"

Lucian adjusts the cravat at his neck. "You really don't know the lengths I would go to to secure your happiness."

I place my hands in Lucian's and squeeze. "You have no idea what this means."

Lucian releases my hands, wraps his arms around my waist and pulls me close. It doesn't go unnoticed how right we feel together, and yet I'm pulling away. Lucian leans forward, his lips locating the shell of my ear.

"I was offered Calloway Housebuilders."

I tense at his words. Lucian's father will never accept me whilst his son is running the Calloways' leading company. "Well done," I say, and attempt to wriggle free of his hold.

"I didn't sign the contract, Chelsea."

My body stills instantly. "What? Why?"

Lucian's emerald gaze connects with mine, and I can feel the deep intensity in his stare. "There is something, or rather someone, I want more." Lucian leans toward me and doesn't stop until his lips are inches from mine. "Tell me to go and I'll walk out of that door and you'll never see me again. Tell me to stay and…"

"Stay." I reach up, fist my fingers in his hair and press my lips against his. We kiss whilst at the same time Lucian walks us deeper inside the room. He doesn't stop walking until my back crashes against a wall. We kiss passionately and angrily. We kiss like it is our first time, and we kiss like it is our last time. So many emotions bunched into one in a crescendo of passion.

Lucian's fingers clutch the taffeta skirt of my gown, such a subtle thing to do, and yet so incredibly sensual. My body tingles with a lust I have never felt before. Our kiss is heated, sensual, and for a moment I forget where we are.

"Sweet Jesus." I hear my sister's words and open my eyes to see her standing with Freja, her hand covering my niece's eyes. I glance up at Lucian and stifle a laugh.

"We were just…" I say, but can't stop laughing long enough to finish the sentence.

"We'll be right with you," Lucian finishes for me. I use his jacket to conceal my embarrassment, seeing as though I no longer have my long hair to hide behind. I only look up when I can no longer hear Freja's giggles and my sister's heels click against the floor.

"I'm curious," I say, while at the same time circling my finger around his cravat. "What would you have done if I asked you to leave?"

Lucian shrugs. "I'd have left, of course. Only…"

"Only what?"

"I'd have looked like a fool boarding the cruise ship tomorrow on my own."

"Cruise ship?" The realisation of Lucian's words hit me. "You mean you're coming with me and Tyler?"

"I'm going instead of Tyler. He is staying here."

As sweet as Lucian is being, this is too much. "Tyler wants to travel just as much as me. It isn't fair he will miss out."

"True," Lucian muses. "But seeing as he's officially the proud owner of Calloway Travel Agency in Heller St Claire, I think he has enough reason to stay."

"The owner of Calloway Travel Agency?" I repeat. "Since when?"

"Since I offered the business to him during our phone call conversation when you arrived in Paris."

Paris? Tyler's known all this time and said nothing to me. The room feels as though it's spinning, and I cling onto Lucian to hold me up when I'm about ready to fall. "I thought you signed the building over to Josh."

"I was about to, until I realised what a lying scumbag he is. Josh of course is still ignorant of the fact. As far as my cousin is aware, I am still sorting the contracts. What a shock Josh will have on Monday morning when Tyler tells him the good news."

I take a few seconds trying to process everything Lucian has told me, and one question still whizzes around in my mind. "So, if you haven't taken on Calloway Housebuilders, which company will you be running?"

"Calloway Cruises. You want to travel the world, and I want to travel the world with you. The sea is our oyster. We will travel until your heart is content, and when you have seen all you want to see, we will return to England and settle down in one of my country estates."

I can't hold back the smile. "Lucian…"

He doesn't wrap his arms around me as I was expecting, and instead takes a step back, putting distance between us. "Two years ago, I went to an art exhibition and became completely captivated by a girl in a photograph. One month ago, that girl became more than an image frozen in time."

I gasp as he crouches down in front of me on one knee. "Lucian, what are you doing?"

Lucian takes my hand in his and gazes up into my eyes. "Thing is, Chelsea, I fell in love with an amazing girl. A girl I cannot get enough of. I'm not too proud to admit that I am greedy, and the photo alone is just not enough. I want the girl who believes in the impossible and is hell-bent on saddle-breaking an unbreakable horse, and I want the girl who does something as whimsical as put a crown of daisies in my hair. I want the girl as well as the photograph. I want it all."

He reaches into the lapels of his jacket and pulls out a small red velvet box. "When we board the cruise tomorrow, I would like you to do so wearing my ring."

Lucian flips the lid, and there lying on the soft cushion is his grandmother's gold engagement ring. *My engagement ring.*

"Chelsea Janssen, will you do me the honour of becoming Mrs Calloway? Of becoming my wife?"

Hot tears stream down my face, and I do nothing to wipe them away. "I will, I do… I do…"

Lucian takes the band from the box and slides it up my finger. He stands up and pulls me into his arms.

I lean forward to kiss him when he pulls away. "Sweetheart, we have all night to celebrate, and believe me when I say that I am going to take my time. But right now, you have a bridesmaid dress to put on, and a wedding you are not going to miss."

I'm flooded with emotion. I have everything I have ever wanted. I look up and meet Lucian's stare and say the words that are long overdue. "I love you, Lucian Calloway."

EPILOGUE

Lucian
Eighteen months later

I push open the door and am greeted with a thick cloud of smoke and the strong scent of tobacco. The blue light from the built-in aquarium shines around the dark room, and my brothers are sitting around the poker table.

"Lucian, what an unexpected surprise," Malachi says, glancing up from his cards. "Kevin, bring my brother a Gurkha Black Dragon."

"Have you come to join us?" Gage asks and pushes out the chair between them.

"I am not stopping, and this isn't a social call." I nod my head toward the window where outside the helicopter is waiting, the engine still on and the blades continuing their slow rotation.

"How's life treating you?" Malachi asks conversationally, though I know he's eager to get back to the game.

I smile big because this is going to feel good. "Save it," I say, and toss a rolled-up magazine on the table from under my arm. The multi-coloured chips that Malachi had stacked so neatly fall to the floor, but Malachi does nothing to retrieve them. Curiosity washes over his face and his gaze is trained on me.

"Nice rack," Gage says, his attention obviously on the busty blonde on the front cover.

Malachi regards the magazine with fading interest, a ghost of a smile tugging on his lips. "Thanks, but *London's Weekly* isn't on the top of my list of reading material."

"It should be," I say, and take the cigar Malachi's butler hands me. I light up and take a slow and controlled inhale. "Page twenty-five."

Gage lifts the magazine and, licking the tip of his finger, begins to flick through. I lean forward and wait for Gage to locate the page, a page I conveniently folded in the corner. "You'll be pleased to know the article hasn't been written by our old friend, Darren Moore."

"Article?" Gage wonders aloud.

I smile. "It would seem I'm not the only brother who makes headlines."

Gage Calloway ties the knot with mystery woman in secret nuptials! is the title that is displayed on the double spread. Gage pales.

"My invitation must have gotten lost in the post," I say.

"It would appear that mine did too." Malachi side-eyes our brother. "Who is this girl? Have you even bothered to run background checks on her?"

Gage and Malachi talk amongst themselves. In the corner of my eye, I can see Alfred, one of Malachi's butlers, enter the room. Josh is walking a few steps behind. I smile because they're right on time.

Conversation stops, and Malachi stands abruptly. "I don't know who invited you here, but you are not welcome."

I raise my hand. "I invited him." I was pleasantly surprised to learn from Natasha's social media that she and Josh are currently holidaying in Scotland. The information presented me the perfect opportunity to kill two birds with one stone.

Malachi retakes his seat, and my brothers sit in silence.

"Thank you so much for giving me a second chance," Josh begins when he is standing feet from me.

"A second chance?" I snort. "No, dear cousin. I only requested your company to return some of your belongings." I reach into my pocket and pull out a small box. I rotate it in my hand several times before I pass it to him. "Here. Inside are all the cufflinks you bought me for my birthdays over the years. Like you, they are fake. I have no use for them, so thought you may want them returning."

"Lucian," Josh begins, but I turn my back on him and head for the door. A hand grabs my shoulder and I spin around and come face to face with Josh. He runs his fingers through his hair, once, twice, before taking a deep breath. "Will you let me explain…"

I consider myself to be a reasonable man, a gentleman. But once in a while a gentleman needs to get his hands dirty. I turn around as though I am continuing on my way, but instead of leaving I throw my arm back and slam my fist into Josh's face.

My cousin stumbles and holds his hand over his nose. "Lucian, what the fuck? I'll sue you for millions." He turns to Malachi and Gage. "You both saw that, didn't you?"

Malachi, whose face is as blasé as ever, shrugs. "I saw you fall and hit your face."

Gage stifles a laugh. "Cousin, you are so clumsy."

Josh turns to me, his eyes wide, as though he expects me to say something. And I would hate to disappoint.

"That's the thing about family. We stick together and have each other's back. But I guess that concept is foreign to you."

I look past Josh and to my brothers, who nod in acknowledgement. I don't say it aloud, but my God, that felt good. I make my way out of Dunmorrow Castle and jump back into the 'copter.

"Where to, sir?" the pilot asks, as I get seated and fasten my belt.

"Swansea. There is an urgent matter I need to discuss with Angus Blackwell."

I became very well acquainted with Angus after the Pink Ribbon Breast Cancer Charity Gala. I sought Angus's help after signing the contracts putting me in charge of Calloway Cruises. We spent a week fishing in his private lake where we discussed tactics, and together we have transformed a once-sinking company into a highly profitable business. Angus is not only a shareholder, but my business partner. As I've learnt, in life and business, it is much better to have someone you trust by your side.

The next morning, I arrive home to Freesdon Hall. After our cruise, Chelsea and I moved about from estate to estate, none of which truly felt like home. I always found a problem, be it not enough land or not enough bedrooms. Truth is that there wasn't a problem with any of my estates. The problem lay with me. They say home is where the heart is, and my heart always has resided and always will reside at Freesdon Hall. I made Samantha an offer she couldn't refuse, and she was only too happy to hand over the keys.

On entering Freesdon Hall, my first port of call is the bedroom where I assume my wife is sleeping.

"Honey, I'm home," I call as I hurry up the flight of stairs.

"She isn't there," Donna calls after me. I turn and see my daughter cradled in our nanny's arms. Annabelle, named after my mother, was a little surprise who first presented herself during our cruise. We were in St Lucia when Chelsea came down with a terrible sickness bug, though it wasn't long after we discovered it wasn't a bug.

Annabelle yawns, and on seeing me her bright blue eyes light up. She has her mother's eyes, and my mother's thick raven hair that sits in tight curls on her head. She has my complexion and disposition. I know I'm biased when I say she is the perfect blend of us.

I look past Annabelle and flash a glance at the photographs of our wedding day hanging on the walls. Seven days after we discovered we were pregnant I made arrangements to fly all our family and friends over to St Lucia for a wedding of a lifetime.

"Pass her here," I say, and open my arms. Donna hands Annabelle over and I hug her close to my chest. "Shall we go and find Mummy?" I ask my six-month-old, who flaps her arms around excitedly.

"Oh, before I forget," Donna says. "Your father called. He asked if he and Julie could come for dinner later."

I take a second to mentally go over my day's itinerary. "Call him back and tell him that's fine, as long as Julie brings Rocky."

My and my father's relationship isn't anywhere near fixed, and it took him time to get used to the idea of me marrying Chelsea. But all his reservations melted away when Annabelle was born. I saw my father cry for the first time when he held his granddaughter in his arms. He dotes on that little girl in a way I didn't think was possible, and in turn she absolutely adores her grandfather.

As for Julie, she will never replace my mother, but as Chelsea requested, I have taken the time to get to know her. Her grandson Rocky is an absolute pleasure to be around, and I thoroughly enjoy our tennis matches. The kid is getting good, and I wouldn't be surprised if one day he played professionally.

I continue down the stairs and, after putting Annabelle's coat on, make my way out into the gardens. The sky is powder blue with sporadic white wisps of cloud. Despite winter's cool breeze hanging in the air, I know where Chelsea is.

I walk toward the hedges cut into the shape of geisha girls, past the tennis courts, and toward the paddock. I stand and watch as my wife feeds Jupiter a carrot whilst Malcolm, our stable boy, sits in the saddle. Jupiter isn't there yet, but I know we will be able to ride her again one day.

Malcolm climbs down when he sees me, and Chelsea

instinctively turns around. On meeting my stare, she runs over. Annabelle bounces in my arms as her mummy approaches. When Chelsea is close enough, I pull her into a hug and place a kiss on the top of her head.

Chelsea pulls back and retrieves a bottle of antibacterial gel from her pocket. "Don't let Annabelle get too close to me, not until I've washed my hands. You know she's constantly sucking her fingers now she's teething."

I don't move Annabelle away and simply ignore Chelsea's complaints. Her OCD has been sparked since having our daughter, whom Chelsea would happily place into a sterile bubble, but that isn't life. If I've learnt anything about my wife's obsession, it's that distraction is key. "My father called. He and Julie are coming for dinner tonight. I thought it would be a good time for you and Julie to discuss your next order."

Julie and Chelsea are the proud owners of a beauty therapy chain named Lotus Flower. They opened their fourth shop last month.

Chelsea holds her hand over her brow to make a visor and peers up at me. "Not tonight. I haven't seen my sister in ages, so I invited her and Rick for dinner."

A smile explodes on my face, because although my father has grown to love Chelsea, the same can't be said for her smart-mouthed older sister. Amber is not afraid of being vocal when it comes to her opinions. An evening with those two in the same room is bound to have fireworks going off.

"Are you going to rearrange dinner with your father?" Chelsea asks.

I laugh. "And miss out on the showdown between him and Amber? Hell no. I'll text Rick and ask him to bring popcorn."

Chelsea nudges me playfully. "What should I ask Mrs Collins to make for dinner?"

I ponder her question. "I was thinking we should give the staff the evening off."

Chelsea raises a brow. "Oh, yeah?"

Annabelle doesn't move when I kiss her crown and it would seem as though she has fallen asleep in my arms. "I thought Farrah could babysit whilst we cook my mother's famous cottage pie."

Chelsea runs her fingers through her hair. "I would like that, only…"

"Only what?"

"The last time we attempted to cook together, we ended up getting takeaway." She flashes me a mischievous grin, because I remember exactly what we got up to.

I flick the end of her nose. "I'll have you know that food from our favourite French restaurant is not what I consider to be takeaway food."

"Well, I do not consider bugs food."

I feign annoyance. "If I've told you once, I've told you a million times. Snails are not bugs, they are invertebrates."

To this day I have not been able to convince Chelsea to try escargot, but I considered it a win when she tried frogs' legs.

Chelsea's pace slows. "I'm going to call Amber and ask her if we can rearrange. She really doesn't like your father, and it would be unfair to expect them to sit in the same room together."

I know Chelsea misses her friends and family, seeing as they're in Cornwall and we're in Knightsbridge. We haven't seen them anywhere near as much as we should—either they are busy, or we are. Kids and work take up so much of our time. We have a family, they have families, it's so easy to get lost in life that we forget to spend time with the people who matter.

"How about I invite everyone over to stay for the weekend? We have enough spare rooms to sleep all of our family and friends. What do you say?"

"Even Tyler and Jean-Paul?"

"Even Tyler and Jean-Paul," I concur. "What do you think about a couples' game of charades this evening?"

Chelsea nods. "That could be fun, as long as you don't complain when Farrah teams up with Dante."

"Dante is Farrah's bodyguard; they cannot play as a couple."

"What about Pictionary?"

I laugh aloud because the last time we attempted that, the children ran off with the marker, and Amber's daughter thought it would be a good idea to draw a life-sized treasure map on the walls in the hallway.

"I have a better idea. How about we disappear upstairs and leave Annabelle with my father whilst he and Amber argue over politics and her delightful daughter draws all over the walls?"

"Now that sounds like my sort of evening." Chelsea laughs.

"Mine too," I agree.

Everything around me fades into insignificance as I stare at the woman who owns my heart. I can't help thinking how the hell did I get so lucky? The wind blows short tendrils of hair into her eyes, and without hesitation I reach up to brush her hair behind her ear when she captures my hand.

"This is too good to be true," Chelsea says, her words filled with emotion. "This life and us. I'm still waiting for you to wake up one day and figure out this isn't what you want and leave."

"I'm afraid you will have an awfully long wait, because that, my dear, is never going to happen."

Although Chelsea smiles, I know there will always be a deep-rooted doubt in her mind. But I have no problem spending every day of my natural life proving her wrong. Which reminds me. "I never told you about the message engraved on the inside of my Calloway crested ring, did I?"

Chelsea shakes her head. "No, what does it say?"

Careful not to wake Annabelle, I slip off the ring and pass it to Chelsea. She tilts the band several times as she tries to make out the inscription.

"Read it," I whisper.

A smile tugs at her lips. "'Make life the dream you never want to wake from.'" She passes me the ring and I slip it on.

"I really am living the dream," I say and, snaking my arm around Chelsea's waist, we take a slow walk back to the house. Back to our today, our tomorrow and our forever.

I always believed that my life would revolve around money and that everything was just a simple transaction. But love doesn't come with a price tag because no matter how rich you are, you can't buy true happiness, and I know this first-hand.

My beautiful wife, my baby girl, and our slightly dysfunctional family all under one roof. I have everything I could possibly want and more.

Life really doesn't get any better than this.

The end

Thank you for reading *A Billionaire's Vow*. I hope you loved Chelsea and Lucian's story. If you'd be so kind, please leave a review.

Watch out for Gage's story from the Calloway series. For updates about the release of his book, make sure you join my newsletter at http://eepurl.com/ds_fXj.

BOOKS BY LAURA RILEY

British Billionaire Romance

Charmed (co-written with April Wilson)
Captivated (co-written with April Wilson)

Stepping Stones Series

Finding Our Forever
Yours to Keep
Falling Into Us

The Calloways

A Billionaire's Vow
A Billionaire's Promise (coming next)

ACKNOWLEDGEMENTS

First of all I want to thank Aoife Marie Proudfoot, my amazing friend and critique partner. She has always there for me, no matter what. I want to thank April Wilson for being an amazing friend and a huge support in the book world. Also Vi Carter for being an amazing support.

I want to thank my 'sassy book ladies'—you know who you are. Love you, ladies.

A big shout-out to everyone in my Facebook group, the Author Laura Riley Fan group. Also my PA, Tami Thomason, who is amazing in helping to run my group.

I want to thank my beta readers, Jenny Hughes, Emma Westell, Annmarie Spiby, April Wilson and Aoife Marie Proudfoot.

To RJ Locksley, my amazing editor and proofreader, Wander Aguiar for my amazing cover image, Lucas Loyola, my handsome cover model, Steamy Book Designs for my cover, and Champagne Formatting for my beautiful book format.

CONTACT ME

Join Laura Riley's mailing list at
http://eepurl.com/ds_fXj
for news and exclusive material.

Reading group
www.facebook.com/groups/1116820285338874

Facebook
www.facebook.com/authorlaurariley

Website
www.authorlaurariley.com

Instagram
www.instagram.com/author_laura_riley

TikTok
www.tiktok.com/@author_laura_riley

Printed in Great Britain
by Amazon